"THE DRAGON OF THE ISHTAR GATE...

is a remarkably convincing recreation of the third century B.C. in Persia in the reign of Xerxes. . . . It is a picaresque story much in the vein of THE ARABIAN NIGHTS. . . . Bessas' adventures are a chronicle of the deceit, trickery, cruelty and raw courage that has always been the hallmark of the Middle East. Strange, fantastic and marvelous things happen along his route beset by gods, demons, and sorcerors and the reader is irresistibly drawn into the reality of the superstition by a devout believer in it."

—Dr. George Woodbury

"A flashy farrago of fights, feints, flights, fornication, fevers, feasts, facts, folklore, fun, and ferocity is this historical romance from the prolific pen of an author better known for science fiction, fantasy, and solid volumes like LOST CONTINENTS and handbooks on inventions."

—Library Journal

To Sam Freiha of Beirut,
the best tourist guide in the whole Middle East.

THE DRAGON OF THE ISHTAR GATE

L. SPRAGUE DE CAMP

LANCER BOOKS — NEW YORK

A LANCER BOOK • 1968

THE DRAGON OF THE ISHTAR GATE

Library of Congress Catalog Card Number 61-12511
Copyright © 1961 by L. Sprague de Camp
All rights reserved
Printed in the U.S.A.

LANCER BOOKS, INC. • 1560 BROADWAY •
NEW YORK, N.Y. 10036

Contents

I The Chamber of the Wizard

GOLDEN LAMPS, hung by chains from the sooty ceiling, smoked and flickered, sending forth an olivine odor. The little yellow flames burnt steadily for a time, then writhed and fluttered as though struck by a sudden draft. Yet no breeze could penetrate to this secluded chamber, whose only opening to the outer world was a doorway closed by a heavy, wooden, copper-studded door.

At one end of the cluttered room, a striped hyena paced to and fro in its cage. Its claws clicked on the stone and, as it turned at the end of its walk, its eyes shone green in the lamplight.

The time was before dawn on the morning of the third day of the month Nisanu, in the twentieth year of the reign of Xerxes—the Great King, the King of All Kings, the King of the Persians and the Medes, the King of the Wide World, the son of Darius, the chief of the Achaemenid clan. The place was a chamber of the west side of the small palace of Darius at Persepolis, in the rugged mountains of Parsa.

Two men, seated on stools, faced each other across a massive table, on which lay three dead mice.

One of these men was King Xerxes himself. The Great King was a tall, strong man, albeit somewhat stooped and paunchy. Instead of his purple robe of royalty he wore a white gown over crimson trousers and pointed saffron shoes. Instead of the towering royal tiara, his head bore only a blue polka-dotted fillet to confine his long, curled hair.

Beneath heavy black brows, his bloodshot eyes bulged slightly. Below the long, hooked Achaemenid nose, a firm, thin-lipped mouth was shadowed by a heavy mustache with sweeping ends waxed to spikes. A curled, graying beard fell to his breast.

7

The king's expression was morose, discontented, and weary. He looked older than his fifty-five years as he peered nearsightedly at the mice, then at the man across the table.

This man was taller, leaner, and older than Xerxes. A long white beard was tucked into the bosom of his dusty black robe, and from his head rose a conical black hat.

"Then," said the king, "you have failed again?"

The other spread his hands, smiling with raised eyebrows. "The Good God did not wish me to find my goal by this route, sire. Yet will your slave persevere, trying each——"

"Ahriman smite you!" roared Xerxes, striking the table with his fist, so that the corpses of the mice sprang into the air as if called back to life. "Promises, promises; of those you have a muchel. But when will you show me some results? Belike the touch of hot iron would speed your quest——"

"Oh, Great King!" cried the other in a broad Medic accent, bowing again and again like a puppet worked by strings. "I do my best, truly I do. Be it as you wish—but who can compel the gods to reveal hidden truths? This time, however, your slave is verily on the scent of success. Fry my guts if it come to nought, sire! I assure my lord and master——"

"There, there," said the king. "I meant not to frighten you, my good Ostanas. Never would I harm a faithful servant and friend. Am I forgiven?"

Ostanas drew a long breath. "Whatever the king does pleases his slave. As for my fright,"—he smiled slyly—"that, I ween, is but the normal hazard of being the king's gossip."

Xerxes said: "I would not drive away my one true friend, for loneliness is the lot of kings. But it roils my temper when day by day I feel my powers waning. Here am I, ruler of the civilized world, commanding riches beyond those of any king before me. Yet year by year my teeth decay, my hair falls out, my breath grows short,

8

and my sight grows dim, as if I were the commonest clod."

"The God of the Aryans give you life, sire! No one would think my master a day over forty——"

"Save your flattery, good Ostanas; I can see the plaster on my pate as well as the next man. My hairdresser does his best, but I do not think he befools anybody with all his powders, paints, and hair dyes. My father—God welcome him—thought it a pretty conceit to keep three hundred and sixty-five royal concubines. But what good does that number do me? I could get along with a mere score and never summon the same one twice in a year. So what can all my wealth and power do to stay the march of time?"

A low laugh came from the end of the room, a mirthless ha-ha-ha-ha on a rising scale. The king whirled about on his stool. The hyena stared greenly at him and resumed its pacing.

"I wish you would get rid of that thing," said Xerxes. "I swear by the golden heels of Gandareva that he understands my words and mocks them. Besides, he stinks."

"Mighty medicines are made from the organs of the hyena," said Ostanas. "So my pet may some day have his uses. As I was about to——"

"Tell me," interrupted the king, "I reign by the grace of Auramazda—the one and only true God, all-seeing and omnipotent—and I have tried to be a good king. Then why, by the Holy Ox Soul, am I so unhappy? I have flunkies and flatterers galore but no real friends save you. My sons—the legitimate ones—watch me like vultures watching a dying camel. And you know how it is with the queen and me. I sleep badly and, when I do snatch some slumber, *he* visits me in dreams, dripping black blood. And *she*——" The king covered his eyes and shuddered.

"If it please Your Majesty," said Ostanas, "your slave will tell you of his discovery, which, if true, will relieve your heartache and restore your youth."

"Speak, man."

9

"I have read crumbling scrolls of cured human hide, writ in blood in the ancient picture language of Egypt. I have communed by the light of gibbous moons with unseen presences in the ruins of ancient fanes. I have cast up the signs of the glittering stars according to the arcane rules of the wise Babylonians. I have sought the guidance of gods in sleep induced by dire drugs from Kush and Hind. I——"

"I know you have done portentous things," said the king, "but come to the point."

"At last my unworthy self has found the formula for the true elixir."

"Then why have you not made it?" Xerxes extended a hand, glowing with rings, towards the three dead mice.

"Because, sire, some of the ingredients are so rare and outlandish that I know not if they can be had. Ancient lore and modern science alike assert that these things must needs be obtained if the great work shall succeed. Moreover, a holy spirit has appeared to me in a dream and assured me that my plan is right."

"What are these ingredients?"

"My lord will not think that I mock him?"

"Have done with evasions, good Ostanas. If you tell me that you need a piece of the moon, then by the Mountain of Lapis Lazuli I swear I will send men to fetch it."

"Know then, Great King, that the elixir must be compounded of three rare ingredients, besides the commoner stuffs like powdered emerald. These three things are: first, the blood of a dragon; second, the ear of a king; and third, the heart of a hero."

Xerxes laughed heartily, showing stained and blackened teeth. "Perfay, but that is a fine bird to pluck! I thank the Lord of Light that you asked me not for milk of a virgin or fur of a fish. Rehearse me the details."

"The blood of a dragon is needed because the vital element of life is heat, and the blood of dragons contains the most ardent heat of any living——"

10

"What kind of dragon? One of the winged serpents of Araby?"

"That were too small. Nor would any common lizard or cockadrill suffice, sire. Know you the reptile that the Babylonians represent as the sacred beast of their false god Marduk?"

"And which they depict in glazed brick on the Great Gate of Ishtar? Aye; I have seen a live one."

"You have? When?"

"Or ever the Babylonians revolted in the fifth year of My Majesty's reign, I entered the temple of Marduk to pay my respects to the priests; for, even though we Aryans have received the true faith from the inspired Zoroaster, statecraft compels us to tolerate the false gods of foreign nations under our sway. Seeing this same monster, portrayed in enameled brick on the walls of the temple, I asked the priests about it.

"This was, they said, a *sirrush*, the divine beast of Marduk. Moreover, they offered to show me a living sirrush. Nothing loath, I followed them into a dark little room below the cella. There, in a cage, lay something that looked for all the world like a large gray lizard, above three cubits* in length.

"When I remarked on this, the priests assured me that the creature was a mere chick, which would in time attain the stature of a camel and the bulk of a buffalo; also, that it would grow the horns and other appendages shown in the reliefs."

"Where is this beast now?" Ostanas leaned forward in his eagerness.

"I wot not; it vanished during the sack of Babylon after the revolt. But I was told where these animals live."

"Indeed, sire?"

"Aye. When I asked where I might obtain such a beast for my menagerie, the priests averred that it dwelt at the source of the river Nile."

* 1 cubit = 1½ feet.

11

"God befriend you!" cried Ostanas. "That is farther than the kite flies. Who has ever been to the headwaters of the Nile? Not even the Egyptians, who live along this river, know whence it comes."

"That is the point," said the king. "None has, at least to my knowledge. But what of your other components?"

"Well, sire, we need the ear of a king for the following reason: Wise men believe that sound makes a permanent imprint upon whatever it passes through. To assure that the elixir shall strengthen the wisdom and mental powers of him who quaffs it, we must include a piece of matter through which spoken words of grave import have passed. And who hears words of more grave import than a king?"

"That were hardly practical," said Xerxes. "I cannot very well call in the tributary king of Cilicia and cut off his ear. Such ungentle treatment would surely drive him to revolt."

"Then my master must obtain this ear from outside his empire. Lastly there is the heart of a hero. The heart is the seat of the passions, affections, sentiments, and virtues. Therefore, to imbue the patient with perfect courage and greatness of soul, we require the heart of a fearless hero."

"That were even less easy," said the king. "Whilst I have some good men amongst my satraps and generals, I should be loath to sacrifice any one of them; nor were such treatment just. Whereas those who merit death for their crimes would not possess hearts of the requisite quality."

Ostanas smiled thinly. "Sire, if you could find a man who would fetch hither a sirrush—alive, of course, so that its blood should be fresh—and the ear of a king, the third requirement would take care of itself."

Xerxes scowled, then laughed. "Ostanas, you shock me. For one who was taught by a pupil of the Great Magus himself, you are a wicked old scoundrel."

12

"It were for the good of the realm, sire. In such cases, private welfare must give way."

"Nay, nay, the Lord of Light would hate me for such perfidy. We must find another——"

The private knock, used by the king's bodyguards and trusted intimates, sounded.

"Come in!" said the king.

The door creaked open, and one of the bodyguards thrust in his beard. "O King! Prince Tithraustes seeks audience."

"At this hour? By the breasts of Anahita! What wishes he?"

There were murmurs in the hall outside. The guard said: "It is not for himself, sire, but for Myron the Milesian."

"The tutor? Well, what does *he* want?"

More murmurs; then: "It has to do with Bessas of Zariaspa."

"Ahriman!" swore the king. "I have given my decision, and the law of the Persians and Medes cannot be set aside——"

Xerxes paused and stared through slitted eyelids at Ostanas. He said: "Know, old friend, that meseems the Good God has sent us the answer to our problem." He turned back to the door. "Say that the king will speak with Tithraustes and Myron in the audience chamber forthwith." Picking up his jeweled, gold-headed walking stick, Xerxes rose and left the chamber.

Ostanas gazed after him, still smiling. From its cage the hyena laughed. The magus swept up the three dead mice, stepped to the cage, and tossed them in. There were soft mouthing sounds and a faint crunch of small bones; then silence.

The former palace of Darius the Great stood on a spacious platform of scarped natural rock and limestone blocks, which towered forty feet above the plain and was in turn overshadowed by the Mountain of Mercy behind it. North, south, and east of Darius' palace loomed the other royal structures, most of them far larger than that modest edifice. Some, unfinished, were still spinous with scaffolding.

Clustered below the platform on the plain stood the mansions of Xerxes' nobles, the huts of their servants, and the shops and houses owned by the local people. Persepolis was only a small town. The king had other palaces in the teeming cities of Shushan and Babylon and Hagmatana. When, as happened several times each year, the king removed from one to another, his host of kinsmen, women, slaves, advisers, officials, generals, and grandees perforce moved with him.

On the night that King Xerxes consulted Ostanas, another man slept in a room that he leased from a Persepolitan shopkeeper. A violent knocking awoke this man. Yawning and cursing, he got up, stubbed his toe, and stumbled to the door. A glance through the peephole showed a veiled woman and, behind her, a slave upholding a burning link of rope and asphalt.

"Myron of Míletos!" cried the woman. "This is your dwelling, is it not?" She spoke Persian, in the dialect of the far northeast, pronouncing "Miletos" as "Miretush."

"Yes. Who are you, madam?"

"I am Zarina the widow of Phraates and mother of Bessas. Let me in! It is a matter of my son's life."

"Wait till I don some garments." Presently Myron slid back the bolt. Entering, the woman threw back her veil, showing abundant white hair. The light of a freshly lighted lamp revealed an austerely furnished chamber littered with manuscripts. Myron, a broad-shouldered man of medium height, wearing a Greek tunic over Persian pantaloons, said:

"It has been months since your slave has seen you, Lady Zarina. What is this about Bessas?"

"He—he is to be impaled at dawn for his part in the rape of Tamyra the Daduchid."

14

"What!" cried Myron. "I heard a rumor of the arrest of Sataspes, but I did not know that Bessas——"

"He was not—that is, he knew not——" Zarina began to weep and moan incoherently.

"Madam," said Myron, "dawn is not many hours off. Be seated and, if you wish assistance, try to give me an intelligible explanation."

Zarina brought herself under control and sat with a clatter of bangles. "I know not what you have heard. Two days past, the king received the acclaim of his nobles and the gifts of the bearers of tribute for the New Year——"

"I witnessed it," said Myron.

"Afterwards came the New Year's banquet. The nobles gorged and caroused, as is the custom, in the main dining hall. Know you the king's cousin Sataspes son of Teaspes?"

"I have seen him," said Myron.

"Well, this fool got even drunker than is to be expected and wandered out of the feast. In the halls he came upon Tamyra daughter of Zopyrus. Just how things went we know not, because Sataspes told divers tales, and the girl was too frightened to tell any sensible story at all.

"It seems he sat down and held her in his lap in an empty anteroom, in fatherly fashion. After all, he has children older than she. But presently his passions rose, and he flung her down, tore off her trousers, and had his will of her. At least, he sought to do so, though what of her struggling and his unsteadiness I do not think he truly——"

"*Aiai!*" Myron broke in. "Why must he pick the worst victim in the entire Empire? Not that I should ever condone rape, even of a humble serving maid; but the virgin daughter of the Daduchids! He must have been as mad as a maenad. Then what happened?"

"Tamyra's screams attracted the guards. Their coming sobered Sataspes, for as they entered the chamber he confronted them with a tale of the child's being frightened by a demon. Whilst they, knowing him for an Achae-

15

menid, hesitated, he dashed off and sought sanctuary at our house as an old friend and distant cousin. I was out visiting my gossips. Bessas tried to smuggle Sataspes out of Persepolis, and both were caught."

As Zarina paused, Myron said: "Folly is mortals' self-chosen misfortune. Go on."

"This afternoon past, the king judged the matter. The Daduchids wanted the boats or the ashes for Sataspes. The king had compromised on the stake, when Sataspes' mother burst in. Such shouting in the king's presence has not been heard since Salamis!

"But the king could not turn out his aunt without giving her her say. She proposed that Sataspes earn his life by sailing around Africa and reporting on what he found, as Phoenicians are said to have done in the reign of some old Egyptian king. After more shouting, Bagabyxas and Zopyrus agreed, albeit with ill grace."

"Then what?" said Myron.

"That left my son. Bessas asserts he knew nought of the rape; that Sataspes told him only that the Daduchids had their knives out for him and he must needs flee. I thought that, in view of the king's lenience towards Sataspes, he would let Bessas off with a mere loss of his commission in the Immortals. But, as Bessas has neither wealth nor influence and nobody to plead for him but me, it took the king but ten heartbeats to sentence him to the stake."

"Beshrew me, but this is a dreadful business!" said Myron soberly. "What does my mistress wish?"

"Save him!" cried Zarina. "Save my only son!"

"I? Good gods, how?"

"How should I know? You, Master Myron, are notorious as one of the cleverest men of your crafty race. You can find a way; but save my boy!"

Myron sighed. "You Persians speak of ordinary human intelligence as if it were a criminal attribute. I grieve with you, madam. But I am neither so rich as Croesus nor so brave as Kodros. I am only a poor schoolmaster, with less influence at court than Bessas. I am not even an

16

Aryan, let alone a Persian grandee. Can you give me a logical reason why I should risk my neck in a probably futile effort to save your whipworthy young——"

"May Ghu the demon king boil you in oil, you greedy Greek!" spat Zarina. "So you are fain to be bribed! Here, take my earrings——"

"Mistress Zarina!" cried Myron. "You utterly wrong me! Keep your earrings, pray. I merely asked for a logical——"

"You and your logic!" screamed Zarina, wringing her hands. "Does not your heart tell you what to do? Or have you none?"

An agony of indecision screwed Myron's face into wrinkles. "It is not lack of heart, dear lady, but a certain lingering affection for my own hide. Though others may not think it worth taking off to make wallets of, I like the old thing. Besides, I have no skill at swaying the minds of the mighty."

Zarina leaned towards Myron, to whom her large dark eyes seemed like bottomless pools of blackness, reflecting the wavering yellow flame of the little lamp. "If you must have logic, consider this, good my sir. When one of your former pupils comes to a bad end, it reflects upon your teaching. You claim to impart wisdom; yet events give your words the lie. Had Bessas possessed wisdom, he would not now face a mean and agonizing death."

Myron drew a deep breath as his face cleared. "Your arguments are irrefutable, lady. I will do what I can. How shall we proceed? Let me think."

For a time Myron sat, fingering his short brown beard flecked with gray. The widow fidgeted. At last the Hellene said:

"Why not urge the king to send Bessas on an expedition like that of Sataspes?"

Zarina clapped her hands together. "The very thing! And you can go with him, to keep him out of trouble."

Myron started so violently that he choked upon a drop of spittle in his windpipe. When he had finished cough-

17

ing, he said: "My hearing must fail me, dear lady! I thought you said that I was to accompany your young hellion on his expedition. Such an absurd idea——"

"Your hearing deceived you not. Think, now! Do you recall the time last year when Bessas brought you to our house to dinner? You talked at length. You told us how much unrelieved schoolteaching bored you. You spoke of the great explorers, like Skylax and Kolaios, and how you envied them their chance to advance the knowledge of mankind. Remember?"

"Sometimes I talk too much, especially when stimulated by fine Syrian wine. But really, I am a man of middle age! I am past the time for deeds of derring-do——"

"Rubbish, my dear Myron! You are a mere youth in your forties. At my age it were different. But, like the rest of us, you grow no younger by the year. Here is a chance not likely to come again! Will you not hate yourself for the rest of your wretched life if you forgo it?"

Myron sighed. "Madam, in deference to your rank I forbear to use some fine picturesque curses, which I learnt in Babylon. You must be a veritable witch, so shrewdly to divine all a man's secret weaknesses and so mercilessly to play upon them! Though I be the cosmos' greatest fool, I will go if it be possible. Now let us to our next step."

Zarina: "But what step? Midnight has passed. The king sleeps, as do most honest folk. It would take a Scythian invasion to persuade his people to rouse him now. And by the time he rises, my baby will have sat upon the stake."

Myron said: "My pupils bring me gossip, and this gossip says that the king is not so regular a sleeper as that. Many nights he spends closeted with Ostanas. The old he-witch has probably cozened the king into thinking that he can turn excrement into gold—but that gives us one hairsbreadth of a chance. Through whom can we approach the king?"

18

"I suppose we could appeal to the commander in chief."

Myron tossed his head in the Greek negative. "Artabanus is no more enamored of being aroused from slumber than the king. Moreover, even if we gained his ear, he would extort monstrous bribes and put us off, day by day, before we attained our audience. We must think of something else."

"Oh, hasten!" said Zarina. "Mithra! Will you waste the entire night in talk?"

"Calm yourself, madam. There is no point in rushing heedlessly about the streets and shouting gibberish. Who besides Artabanus?"

"How about Aspamitres?"

"Gods forbid! Once you get into the hands of the eunuchs, they'll bleed you whiter and delay you longer than Artabanus. In the palace, there's a scorpion beneath every stone."

"Have you tutored any of the king's sons?"

Myron pondered. "Not to speak of—I taught the young Darius for a ten-day, and then we parted because I insisted upon classroom discipline and he upon his royal prerogatives. But wait! I once tutored the king's bastard Tithraustes. He is not a bad sort, for a prince."

"They do say the king dotes upon Master Tithraustes, despite the thrashing that the Hellenes gave him in that affair off Cyprus."

"The reason is obvious," said Myron. "Being illegitimate, Tithraustes has no claim upon the throne. So, when he says 'dear Father,' Xerxes knows that he means it and is not using his love as a ruse for slipping a knife into the royal ribs." He rose and took his plain brown cloak off the peg. "My dear madam, I think we have it. I am informed that the bastard prince is a nocturnal bird, who makes the rounds of the taverns until false morn rises in the eastern sky. So let us go to find Tithraustes."

19

The night was dark with an overcast that promised one of spring's last rains. Myron and his companion went warily, holding two links high, lest some nervous Immortal mistake them for robbers and loose a shaft.

An hour and three taverns after they had left Myron's room, they entered the wineshop of Hutrara on the outskirts of Persepolis. Hutrara, a stout bald Elamite, leaned one elbow on his wine counter and eyed his few remaining customers with patient impassiveness.

Two of the tables were empty. At another, a stout Babylonian banker held a heated discussion in frantic whispers with a lean man who looked like a Kossian cutthroat. At another, three Parthian cameleers sat with arms about one another's necks, singing a song with a wailing tune.

A black-browed soldier in the short white jacket, white pantaloons, and golden necklet of the Median battalion of the Immortals, his costume wine-stained and his bulbous white felt hat awry, had another table to himself. Thence, over his winecup, he glowered to right and left as if seeking a quarrel.

The remaining table was occupied by a plump young Persian and a heavily painted strumpet. The man, with rouged cheeks, waxed mustaches, and a golden chain around his neck, sat with his arm about the giggling woman. He alternately sipped wine and nuzzled his companion, whispering in her ear and tickling her with his beard.

"There is our man," murmured Myron, squeezing past the other table. "Hail, noble Tithraustes!"

The Persian looked up, blinking and moving his eyebrows as if he had trouble in focusing. "Who are you?"

"I am your old tutor, Myron Perseôs by name—Myron the Milesian."

"Oh? Well. Great pleasure. Great pleasure. Sit down."

"Thank you. This is the noble lady Zarina. Your slaves need your help."

The Persian, who had gone back to nuzzling the whore, looked around. "Help? Thank you, my master,

20

but I need no help. Doing fine by myself." He hiccupped.

"No, sir, it is *we* who need *your* help. You can assist *us*. Now do you understand?"

"Who are *you?*"

"Zeus, Apollon, and Demeter!" muttered Myron. He took a draft of wine and addressed the Persian anew. "I am your old tutor Myron. You remember him, do you not?"

"Aye. Whatever befell him?"

"Nothing befell him; here he is. Well then, I require your help."

"I told you, I need no help," said Tithraustes, fingering the emerald in the lobe of his left ear.

Zarina whispered loudly over Myron's shoulder: "Knock the lout senseless, and we will drag him outside and revive him."

"Go away and mind your business," said the whore, "or I will scratch your eyes out."

"Try it, hussy!" said Zarina. "I will pull off that wig of yours."

"Mistress Zarina," said Myron, "do me the favor of sitting at that empty table. Order something. This may take time. Now," said Myron to Tithraustes, "Your Highness is a true Persian gentleman, are you not?"

"Does any scum deny it?" growled Tithraustes.

"Right. Now, that means that you have a keen sense of honor, does it not?"

"Plague! Any ninny knows that."

"Then, when your old tutor appeals to you for help, honor compels you to help him. Is that not so?"

Tithraustes pondered this for an instant, then said: "And who are *you?*"

Myron closed his eyes and passed a hand across his forehead. "Sometimes, by Earth and the gods, I wonder." Then his manner changed. From intensely serious he became boisterously jovial. He laughed loudly and clapped Tithraustes on the shoulder.

21

"Look, son," he said, "do you know what I can get you?"

"Nay; what?"

"I can lead you to a woman whose cleft runs cross-wise"—he made slicing motions—"instead of up and down. Are you game?"

"Am I?" Tithraustes fumbled in his purse and slapped a small coin on the table. "Lead on!"

Myron rose and started for the door. The whore spat a curse after him. A hand caught his cloak and turned him half around. It was the sullen Median soldier.

"Did you say aught to me?" snarled the Mede.

"No, general, your slave did not," said Myron. "It is my misfortune that I do not know you. No doubt the man beside you said something."

The Mede turned to stare into the empty air beside him. He was still staring when Myron and his companions passed out of the wineshop, leaving Hutrara and the hussy to quarrel over the money on the table.

A few blocks towards the palaces, Tithraustes stared at the Greek and cried: "Why, Master Myron! Fry my balls if it be not good old Myron! Whence came you?"

"Well, thank all the gods and goddesses!" said Myron. "I am in desperate need. . . ."

Myron followed Tithraustes up the broad reversing stairway on the western side of the platform. The first faint light appeared in the east, revealing the outlines of the Mount of Mercy towering jaggedly above the palaces.

"Hasten!" breathed Zarina. "Dawn comes on apace."

At the top, a sentry challenged, bringing his partisan to port. This was a broad-bladed polearm, a clumsy weapon meant more for impressing the Great King's subjects than for serious fighting.

Tithraustes conversed in murmurs with the guard. Then he led his companions into the huge Gate of All Nations, flanked by limestone bulls twenty feet high.

"Sit and wait," he said, indicating a bench along the wall.

The bastard prince disappeared, while the sentry watched them, leaning on his partisan. The torchlight flickered ocherously on the gilding of the winged disk of Auramazda, above which rose the crowned and bearded head and upper body of the Lord of Light.

They sat while Zarina gnawed her knuckles. "If he keeps us waiting much longer," she murmured, "I shall scream, king or no king."

Myron said: "Hurrying a king, my dear Zarina, is like trying to contain the wind in a goatskin."

"You can be patient. It is not your son."

"I have none, alas. But I will do my poor best for yours."

"Try to have Bessas sent on an expedition to some safe, peaceful land."

"Do you know of any?" said Myron dryly. "Even the royal realm of Parsa has proved less safe than lying in bed."

Somewhere in the maze of palaces, the king's pet lion, Rustam, gave a moaning roar. The light was stronger when Tithraustes reappeared.

"Come this way," he said.

Leaving Zarina's slave in the gate, Tithraustes led them out the rear, where stood a pair of winged, human-headed bulls of stone. Two guards trailed after them. The soldiers' leathern bow cases, gay with glued-on bits of colored leather, bumped against their hips.

A pair of palace servants stood yawning by a basin on a pedestal. They washed the hands of Myron and Zarina and put long loose white robes upon them.

The petitioners climbed the stairs on the northern side of the audience hall, where sculptured soldiers of the Immortals, noblemen, and delegations bearing tribute from all over the Empire marched in stony files in low relief along the retaining walls. Then before the party rose the portico of the great Apadana, begun by Darius and com-

23

pleted by Xerxes. Slender columns, soaring sixty-five feet into the air, upheld the roof. The capitals of these columns took the form of the forequarters of kneeling beasts—bulls and horned lions—in pairs, back to back.

Within the audience hall rose a shadowy forest of pillars with similar capitals. The light of torches and cressets glimmered redly on the bronzen horns and the golden eyes of the sculptured beasts; it gleamed on the gilded arms and armor of motionless guards.

Beyond this forest of columns, at the southern end of the hall, stood a golden chair of pretense on a dais. Above it, supported on golden pillars, rose a jeweled canopy, glimmering with gems of many hues. Here the petitioners waited again, while a slave lit the tall golden incense burners flanking the throne.

At last Aspamitres, the chief eunuch, entered. He smote the pave with his staff and cried:

"Silence! Bow down before the Awful Royal Glory!"

Myron, Zarina, and the bastard prince sank to their knees and touched their foreheads to the floor. Zarina's jewelry clanked as she knelt. A tramp of feet, a swish of garments, and a heavy smell of perfume told of the king's arrival. The voice of the king said: "Rise!"

Xerxes sat on his throne, with his feet on a golden footstool footed with golden bulls' hooves. Two attendants flanked him. Although it was night and indoors, one held the royal parasol over his head, while the other stood by with a fly swatter and a napkin, in case the king were troubled by a noxious insect or wished to blow his nose.

Farther to either side stood guards from the Elamite battalion of the Immortals, wearing embroidered knee-length coats, close-fitting trousers, and low twisted turbans. They rested on their toes the golden balls on the butts of their spears. A score of slaves, trying to look inconspicuous while standing by in case the king wished an errand run, clustered in corners.

The king's prominent eyes were more bloodshot than

24

ever, and a hasty job with paint and powder merely added to his years. He wore an old robe of state, dimmed by dirt and dotted with food stains. He peered myopically and rasped:

"You are Myron the tutor, are you not?"

Myron and Zarina had, upon rising, thrust their hands into their sleeves as court procedure required. Myron spoke: "It is as the Great King says."

"Well, speak up!"

"God give Your Highness life——"

"Never mind that, Ionian; say what you mean."

"It is well known that my master fosters the increase of human knowledge. Where your great father sent Skylax down the——"

Zarina broke in to cry: "King of All Kings, spare my baby! He has fought bravely for you——"

"Guard!" said Xerxes. "Take the lady Zarina to an anteroom and keep her there until I command otherwise. Go on, Ionian."

"As your slave was saying, where the great Darius sent Skylax down the Indus, you have dispatched Sataspes to circumnavigate Africa. But more could be done to glorify the royal name and benefit the realm; namely, to send out another such expedition. It is an old and excellent Persian custom to do things in pairs, so that if one fail——"

"What had you in mind?"

"There are several possibilities. One is the circumnavigation of the Hyrkanian Sea to determine whether, as some aver, it communicates with the ocean. But my main argument concerns not the direction of the effort, but its leadership. If——"

"No doubt you are thinking of young Bessas," said Xerxes.

"True, sire; how did you know?"

"Much is known to My Majesty."

"Well, here is a man of extraordinary size and strength, a ferocious fighter and a seasoned——"

25

Xerxes held up his golden scepter. "Enough, my good Myron. My Majesty has already decided. Justice requires that Bessas be given the same chance to earn his life as his fellow criminal. He shall not, however, sail the stormy Sea of Varkana. I have another task for him. What know you of the sources of the Nile?"

Myron: "An Egyptian has informed your slave that, beyond Kush, the Nile rises from a pair of conical mountains, formed like the paps of a woman, each with a fountain at the top."

"Very well. My man of science, Ostanas, requires two rare things for his work. One is the ear of a king."

"Did you say the ear of a king, sire?"

"You heard me aright. The other is a dragon like those depicted on the Ishtar Gate in Babylon. . . ."

Xerxes repeated what he had earlier told Ostanas about the sirrush.

". . . so the beast must be brought hither alive," he concluded. "It is no small thing that I command; but there is no help for it. If Bessas would live, let him perform this service."

Myron, his heart pounding, drew a deep breath and gathered his courage. "May I, too, go on this expedition, sire?"

"Wherefore should you wish to do that?"

"Well—Bessas is a mighty warrior whose glance flashes lightning, but literary he is not, and you will wish a well-written account of the journey for the archives."

The king smiled faintly. "That is not a bad reason. But I will wager that you have a better one—one concerning your own advantage. Tell me what it is."

Myron smiled in turn. "Your Majesty can see a mouse through a millstone. I wish to observe things that no man has yet seen and learn things that no man yet knows. Besides, I come of a people who number many heroes among their forebears. Teaching in the capitals of the Empire is pleasant—especially when I can catch glimpses

26

of Your Majesty—but hardly heroic. So pray let your slave accompany Bessas."

"I see no objection."

"Then may I——" Myron began, eager to start for the execution ground to save Bessas, whose time must be drawing short. But the king spoke:

"This Hellenic passion to see all and pry into all is a curious new form of insanity. I am told that there are even people among you called wisdom-lovers, who devote their entire lives to this pursuit. How do you pronounce it? Fir—firos——"

"Philosophers, sire. Your slave studied under one of the great ones, Herakleitos of Ephesos. I hope some day to be considered a wisdom-lover myself. And now may——"

"Curious," persisted Xerxes, running his fingers through his beard. "I should not care to rule an entire nation of these wisdom-lovers. They would demand a reason for every command or ever they obeyed it, and nought would get done.

"Meanwhile we must set a time limit to this expedition, or Bessas may think to disappear into the wilds of Africa and never return. How far is this land of dragons?"

Myron scowled in concentration. "I could tell better in the archives, Highness, where the maps and manuscripts lie. But, as a rough estimate, I should say it were about four hundred leagues from here to Memphis; three hundred more to Kush; and several hundred—no man knows how many—thence to the source of the Nile. I would allow at least a thousand leagues each way. If I may——"

"At ten leagues a day, you could make the journey each way in a hundred days, or two hundred altogether. Allowing for stops, you can easily catch your dragon and be back by this date next year."

"O King!" cried Myron. "We could never do it so quickly."

"Why not? My postmen cover twenty or thirty leagues every day."

"But sire! Your couriers follow well-trodden routes, and when one mount or team becomes fatigued they change it at a relay station. We shall command no such facilities, and we shall be burdened with extra people, weapons, and other necessary things. We cannot cover the whole vast distance at a gallop. Moreover, the latter part of our journey lies deep into unknown country, where roads may not exist, and where we may be imprisoned by some barbarian king or attacked by some wild tribe. By straining every sinew, perhaps we can return in two years. Now, with Your Majesty's permission——"

"Ridiculous!" growled the king. "At worst, I see not how you would need more than a year and a quarter. I will tell you. Be at Persepolis on the first of Duuzu of next year, with your dragon. Now, you will require documents—man, why do you hop and fidget like a mouse in a chamber pot? Have you a flux of the bowels?"

"Great King!" cried Myron, who had been glancing with growing nervousness at the waxing light that came through the door of the great hall. "Bessas is to be executed at dawn, and dawn is upon us!"

"Well, why said you not so sooner? Begone! You will arrive in time, as nought begins when it is supposed to. *Here!* Come back! You do not think the executioners will halt on your mere word, do you? Show them this ring. Fetch it back, together with your man!"

Xerxes tossed his seal ring. Myron leaped, caught it, and dashed out. It was raining. He slipped on the wet steps of the Apadana and almost fell off the platform, but saved himself by catching one of the stepped triangular crenelations of the parapet. He dodged around a group of stonecutters, who had arrived early to work on an uncompleted relief, and ran down the stair to the Gate of All Nations. Here a pair of guards thrust themselves in his way until another guard called down from the platform of the Apadana that all was well.

28

"Master Myron!" shrilled a eunuch. "You must leave your robe of audience!"

Myron tore off the white robe, threw it at the eunuch, snatched up his plain brown cloak from the bench, and ran on. At the bottom of the main stair he looked about for a horse, mule, or cart, but none was in sight.

He ran westward, taking what he hoped was the shortest route. Persepolis was beginning to stir for its day's work. Myron dodged slave girls walking towards the town well with jars on their heads.

In a narrow alley he found himself behind a huge dark-brown two-humped camel, whose coat of winter wool was peeling off in patches. The beast plodded slowly on, filling the alley. The cameleer, a turbaned Arachosian in baggy trousers and sheepskin coat, looked down impassively from atop a pile of merchandise.

"Get that abandoned beast out of the way!" cried Myron, waving the seal ring. "I am on the king's business!"

The cameleer spat and looked away. The camel ambled on.

Myron drew his knife, reached up, and jabbed the beast in the haunch. The camel gave a bubbling roar and broke into a jouncing trot, banging its load against the house fronts. The load began to slide. The cameleer grabbed for handholds, shrieking curses in the names of Imrâ, Gîsh, and other elder gods who reigned before the coming of the Aryans. At the next corner, Myron slipped past, dodging a kick that the driver aimed at his head.

Myron ran on. His breath began to labor; he had not run like this for years. The universe swam before his eyes.

Soon he reached the wall. This was a small wall as such things went: a mere ten or twelve feet of mud brick, counting the parapet. At the Shushan Gate, a flourish of the ring got Myron past the sentries. He ran out upon the Shushan road, through a scattering of houses and plowed fields. Ahead, he saw a multitude gathered at the drill field, some holding umbrellas and some with hoods pulled over heads.

As Myron drew near, he was vastly relieved to see that the execution had not yet taken place. He pushed roughly through the crowd to the front, ignoring curses and threats from those whom he elbowed aside.

On the ground, a dozen paces in front of him, lay Bessas of Zariaspa, naked and bound. A few feet away rose the stake. It had been rammed into the earth at a low angle, so that its point, gleaming with the creamy hue of freshly whittled wood, was only a foot above the earth. Two great gray oxen stood, one on each side of the stake. The crew were tying Bessas' ankles to the harness of the beasts, one to each ox.

When the point of the stake had been inserted, the oxen would pull Bessas until the point had pierced upward into his vitals for a little more than a foot. Then the tackle would be removed from the victim and attached to the stake itself, so that the oxen could pull the stake and its victim into an upright position. It would then be wedged into place.

Myron faced an Immortal, who held a spear level to keep back the crowd. Waving the king's ring, Myron tried to talk but could not get his breath.

"You—the king—pardon——" he gasped. Then he went into a fit of coughing.

"Stand back and stop pushing, you!" said the soldier.

The executioners finished tying Bessas' ankles. One grasped each ankle and began to haul the prostrate man towards the stake. Bessas jerked a leg loose, whereupon another executioner kicked him in the ribs. More hands seized his legs and pulled until the point of the stake touched his flesh. Those holding the oxen pulled them forward, to tauten the ropes running back from them to the victim, and lined the animals up. The chief executioner, a brawny, bare-armed man in brown leather, raised an arm.

"Commutation of sentence!" gasped Myron. "Let me through, in the name of the king!"

"Let a Hellene through with such a tale?" said the soldier. "We all know what liars——"

Myron ducked under the spear and ran towards the executioners. The soldier shouted angrily over his shoulder but did not leave his post in the line for fear that the whole crowd would surge through the gap thus opened. The other Immortals took up the shout. An officer started towards Myron, half drawing his sword.

The chief executioner lowered his arm. The men tending the oxen stepped back and raised their whips.

Myron ran in front of the oxen, unfurled his cloak, and flapped it in the animals' faces. With startled snorts and rolling eyes, the beasts gave back, turning in their traces.

"Cut down that madman!" shouted a voice.

The officer came close, sword out. Myron thrust the king's ring into his face, shouting:

"Behold the king's seal! The sentence has been commuted!"

When Myron said it for the third time, the officer grasped the idea. Soon Bessas' ankles were unbound, though his wrists remained fettered. An angry mutter arose from the crowd.

"My trousers, curse you!" roared the prostrate man in a Bactrian accent.

Soon Bessas was on his feet again. His teeth flashed through a mass of dirty black beard. "Good old Myron!" he cried. "When I'm free, I'll buy you enough wine of Halpa to drown an elephant in!"

Bessas son of Phraates towered over all the rest. Zarina's baby was a heavy-featured man, six and a half feet tall and massively muscled. Under a disordered mop of black hair were a broad forehead, heavy black brows, deep-set brown eyes, wide cheekbones, a long nose (which had been straight until a sword cut had put a kink in it),

31

and full lips. A short beard masked his massive jaw. But for the pocks that marked his face, he would have been handsome in a rugged, somber way.

Although but thirty, Bessas bore the scars of a veteran. One ran from the left temple down into the beard, another across the right cheek, and others were to be seen on neck and arms and running through the mat of curly black fur that covered his chest.

In stripping the Bactrian, the executioners, not daring to untie his hands, had cut his jacket to pieces. So Myron cast his cloak over Bessas' bare shoulders.

"I do not mind the rain," said Bessas. "It might wash some of the muck off me. You there!" he snarled at the head executioner. "Will you keep us standing here all morning? You stinking slob, haven't you heard that the king awaits me?"

The executioner tightened his lips and took a step forward as if to punish the Bactrian's insolence. Bessas bared his gleaming teeth. The executioner turned away to supervise the packing up of the stake and its gear. Soon spectators, soldiers, executioners, Bessas, and Myron were all slopping through the mud back towards the city.

II   The Rim of the World

WHILE THE KING'S BARBER and bath attendant made Bessas presentable, Myron talked with his former pupil. Since he was sure the attendants did not know Greek, he spoke in his native tongue.

". . . so you will be liberated on condition that you procure these two rarities," said Myron. "How does it strike you?"

"It sounds like a quest for the fabled castle of Kangdiz," said Bessas in slow, heavily accented Greek, "but it's better than being buggered by the Ionian." He called the stake by its Persian nickname. "I am no puling infant

but, by Mithra, the touch of that damned toothpick un-
manned me!"

"Your Greek has deteriorated," said Myron. "It's *mè*,
not *moì*."

Bessas gave a low rumble of laughter. "Same old Myron! It is well that you're not going on this journey.
Else, when some savage chieftain is making up his mind
whether to chop our heads off, you would correct his
speech and get us slain for sure."

"Oh, but my dear fellow, I am too going!"

"*What?*"

"Yes; the king has already given his permission."

Bessas groaned. "What in the name of the Seven
Guardian Stars put that thought into your mind?"

"For nearly thirty years I have taught in Shushan and
other cities of the Empire: first as Arsaces' slave, then as
a freedman. You, who are young enough to be my son,
have undergone desperate adventures all over the eastern
marches of the Empire. Before I die, I intend to experience some action and adventure, also. And I mean to see
some far countries and learn new truths, that the Milesians shall remember my name. To the crows with trying
to beat culture into these insolent brats!"

"But look you, O Myron, you must be an old man of
fifty. How could you survive such a rigorous journey?"

"First, I am not yet fifty, albeit near enough to it. Second, I have kept up my physique in our little gymnasium
in Shushan."

"Wearing a breechclout so as not to shock our Persian
modesty, I trust," said Bessas with a grin. The first attempts of the Hellenes of Shushan to keep up their athletic customs had caused a mighty scandal, because of
the innocent Greek attitude towards nudity.

"And third," continued Myron, "I was in condition to
run all the way from the palace to the drill field this
morning, to rescue you from the spike. Lastly, who else
in his right mind would accompany you at all, let alone
seek to do so?"

"You have a point," rumbled Bessas, "and I admit you are cleverer than I in many ways. Even if you weren't, I could hardly deny the man who has just saved my life. Still and all——"

"Furthermore, your mother urged this course upon me."

"Oh. That's different. No paint or powder!" he commanded the attendants. "But put on more of that scent. By the claws of the Corpse Fiend, 'twill take a quart of perfume to cover the prison stench!"

As the attendants rubbed more salve on his hairy chest, Bessas went on: "Well, our next step is to find ways and means. Who is to pay for this daft jape?"

"Rise!" said the king.

Having slept and rightly arrayed himself, Xerxes was now more impressive than he had been at the meeting before the dawn. Over a purple shirt with white dots he wore his best robe, the great purple-dyed kandys, heavy with golden embroidery representing gryphons and other monsters in combat. Rumor said that this garment, woven by the most skilled embroiderers of Babylon, had cost twelve thousand talents. Jewels winked from the golden earring in his left ear and from the rings on his fingers. A tiara of thin gold, adorned with a circle of upright golden feathers, rose from his head.

"May the gods give the Great King life!" said Myron. "Your slave has explained to Bessas the conditions of the commutation of his sentence."

"Do you accept, O Bessas?" asked the king, popping his still bloodshot eyes at the Bactrian.

"Your slave accepts," said Bessas.

Xerxes smiled a wry little smile. "And think not to flee, once you are over the borders of the Empire. I hold your mother as security for your return."

"You——" Bessas started to burst out violently but choked back his words. His lips writhed and the veins

34

stood out on his forehead with passion. Myron feared for a moment that Xerxes would punish the Bactrian for lèse-majesté, so patent were his feelings even though he spoke not a word.

Then Bessas' pock-pitted face fell. Myron, keenly watching, was sure that Bessas had had some such plan of escape in mind.

"Your slave understands," the young man choked out at last. "But how are the costs of this journey to be met? Whereas Lord Sataspes is rich, I have nought but my pay as troop leader."

Xerxes frowned. "I thought you possessed an estate in Bactria."

"Nay, Majesty. The Toktarians overran that part of the land when they slew my father."

"Oh, I see. Your father was *that* Phraates. Well, My Majesty will authorize you to draw ten darics from the treasurer."

"Ten? That will not take us far, sire. You speak of a journey of thousands of leagues."

"Well, fifteen then, but no more."

"Great King!" said Myron, terrified at his own daring. "My master truly wishes this expedition to succeed, does he not? Well, no obstacle is so great as inability. What good will it do to struggle through hundreds of leagues of wild, exotic lands, only to be stranded for want of resources? To be safe, we shall require at least fifty——"

"Twenty-five, and not a shekel more," said Xerxes. "If Bessas succeed, I will not only pardon him; I will also see that he gets back his father's barony. And I will give him a document to this effect. By presenting this document he can borrow such further sums as he needs from the bankers of Babylon, putting up the estate as security."

"But sire!" said Bessas. "To recover our lands would take an army——"

"Do you question the Great King's power, sirrah? Anyway, even if it prove impracticable, I can always give you

35

life tenure to an equivalent tract from the crown lands, to provide for your needs. Nay, not another word of this. Is the King of All Kings a Tyrian haggler?

"Now go your ways. Aspamitres shall furnish you with documents to commend you to the satraps and authorize you to draw food and fodder from the royal stores. May God befriend you; for you will need the favor of Auramazda on this journey."

The Daduchid mansion stood near the base of the great platform of Persepolis. As torches flared against the dark of the evening, the lordly owners sat in their counting room. Costly hangings covered the walls, and weapons hung from the undraped strips between the hangings. Yellow lamplight winked from jewels and golden filigree on the hilts of swords and daggers. A rich rug, whose pattern depicted the hero Haoshyaha destroying the wizards of Hyrkania, covered the floor.

Bagabyxas, ranking member of the clan, commander of one of the six army corps, member of the Council of Seven, and fourth most powerful man in the Empire, was about Myron's age. He was a lean, sinewy man with a sharp, narrow face, who moved with smooth control. Although he painted his face in the manner of a Persian gentleman, he gave the impression of hardness, shrewdness, and immense controlled power.

Zopyrus son of Bagabyxas was much like his sire, albeit younger and heavier. He ran his fingers through the curls of his beard as he spoke:

"You may talk of temporizing and accepting an indemnity, Father. Were Tamyra a grown woman who had enticed that blackguard, I might be so persuaded. But a child of eleven! Nay, this is a matter of honor—of my honor and the clan's. I should count myself worse than a woman, did I not strive to sunder these men's god-detested souls from their stinking bodies."

"They may both perish on their expeditions," said Bagabyxas. "Why not leave it to the gods———"

36

"Because, by the hairs of Auramazda's beard, I want revenge!" roared Zopyrus. Leaping up, he paced like a captive leopard. "I am fain to see their blood flow, to relish their screams of pain, to play stick-and-ball with their heads, to hang their fresh-flayed hides on the wall. If fate prevent me from putting them to the torture myself, I will work through others. Now do you understand?"

"Aye. But how will you catch the departed Sataspes? A stern chase is a long chase."

"I know one in Shushan who can overcome the barriers of time and distance."

"Mean you Ardigula of Baghdad?"

"Aye. Know you him?"

"I have heard of him and not to his credit. We risk our souls in dealing with this demon-worshiper."

"I fear neither man nor demon."

"He who hugs hot coals to his bosom will surely have his raiment scorched," persisted the older man. "Were it not better to wait until Sataspes be on his way back and hire men to waylay him?"

The younger Persian snorted. "How could we post men at the right time and place, not knowing when or whence the man will come? Nay, this is the only way left to restore the honor of the house of Daduchus." Zopyrus seated himself again, held a pomegranate to his nose, and inhaled. "What stirs my bile the most is the king's letting these scum off without even sending word to us. If Xerxes—Ahriman smite him!—had not given the scoundrels these tasks to perform, I had sought them out and slain them myself. As it is, I shall make arrangements to dispose of Master Bessas on my way to Shushan."

"No deeds of blood in Persepolis!" said Bagabyxas.

Zopyrus grinned. "Fear not. I shall merely collect the debt of gratitude owed me by Puzur the Ouxian."

When Myron opened the door of Hutrara's wineshop, the blast of noise and the smell of sweat and stale beer struck him in the face like a blow. The place was jammed. All those within appeared to be drinking and shouting at the same time. Some, having brought their suppers, were eating as well. At last Myron made out Bassas' heavy, pock-marked visage in a distant corner.

"Make room for my friend!" roared Bessas.

When those on the bench beside him did not respond, he pushed against the nearest with his shoulder, so that all slid down the bench and the last man fell off the end. The fallen man scrambled up with a curse, feeling for his knife. Then he recognized Bessas and subsided.

"Heed these knaves not," said Bessas. "Squeeze in here and have some beer. Greek or no, you had better learn to like beer, for that's all they have in Egypt."

"Thank you," said Myron, "but I think it were desirable to go out to talk. One must shout to make oneself heard here, and we would not reveal our plans to everyone from Karia to Carthage——"

"To Ahriman with your Greek moderation! This is my last chance for a decent carouse, and I mean to make the most of it." Bessas wiped the froth from his mustache, closed his eyes, and silently moved his fingers and lips. Then he spoke:

> The moving shadow saith: "Swift Time doth run,
> And soon he'll hale thee where there is no sun."
> Well then, am I Time's slave? I'll mock the fiend,
> And gaily revel till my course be done!

"We can return to drink anon, when the crowd has thinned," said Myron. "If you become intoxicated now, you'll not understand me when——"

Bessas made a vulgar noise. "Either drink here with me, or go jump in the Kurush."

"So you don't care what befalls your mother?"

Bessas glowered at the older man. "May you be kinless! You would think of that. I'll come."

The Bactrian rose with a belch and staggered towards the door. Outside, he said:

38

"Because I obey you this time, do not think that you are the leader. This is my expedition and I command it, do you understand?"

"How did you do for money?" asked Myron.

They climbed the stair leading to the top of the city wall and, leaning their elbows on the crenelations of the parapet, looked out over the plain. The sky had cleared. A narrow stripe of gold and apple-green along the jagged western horizon told of the departure of the day. Overhead the stars had come out; a silver scimitar of a moon hung a hand's breadth above the western peaks. Bats wheeled overhead as the darkness deepened. From the cultivated fields that spread out before them came the buzz and chirp of insects and the cries of night birds. Jackals yelped in the distance.

"I got the twenty-five darics out of Vaus," said Bessas, "and I talked another five out of my battalion commander as an advance against my pay. I had to argue my throat sore to get part of it in gold, so as not to have to haul ten pounds of silver all over the world. Those knaves in the treasury love to give up their gold as Xerxes loves the Athenians."

"Have you nothing saved up?"

"A few shekels only, and those I must leave with Norax to buy things for Mother." Norax was Bessas' Sardinian slave, who had lighted the way to Myron's house for Zarina. "If I had more money, I should have bought horses."

Myron slapped a mosquito. "It's too bad that all this had to happen when you had gambled away your horses."

"Yes, teacher. And twit me not on my follies, unless you wish a tumble from the wall. Oh, well, we may stumble upon a chance to loot the treasure of some foreign king or nobleman. But I have got us passage as far as Shushan, at least."

"How?"

"One of my brother officers agreed to let me take two of his horses to Shushan and deliver them to his groom

39

there. Soon the court will move to Hagmatana for the summer months, and my friend will pick up his horses on the way thither. I promised not to race the nags."

Myron said: "I don't suppose they would permit you to take your Nisaean stallion?"

"Varuna, no! The king won't let one of those steeds out of his grip. My trouble is that a horse, to do me any good, must be nigh as big as a Nisaean. If you put me on some little pony, the beast drops dead within the first league."

"We could have used that pair the king sacrificed to Mithra the day before yesterday."

"Grudge not the Lord of the Wide Pastures his meed. How fared you in the archives?"

"I obtained lists of towns as far as Meroê, in Kush, with notes on distances and dangers. Nobody seems to know what lies beyond Meroê. And I made a rough map of our route. Did you see your mother?"

"Aye." The Bactrian fell silent. Myron knew that his feeling for his mother was a subject on which Bessas would not wish to speak.

Myron began: "And I have a letter from a friend in Shushan, Uni the Egyp——"

He stopped as light, sound, and motion came from the Shushan Gate below them and a score of paces to their right. Torchlight flickered redly; fragments of words drifted up on the still night air.

Two horsemen rode out from the gate, one carrying a torch. They spurred to a canter and headed westward on the Shushan road. The torch flared as the riders began to move rapidly, then dwindled to an orange speck, like a sluggish shooting star. Myron said:

"I could swear I knew the leading horseman. But I cannot quite——"

Bessas grunted. "Dip me in dung if that be not Zopyrus son of Bagabyxas, with his beard in a bag! After he was so eager to see me impaled, I could not help knowing him, even by torchlight. And the other is his armor bearer."

"Would that I had your eyes!" said Myron. "I trust Zopyrus' errand has nothing to do with us. He would not gallop the length of the Empire to fetch us Hippolyta's belt, I'm sure."

"I like it not either. Whatever it be, it must be urgent, to set out at a run on a moonless night on these polluted roads. My *fravashi* tells me that we had better be off soon, too."

"How about equipment?"

"We'll buy it in Babylon, where they have proper markets. Let's catch some sleep and be off with the false dawn. You have no family to concern you, have you?"

"No. I have a woman friend, but a hasty farewell must suffice her. I must, however, make arrangements for my pupils and take time to gather writing materials."

"What for? I've galloped all over the eastern marches of the Empire and led troops of the king's horse without writing a word. Not that anybody can read my writing anyway."

"Bessas!" said Myron in a pained tone. "After all the trouble I took over your penmanship!"

Bessas clapped his smaller companion on the back. "Cheer up; I'm happy to be unlettered in half a dozen tongues. I find sharp steel of more avail in my trade than pen and parchment, and so will you on this journey."

"But somebody must keep a journal! Otherwise we shall never know if we are returning in time. Moreover, the king expects a report on the foreign lands we visit."

"*Vaush;* see you to it. One more thing!"

"What's that?"

"We must swear fidelity to each other, lest we break up over some petty quarrel halfway to our goal. I have not the sweetest nature in the world, and I know how fickle you Hellenes are."

"*Ea!* We are not! What makes you——"

"Ha! What of Pausanias the Spartan king? What of the treachery of the Samians at Ladê? Now, cut your arm a little and swear by all your gods that you will adhere faithfully to me and be my friend, helper, and defender, sharing in need and standing fast in danger, until our quest be done or until death part us!"

"If you like; though it's the man who makes us believe the oath, not the oath the man."

Each made a nick in his arm, sucked the other's blood, and swore a mighty oath. Far away a lion roared, and overhead great white stars shone coldly.

Next morning, in a glow of quiet self-satisfaction, Myron returned to his room from his farewell to his lady friend. He paid off his landlord, gathered his gear, and went to the barracks to find Bessas.

The Bactrian was not there. After waiting for a Babylonian double hour, Myron learnt that Bessas was bidding his mother farewell.

Zarina was settled in a room, small but not uncomfortable, in the palace of Darius. A pair of burly guards stood before the door. Inside, Myron found the lady and her son seated side by side on the bed and weeping. Zarina was saying:

". . . if an old woman like me die a year sooner or later it matters not. But you are young; you must live out your life——"

"I will not live it out without you!" said Bessas. "If you die thus, I will die, too!"

"What is all this dismal talk of dying?" said Myron.

"My mother," said Bessas, "has a mad idea, to wit: after I have been gone for a few months, to give me a good start for the frontiers, she'll slay herself, thus robbing Xerxes of his hold over me. I tell her that, if she do any such thing, I will slay myself when I learn of it."

"It is the only way——" began Zarina, but Myron broke in:

"My dear Lady Zarina! We must all die, and let us hope we shall face death with fortitude. But let us not

42

hasten our terminus. I didn't save your son just to have the pair of you threaten each other with suicide. You remind me of a story I heard in Babylon."

"What is that?" asked Zarina.

"When I studied there under the astronomer Naburimanni, I once became despondent because I could not seem to master the arcane Babylonian art of long division. But, when I uttered some such foolish threat as yours, my wise old teacher told me this tale, of the times of the great King Nebuchadrezzar.

"It seems that a third assistant pastry cook in the royal kitchens was caught in the act of stealing a lamb, which was to have been cooked for the king's supper. So the king, full of righteous wrath, ordered that the felon be flayed alive the next day.

"As the thief was being led out to execution, the king passed by in his chariot. And the condemned man called out: 'O King! If you will grant me a reprieve, I will teach one of your horses to sing a hymn to Nabu, which will greatly please the god.'

" 'Are you mad?' said the king.

" 'Nay, sire,' said the thief; 'I do but make you a sporting offer.'

" 'How long would this course of instruction take?' said the king.

" 'Give me a year, Your Majesty,' said the thief.

" 'So be it,' said the king. 'But, if you fail, know that you shall die as before.'

"So the thief was established in a place near the stables, to begin teaching the horse. And one of the guards posted over him asked: 'What silly business is this, about teaching a horse to sing hymns? You know you cannot do it.'

" 'Well, perhaps I can and perhaps I cannot,' said the thief. 'But even if I fail, I have a year. And during that year the king may die, or the horse may die, or I may die; and in any of these cases I shall be better off. And who knows? Peradventure I shall teach the horse to sing hymns after all!'

43

"So, my dear but foolish friends, let us not anticipate more troubles than we must. Who knows? Perhaps we shall find our dragon and win Xerxes' gratitude after all."

Bessas and his mother dried their tears, smiled wan smiles, and embraced for the last time. Then Bessas followed his teacher back to the barracks.

Again, King Xerxes sat in Ostanas' chamber, facing the wizard across the table. On the table stood a small brazier with three bronzen legs, which ended in reptilian claws. In the brazier glowed a small fire of charcoal. Ostanas fanned the flame until the lumps of charcoal brightened from red to vermilion.

Then the magician began dropping jasmine seeds into the charcoal, one at a time. There was a delicate hiss and crackle. Otherwise all was silent, save for the breathing of the men and the click of the hyena's claws as it paced its cage.

A thread of blue smoke arose from the brazier, to curl back upon itself in coils and arabesques. At times the column rose straight to above the level of the watchers' eyes; then it broke into a mass of writhing coils. Ostanas' eyes gleamed beneath his shaggy white brows.

"What says the smoke?" demanded Xerxes.

Ostanas took his time. At last he said: "They may succeed; but only if the gods so will it."

Xerxes snorted. "A prophetic ambiguity worthy of Delphoi! How could you lose?"

Ostanas spread his hands. "Your slave does his best, but the world of magical science is not to be coerced."

"Can you give me the details?"

"I was coming to that, my master. I saw them returning with a monster. Yet something—perhaps my *fravashi* —told me that dangers hem their path and may destroy them ere they reach us."

"What shall we do?"

44

"The unseen powers have not yet informed me. I will seek enlightenment in dreams and consult the glittering stars."

"Speaking of dreams," said the king, "I had a hideous one ere I awoke. I dreamt that I lay on my bed, with one of my women beside me. A man stooped over the bed, raising a knife to plunge it into my heart. At first I weened it was my brother Masistes, red with blood. Then I saw that the face of the figure was but a mask, like those which actors wear on the Greek stage. I struggled, with one hand to hold back the knife and with the other to tear away the mask. But the mask would not move, whilst the knife came ever closer. I awoke screaming, with the eunuchs running to and fro in the chamber like frightened Indian fowl. What make you of it?"

"That will require study of the records of ancient oneiromancers. If my master——"

The king's private knock interrupted. Xerxes called: "Enter!"

A stout Persian, with a permanent smile and darkly darting eyes, stood bowing in the door. "Your slave, Great King!"

"Aye, Artabanus?"

"Your slave has been reliably informed that the persons after whom the King of Kings inquired—Bessas son of Phraates and Myron son of Perseus—departed according to plan, one hour after noon, on the Shushan road."

"Thank you, good Artabanus."

"The utmost appreciation is hereby expressed by your slave, that this small piece of information should have met with my lord and master's approbation. And now, if my unworthy self may present this report whereof I have spoken——"

"I want the King's Eye named Datas!"

"But, sire, this said report is considered to be of the utmost moment, dealing as it does with alleged unrest in the province of Egypt. Your slave estimates that it will not consume above two hours——"

"Curse you, get me Datas!" shouted Xerxes, almost in a scream.

When Artabanus had bowed himself out, the king said: "I know not why he so provokes me. The *hazarapat* is a brave warrior and a competent governor. Yet his way of wrapping every word in a thick layer of unctuous formality renders dealing with him repulsive. I verily believe he desires to slay me by boredom."

"We must maintain the royal dignity," said Ostanas.

"Certes, but Artabanus lays it on so thickly that I suspect him of laughing in his beard at me. And yet, he knows all the threads of authority and influence so well that I could not replace him."

"Of course," murmured Ostanas, "if Your Majesty took a more active part in administration, as once you did——"

"Ahriman take you, Ostanas; tell me not how to run my realm! If the quest prove successful, I shall have things to consider of more moment than these endless, tedious reports on unrest in Egypt, drouth in Chorasmia, nomadic raids in Bactria, and——"

The knock sounded again. This time the visitor was a man of less than average height, so ordinary-looking that he were hard to describe further.

"Your slave, Datas by name, awaits the Great King's command," murmured the man, touching his forehead to the floor.

"Good." Xerxes briefly described Bessas, Myron, and their quest, adding: "I trust not this Bessas. Not only is he a daring and hard-bitten rogue, but his father, also, was a factionary of my traitorous brother Masistes. So I wish you to follow them."

"Aye, Majesty?"

"You shall watch for three things. First: Bessas adheres to the outlawed cult of Mithraism, as did his father before him; Baron Phraates was a notorious coddler and fautor of heretics. Instead of joining the reformed and united true faith of Zoroastrian Mazdaism, he clings to the remnants of schismatic superstition. Were he some flea-bitten Syrian or Arab, that would not matter; but we cannot tolerate such heresy in an Aryan. I wish you to watch for evidence of his dealing with hidden Mithraists. Mayhap he will discover us their leaders, so that we can scotch this serpent of daiva-worship once and for all.

"Secondly, I hear rumors of a pretender: one Orontes, claiming to be a son of Cambyses. His emissaries approach daring and able Aryans to seduce them into conspiracy. Watch for signs of this plot, also.

"Lastly, some are displeased that Bessas should have escaped the stake. Bagabyxas the Daduchid, I am told, is one such. Knowing Bagabyxas, it would not astony me if he sought by subtle means to make away with Bessas and Sataspes ere they return. Watch for such an attempt and, if need be, do your utmost to thwart it. The final disposal of Bessas is mine, and I will not have one of my subjects take private vengeance upon him! Do you understand all?"

"Aye, sire."

"Then may God befriend you. Get yourself upon the road whilst the trail is still warm!"

As the agent departed, Xerxes turned again to the wizard. "Tell me, good Ostanas, why should any sane man wish to take my place as king? For twenty years I have striven to be a greater king than my noble sire; yet my loftiest schemes have gone awry." He held up a hand at Ostanas' protest. "Save your flattery, my friend. I would not admit this to any other, but I know fire from flood.

"I reformed the currency—and the plaints of the merchants that they can no longer make a profit are louder than ever. I reformed religion, uniting the quarreling sects of the Aryan faith according to the teaching of the Great Magus—and the Mithraists and Anahitists and others remain stubbornly outside the fold, worshiping in secret and plotting with would-be usurpers. I beat down two great rebellions, smashing mighty armies—and the barbarous brigands of Hellas cut two of my army corps to

47

shreds and slay three of my brothers and my finest general. What have the gods against me?

"At first I worked myself nigh unto death, and the people said: What does this royal busybody, thrusting that long nose of his into our business day and night? Why does he not leave us alone to mind our affairs? Now that I rule through Artabanus and the rest, they say: What does the royal lecher, lurking slothfully in his harem when he should be leading the Empire and smiting wrongdoers night and day? None values me at my true worth. Suspicion and hatred divide me from my family. Women have been my curse; I cannot wait to finish my new palace, to get away from the clack of their venomous tongues.

"Would the great Cyrus had remained a petty kinglet in the hills of Parsa, without imperial ambitions! Yet, having mounted the tiger, I must needs ride the full nine circuits."

In the barren, rugged Ouxian mountains, where cold winds whistled through a vast blue sky and vultures and eagles circled forever on broad brown wings, a ring of hillmen squatted. They were a wild-looking lot with long tangled hair, ragged tunics, and patched pantaloons. One, however, was clad in new if dirty garments, with his hair confined by a low twisted turban. They listened to Zopyrus, who said:

"Tell me, friend Puzur, if it be not true that, when the Great King would have seated you on the stake, I prevailed upon him to let you go?"

"You speak sooth," said he of the turban. "And now, I doubt not, you wish a return for your boon. Have you fallen out with the Great King, so that you must hide in the hills?"

Zopyrus smiled thinly. "Not yet. I do but wish you to waylay a brace of travelers."

"As Lagamar is my witness, that were no favor at all!"

48

cried the hill chief. "We do that anyway. Ask a boon worthy of Puzur the Ouxian."

"Fear not, this will do admirably. Moreover, you may keep all the loot that you find upon them, with one exception."

"And that is?"

"Their heads. These you shall send to me, at my house in Shushan."

"When will these travelers appear?"

"At any time, but I should think within the next day or two. Thus shall you know them. . . ."

Bessas and Myron rode up the valley of the Kurush. Rugged mountains towered to right and left in long brown ridges, running from southeast to northwest and seeming closer in the clear Iranian air than they really were.

Bessas wore a short Median jacket, baggy leathern riding breeches, and over his head a bashlyk, or cloth hood. This hood hid most of his beard and could be pulled up to the eyes at need. At his left side swung a straight horseman's sword of Indian steel, a full three feet long including the hilt. The teakwood scabbard bore a row of little silver tahrs, or Himalayan wild goats, and ended in a silver tiger's head. The pommel took the form of a gryphon's head of crystal. From his other side hung a dagger with a large turquoise roundel; a lacquered bow-and-arrow case bumped against his back.

With leathern trousers and boots on his legs and a bashlyk on his head, Myron looked like a Persian, except that his skin shone with fresh oil. As he rode, he felt pleased with himself for having kept his courage up, to the time of departure. This adventure was something of which he had long dreamt and talked. But, when it bade fair to come true, he approached it with hesitation and dread. A dozen times he had almost backed out; but now, thank Hera, he had taken the plunge.

He stared intently at the vast, dust-colored land, speckled with the red and blue and yellow flecks of short-lived spring flowers. He gazed at the clouds and the birds and the mountaintops. He looked about him keenly for any odd fact or new phenomenon to add to his store of knowledge.

For Myron Perseôs was a collector of facts, as other men collected concubines or horses or gold. Sometimes he temporarily forgot them, as does a squirrel the nuts it has buried. But the facts were all there, locked away in his squarish skull, waiting for some reminder to call them forth. He secretly hoped that some day these facts would fall into a pattern—a pattern that should give a profound new insight into the nature of things and place his name with those of Thales and Herakleitos among the great lovers of wisdom. Although it had never occurred, and Myron sometimes feared he was simply not clever enough to build a noble edifice of thought from his myriad bricks of fact, he never completely gave up hope.

At the end of the first day out of Persepolis, Myron and Bessas crossed into the valley of the Ulai. Near its source the Ulai was a mere trickle, whose tributaries ran water only after a rain. The snows of winter still crested the higher ridges.

Once or twice a day a Persian post rider passed them, racing along at full gallop with his bashlyk pulled up to his eyes and his mailbags flapping against his horse's flanks. Now and then they encountered a string of camels, swaying slowly under high-piled loads, or a pair of road guards cantering by and watching the heights. Once they passed a knot of sullen peasants, lackadaisically filling holes in the road, while a royal officer barked himself hoarse at them.

Bessas set the pace by alternately cantering and walking. Betimes he stopped to let the horses graze, while he and Myron sat on stones and munched salt meat and hard biscuits. By the second day Myron could hardly walk, let alone mount and dismount. Therefore his giant companion had to give him a leg-up.

"A mule at a gentle walk is more my speed," groaned Myron.

"You need a few more calluses on your arse," said the Bactrian. "You'll have them by the time we get to Kush."

"Or else I shall be dead, as dead as Odysseus' dog."

"Ha! Shall I then bury you, burn you, or throw you away as do the Magi?"

"Do as you like. As Herakleitos says, a corpse is worth no more than so much excrement."

"Good for him!" Bessas sang:

> Some give their dead to earth, and some to fire,
> And some to beasts that roam the deserts dire;
> But since the dead do not return to rail,
> For aught I care, my guts may string a lyre!

Myron observed that, while his companion had been morose and irritable in Persepolis, under the strict routine of the Immortals, he became buoyantly and boisterously cheerful once they were out on the royal road, owning no master and bound for the rim of the world. The Bactrian cracked coarse jokes, at which he laughed thunderously. He lectured on his favorite subject: the care of horses.

"For look you, O Myron," he said, "I have seen you tie your horse to a low bush when the branch of a tree was to hand. In tethering a horse, the halter or reins should be tied, when possible, to a place above the animal's head. For it is the wont of the horse, when aught annoys his face, to strive to rid himself of it by tossing his head. If the halter be tied low, this jerk is likely to tear it loose or break it; whereas, if it be tied high, it is merely tossed out of the way, and the beast remains tethered.

"Now, in rubbing down a horse, one should start at the head and mane, taking care not to use any instrument of wood or iron on the animal's head; for here the skin, being stretched tightly over the skull, is easily injured. . . ."

They drew up at a fortified post of dun mud brick.

51

Here was a postal station, with remounts for the post riders. Here also was a tiny inn and the divisional guardhouse of the road guards. At Bessas' bellow, a groom took their bridles. Bessas leaped down, his heavy boots striking the ground with an earth-shaking thump. Myron slid off his mount, almost collapsed, and straightened up with effort.

In the inn, Bessas was soon deep in a jug of yellow beer with the officer in command of the road guards. The latter said:

"Bessas son of Phraates, of Zariaspa? Spit in my face if my cousin Arsames did not serve with you in Gandara, in the fifteenth year of King Xerxes. . . ."

They went into a long dialogue of pedigree and anecdote. Bessas boasted how he had once played stick-and-ball against the raja of Takshasila and scored five goals in the first chakkar. At last he said:

"Damn me for a mannerless barbarian, but I have not presented my companion, Myron of Miletos. Myron, meet my old friend, Troop Leader Ochus. Myron is a schoolmaster and, as the Hellenes put it, a lover of wisdom. Wishing to know all, he already knows a hundred times as much as I do, which is a right good start. Such a marvelous memory has he that oft he forgets his own name."

Myron and Ochus each said: "Your slave!" Bessas continued:

"How is the road from here to the Hujan plain?"

"The rains of winter tore many holes," said Ochus, "but the road commissioner will soon have them filled, if he can catch enough of these lazy Ouxian peasants and drive them to the work."

"They might work with more enthusiasm if paid," said Myron.

"*Pay* these baseborn clods? You must be mad, Greek," said the officer. "Once the holes are filled, you will have nought to fear, unless a lion steal your horses whilst you slumber, or unless Puzur choose the day of your passage for one of his raids."

"Who?" said Bessas.

"Puzur, chief of the nearest hill clan. He has taken up his old game."

Myron said: "Was there not some great to-do over Puzur about three years ago? Was he not arrested and later——"

"Aye," said Ochus, wiping the beer foam from his mustache. "Caught he was, for having robbed the Great King's mail and murdered the post rider. I looked to see him dropped into the ashes or sat upon the stake. A month later, however, he was back in his hills, having promised the king most solemnly to reform. Somebody said the Daduchids had pled for him. His reform endured for almost a year. Then, I suppose, his clansmen told him that they were starving and, unless he let them resume raiding, they would cut his throat and find a new chief."

"When will you catch him?" asked Bessas.

Ochus snorted. "Me, with sixteen road guards, catch the chief of a clan that musters above a hundred fighting men? And a man who knows every fold of the land like a mountain goat? Give your slave something easy, like snaring Keresaspa's golden sea serpent with a gossamer! I have wearied the commander in chief and the postmaster general with pleas for more men. . . ."

A reckless light danced in Bessas' dark, deep-set eyes. "By the snows of Mount Hara, fain would I wager with you that I could catch this Puzur, singlehanded!"

"Ha! That I should like to see! How much will you bet, and what time limit will you accept?"

"O Bessas!" Myron spoke in Greek, in his sharpest schoolmaster tone. "Have you gone insane, to forget your mission and all that depends upon it? Wagers, indeed!"

"Yes, teacher," grumbled Bessas. "I am sorry, Captain Ochus, but orders from the king prevent. When I return next year, if Puzur be still at large, we shall come back to this matter."

During the night, Myron awakened shivering, as the scanty fire had gone out. He became aware of a tumult among the animals in the corral behind the guardhouse: the neighing of horses, the braying of asses and mules, and the roaring of camels. When the noise died down, he heard the cause: the coughing snarl of a hunting leopard.

Unable to sleep, Myron walked briskly up and down the road in front of the guardhouse to warm his frozen limbs, bearing a spear in case the leopard were close at hand. And as he walked, he thought upon what he had heard.

An hour later, as the stars were dying and the sky was paling, Bessas was washing by the well, blowing like a porpoise as he buried his face in his cupped hands. Myron spoke:

"I have been reflecting on what I should do in Zopyrus' place."

"A Greek scribbler, taking the place of one of the greatest lords of the Persian realm?" Bessas, wringing water out of his beard, laughed with good-natured contempt. Then the Bactrian's countenance changed as he saw Myron's mouth tighten. "Forgive your slave, old man. I had forgotten my debt to you."

Myron fought down his resentment, as any Hellene living among the haughty Persians learnt perforce to do. "If I wished to destroy a man, and I knew he were going to pass over a road, and I had friends among the bandittical tribes thereabouts, I should ride ahead and arrange an ambush. Zopyrus has ridden ahead, and this Puzur is in his debt. Does it not seem logical——"

Bessas gave Myron a clap on the back that almost sent him sprawling. "*Vaush!* Though betimes your Greek logic drives me mad, I admit that it has its uses. Ochus! My lieutenant thinks there will be an ambush. . . ."

An hour later, Myron and Bessas rode out with a cold windy dawn at their backs. With them went two troopers of the road guard. Bessas ordered one of the guards to ride ahead to scout. When the man understood what was toward, however, he resisted leaving his companions. No matter how the Bactrian roared at him to get on, he persisted in reining in to let the others catch up. Meanwhile, where the slopes of the rugged brown hills allowed, Bessas ordered the second guard to ride up the heights from time to time to look about.

"This robber is no dolt," said the first guard, returning again to report. "He will send men down to the road before and behind us, to be sure of trapping us."

"Then——" began Bessas, but broke off to stare at the heights. "I think," he said, "that I saw a piece of cloth waved on the end of a stick. That were a signal. The tribesmen are probably clustered behind a hillock around the next bend or two; at least that is how such vagabonds do it in Gandara. Is there any way by which we could get behind them?"

"We have just passed a dell that leads away to northward," said the guard.

"Good. We will see where that dell goes."

"Troop Leader Bessas!" said the guard. "Would you attack this whole clan singlehanded?"

"Why not?" grinned Bessas. "If we can get behind and above them, we shall have the advantage."

"You are mad! I will have nought to do with this witless scheme!" The trooper set off at a gallop along the road by which they had come.

"Some day," said Bessas, "I will pull down that lousy craven's breeches and spank him with the flat of my sword. But then, he's not under my orders, and it is better to know the cowards before the fight than later. You!" he barked at the other guard, who rode up from his latest reconnaissance. "Are you rabbit-hearted like your comrade?" Bessas explained his plan.

The man paled but said: "Verethraghna aid us, what a

conceit! Natheless, I will go anywhere you do, Captain Bessas."

Myron's heart rose into his throat. He thought, I am no fleet Achilles, alas; affrays like this affright me witless. But I must not let these foreigners see that a Hellene quails.

They rode up the dell but soon were forced to dismount. The dell narrowed to a ravine, along which they picked their way, squeezing past boulders and hopping from rock to rock. Bessas halted to listen.

"The Corpse Fiend take this wind!" he exclaimed. "A man can't hear himself think. But I hear horses coming down. . . . What are you staring at, Myron?"

"That insect," said Myron. "I have never seen one like it, and I wondered——"

Bessas gave a snarl of nervous exasperation. "Ahriman eat you! Here you're about to fight for your life, and you look at insects! Stay here, you two, and hold the beasts."

Bessas bounded up to the next bend. There he braced himself against the side of the ravine and pulled from its case his powerful Parthian bow, strung with tendons of stag. He took out a fistful of arrows and thrust them, one by one, into a patch of dirt. He slipped a leather bracer over his left wrist.

For a while he leaned unmoving against the rock. The wind whistled among the crags and made the grasses and mountain flowers nod. The horses stretched their necks towards scanty patches of herbage.

Suddenly, Bessas straightened up, bent his bow, and let fly. A hoarse yell sounded from around the bend. Before it had stopped, Bessas had whipped up another arrow from those in the ground and shot. A third and a fourth followed, then a pause.

"Come on up," said Bessas.

Around the bend, Myron saw three men in ragged coats and trousers lying in the bottom of the ravine. Each had an arrow through his ribs. These arrows had been

56

driven with such force that little more than the feathering showed. Crimson stains were spreading on the tribesmen's jackets where the arrows pierced them. One man moved and groaned. Their horses had run back up the dell, then stopped to graze.

"I missed one shot," groaned Bessas. "In broad daylight, at less than twenty paces, I make a clean miss! I must be getting old. But then, a sudden gust carried the shaft aside. Kill that one who lives, trooper, and help me to get these arrows out. They are too good shafts to waste."

The road guard, awe in his face, thrust his spear through the wounded man. Myron winced, though he knew that this was how things were done, that the hillmen would have used him the same way, and that it was not his place to tell Bessas how to manage military matters. Feeling a little shaky, he said:

"Those are the men who were going to take us from behind, as the monkey took the miller's wife. Now what?"

"You shall see," said Bessas.

They followed the Bactrian on an hour's scramble. Then Bessas said: "Hist! We are almost in sight of them. Tie the horses and come on, keeping your heads down. Remember what I told you about tethering high, Myron!"

Soon Myron cautiously thrust his head above a sharp-edged ridge. Before him, the slope fell away gently. Then the ground rose again to another ridge, lower than the first. In the distance beyond, blue mountains towered.

Just behind this more distant ridge, thirty-odd hillmen clustered. The wind whipped the loose ends of their ragged garments. A better-dressed man stood behind them on an outcrop, peering over the lower ridge with fists on hips. Bessas whispered:

"Methinks our road is just beyond the second rise, and the fellow in the turban is our man. Trooper, I am going out to take that rogue. Cover me with your bow as I re-

57

turn, in case the others come after me. Myron, take my bow——"

"I'm no archer, alas!" said the Greek.

"Oh, fiends! Take the spear, then. If I fail, prick a couple of the knaves as they come up, and they may give you time to get to your horse."

Bessas unstrapped his bow case and sword belt but took the crystal-pommeled sword. He stepped across the ridge and started down towards the watching group, hopping lightly from rock to rock. He would have been in plain sight, had any of them looked around. But all eyes were turned away from him; the tribesmen's gaze was fixed on the road below. The howl of the wind muffled Bessas' approach.

Coolly, as if he were but another tribesman late to the muster, Bessas strode up behind Puzur.

Just before Bessas reached him, the Ouxian half turned his head to speak. With one great leap, Bessas was upon him. The Bactrian's left arm swept around and gathered the smaller man in a bear hug, while Bessas brought his sword up under Puzur's beard, so that the edge touched his throat. Puzur screamed something in Elamite.

The tribesmen, who at the first movement had begun to draw knifes and to reach for bows and spears, froze into immobility. Bessas backed up the slope, dragging Puzur with him and keeping the sword blade always against the chieftain's throat.

"Trooper!" said Bessas. "Give me something to bind this knave with and then lasso me one of those loose ponies."

"The Lord of Light preserve us!" gasped the road guard. "You are Rustam come again!"

"Belike; but hurry, lest the tribesmen rush us regardless."

Later the same day, the travelers reached the next relay station. Here Bessas turned his prisoner over to the road guards, despite the outcry of Puzur: "You said you would not slay me if my men did not attack you!"

"I'm not slaying you," said Bessas. "What the king does is between you and him. Myron, give me a sheet of your parchment and a pen."

Myron got out his writing materials and cut a piece off the end of the roll of parchment. He filled a cup with water, dipped a reed pen into it, and rubbed the point of the pen briskly against a block of solid ink. Then he handed the materials to Bessas.

The Bactrian pressed the sheet against the wall of the guardhouse and wrote his message, letter by letter, with terrific concentration. The pen trembled in his mighty fist. As he wrote, he contorted his face into frightful scowls and grimaces, licking his mustache. After a long time, and many re-inkings of the pen, he handed the letter to Myron with a weary sigh.

"Think you he'll be able to read it?"

"With the eyesight of Argos and the wisdom of Nestor, perhaps," said Myron. The letter, a barely literate scrawl, said in Aramaic:

BESSAS SON OF PHRAATES GREETS TROOP LEADER OCHUS
    With this letter I send you the prisoner Puzur. The road guard will tell you how he tried to ambush us. You see, it is not so hard to catch these mountain goats.

As he sealed the letter, Bessas said to Myron: "My only regret is that I let you talk me out of betting with Ochus that I could do it! Next time, stick to things whereof you know."

59

III The Gate of the Gods

ON THE EVENING of the ninth, Myron and Bessas forded the Idide River. Beyond the ford, the road was paved with broad flat bricks set in asphalt. Out of the plain before them, dotted with groves of palm, acacia, tamarisk, and poplar, rose Shushan the Palace, as the Persians called their second capital. Its hills, topped by fortresses, temples, and palaces, stood up in black silhouette against the blood-red sunset.

An indifferent guard waved them through the Persepolis Gate into Shushan. In deepening darkness they rode along an avenue until Myron said:

"I turn off here to get to my friend's house."

"I'll stay with you until you are delivered," said Bessas. "When the king is away, the cutthroats make merry."

They turned down a narrow unpaved lane, the hooves of their horses striking the mud with shapeless wet sounds. Inky blackness closed in upon them. Slinking shapes scurried out of their way, and nauseous stenches assailed their nostrils. On either side the close-set walls reared up above their heads, leaving overhead but a narrow strip of starlit sky, like a gem-studded girdle. There was no light, and no sound but the snarl of pariah dogs fighting for offal.

As Myron's eyes adjusted to the blackness, he made out an occasional window, small and barred, high up; or a small but massive door, set deep in an ancient wall. Down the walls, stinking liquids trickled over coatings of moss, mold, and grime. From one window came the snarl of an angry man, followed by the crack of a whip on flesh and a woman's scream.

Another turn, and Myron said: "Here we are." He dismounted and rapped.

"Who is that?" said a voice through the peephole.

Myron gave his name. The door opened and a shaven-headed man in white linen called out: "Come in, Myron, ere we let all the vermin of the night in with you!"

Myron untied his small bag of possessions from his horse. "This is my friend Uni, the Egyptian priest," he said. "And this wee little fellow is Bessas of Zariaspa."

"Your servant," said Uni.

"God give you long life," said Bessas. "Myron, I am for the barracks. Tomorrow I must deliver these nags and study how to get us farther along on our journey. If you cannot find me elsewhere, come to Indabigas' tavern tomorrow even. Mithra preserve you!"

"The same to you," said Myron. "I shall spend tomorrow in the archives, for ignorance to a traveler is the same as blindness."

The priest touched noses with Myron and called to his wife to get food and drink for the traveler. He said: "A thousand welcomes, old friend! What brings you hither ahead of the Great King and his court?"

Having spilt a small libation, Myron drank deeply. Gazing at the procession of animal-headed gods that paraded stiffly, in red and white and yellow paint, around the walls of the room, he recounted what had befallen. By the time the tale was told, he had eaten and drunk.

"Four and a half days!" said Uni. "Only the postal riders do better."

"*Oimoi!* At the end of the first day I feared I should die, and at the end of the second I hoped I should! However, I have toughened up since. I've led too soft a life these many years."

"How goes the City of the Persians?"

"The same as ever: plots and intrigues in the palace; Persian arrogance in the streets; peasant ignorance in the countryside. By the World Egg of the Orphics, I shall never be happy until I can dwell again in a Greek city!"

"Haven't you made a good living?"

"Yes, but the soul finds refreshment in change. True, the Persian gentry have their good points. They are all

61

brave, mostly well-mannered, and many even honest. The trouble is, there is nobody to converse with. All I hear is court gossip, and hunting, and the great equestrian game of stick-and-ball, which means to them what the Olympics do to us. Nobody has one thought to rub against another, and those who have are looked upon as insane. *Pheu!*"

"You need a wife," said Uni.

"You mean I once did. But try to find one when you live in a foreign city, where there are but a handful of your own kind! Why, fifteen years ago, when I was just past thirty, I courted the daughter of Pythonax the Eretrian here in Shushan. Pythonax was willing, but his daughter would have none of it. She told him I was old, and dull, and worst of all I *thought* all the time! I decided that the gods preferred me to stay a widower, and now, by the Dog, I am accustomed to my single state. I am less subject to

eager desire and passion that wasteth the bodies of mortals

than I was twenty years ago."

"What are your plans?"

"If I survive this journey, I will ask permission to return to Miletos."

"I am told," said Uni, "that Miletos is full of Karians, brought in to replace the enslaved Milesians.'"

"Some true Milesians will have trickled back. Anyway, this hope of future return is one reason for the journey."

"How mean you?"

"I do not desire to return to Ionia as merely one more wandering Greekling, who has tutored noblemen's sons and accumulated a few shekels. I should be as much a nobody then as now. But let me come as the man who has seen lands that no other Hellenic eyes have beheld. . . ."

Uni pursed his lips. "It seems like a desperate risk for a

62

doubtful gain. I had rather search for spiritual perfection in contemplation of the deathless gods."

"Please yourself; but to labor eternally for the same masters is wearisome. Don't you see, man, I might even settle the question of whether the earth is a flat disk as says Thales, or a cylinder as says Anaximandros, or boat-shaped as say the Babylonians?"

"All very interesting, no doubt; but take care that in your searching you fall not over the edge."

"With danger even danger is overcome," said Myron. "And, as says Herakleitos, who hopes for nothing wins nothing."

"I must give you letters to some of my colleagues in Egypt; for, to a traveler in a strange land, next to a well-filled purse a good introduction is the best thing. But, speaking of purses, how do you expect to gain tangible wealth from your wanderings? I would not count upon Xerxes' gratitude. A king's wrath is as lasting as the hills, but his favor is as dew upon the grass."

"You are right. But I may acquire understanding, which to me is more than darics. My master Herakleitos used to say: Most men might as well be blind and deaf, for all that they comprehend what lies about them. If you would gain wisdom, he said, get about, see things for yourself, and subject the impressions thus gained to the divine power of reason. And why should not I be the man to put Herakleitos' advice into effect?"

Later they played sacred way, on a narrow board, three cells by twelve. At length Myron threw the elongated die, cried, "Four!" and took Uni's last piece.

"May Seteh gnaw your bones!" exclaimed the shaven man. "By the rays of Amon-Ra, you have placed a spell upon that die."

"My dear Uni," said Myron, "see for yourself." He held up the die. "It is your own perfect die, and not a flattened one that I have craftily substituted for it."

"True, though a clever man could control the fall of

even a perfect die." The Egyptian finished his cup of Syrian wine and yawned. "Next time we shall play tjau and I shall slaughter you. But I should be abed. I must be full of holy unction for my little flock tomorrow."

Next morning, Myron beat his way through the swarming streets to North Hill, whereon stood the palace of Darius the Great. Myron climbed the stair to the top of the hill, passing brilliant brick reliefs of fantastic animals—winged bulls, and goat-horned lions with hindlegs and wings of eagles, in blue and emerald and crimson and gold. At the top he talked himself into the royal library. The librarian, who knew Myron of old as a respectable bookworm, welcomed him warmly.

Meanwhile, in the Daduchid mansion in Shushan, Zopyrus son of Bagabyxas paced restlessly while listening to his visitor, a fresh-faced young cousin from the barracks.

"There is no doubt at all," said this one, "that it is Bessas son of Phraates. Who else comes roaring in, knocks people over with playful slaps on the back, drinks half the troop's daily allowance of wine at one draft, breaks the troop commander's collarbone in a friendly wrestle, and then snores all night like seven thunderstorms?"

"You have convinced me, cousin, though I see not how—but never mind. *Slave!* Run to the house of Ardigula the Babylonian and fetch him hither. I have a task for him."

The sun had passed the meridian when the slave returned with a small, mouselike, brown man, wrapped in a camel's hair cloak and a shawl. The small one glided in, bowed deeply to Zopyrus, and touched his own nose. "God increase your wealth and family!" he said in Aramaic.

Zopyrus held out his hand for the man to kiss, ordered his servants out, and closed the door himself. Long and earnestly the two conferred. At length the little man, scratching, said:

64

"*Ari!* You drive a hard bargain, my lord. It had been simpler if your highness had spoken yesterday, ere Lord Sataspes left Shushan."

"That could not be helped," said Zopyrus. "I had not found you yesterday. Mean you that you cannot catch up with Sataspes?"

"Nay; there are ways. I shall summon sprites from the sunless North. . . . But give my unworthy self the money at once, that your slave can get about this business. Him whom I serve"—he made a reverential gesture towards the earth—"shall take the honor of the Daduchids into his keeping. He will not fail my master. As for Bessas the Bactrian, that were as simple as spearing fish in a bathtub."

Myron ran Bessas to earth in the tavern of Indabigas. This time he could not get the giant Bactrian to leave until he had sat and drunk with him till his senses swam. Bessas improvised:

> *When I was young, my tutor used to say:*
> *"Waste not thy gold on wine, in revels gay!"*
> *But thieves have stolen all the gold I saved;*
> *Whilst that I spent on wine is mine for aye!*

At last Bessas suffered himself to be dragged forth. They walked towards the river Khavaspa, over which a gibbous moon hung high. Bessas continued:

> *Behold the moon, which monthly swells and shrinks.*
> *It is, they say, a god. 'Tis but, methinks,*
> *A silver dish by goddess hurled at mate,*
> *And which, forever whirling onward, winks!*

Myron said: "You ought to write these down, old boy. They might preserve your name for posterity."

"Nay! That were hard work; it would spoil the fun. Posterity can make up its own rhymes." As they came to the parapet overlooking the Khavaspa, Bessas added: "How did you make out?"

"I unearthed a few more details of our route. How about you?"

"I have—hist!"

"What is it?"

"I thought I heard a man moving stealthily. . . . Be that as it may, I have got us passage as far as Babylon, at least." Bessas hiccupped.

"How?"

"I have a friend in the postal service whose next run was to be tomorrow. He's sick with a cold in the head, and they are short of spare drivers for the mail carts that run from here to Babylon. So the postmaster said I might take the car in my friend's——"

Two shadows moved out from the houses on the landward side of the promenade and rushed towards the twain. Bessas cried:

" 'Ware knives!"

Myron gaped for a heartbeat, then snatched off his cloak, whipped it about his left arm as a shield, and fumbled for his knife. There was a rip of cloth as the man thrust at him, his blade agleam in the moonlight. Myron swept his cloak over his attacker's head and kicked. The man grunted and gave back, tearing himself loose from the folds of wool. Myron got his knife clear at last and thrust, driving his assailant back.

Looking past his assailant's head, Myron saw what happened to the other marauder. The man ran at Bessas with a short sword held out in front of him. Bessas, too, seemed to hesitate. Then he made a tremendous leap, which carried him to the top of the four-foot parapet between the promenade and the river.

Myron expected to see the Bactrian plunge on into the water. Instead, the huge man, balancing as lightly as a dancer, spun on the balls of his feet as he swept out his long horseman's sword. As the attacker plunged in, the sword whirled in a double circle. The first stroke sheared through the wrist that held the short sword; the second came down between shoulder and neck.

The man collapsed with a hoarse, choking cry. Bessas leaped down from his perch and started towards Myron. Myron's opponent, who was still trying to get past Myron's guard, turned and ran. Bessas ran after, but the man vanished. Presently Bessas came back.

"Ducked into an alley and lost me," he growled. "Let's see who this *druj* is."

He turned the dead assassin over. "I cannot be sure in this light, but I don't think I know him. Do you?"

Myron, breathing hard, said: "Not I." They searched in vain for marks of identification. Bessas said:

"We'd better get rid of him, or the watch will hale us into court, and we shall spend a year fighting a murder charge instead of getting to Kush. Take his sword."

Seizing the dead man's collar in one hand and his girdle in the other, Bessas picked up the corpse, swung it in a circle, and tossed it over the parapet. As it struck the river with a splash, shattering the moon's reflection into silvery shards, he threw the severed hand after it. Glancing warily to right and left, he said softly:

"Now I am damned to the Land of Silence for polluting running water. But my *fravashi* tells me that these were no ordinary footpads. Probably, like Puzur, they are creatures of Zopyrus. Let's get home."

Next morning, in the Daduchid mansion, Zopyrus snarled: "Well, Master Ardigula, what have you to say, aside from the fact that you have failed?"

The Babylonian spread his hands. "Take it not so to heart, my master. It is but a temporary check. It cost me a good man to learn that Bessas' guardian spirit, or *fravashi* as you call it, is of outstanding power and must be neutralized by mighty spells——"

"How will you neutralize his spirit when he is on his way to Babylon?"

"Fear not, noble sir. Your slave will communicate with

his colleagues in that city, by the same method that I have used in the case of Sataspes."

"And what is that?"

"A secret cantrip, handed down in my family from the days before the Flood. As seven rare ingredients are required, however, you had better pay me an additional daric——"

"Not another farthing, scum!" said Zopyrus. "You know our bargain."

"Alas, good my lord, too well do I know it! Very well, I will do what I can with cheap ingredients; but blame me not if——"

"Here, take it," growled Zopyrus, tossing a heavy golden coin. "But that is all, do you understand?"

"I wist that my master would see reason. May the earth spirits aid us!"

Back in his own quarters, biting his fingers in anger over Zopyrus' arrogance, Ardigula went to his cabinet and got out writing materials. He penned a letter in tiny writing on a strip of papyrus smaller than his palm. The writing would have baffled any Persian, Elamite, or Babylonian into whose hands it fell. But Uni, the priest who ministered to the religious wants of the small Egyptian colony of Shushan, could have read it at once, for it was in Egyptian demotic.

Ardigula called his servant, saying: "Fetch one of Labashi's birds; a strong one."

Presently the servant appeared with a gray pigeon cradled in his hands. Ardigula rolled the strip of papyrus around the bird's leg, tied it fast with a length of thread, and secured it with a dab of gum. He went to the roof and tossed the bird into the air. The pigeon circled over the city three times and flew off to westward.

Ardigula went back to his cabinet and began mixing powders for a mighty incantation. This, he thought, should do the work without the pigeon; likewise the pigeon should do the work without the spell. But there was no point in taking chances.

68

Night, like a black cloak spangled with diamonds, lay across the vast Euphratean plain. The wind from the desert rustled the fronds of the date palms, which marched along the banks of the irrigation canals in endless rows, like King Xerxes' Immortals.

Along the royal road from Shusan, at a lively trot, came a two-mule chariot. The nailheads that studded its bronzen tires rumbled along the paving of brick. Ever and anon, the rumble was hushed as the vehicle crossed a patch of drifted sand.

Moonlight showed the towering form of Bessas at the reins, while the smaller Myron sat on a roll of baggage with his back against the side of the car. He chewed on a biscuit. Other sacks and rolls of gear, including a royal mailbag, heaped the floor behind the driver's wide-braced feet.

As the chariot neared the town of Kish, three leagues short of Babylon, cultivation became thicker and houses more frequent. Some houses clustered in hamlets.

As the car entered one of these villages, there was a stir in the darkness. From two houses facing each other across the highway, men darted out. Torches in the hands of two of them stabbed the dark with fluttering yellow beams.

The torchbearers dashed in front of the team, thrusting their torches into the animals' faces. The mules skidded and reared, snorting, squealing, and pawing.

Other men scurried in from the sides. Some reached for the animals' bridles, others for the men in the car.

"Mithra smite you!" roared Bessas. His right arm flew out. The long whip cracked like a thunderbolt. One of the torch-bearers dropped his stick and reeled off, screaming, with both hands clapped over one eye.

The others continued to close. They needed but a few steps to swarm over the chariot and its occupants.

Again the whip cracked. The other torch was snatched from its holder's hand and flew into the air with a shower of sparks.

69

A lariat hissed out of the darkness and settled over Bessas' shoulders. As the giant Bactrian clutched the forewall of the chariot, Myron, who had risen unsteadily, made a wild, half-blind swipe with the sword he had taken from the assassin in Shushan.

The lariat parted, and Myron shouted: *"Iai!"*

Bessas, recovering his balance, lashed his mules with frenzied force. They screamed and bounded forward. The jerk unbalanced Myron, who had to drop his sword to the floor of the car and clutch with both hands at the chariot's side to save himself. Several attackers, who had reached the vehicle and grasped its sides, were thrown to the road. One shrieked as a wheel crunched over his foot.

Bessas cried: *"Yâ ahî!"* and the mules broke away at a wild gallop. Behind, the two dropped torches dwindled to ruddy specks, while the shadowy forms of the waylayers faded into the darkness. Night resumed its rule.

On the east branch of the Euphrates, three leagues beyond Kish, rose mighty Babylon—Bâb-ilâni, the Gate of the Gods, the metropolis of the world, the center of the universe. To Myron, approaching it at night, it seemed an immense, angular black mass—mysterious, illimitable, overwhelming.

Although he had been here before, the sight of this city inspired in Myron a curious mixture of feelings, compounded of awe, repulsion, and fascination. It differed so utterly from his bright little Ionian cities with their theaters, their tight civic organization, and their intense political life.

Although laid out in more orderly fashion than any Greek city, Babylon had no true civic life and so was not, in the strict Greek sense of the word, a city at all. Here were hundreds of thousands of human beings, whose only concern with the government of their city was to avoid the police and cheat the tax gatherers. It reminded Myron of the swarming life sometimes found under a flat stone.

A few pinpoints of ruddy light winked from the towering walls, where Persian sentries paced with torches. These walls had been one of the world's wonders. Now they were partly demolished. As punishment for Babylon's revolt, King Xerxes had razed several sections. Thus the remaining stretches of wall, while still a mighty monument to the great Nebuchadrezzar, were useless for defense.

Before the chariot reached the outer wall of the city, a row of crosses loomed up in the moonlight beside the road. On these crosses hung the bodies of felons, in various stage of disrepair. Myron held his nose until they passed the place.

They entered the gate in the outer wall with no more than a wave from the guards. For ten furlongs they trotted along Zababa Street, through sprawling suburbs and across a canal. Betimes a little square of yellow light appeared amid the blackness of the buildings, where a small, high-set window of a lighted chamber fronted on the avenue. Otherwise the suburbs were dark, and Bessas guided his car by moonlight. Now and then the furtive figure of a prowler slunk out of sight as the chariot neared it.

Then the more massive inner wall loomed across the moat. The stench of stagnant water came to Myron's nostrils as the bridge timbers boomed beneath their wheels. At the Zababa Gate the guards halted them to peer by torchlight at the golden eagle on the end of the chariot pole and the golden winged disks on the sides of the car before waving them on. Myron said:

"I think the Post Office is in the citadels. Take a fork to the right; there's a diagonal street along the canal. . . ."

In the central city, lights were more frequent. They rumbled past late-closing wineshops and brothels. Apartment houses of three or four stories rose like black cliffs on either hand.

Half an hour after they passed the inner wall, they sat in the office of Earimut, chief clerk of the postmaster of

71

Babylon. Earimut, wearing an old robe and with hair and beard uncombed, squinted sourly in the lamplight.

"We did not look for this car until the morrow," he said.

Bessas shrugged. "We had made such good time by sunset that I saw no reason not to continue on. Does not the motto of the service say we stop not for snow, rain, heat, or gloom of night?"

Earimut yawned. "And the mules are lathered. Even if you are but a substitute driver, you should know better than to race these costly governmental animals."

"Race, plague!" Bessas burst out. "We were attacked near Kish. What do you expect me to do, sit down to throw dice with the robbers?"

"Attacked!" cried Earimut. "*Ari!* This is serious. Tell me what befell."

When Bessas had told his tale, Earimut said: "Well then, we will excuse your haste. Did you know these rogues? We must get the soldiers out to search for them."

"It happened so fast that I do not think I should have known my own brother, even with a moon," said Bessas.

"Wait here," said the Babylonian. When Earimut returned, he went on: "The soldiers have been sent out. Now, Master Bessas, what of this other man, this Hellene who came with you? Nought in the rules allows you to carry private passengers. What have you to say?"

"Postmaster Haraspas in Shushan said it were allowable, because of their urgent need for a driver and ours for carriage. Besides, we are both on a mission from the king. Argue with Haraspas, not with me."

Earimut clucked in an agitated manner. "It is not right to twist the regulations thus. Haraspas will get himself into trouble. But I have too many other cares to press the matter, so I bid you good-night——"

"One more thing," said Bessas. "My pay."

"Ask me in the morning——"

"No; right now, my friend! In the morning we may be on our way to Egypt."

72

"Oh, very well, though I think you are inconsiderate. Will you have it in barley, wheat, or wine?"

"In silver. I am for far countries, and I cannot carry a year's harvest on my back."

"Silver? But, my dear Captain Bessas, that is not how things are done. There is a shortage of silver, and all payments are made in kind. Withal, there will be a deduction for the fare of Master Myron——"

"May Ghu skin you alive and dip you in salt!" Taking the mailbag in one hand and the lamp in the other, Bessas said: "I have here the day's official mail from Shushan to Babylon. I shall count ten, and if by then I do not have my whole shekel, in silver, I shall begin to burn the dispatches, one by one. Take your choice."

"You—would burn the king's mail?" said Earimut, eyes popping.

"Aye, and if you call your men I'll burn the whole lot and cut my way out." Bessas took out a letter and squinted in the yellow lamplight. "This is addressed to —hmm—General Pacoras, commander of the garrison. One—two—three——"

"Stop, madman! Here is your money, and may your canal be filled with sand! You shall certainly never be hired as a driver by this office, not whilst I draw breath."

"That's better. And now to find a pallet." Bessas grinned at Myron and said in Greek: "Do not look so terrified, teacher. We must needs take a firm stand with these clerkly types."

The barracks at Babylon were like all the others in the great cities of the Empire: a row of cubical, graceless brick structures without, dirty and dingy within. Bessas' status as an officer on inactive duty entitled him to a room for himself and one slave in the officers' quarters. As he and Myron were making do without servants, Myron shared Bessas' room, no larger or more luxurious than the cubicle that Myron had rented in Persepolis.

"The king believes," said Bessas, "that officers and men

should not be tempted into indolence by luxurious quarters. He would have them spend their free hours out-of-doors—preferably in hearty sports, like racing, hunting, and stick-and-ball. *Yá ahí!*" He whirled an imaginary polo mallet.

The next morning Myron and Bessas came out of the barracks and wound their way through many alleys and passages, with much asking of directions, to the mighty Ishtar Gate.

This colossal portal, on the northern side of the inner wall, comprised an immense square tower of brick, seventy feet high and even larger in plan. Processional Way led through an archway in this tower, closed by two pairs of huge wooden doors reinforced with bronze. On the northward side of the gate proper, flanking the approach, were two lofty, slender towers. North of these, as a first line of defense, stood two smaller towers.

The entire structure was finished with enameled bricks, of a deep-sea blue on the towers and of grass greens and delicate pinks on the connecting curtain walls. On each tower were several vertical rows of bulls and dragons in low brick relief, repelling hostile supernatural forces from the city by their frowning glance. The beasts alternated in each row; they also alternated as to color. Half the animals were a gleaming white with golden claws, hooves, manes, and other parts, while the other half were a rich reddish brown with blue-green parts. Around the upper levels of the towers ran a row of glowing rosettes.

Myron and Bessas strolled about this vast structure, avoiding the traffic that streamed in and out. They ignored the cripples who, having been convicted of misdemeanors, had been deprived of eyes, hands, or feet by Xerxes' judges, and who now squatted and begged about the great gate.

Myron fixed his attention on one sirrush at eye level and got out his writing materials. "O Bessas," he said, "you will have to kneel."

"Why?"

"We require some sketches of this dragon, and I have no table whereon to rest my parchment. So your broad back will have to serve."

"Well, tan my hide for shoe leather, if this be not a fine occupation for a noble Aryan!" grumbled Bessas. But he knelt.

The relief was about five feet long and four feet high. The slender white body and forelegs were like those of a cheetah except that the body was covered with reptilian scales. The hindlegs terminated in the talons of a bird of prey. A long tail, catlike but for its scales, ended in a small scorpion's sting, while a slender scaly neck supported a small serpentine head.

Above the large, round, black, lustrous eye rose a golden spike of a horn. Myron surmised that, as in the case of the bulls, one horn did artistic service for two, for the beast was shown in pure profile. Behind the eye were several projecting appendages: a curly crest, like that of some bird, and dangling wattle-like parts. A forked tongue played about the creature's scaly snout. Tongue, wattles, mane, and claws, as well as the horn, were picked out in golden yellow.

"Must you take all day?" complained Bessas.

"Perhaps. Rejoice; you're no worse off than standing at attention in front of the Apadana, and you serve a more useful end."

Finished at last, the twain strolled through the Ishtar Gate and south along Processional Way. On either hand, rows of life-sized lions in bright enameled brick relief prowled along the walls that flanked the street, red-maned yellow lions alternating with yellow-maned white lions.

The travelers dodged chariots, ox carts, and camel trains. Some of the camels, to cure them of the mange, had been shaved all over and painted black with mineral pitch of Id, so that they looked like animals made of asphalt.

The swarming Babylonians, in long tunics and knitted caps with dangling tails, were leavened by a sprinkling of trousered Persians and other Aryans, shaven Egyptians, Syrians in tall spiral hats, cloaked and skirted Arabs, robed Judaeans, booted Sakas in pointed hoods, turbaned Carduchians, felt-capped Armenians, Greeks in broad-brimmed hats, and men in the garb of even more distant lands. Beggars whined, catamites smirked, hawkers cried their wares, and pimps extolled the beauty and cleanliness of their girls. Persian soldiers strolled in pairs, arrogantly shouldering other folk out of the way.

"People, people, people!" growled Bessas, plowing through the ruck of officials and tradesfolk, soldiers and slaves, peasants and prostitutes. "I feel as if I were being smothered in people."

Now and then Myron caught a scowl or a sneer from one of the Babylonians. For Persians had been hated in Babylon ever since the great rebellion, when Xerxes had opened breaches in the city's magnificent walls, carried off the golden eight-hundred-talent statue of Marduk, confiscated the property of the leading citizens, given their houses and lands to Persians, and degraded Babylonia from a kingdom in its own right to a mere province.

King Xerxes, returning the Babylonians' dislike, no longer spent his entire winters there, as had the great Darius. In fact, Xerxes seldom visited the city at all. Each successive year he passed more of his time at remote Persepolis, overseeing his grandiose building projects: the mighty Hall of a Hundred Columns and the new private palace.

There were many signs of dire poverty among Babylon's swarming thousands. A man lay dead of starvation in the gutter. People stepped around the corpse until a Persian soldier shouted to a patrolling member of the civic guard:

"You there! Fetch a detail to remove this offal!"

Begging children thrust out arms of skin and bone. Myron gave a slug of trade copper to one. She at once set

76

off at a run, with several older children pelting after her in hopes of possessing themselves of Myron's alms.

At the same time, hundreds of other children converged on the travelers, all screaming, "Give!" Myron found himself surrounded by a seething crowd. Older beggars, too, came shuffling and hobbling forward, kicking and beating the children out of their way.

"Now see what you did!" said Bessas.

At last the two took refuge in a tavern, where they sat drinking beer while waiting for the mendicatory horde to go away.

"This," said Bessas, "should be a lesson to you."

"But I cannot bear to see the little creatures starve!"

"If you save one, it will only grow up to beget more beggars. Babylonia has more people now than it knows what to do with."

They had to wait a full Babylonian double hour before the last of the suppliants drifted off and they could resume their walk unmolested.

On Myron's right rose the great ziggurat of Babylon. This was Etemenanki, the Cornerstone of the Universe, towering two hundred cubits into a bright blue sky flecked with streamers of thin white cloud. The tower gleamed with enameled bricks in dazzling patterns of white and gold and blue and green and scarlet, as if it had been covered with the scaly hide of some fabulous reptile. A closer view showed that many of the gaily colored tiles had fallen out, exposing the brown mud brick beneath. The neglected structure was fast decaying into shabbiness. Myron said:

"I should like to learn more about that edifice. When I was here before, I studied the Babylonian system of arithmetic under the great Nabu-rimanni. I could look the old boy up, if he is still——"

"We have no time for such leisurely pursuits," snapped Bessas. "Come along."

South of the ziggurat, also on Myron's right, stretched

the temenos of Marduk of Babylon. Myron entered, followed by an apprehensive-looking Bessas.

"These foreign gods make me nervous," grumbled the Bactrian. "I am never sure of the right way to handle them."

Myron brushed aside the swarm of beggars and sellers of votive offerings and headed for the naos, which rose amid the groves. He stared at the temple. As usual when Myron was on the track of knowledge, his faculties were alert and keyed up. Whereas he tended to become vague and absent-minded when bored by the ordinary routines of life, the promise of discovery roused him to foxy keenness.

The huge old temple of Marduk was well kept. Gilded ornaments gleamed from its cornices. Dragons in reliefs of white and gold paraded around its walls, lashing their scorpion tails. Myron compared these reliefs to the drawings of the sirrush that he had made at the Ishtar Gate.

"I don't think we need any more pictures," he said, "but—— Oh, Father!" he cried in Aramaic.

A Babylonian, distinguishable as a priest by his vestments and shaven face, turned. "What is it?" he said in no very friendly tone.

"May I ask Your Holiness some questions about this reptile, pray?"

The priest pulled himself together and touched his ivory-headed walking stick to his nose. "Your pardon, my son. Yesterday was the last day of our New Year's festival, and some of us suffer from an excess of—ah—holy spirit." He cleared his throat. "This is the sirrush, the sacred beast of the supreme god Marduk, symbolizing the powers of Marduk as the lion does those of our Lady Ishtar and the bull those of the mighty Adad——"

"Yes, sir, this I know. But I seek to learn about the living, earthly sirrush." Myron explained the quest on which he and Bessas were embarked.

The priest looked thoughtful. "This calls for consideration. I cannot ask you into the temple, since you are not purified initiates. But perchance you will do me the honor to step into the presbytery where we can talk. I am Father Nadinnu."

The presbytery was a building on the edge of the temenos, or sacred precinct, wherein dwelt several minor priests with their families. Nadinnu led the twain to a reception room and ordered a temple servant to bring wine, which was poured into light, gracefully curved silver cups. A taste showed Myron that it was date wine, which he did not much like; but he drank it with good grace. After a long silence the priest began, seeming to pick his words with care.

"Once upon a time," said he, "according to our ancient records, the sirrush abounded in the Land of the Two Rivers, as the lion does today. In those days, I suppose, the priests of Marduk had no trouble in keeping a living sirrush for the edification of the faithful.

"But then came the Flood, and all the animals perished save those that could reach the tops of mountains, or those that Ziusudra, the protected of the gods, had with him in the Ark. The sirrush vanished forever from Babylonia. Howsomever, after the Flood, as civilization revived and travel and trade spread geographical knowledge among mankind, it transpired that these beasts still lived in Africa, at the headwaters of the Nile.

"Now, no man in Babylonia, to my knowledge, has ever seen this fabled region. So I cannot forewarn you of what you will find there. But once in a century, more or less, some trader obtains a young sirrush that has been taken alive by the black barbarians of that land. Knowing that we pay well for the beast, the trader brings it by river raft and camel train and ox wain for many hundreds of leagues to holy Babylon.

"The last live sirrush that we possessed arrived here early in King Xerxes' reign. It was this one that the king

79

saw, whilst it was still but a chick. But alas! During the sack, the beast disappeared. For aught we know, it may have escaped to the river, or it may have been eaten by some starving citizen. And we have not yet found another to take its place. If you can fetch back two, we will gladly buy the one that the king wants not."

Myron, staring at the distorted reflection of his face in the polished, curving surface of the silver cup, asked a few more questions. But Nadinnu made it plain that he had told all he knew, or at least all he would admit. Then Myron asked:

"Is it true that the temple lends money?"

"Aye. What sort of loan had you in mind?"

When Myron explained about the security that Bessas had to offer—an estate in Bactria now overrun by hostile nomads—Nadinnu said: "I fear me that such a loan were too speculative for us. Try the private bankers."

"Who are they?"

"The two leading firms are Iranu and Murashu of Nippur. Iranu's office is in the New City, at the corner of Adad and Shamash streets. Murashu you will find in the old business center, near Marduk and Enlil."

The travelers took a ceremonious leave. As soon as they had gone, Nadinnu dropped his air of benign imperturbability. Without trying to hide his agitation, he hitched up his robe, ran to the manse of the high priest, and sought out his superior, to whom he told the events just past.

Belkishir, high priest of Marduk of Babylon, said: "Aye, it behooved you to say something. But why are you so fearful?"

"See you not, sir, what will happen? These barbarians will go to Africa, reach the headwaters of the Nile, learn that no such beast exists, return, and discover this fact to the king. The king, resenting the tale we told him——"

"What mean you, *we* told him?" interrupted Belkishir. "That conceit was wholly yours."

"Well, who installed that accursed Chaldean marsh

80

lizard in the first place? So when the king asked me about it, I could not say: O King, this is but a wile of guile, wherewith to chouse our gullible worshipers of a few more ha'pence——"

"Nadinnu! I forbid you to use such unseemly language about our holy church!"

"Well, it is true natheless. But let us not waste time in futile recriminations. The king, enraged at having been befooled, will come down upon us like a winter tempest. He loves us not and would like nought better than a pretext to crush us utterly."

Belkishir mused: "Mayhap on their godless quest they will perish."

"Oh, aye, and mayhap they will find that the sirrush does forsooth dwell in the lands beyond Kush after all. But let us not upon either alternative count. They seemed to me a pair of hardy and resolute masterless rogues."

"Then belike we had better help them perish."

"My thought also, sir. One of our worshipers has underworld connections——"

Belkishir: "Nay, not in Babylon."

"It could be so arranged that the deed could not be traced to us."

"That is not the point. If some infortune befall our friends so close to their starting point, the king will hear of it and, like as not, send forth another expedition. But if it happen a goodly distance hence—in Africa, let us say—His Majesty may never hear of it at all. By the time he has waxed inquisitive enough to look into his explorers' evanescence, or to send out another party, many things may have occurred. He might even forget the whole business."

"How can we arrange such a disappearance at such a distance?"

Belkishir smiled. "Have I spoken to you of Kothar of Qadesh?"

"Nay."

81

"He is—ah—a political correspondent of mine in Syria. Through him I ofttimes know of developments in the western region or ever the king himself does. Kothar is a queer individual but useful in his way. I would ask him to do the deed himself did I not know him for an arrant coward. But if any man can arrange that things shall fall out as we wish, it is he. And the gods will forgive us, because the blow will be struck in defense of our sacred faith."

"How will you get word to him ere the barbarians have passed through Syria?"

"Through Shaykh Alman of Thadamora, who carries our letters across the Syrian desert. Marduk strengthen his camels' sinews!"

IV The Shrine of the Sleepless One

LEAVING THE SITE of the Lofty-Headed Temple, Myron and Bessas crossed the Euphrates by Nabopolassar's great seven-piered bridge and entered the New City. They had no trouble in finding Iranu's bank, as all the folk of Babylon spoke Aramaic in addition to whatever other speech they used at home. Furthermore, most of the street crossings of Babylon were at right angles, so that it was easy to pick one's way.

"Natheless," said Bessas, "I like not being in debt. A loan is pleasant when there is need, but the repayment of it is like the filling of a house."

At the banker's office, however, they were disappointed. Iranu himself had gone to Uruk on business and might not be back for a month, while his subordinate would have nothing to do with a loan on such odd security.

An hour later, footsore and somewhat restored by a loaf and a sausage bought from an old peddler woman, the explorers arrived at the office of Murashu of Nippur.

A young man whose beard was beginning to burgeon

ushered them into the inner office, where a
bearded man sat behind a table. The office w̶
with objects from many lands: a statuette
headed god from Egypt; a red-figured Attic
which was pictured the combat of Herakles an̶
polyta; a mailshirt from the land of the Sauromat̶, armored with scales made from horses' hooves; and other
curios. Tables were heaped with sheets of papyrus and
parchment bearing writings in Aramaic, and dried slabs
of clay inscribed with the complex signs of Akkadian, so
that they looked as if they were covered with the tracks
of tiny birds.

"God prosper you, my masters!" said the fat man.
"Your servant is Murashu of Nippur, and the young fellow who showed you in is my elder son, Belhatin. How
can I serve you?" A golden amulet in the form of Pa-
zuzu the wind demon—winged, fanged, and taloned—
hung round his neck.

Myron explained. Murashu frowned over the king's
letter, which Bessas produced from his scrip.

"This is strange security! Title to an estate in Bactria,
now overrun by wild stinking nomads, were of no use to
me. If you defaulted, can you imagine me, vaulting
aboard my Nisaean charger and scattering the savages
with lance and sword?" The banker uttered a short, mock-
ing laugh. "Were you permanent dwellers in Babylon,
with masters, families, and other ties to fix you in place,
we could arrange it, but——"

"Do you doubt the word of a Bactrian gentleman?"
said Bessas ominously.

"Nay, but you are mortal like the rest of us, are you
not?"

Bessas grunted. Murashu continued: "Now, in view
of the lack of solid security, I should be compelled, alas!
to charge you a higher rate of interest than the standard
twenty parts in a hundred; double, in fact. If you wish
fifty darics, you must pay back seventy within a year. I
rely upon your Bactrian word of honor not to get your-

...eedlessly and needlessly slain, Master Bessas."
..urashu laughed and twiddled his thick fingers on his paunch.

Bessas scowled. "I trust, sir banker, that you seek not to take advantage of our simplicity to squeeze unwonted wealth from us. You money-grubbers would pick a farthing from a dunghill with your teeth."

Murashu's smile vanished. "My good Captain Bessas, if you like not my terms, you are at liberty to try elsewhere." His dark eyes flashed hatred as he burst out: "Unwonted wealth! Money-grubber, forsooth! As if my life were not a never-ending struggle to keep out of debt slavery! Know that I am pursued by night and by day by your Persian king's tax gatherers, who seek to wring the last shekel out of Babylonia as a man wrings water from a towel! Why think you there is such wretched poverty here? Because your foolish Persians fancy that gold and silver are true wealth, and that the more they squeeze out of us the better off they will be!"

Bessas looked bewildered. "What, are not gold and silver wealth?"

"Can you eat them? Can you weave a warm garment of them? Can you build a house of them? Do they make good sword blades or plowshares?"

"Nay, but——"

"So then, what are they? I will tell you! They are the counters in the game of commerce. Though they have but little value in themselves, save for rings and such gewgaws, they make the wheels of trade turn smoothly, as grease helps the wheels of a carriage to spin. And now the Persians tax and tax, withdrawing these ointments from the wheels of commerce. Instead of putting these metals back into use, they take them to Persepolis the Treasury, Shushan the Palace, and Hagmatana the Fortress. There they cast them into massy ingots and store them in the Great King's cellars. So, without its hub grease, the chariot of commerce runs slower and slower, and you wonder why business is bad!"

"I never thought of it thus," said Bessas. "And pardon me if I spoke discourteously. In matters of money I am the veriest clod."

"It is nothing. Now, what say you to this deal?"

Myron spoke up crisply: "We shall think about it and let you know, Master Murashu." He rose.

"By all means," grinned the banker. "Think hard, as any prudent financier would do. But think not to beat down my interest rate. I have cast up the reckoning of my risks, and I cannot let you have the money for less."

Outside in the swarming street, Bessas said: "What is it, Myron? Think you he tried to swindle us?"

"I am not sure. That interest rate is murderous, especially as we may be more than a year in getting back."

"But that would mean only another forty parts in a hundred, would it not?"

"No! You don't understand. The second year's forty parts in a hundred would be calculated on the total you owed Murashu at the end of the first year—not on the amount you originally borrowed. On fifty darics that would be—let me think—twenty-eight darics more, instead of twenty, making a total of ninety-eight. In other words, we should owe Master Murashu almost double what we borrowed. In three years our debt would almost triple."

Bessas looked at Myron with awe. "I was wiser than I thought, to persuade you to come with me. Never could I fathom those higher computations if it were the only escape from the seven Babylonian hells." He glanced at his huge hairy fist. "Methinks Master Murashu wants a lesson in what happens to those who cheat noble Aryans."

"No, you thick-skinned idiot! He hasn't cheated us; he has merely made us an offer, which we are free to decline. With care and consideration, we may yet discover a way to obtain our money at lower rental."

"Meanwhile we might as well buy our other stuff——" Bessas broke off.

"What is it? Are we followed?" asked Myron.

"There's an ordinary-looking little man, so common-place that he were hard to describe, loitering across Enlil Street. . . . Now he's gone. I would swear by the demon Azi Dahaka's three heads that I have seen him before, following us about."

"*Papai!* Another man sent by the Daduchids?"

"No doubt. If we are to be harried from Kissia to Kush by slinking shadows, we'd better buy some weapons and defenses now." While they sought out an armer's shop, Bessas asked Myron: "What weapons are you seasoned in the use of?"

"None, I fear. As a youth in Miletos I learnt to march in step, keep in line, and thrust with the spear. But that was long ago; and, when the Persians stormed my city, all was over before I had an opportunity to fight. Being taken in arms, I was auctioned off. Although Lord Arsaces, liking the way I tutored his sons, liberated me after a few years' service, I have not had occasion to handle weapons since."

"Hmp. That sword you took from the murderer will be useful, but it's too short to use from horseback. Let us see what this fellow has to offer." Bessas turned in at a shop whose signboard bore a crude painting of a sword and a battle-ax crossed in front of a circular shield, and a helmet surmounting the whole.

The Bactrian's eyes gleamed with eagerness as he entered the armer's shop, where dully gleaming weapons hung in rows and the clang of the smithy came from the rear. He bandied weapon talk with the armer, bent bows, poised javelins, and swished swords and axes through the air until Myron reminded him that they had business.

"For you, I shall buy this mace," said Bessas, handing Myron a weapon with a two-foot hardwood shaft and a wickedly spiked bronze head. "That's the weapon for a tyro. You need not worry about its turning in your grip, as with a sword or ax; just hit hard with it. Now, armer, let me see a couple of spears: heavy enough to thrust,

86

light enough to throw, short enough to handle easily, yet long enough to hold off a lion. . . ."

"Now for armor," said Bessas when he had chosen the spears. "A pair of helmets—none of your fancy Karian cockscomb crests, either, but a couple of plain bronzen pots to keep our brains from being spattered. . . . For body armor, let's see a couple of leather jacks."

Myron looked dubiously at the bronze-studded leather cuirass, of a deep, shiny, reddish brown. "A forceful thrust would go through this stuff. Why don't we purchase bronze cuirasses, such as they wear in Ionia, or those Persian mailshirts with iron scales?"

"Because we are riding, little man, and on ordinary horses, not Nisaean giants. If we load ourselves down with the whole bronzen panoply of a Greek spearman, our beasts will founder from the weight."

By the time that Bessas completed his purchases with a pair of light leather bucklers and some extra arrows, and his cuirass had been altered to fit his huge torso, the afternoon had fled. Back at barracks, as Myron prepared to write up the log for the day, he asked:

"How much more purchasing must we do?"

"Tomorrow morn we shall try the horse mart for mounts. That leaves but a few items of harness, a tent, and the like."

"Will you buy a slave or hire guides or men-at-arms?"

"Time enough for such fripperies in Egypt. Until we get there, we can find our way by asking. I have been on many such journeys—as the time my half brother Moccus and I beat our way across Hind—and I have seen what happens. The leader, too proud to saddle and feed and water his beasts, procures a groom. Then, misliking cold victuals, he must needs have a cook; and a body slave to brush his garments and shine his shoes; and a woman to keep him warm at night.

"Then he must hire guards to protect these unfighters. That means more animals, and they in turn require more

87

grooms, who need camp men to care for their tents and baggage, who require more men-at-arms to guard them, and so on until we have a small army, straggling over the countryside at a snail's pace, getting lost, taking sick, robbing the natives, and being attacked by them in turn. By keeping our numbers down to the twain of us, we shall move far faster and more cheaply. Speaking of cost, have you found a way to get us our money at lower interest?"

Myron had to admit that he had not. The next morning they spent in the horse market. Here Bessas, who usually claimed to know and care nothing about trade and money, revealed himself as a very sharp bargainer. When Myron twitted him, he said with a shamefaced grin:

"Oh, well, a Bactrian can trade in horses and still be deemed a gentleman."

In the end, Bessas bought two horses—a powerful destrier named Vayu for himself and a smaller Cilician bay for his companion—and two mules to bear their belongings. "How is our store of darics holding out?" he asked.

Myron did a hasty computation. "They are half consumed."

"Plague! Riches certainly fly away, as the eagle flies into the heavens. We had better get some more money, if we must needs rob the temple of Marduk."

They made a few more purchases during the afternoon. Bessas, for instance, bought a silver whistle to hang around his neck. "It utters as loud a blast as a trumpet," he said, "with far less bulk."

Every coin had to be weighed out. Change was made in bits of silver, copper, and lead: rings, bars, squares, and irregular lumps, all of which had to be weighed in their turn; for the Babylonians had not yet come to the use of small coins.

Their last stop was at the saddler's shop of Shamu and Zeria. This was a large establishment, selling not only bits, bridles, and saddles, but also chariots and wagons. Horse trappings, smelling of freshly oiled leather and gleaming with polished bronze, hung from the walls.

Sounds of carriage-making came from the rear. A stout, blue-eyed man with a cheerful round face took them in charge.

"Why, if you go to Egypt, do you not drive instead of riding?" he said. "We could build you our special chariot with an attachable trailer, ideal for such journeys. We made one for Lord Masdaeus last year, and he will tell you how well it has pleased him."

"We lack time for the filling of such an order," said Bessas.

"Well then, we have a harmanaxa of a late model, repossessed from an owner who could not pay for it——"

"A woman's wagon?" said Bessas in tones of deep scorn. "Do you take me for a dotard who can no longer sit a horse?"

"Nay, sir, your slave thought no such thing. My reasons are practical, to wit: that a horse can pull twice the load on wheels that it can bear on its back. So you could thus save the price of an extra horse to count against the cost of the vehicle. Also, you could go all day at a trot. . . ."

Bessas and the man fell into a long argument about horses, mules, and asses, and the proper loading and harness for each under every condition. At last Bessas said:

"You seem to know a thing or two about this business, my friend. Who are you?"

"Your servant is Daniel bar-Malko, once of Qadesh but now master wainwright for Shamu and Zeria."

When Bessas and Myron made themselves known, the latter said: "Your carriage is an attractive idea, Master Daniel, but I fear me the roads would not allow it. The postal people inform me that there is no paving beyond Kounaxa, only tracks in soft sand. Also, they say that some of the roads in Phoenicia are impassable to wheels because they go up and down the faces of crags by means of stone steps. We should need, instead of horses, a team of trained eagles, like those which bore aloft the flying throne of King Usan."

"I am sure you could get a well-made carriage over

89

the roads, with a little local help to push you over the bad spots," said the Syrian. "After all, the king rides chariots and carriages all over the Persian Empire. When he finds a stretch of bad road he has it fixed, or somebody loses his head. . . ."

When the harness had been bought and paid for, Daniel bar-Malko invited Myron and Bessas to his house for dinner; for a warm friendship had sprung up between the friendly and voluble wainwright and the moody Bactrian.

At Daniel's house, near the Enlil Gate, the Syrian's women glided about, plying the three men with food and wine while Daniel held forth:

". . . if I could only get capital to start in business for myself, I should soon show these stodgy Babylonians a thing or two. What is wanted here is the light sporting chariot of the Egyptian type. Know you, my masters, that no less than six such chariots have been brought all the way from Egypt to Babylon in the past year, for sale to rich youths who are fain to cut a dash? I have talked my tongue off to make Shamu see the light; but no, he insists that the traditional Babylonian chariot—a slightly refined ox cart, in my opinion—has sold well ever since the Flood. . . ."

When his turn to speak came, Bessas told of some of his wild adventures on the eastern frontiers. He told, for instance, of the time some Massagetai caught him and stripped him for torture. He told how he broke away, vaulted on one of their horses, and galloped fifty miles with the whole tribe pounding after him. When his horse foundered, he escaped by diving into the Oxus River, coming up under a pile of driftwood, and spending a whole day there with his nose alone out of the icy water while the nomads raged up and down the banks in search of him.

At parting, Daniel lit the end of a link in the hearth fire and thrust it into Bessas' hand. "This will see you back to the barracks," he said. "Turn right as you go out, walk thirty paces, and you will be on Enlil Street. Oh— if you are fain to hire a guide in Syria, you could do worse than to obtain my brother's services."

"Oh?" said Myron.

"Aye. Ask in Qadesh for Kothar bar-Malko." Daniel chuckled. "You will find my brother a strange man. He is a former priest of El, cast out of his priesthood for unlawful magic. His family disowned him. Since then he has made a chancy living as a guide, trader, and wandering wizard. He is not what you would call respectable, but he is an able guide. He has been to Egypt several times and fluently speaks the speech of that land."

Daniel kissed his guests good-by and showed them out, saying: "May honey drip upon you, my friends! Tell me of your adventures when you return. Remember the name, Kothar bar-Malko."

A light overcast veiled the moon and transformed it into a faint opalescence high in the heavens. The link burnt with a smoky red flame, which threw writhing, misshapen shadows as Myron and Bessas, laden with their purchases of the afternoon, picked their way along Enlil Street.

Once they came upon a detachment of the night watch: four men of the merchant class, wearing pointed helms of an antique pattern and carrying pikes. These halted the travelers at the sight of the gear they bore and the swords they wore. But a flourish of documents from Myron, some gruff replies by Bessas, and the mention of their recent host convinced the watchmen of their honesty.

"We all know Master Daniel," said one. "Anyway, thieves do not carry links to light their way."

The twain continued northward until Bessas halted, saying: "By Mithra and Verethraghna, we are followed!"

Myron listened but heard nothing. They walked forward again, and this time he thought he heard stealthy footsteps beind them. When they halted, the footsteps halted.

91

"Are you sure it's not the echo of our own feet on the walls across the street?" whispered Myron.

"Not unless I'm growing deaf with age. But I have a trick for that. Come along."

They hurried ahead and soon reached the crossing of Marduk Street. Here Enlil Street ended, unless an alley opening on the north side of Marduk Street were to be deemed a continuation of Enlil Street.

Bessas turned to the right on Marduk Street, as if to take in the jog to Sin Street, where the diagonal road from the Zababa Gate crossed Marduk. Then he halted and set down the link, carefully so it continued to burn.

"Now run!" he breathed.

Bessas crossed Marduk Street with giant strides and turned left. He plunged into the alley that continued Enlil Street. Myron panted after him, staggering under his burden.

Darkness closed in about them. Noisome stenches made Myron gasp; he felt soft nameless substances under his boots. Ahead, Bessas stumbled and cursed luridly under his breath.

"This should be a short cut through to the diagonal road," muttered the Bactrian.

The alley bent this way and that and forked. Bessas halted, so suddenly that Myron blundered into him in the dark. In the instant that he stood silently, panting, Myron heard the sound of many running feet, from no definite direction.

"Take the right," said Bessas. "The other way will get us lost in the alleys."

They plunged off to the right but soon halted again. "The gods damn me to the House of the Lie for a stupid oaf!" breathed Bessas. "This is a bag-end. We shall have to try the other——"

"Too late," said Myron. Sound and motion from the mouth of the close revealed that their pursuers had trapped them.

Bessas dropped his burden, doffed his cloak, wrapped

it around his left arm, and drew his sword. Myron did likewise, desperately wishing that they had with them the warlike gear they had bought the previous day, which now reposed in the barracks.

"Keep on my left and a little behind me," said Bessas. "Guard my back, and let them not grapple us."

"Well, don't amputate my head with one of those wild swings," said Myron, whose heart was pounding with painful intensity.

Without further words, Bessas charged their pursuers, who had penetrated only a few paces into the close. They were shadowy figures. Nothing about them stood out definitely, save that the faint traces of moonlight that seeped down between the high dark walls struck feeble gleams from their blades.

The Bactrian, moving with the swiftness of a storm wind, was upon them before they could brace themselves. The long Indian sword whistled. There was a hard sound of cloven bone, and the first man was down with a split skull.

Little clash of steel was heard. The attackers seemed to be armed with knives and short swords, but none had a weapon of the reach of Bessas' blade, and in the darkness there was little opportunity for fencing.

Myron, pressing after Bessas, stumbled over a form and stabbed downward, fetching a groan from the victim. He lunged at the man before him. The man gave back, and Myron heard and felt his own cloak rip as a foe's blade caught in it. Another man screamed and fell back before Bessas' attack. There was a slap of sandals and a hiss of hard breathing.

"*Got* you!" said Bessas. Another man shrieked.

From behind the throng at the mouth of the close came a voice, urging on the attackers: "Go on, fight! Get in close! They are but two! Go in low and stab upward! Seize them about the knees and throw them!"

"If you'll step up, General," snarled Bessas, "I will give you a chance to demonstrate."

93

The mob surged forward again. They could not get behind the travelers, as they could not advance more than three abreast. Bessas and Myron between them filled the alley from wall to wall, the Bactrian taking up the space of two ordinary men.

However, a man lunged forward in a crouch, aiming a stab at Bessas' midriff. Myron saw the blade go home and thought they were done for. But the Bactrian skipped lightly backward, knocking the man flat with a sword blow. He and Myron had now lost several feet of fighting space.

"You rear men, push forward and give the others a rest!" came the voice of the unseen leader.

"They'll wear us down," panted Myron.

Bessas, dancing, thrusting, and slashing, did not answer. Little by little he and Myron were forced back down the close. Soon, thought Myron, they would have their backs to the wall at the end. He shouted:

"Help! Murder!"

There was no reply. The dwellers in houses along the close, if they heard the call, would only brace things against their doors.

Then came a new trampling of feet, a clash of steel, and cries from the mouth of the close. The attackers melted away. They turned their backs and bolted out of the close in a jostling mob. Myron and Bessas were too winded for the moment to pursue them.

Another group of dark figures entered the close. Bessas brought his sword up to guard, but the first newcomer said: "Bessas of Zariaspa?"

"Who in demon land are you?"

"Friends. Come quickly! The gang outnumbers us and will soon return in force."

"All right, but do not get too close. No tricks!"

Myron followed Bessas, who followed the hooded newcomer. Others fell in behind Myron, who judged that there were about half a dozen of them. They went swiftly, sometimes walking and sometimes breaking into a trot.

They zigzagged among the alleys until Myron had no idea of where he was.

A door opened in a blank wall. A gleam of yellow lamplight momentarily splashed across the alley, showing a dead dog lying in the dirt.

Myron, still clutching his sword, filed in with the rest. He found himself in a narrow passage, at the far end of which a lamp smoked and guttered in a wall bracket. The leader lit a rushlight at the flame of the lamp and led on by this feeble illumination. The passage descended by steps below street level and wound this way and that. Occasional doors of crude, heavy timbers appeared on the side walls. They passed through a confusing sequence of doors, rooms, and corridors.

Then Myron found himself in a long chamber, lit by several petroleum-burning bronzen lamps. Benches ran along its sides, leaving a wide clear center aisle with a stair well in it. A narrow stair ran down from this opening out of sight.

On either side of the chamber, a statue stood in a niche. Each statue was that of a nude winged man with a lion's head, around whom a large serpent was entwined. Each leontocephalus stood on a globe and held a scepter in one hand and a thunderbolt in the other.

At the far end of the chamber rose an altar. Behind the altar, on the far wall, a scene was carved in low relief. Artistically, Myron thought it simply another example of stiff, lifeless Persian art. The subjects, however, excited his interest.

The relief showed a bull, which had been forced to its knees by a trousered youth. The man wore a cap with lappets, of the sort encountered among the more northerly Aryans. He gripped the bull's muzzle with his left hand and stabbed the beast with a knife in his right. A dog lapped the blood that flowed from the wound; a serpent writhed about the bull's legs; and a scorpion clawed at the dying animal's scrotum.

Myron brought his attention back to his human surroundings in time to see the hooded leader of their rescuers make a quick ritualistic gesture to Bessas, who made a responding gesture. Then the two men solemnly kissed each other's cheeks. The leader pushed back his hood, showing a lean, refined face. He gestured towards Myron.

"Can we trust the Hellene?"

"I think so," replied Bessas. "He is my lieutenant, and if he blabs——" Bessas grinned horribly and drew a finger across his throat. "How did you happen by just then?"

"Your slaves heard that you were passing through Babylon and were likely to be beset. Remembering the great good that Phraates did for our brethren, years ago, we set men to watch you. Several times we lost you, what of that giant stride of yours. But we caught up with you just in time."

"Was one of your men a rather small fellow, very ordinary-looking, with dark hair and beard, wearing a shabby brown jacket and patched green trousers?"

The other frowned. "None of my men answers that description. But one of them did report that others besides themselves seemed to be following you. I——"

There came a disturbance. Four more men entered. Two of them dragged a ragged, ruffianly looking fellow, bleeding from a wound in his chest. The fourth man carried the gear that Myron and Bessas had dropped.

"This one still lives, Father," said one of those bearing the wounded man, "but not for long, methinks. There were three dead, and several of the knaves bore wounds away with them."

The leader said: "Take him below and see if you can get some truth out of him ere he dies. Yes, O Myron?"

Myron, who had been fidgeting, said: "Sir, I burst with curiosity. Be it as you wish, but at least tell me this: Are you not Mithraists?"

"Aye. As you see, the persecution of the usurper's son has forced us to hide our places of worship. However, it will do no harm to tell you that——"

A shriek from the chamber below cut off the leader's speech. When all had recovered their poise, Myron asked:

"What may your servant call you?"

"Call me Embas. How did you manage with Murashu the banker?"

Myron told him of the difficulty over interest rates. Embas thought awhile, then said:

"Murashu is a hard man. Perhaps the Lord of the Farmyard can aid in this matter."

More screams came from below. Presently one of the hooded Mithraists came up the stairs with bloody hands and said:

"Father Embas, the robber is dead. Before he passed to the Land of Silence, he told us that he was one of Labashi's retainers."

"What else?"

"Little, save that two days past Labashi got word from Shushan, urging him to slay Bessas son of Phraates and promising rich rewards."

"That means Ardigula," said Embas. "Know you Ardigula of Baghdad, either of you?"

"Not I," said Bessas. "What is Baghdad?"

"A village on the Tigris, fifteen leagues or so to northward. You, Myron?"

"Nor I," said Myron. "But wait—the name is somehow familiar. I may have heard him referred to as a wizard and occultist. I paid no heed at the time, as I have nothing to do with such people."

"Know you any reason why he might wish you ill?"

"No, unless he were retained by someone with a grudge—say, the House of Daduchus. But I do know that we have been attacked four times in ten days, the first time definitely by emissaries of the Daduchids. We captured the leader and made him confess. At that rate, we shall sustain a hundred or more attacks before we return. And, even though Captain Bessas be a fell fighter with the might of Rustam and the luck of Odysseus, I doubt if we should survive them all."

"Rehearse me the whole tale," said Embas.

Bessas narrated the story of the rape of Tamyra. When he had finished, Embas said:

"The connection is plausible, though not proven. In any case, you will not wish to lurk for aye in our crypts; whereas, if you wander abroad in Babylon, we cannot forever protect you. You had better be on your way to Kush. Ardigula can scarce pursue you beyond the Syrian desert."

"But," said Myron, "how can we go without sufficient funds? And how do we get our beasts and our gear from the barracks? A bird cannot fly without wings."

Embas smiled thinly. "Snatch yourselves a few hours' sleep. You will be surprised at the succor the Sleepless One can render to those whom he loves."

As Myron and Bessas prepared to sleep in a small chamber off the Mithraeum, the Greek said: "How in Hera's name did you avoid that stab, which the fellow sent home against your middle? I thought you a dead man."

Bessas, with a deep chuckle, reached inside his trousers and brought forth a long girdle of stout cloth. When he unfolded it, golden coins winked yellowly in the lamplight.

"One of Xerxes' golden archers stopped the point," he said. "And belike my little prayer to Mithra helped."

On the next morning, an hour before the first light of dawn appeared above the canal-stitched Euphratean plain, Myron and Bessas joined a caravan setting out for Damascus. Yawning and shivering, each rode one of the horses that Bessas had bought and led one of the mules. To each mule's back was lashed one of the two spears. Myron wore his short sword in Median fashion, low on the right side, with the thong on the end of the scabbard tied around his thigh.

The caravan sorted itself out into a straggling serpentine column. Asses brayed, camels gargled and roared, horses whinnied, and caravaneers shouted commands, advice, and curses.

The column trailed northward along Processional Way and through the mighty Ishtar Gate, where sleepy Persian soldiers stamped their frozen feet and blew on their hands. Torchlight flickered on the bulls and dragons of the great blue gate; the nearest sirrush seemed to Myron to leer at him. Each caravaneer, as he passed through the gate, uttered a prayer to his favorite god.

Out through the northern suburbs they trailed and along the river road, into the morning mist. The city faded into the murk behind them.

In Myron's scrip reposed a parchment copy of their contract with Murashu and Sons, promising to pay back fifty darics with annual interest at twenty parts in a hundred. Myron had a blurred recollection of Bessas, leaning over both copies and signing by rushlight, scowling and licking his bearded lips as he painfully traced out each letter. Embas had explained that the temple of Mithra had guaranteed the loan. This brought Murashu down to the normal interest rate, even though the emissaries of the Mithraeum had hauled the banker out of bed to close the deal.

"Most of it is in bar silver," said Embas, "because such silver commands a premium in Egypt above the monetary value of the coinage. The Egyptians dislike coins, holding them a newfangled scheme to enable rascals to cheat honest men."

"I found the same stupidity in India," said Bessas.

"Then why cannot the traveler simply melt down his shekels in Egypt?" asked Myron.

"Because such defacement of the royal coinage, if found out, would only cost you your heads, as it cost the satrap Aryandes his."

When the sun stood high, Bessas said: "I see no sign of pursuit. Let's not loaf along with these stinking camels all the way to Id, but seek our own gait."

The travelers pulled out of line, spurred to a canter,

and soon neared the head of the line of camels. Then, however, a man on an ass—a smallish, nondescript man —rode out in front of them.

"My masters!" he called. "Do you follow the Euphrates to Barbalissos?"

"What is that to you?" asked Bessas with a scowl.

"I thought you might permit your slave to go with you. I cannot stay with the caravan beyond Sirki, for there they take the desert road to Thadamora, and that road is impassable save to camels. Withal, one must pay a caravan toll to Shaykh Alman. So meseemed——"

Bessas began to slide his Parthian bow from its case, muttering: "By the waters of Ardvi, it is time we ended this damned——"

"Not so precipitate!" said Myron in Greek. "We don't even know whose side he is on."

"Well, then?"

"We can easily outrun him. That ass is no Pegasos."

Bessas grinned and called out: "You are welcome to stay with us whilst you can!"

Bessas and Myron clapped spurs to their steeds. Leading their pack mules at full gallop, they raced on up the palm-lined left bank of the Euphrates and were soon out of sight of the caravan and of the man on the ass as well.

Meanwhile, in another room in Babylon, as difficult of access as the Mithraeum but very differently appointed, Labashi received his minions. The room, though small, was hung with costly stuffs and gleaming ornaments. The air was thick with incense. Tables and floor were heaped with masses of documents: sheets of papyrus and sheepskin and clay tablets. Astrological charts were pinned to the wall hangings.

Labashi sat on a raised chair, clad in raiment of a thin shiny unknown stuff that had come from far to the east. Nobody else, not even the king, as yet possessed a garment of this lustrous material. Labashi was a hunchback, with

100

a large head and regular features, which he shaved in priestly style.

As Labashi's lieutenant, limping from wounds, gave his report, Labashi's black eyes bored into him with an unwinking basilisk stare. Once Labashi slapped his thigh with anger when the lieutenant told of the arrival of rescuers. When he had finished, the lieutenant stood with bowed head, awaiting the blast.

It never came. Instead, Labashi said softly: "Well, then, another scheme we must try. Honor demands that we persevere and do not our colleague Ardigula disappoint." He rose and walked to one of the star charts, which he studied for several ush.* At last he said: "Find me one of Shaykh Waliq's tribesmen, that I may send a message to the shaykh."

V   The Temple of the Harlots

UP THE MIGHTY RIVER rode Myron and Bessas, past endless lines of date palms, past creaking swapes by which early-rising peasants hoisted water from the public canals to the heads of their irrigation ditches, past fields of young wheat and barley, past lakes and marshes whence waterfowl rose with a thunder of wings. They passed Agade with its massive wall and dreams of ancient greatness, and Sippar with its many-storied ziggurat. They crossed canals and passed mud-walled villages innumerable.

At Kounaxa they waited for a string of dromedaries to plod across the floating bridge that spanned the Euphrates, their bells emitting a melancholy tune. Myron, looking apprehensively at the structure, remarked to the villager who took the bridge tolls:

"Your bridge doesn't look particularly secure. The planks sag, and half the boats are low in the water."

* 1 ush = 4 minutes.

"Oh, good and great master!" said the peasant with the air of fawning servility that subjects of the Persian Empire were wont to adopt towards the Great King's servants. "That will soon be mended. The King of All Kings —may the gods preserve him—has promised your vile and unworthy slaves a new bridge."

As they crossed the rickety structure, Myron said: "Let's hope they get their new bridge before this one sinks with a quiet gurgle beneath its users."

Bessas replied: "Three things should not be counted upon: the level of a river, the tameness of a lion, and the promise of a king. Especially a king like our popeyed friend."

"Embas spoke of—ah—that same man as the son of a usurper. What did he mean?"

Bessas lowered his voice. "Repeat this not, lest your head fly off like the ball in a game of stick-and-ball. Some think the supposed false Bardias, whom Darius claimed to have slain ere he took the throne after Cambyses' death, was not false at all. They think he was Cambyses' veritable brother, whom Cambyses had never slain as Darius claimed."

"My dear fellow! Do you mean that story of Gomates the Mage, who took the place of Bardias after the latter's murder and even fooled Bardias' wives, is a lot of cock and bull?"

"So some believe. But there is no tale more dangerous to relate. You know the saying: He that keeps his mouth tightly shut shall live, while he that blathers shall meet destruction."

They rode on. At Id, Myron insisted on stopping to see the asphalt wells and to watch the Idites scooping the sticky black stuff into baskets. Bessas, fuming, growled:

"If you stop to look at every new sight along the way, we shall be dead of old age ere we return."

"What I do," said Myron, "is quite as important as our wretched little lives."

102

"Mean you looking at asphalt wells?"

"No; I mean reviving the glory of Miletos."

"With asphalt? Are you mad?"

"You no more understand than your horse understands astronomy. The glory of Miletos was the glory of the mind. We Milesians were the first folk ever seriously to ask how the universe is made and how it works. What shape is the earth? Where does the sun go at night? What is the basic substance of all things: fire, air, or water? Whence came mankind? We may not know the final answers to these questions, but at least we have sought the solutions, instead of swallowing the many and inconsitent myths purveyed by the priests.

"When Darius' generals crushed the first Ionian revolt, some of the Milesians were massacred; some like myself were enslaved; some were deported to Chaldea; some fled to Sicily. The city was utterly depopulated. Other people have moved into Miletos since then, but they lack our tradition of wisdom-seeking. If I can learn enough in my travels, I might yet revive the wisdom-loving tradition, which was the glory of my city."

"It sounds noble but not practical," said Bessas. "Most men, you will find, care not a whit if the earth be shaped like a plate, or a cup, or even round like a ball." He guffawed at the absurdity. "Therefore, instead of honoring you for your deep thinking, they'll scorn you as a bookish fool."

"Dogs also bark at what they do not know," bridled Myron. "Besides, wisdom-lovers can be practical when necessary. Thales, who first laid down the laws of geometry and determined the sun's course from solstice to soltice, was once annoyed by people who said: 'If you are so clever, why aren't you rich?' So he rented all the olive mills for one season and, having thus cornered the sources of oil, earned a large fortune. Then he went back to philosophy."

"Mithra prosper your enterprise. When you have made such a fortune yourself, you might ask Bessas of Zariaspa

103

to help you spend it. Meanwhile, if you do not leave your asphalt well and come along, I will toss you in head foremost, so that you shall learn the properties of mineral pitch at first hand."

Northwest of Id, the landscape became more barren. When Myron and Bessas arrived at Baia Malcha, the desert had almost crept to the river's edge, where poplars and tamarisks grew in clumps along the margins of the flume and on the islands in the river.

Towns were few and small. Most of the people were either nomads or dwellers in huts of reeds and dried mud among the feathery tamarisks. They pastured sheep on the scanty strips of grass, speared fish in the shallows, and beat up the thickets for wild pig.

The next day the travelers toiled through a desolate land of sand and rock, which rolled away gently to the horizon save when broken by outcrop or hill. Short-lived spring grasses, not yet browned by the summer sun, carpeted patches of desert with gray-green films, in which the wild flowers shone like gems. Groups of gazelles and ostriches appeared, to bolt off into the blue when the travelers turned towards them.

A little yellow whirlwind arose in the middle distance, drifting this way and that. When it dissipated, another took its place. After these dust whirls had been in sight for some time, Bessas said:

"By the four teats of Ishtar, I'll wager that is a spirit sent to spy upon us by that Labashi fellow! I'll teach the demon to pester *me!*"

The Bactrian spurred off into the desert, drawing his bow and an arrow. As he galloped past the dust whirl, he loosed. The arrow went through the column, which faded and died at once. Bessas circled, picked up his arrow, and rode back grinning. "What did I say?"

"I fear you but winged it," said Myron. "There's another—or perhaps the same one farther off."

Another dust whirl danced in the distance.

104

"I taught it a lesson, anyway," growled Bessas. "I suppose if I slay one, the wizard can always conjure up another, like that Kasmirian sorcerer I told you about, the one who sat on a Himalayan peak and collected human hides for a hobby."

"Personally," said Myron, "I should say that they were a natural phenomenon. Herakleitos insisted that most things have rational explanations, if only men took the trouble to seek them out."

"Where do the gods fit into this rational world of your Herakleitos?"

Myron shrugged. "I have heard tales of the gods of many lands, all of which can hardly be true at once. As Xenophanes said, if the horses had a god, they would visualize him with mane, tail, and hooves. I suspect that whatever gods exist are beyond our comprehension, just as we are beyond the comprehension of that butterfly." He pointed at a black and golden insect, which fluttered across their path. "To him we should no doubt seem almighty, immortal, and incomprehensible, just as the gods seem to us."

"Mean you that the gods are really mortal, though their span be greater than ours?"

"I don't know, Bessas; no god has confided in me. I merely point out a possibility."

"Take heed that, in all your pointing out and surmising, you rouse not the ire of these gods, who all the myths agree are a fractious and touchy lot." Bessas sang in his booming bass:

Some men adore the gods on bended knee,
While some to their inmost secrets seek the key.
I go my gait and leave the gods alone,
In hope that they will do the like to me!

"Are you not a Mithraist?" asked Myron.

"Aye; but I do not importune the god to the point of

105

boring him. When he receives a prayer from me, he knows it's about a really urgent matter."

"King Xerxes sacrifices horses to Mithra at the New Year. Wherein, then, does your creed differ from his?"

"Oh, Xerxes worships Mithra, just as we Mithraists also believe in Auramazda. The difference lies in this: that we don't think the Lord of Light bothers himself with men's personal problems, any more than King Xerxes can personally comfort every afflicted peasant in his Empire. Auramazda is remote and withdrawn from these material things; Mithra truly governs the world. So our prayers are directed to Mithra. But the Zoroastrians would lower Mithra to the rank of a mere angel. If Xerxes is fain to belittle Mithra and address Auramazda directly, that is his business, but what call does that give him to interfere with us?"

"I suppose he desires to strengthen his Empire by unifying the Aryan religion."

Bessas spat. "If he would please the unseen powers, let him begin by acting justly himself, not by causing my mother and me to suffer for others' misdeeds."

They stopped at Ana with its palm groves and its fort on an island in the river. Bessas gave Myron lessons in archery and, using sticks whittled from tamarisk stems, in sword fighting. On the morrow, Myron awoke with bruised knuckles to hear Bessas say:

"Perhaps no god has confided in you, but one of them visited me in dreams last night."

"Indeed?"

"Aye; 'twas the hero Artagnes. He said——" (Bessas closed his eyes):

> *O man, who seeketh what is sought in vain,*
> *For thee Hvareno doth this fate ordain:*
> *Red shall engender red, blood call to blood,*
> *And that which dwelleth far above the flood*
> *Shall not avail to save thee; put thy faith*

In that to trust which were to grasp a wraith.
A dreadful deed within a narrow room
May yet by devious ways avert thy doom!

"It sounds ominous. Who is Hvareno?" asked Myron.

"Our goddess of fortune—our Tychê. What make you of it?"

"Nothing at the moment; but I have too often seen how oracles are manipulated to take much account of them."

"Scorn not divine warnings. We are not so sure of our way and our fate as lightly to cast aside any helpful signs."

Myron slowly repeated the poem in Persian. "So we seek something in vain? That would mean that the dragon is not to be captured at the Nile's headwaters after all."

"It might mean, not that it cannot be caught, but only that it never has been caught, by reason of its strength and ferocity."

"Or that something else—life for your mother, which you seek, and eminence as a philosopher, for me—are not to be had by searching. Well, it's true enough, I suppose —Zarina is mortal like the rest of us—but the remainder of the verse is so confused that I can make nothing of it."

Bessas sighed. "No doubt, when all is over, the meaning will stand out as plainly as the noses on the Achaemenids' faces, and we shall berate ourselves as dunces for not having seen it. Meantime we had better be on the road."

They passed Mari, a cluster of huts and a caravan station amidst the ruins of a great city. Myron rummaged through the buff-brown piles of debris with his head down, like a dog with its nose on a scent, until Bessas bellowed:

"By the bronzen balls of Ahriman, why do you waste time there?"

107

"I hope to find a clue to the history of this city. The people hereabouts know nothing."

"The wiser folk they. Besides, if you fool around these places long enough, you might scare up the ghost of some long-dead king. These are uncanny places. Many deeds of blood and darkness have been done in them, and evil influences last down the ages. The Corpse Fiend take your curiosity; come along!"

They passed Dura on its towering cliff, with the crumbling ruins of an Assyrian fortress. And every day, dust devils danced upon the horizon. Bessas, more and more uneasy, muttered spells of exorcism and became punctilious in his prayers to Mithra. He also exercised Vayu who, like a proper war horse, had been trained to assail his rider's foes with teeth and hooves and, if his rider fell, to stand over and protect him.

A dust storm swooped upon them, forcing them to huddle in their tent for half a day, while they listened to the howls and fiendish laughter of the demons of the waste. During the lulls in the storm, Bessas told of demons he had encountered on the fringes of the Empire. One especially unpleasant one, nine feet tall and covered with long white hair, dwelt in the mountains of the Austanes east of Bactria. This fiend could suck all the bones out of a man's body without breaking his skin. He had not, said Bessas, actually seen this demon, but he had heard it shuffling about his hut at night and seen its footprints in the snow the next day. Only the drumming and incantations of the village shaman had kept the demon from breaking into the hut. Although skeptical towards tales of demons and other spooks, Myron thought it more tactful to keep his doubts to himself.

They passed Sirki, where the Araxes adds its flood to the Euphrates, and whence the caravans set out for lone Thadamora in the waste. Here they heard how things went in the Desert of Aram. By protecting the caravans, Shaykh Alman, lord of Thadamora, was trying to build up caravan trade through his oasis. At the same time the nomadic Shaykh Waliq, at feud with the Thadamorites, attacked these same caravans, making the short cut across the Syrian desert an exciting passage.

Beyond Azaura, human habitations became more frequent. Hills and ridges appeared to the south. Blue lagoons fringed the Euphrates, in which mud shoals lay like colossal crocodiles. The land became more fertile, and the date palm gave way to the olive tree. Dust devils ceased to shadow the travelers.

Myron, gazing at some curious flat-topped hills that rose over a hundred feet from the banks of the river, said: "I wonder what could have given those hills that curious shape, like tables——"

"Oh, hold your tongue, Greekling!" snapped Bessas. "Your everlasting questions irk me."

Myron looked sharply at his companion. During the first part of their journey up the Euphrates, Bessas had been cheerful and good company. Now he showed increasing irascibility. Once he wept for a solid hour but refused to give any reasons for his sorrow.

The night of the twenty-ninth of Nisanu they spent at the ford of Tiphsah. Noon of the next day found them in Barbalissos. Here the Euphrates, descending from the north, bends around to eastward on its way to Sippar and Babylon, and here a steep escarpment rises on the south and west of the river.

In the tavern, Bessas cocked an ear at the buzz of talk and asked: "O Myron, what language do these folk speak? I know it not."

"Neither do I." Myron spoke in Aramaic to a short, stout youth who wore a necklace of amulets of copper and crystal: "Your pardon, sir, but do you understand me?"

"Aye; I speak the Syrian tongue. How can your slave serve you?"

"By sitting down, having a mug of wine at our expense, and telling us what travelers in the region ought to know. For one thing, what language do we hear about us?"

109

"Karian. Our forebears were mercenaries serving Croesus of Lydia, who fell into Cyrus' hands at the downfall of Sardeis. King Cyrus settled us here in Barbalissos, far from our native heath. Whither are you bound, my masters?"

Myron told briefly of their mission and asked about roads and accommodations in Syria. The youth answered, but then burst out:

"Masters, for such a journey you will have to hire more men ere you reach your goal, will you not? I am told that in Africa live wild black men, who eat other men when they catch them. You will need strong arms besides your own to force your way through such perilous country."

"We shall see what we need when we get there," said Bessas. "Why?"

The youth held out his hands. "Oh, my masters, take me with you! I will not even ask for pay until we reach Egypt, so long as I can go."

"We are not——" began Bessas, but Myron interrupted:

"Why are you so eager, Master—what's your name?"

"Your servant is clept Skhâ son of Thuvlo. My father is the fuller and dyer of Barbalissos and, by Teshub's beard, I tire of the stench of urine in my nostrils! Naturally, he expects me to follow in his trade. But he has two other strong sons, and I am fain to leave this dull little puddle of a town, see the world, and peradventure become a warrior as were my forefathers."

"You're a little pudgy for that sort of work, youngster," said Bessas.

"I am no weakling, even if not so long in the limbs as you! I serve in the town guard and practice with warlike gear."

"Hold out your hand," said Bessas. "Now grip mine."

Skhâ squeezed Bessas' great paw, clamping down until the sweat ran down his face into the fuzzy young beard. Bessas easily matched the pressure. Then the Bactrian be-

110

gan to squeeze in his turn, until at last he fetched a grunt of pain from the youth. Bessas at once released the hand, whose fingers were now swollen and purple.

"Not bad for a townsman," said Bessas.

"Then take me, I beg!" cried Skhâ. "I work hard, and I shall certainly be a brave fighter when the need arises. I fear nought, for these"—he touched the necklace of amulets—"protect me. All I shall cost you is food until we reach Egypt. Then you may pay me the going wage."

Bessas twisted a strand of his beard around his forefinger. "Master Skhâ, you say you will cost us only bread and wine from here to Egypt. But we have no spare beast to bear you, nor spare arms to arm you with."

"True," said Skhâ, his mouth turning down. "Ah, woe and misfortune!"

"Well then," continued Bessas, "we leave for Halpa at dawn tomorrow. If you would go with us, join us, armed and mounted, within an hour of our departure."

"But how——"

"How you do it is your affair. On such a journey, we need resource. Good night."

The next morning, the travelers took their way across the grassy downs of northern Syria, past villages like clusters of stone beehives. Within an hour of departure, a drumming of hooves made them turn. Along came Skhâ on a piebald pony, waving a spear. He bore a light leather buckler, like those which Myron and Bessas carried. On his head was a crested leather helmet stiffened with strips of bronze. As this helmet was too large for its wearer, it came down over his eyes. He had to tilt his head backwards to see. The pony was small beside Bessas' big charger, but as Skhâ was the shortest of the three men this made little difference.

Bessas looked slit-eyed at his recruit. "Well," he said, "where did you get the arms and the horse?"

"You said it was my affair how I——" began Skhâ, but Bessas cut him off with a roar.

111

"No arguments! I know what I said, but today I am asking a question, and I want a straight answer!" Skhâ bit his lips, gulped, and finally answered. "The arms I b-borrowed from the town armory, and the horse belongs to my elder brother."

"All right. We may have to borrow a thing or two ere the course be run. But that does not mean pilfering within the company! We have a short way with the light-fingered." Bessas drew the edge of his hand across his throat. "Now, think well ere you make your decision. The way will be longer and harder than you can imagine, and we may all go the Bridge of Judgment. Nor will you find me an easy, kindly leader. I will try to use you justly, but sweet-tempered and long-suffering I am not. When I command, I expect you to jump to obey. Our lives may hang upon the speed of your compliance. Do you understand?"

"Aye, my master. Your servant has already decided. I will go with you, though you be the dragon Illuyanka in disguise."

"Then swear!" Bessas administered to Skhâ an oath like those that he had exchanged with Myron.

Skhâ proved a garrulous young man, incessantly questioning his companions and chattering about his personal affairs. "By what route do you plan to reach Egypt?" he asked.

"By way of Phoenicia and Judaea," said Myron, "or the land of Canaan, as the older manuscripts call those countries."

"By land? Let me tell you: I have spoken to many travelers, and they agree that it is quicker and less arduous to take ship from one of the Phoenician ports."

"We go by land," said Bessas. "Horses and mules do not travel well by sea."

"Or perhaps it is that noble Persians, who mortally fear

water, do not travel well by sea either?" Skhâ grinned impudently.

"Do you call me coward?" roared Bessas, grasping his hilt. His face became convulsed with passion.

"Oh, no, sir! But you——"

"Quiet, both of you!" cried Myron. "Bessas, you warned me at the outset against disputes within the ranks. Would you quarrel over the shadow of an ass? Now, can you swim or can't you?"

"No, but what business is that of yours? That ducking I took in the Oxus, when the Massagetai were after me, will suffice me the rest of my life."

"Do you swim, Skhâ?"

Skhâ toyed with his copper and crystal amulets. "Nay. But I fear not ship travel——"

"Harken! Bessas has been teaching me archery and swordplay, on the ground that these skills may come in useful. But knowledge of swimming will be just as useful, because of the many rivers and lakes that lie before us. So, my dear fellows, since all Milesians learn to swim, I shall teach you two the art the first time we encounter a body of water deep enough for the purpose. No objections, pupils," he said firmly, as the others began to protest, "or you must confess not only that you're ignorant of a useful skill, but also that you are too timid to remedy your ignorance."

They subsided. As the sun sank, they rode down a gentle, sparsely grassed slope into a broad shallow basin. Here, rising amid its orchards and vineyards by the sluggish Chalos, stood Halpa. From the center of the town arose a steep-sided frowning citadel.

They put up at a khan. A turbaned porter with boils on his face let them in through a gate in a high, blank stone wall.

Inside was a spacious quadrangle. A fountain gurgled in the center of the quadrangle, while stalls for travelers' beasts comprised its periphery. In back of each stall was a large locker for the traveler's gear. Above each space, opening on a balcony that ran around the quadrangle, was a sleeping chamber. A cubical brown brick building, with a tavern on the ground floor and the owner's quarters above, filled a corner of the quadrangle.

Having tethered their beasts and stowed their gear, the three travelers betook themselves to the tavern to enjoy the famous wine of Halpa. When they had drunk deeply, Skhâ said:

"Master Bessas, give me, pray, a small advance—say half a shekel—on the money you will pay me in Egypt."

"Why, you little beggar! You can go to the House of the Lie."

"But, sir——"

"Shut up, curse you!"

"But——"

"Just a minute," said Myron. "What do you want this money for, Skhâ?"

"Well—ah—this is the season when the unwed girls of Halpa go to the temple of Ashtarth—or Ishtar as you easterners call her—to earn dowries as temple whores. In Barbalissos we have no such temple, so I am fain to seize my opportunity here."

Myron said: "Why not make a celebration of it? Although I am no three-ball man, I think my old yard retains a stand or two. How about it, Bessas?"

The giant sat with darkened face and clenched fists, breathing heavily. He scowled, bit his lips, hesitated, but said at last:

"I'm with you—after dinner, that is. Is your temple open of nights, Skhâ?"

"Until midnight. But, sir, if I may say so—ah——"

"Speak up, lad!"

"Think you not that we should visit the bathhouse first? I mean no offense, but you know how fussy some women are——"

Bessas, in another unpredictable change of mood, gave

114

a rumble of laughter. "Aye, youngling, I see what you mean. Myself, I take a bath every month whether I need it or not. But this were a special occasion, eh?"

Torchlight flickered about the temple of Ashtarth to the west of the citadel. From the citadel wall came the wailing call of the Announcer of Moons and the flat blare of rams' horns saluting the thin silver sickle which, low in the western sky, marked the coming of a new month.

As Bessas and his followers entered the spacious temenos of Ashtarth, they stared about. Directly before them lay the sacred pool, in which swam fat old carp, some as long as a man's arm, bearing jewels affixed to their fins by golden clips.

A clank drew the travelers' regard to the left. There, at a safe distance from the gate, was tethered the living symbol of the goddess: an aged lion, sway-backed and gray-muzzled, fastened to a stake by a golden chain. He plodded back and forth with the air of a fat old man feebly exercising in the gymnasium.

To the right rose a great wooden pillar, twenty cubits tall and shaped from the trunk of a cedar of Mount Libanos. The pillar was roughly but unmistakably carved into the form of an erect phallus. A crowd of Syrians stood around its base, while on its top stood a priest, who had climbed to his risky perch by means of pegs driven into the sides of the pillar. This priest, making a trumpet of his hands, shouted prayers upwards into the star-spangled sky.

Next to the base of the pillar stood another priest holding an offering bowl. As each offering from the faithful tinkled into the bowl, the priest on the ground shouted up to the priest on the pillar the name of the petitioner and his particular desire. The priest above then shouted his prayer to the gods, who presumably could hear him the better because of his height. As he finished each prayer, he shook a sistrum, for the silvery clang of the in-

115

strument was known to be an effective demon repellent.

Beyond the fishpond, a small temple rose amid the sacred grove. In front of the naos stood an altar and a sacred basin, overshadowed by an ancient oak. From the lower branches of this tree depended hundreds of necklaces, trinkets, and strips of cloth, hung up by the faithful in gratitude for former benefits or in hope of future ones. From somewhere wafted a wailing hymn, sung to the tune of a lyre. Mingled with this sound and the shouts of the priests at the pillar was the bleating of sheep, kept in a fold at the back of the naos to sell to worshipers for burnt offerings.

The travelers stood in line before the basin wherein, when their turns came, their hands were washed by eunuch priests with painted faces. While waiting, Bessas muttered to Myron:

"Let's hope these lassies be not like that witch I knew in Patala, whose wont it was to turn herself into a cobra in the midst of copulation. Albeit the Indians' ways are not ours, I still think this an uncouth habit."

One of the priests, fat and beardless and clanking with jewelry, led them to the western side of the temple. Here cords attached to stakes marked out a path. The path zigzagged past a series of benches on which sat a score of young women in their finery, wearing bright-colored dresses and strings of beads about their heads and necks.

Myron took his time, strolling back and forth past the girls. He found it hard to discern their features in the dim, ruddy light. But this, he told himself, was often just as well. Some of the women smiled invitingly; some lowered demure eyelashes; some looked unhappily apprehensive. At last Myron chose one who gave back a challenging stare. He tossed his threepence into her lap, saying:

"I summon you in the name of the goddess."

The girl put away the coin, rose, and led Myron to a row of huts, built against the wall of the temenos.

116

Half an hour later, Myron and Skhâ awaited their leader at the entrance to the temenos. Skhâ, grinning, asked:

"How did you make out?"

"I managed, though nowadays I find the early morning more propitious for such sport. And you?"

"I had a fine time; she was frightened at first. . . ." Skhâ launched into a verbose account of his experience, detailing every thrust and parry. Then he began to tell of a great-uncle named Mizai, who served as a mercenary in Egypt before the Persian conquest of that land, and whose principal prowess was lectual rather than warlike. He rattled on for half an hour, while Myron became uneasy about Bessas' long absence. To Myron's anxious questioning, Skhâ replied:

"Oh, such a mighty man will wish to prang his lass several times in a row. So there was my great-uncle Mizai, safely hidden in King Aahmes' harem. But the women would not leave him alone for an ush; for, while a hundred wives and concubines may satisfy the vanity of a king, you would search the wide world over ere you found a king who could satisfy a hundred wives and concubines.

"But for six days Mizai did the best he could, which was no more than three ordinary men could have done. And whilst he was pleasuring the women and pacifying those who quarreled over which should have the next turn at him, a woman came running in, crying that King Aahmes had returned early from his campaign and was even now dismounting from his chariot before the palace at Memphis."

"What did they do, smuggle Mizai out in a laundry basket?" said Myron.

"Nay. They thought of that, and many other dodges, but for one reason or another none could be brought to pass. So my great-uncle, thinking valor the better part of discretion, armed himself and ran through the halls and chambers of the palace, shouting: 'Stop the intruder! Catch the skulker! A villain is sneaking into the harem!

117

Seize him to guard the sanctity of our divine king's dwelling!'

"Whilst thus running and shouting, Mizai met the king, who demanded to know the cause of this uproar. Mizai stammered out a story, that he had been walking his post when a eunuch called to him to come because a burglar had been espied in the palace. In the midst of which tale, Mizai swooned dead away and fell to the floor with a crash. The cause of this faint was Mizai's exhaustion from his exertions among the king's women. But the king, thinking it a result of Mizai's strenuous efforts on His Majesty's behalf, promoted him to—— Good gods, look!"

Skhâ stared past Myron with popping eyes. Myron spun and gaped in turn.

Coming at a trot from the women's huts was Bessas, with a girl on his shoulder. Although Bessas was fully clad, the woman was naked. As the Bactrian passed Myron and Skhâ he shouted:

"Come on, you whoresons! This is a rescue!"

"Zeus almighty!" breathed Myron.

Not knowing what else to do, he ran after his leader. So did Skhâ; and so, shortly, did the temple guards and the eunuch priests, the latter squealing: "Stop! Rape! Kidnapping!" The lion uttered a groan.

Others took up the chase until Bessas led a procession three blocks long, some carrying torches and all screaming threats and imprecations against the foreigner. They zigzagged through narrow vaulted alleys where the only light was the ruddy, pulsing beams of the torches borne by the pursuers. They ran through the stinking tannery district, whence came Halpa's famous leather goods.

A thrown stone grazed Myron's hair. He imagined clawlike hands reaching for his back, though he did not dare to turn for fear of tripping. He drew deep, rasping breaths and pounded the pavement in an effort to catch up with Bessas. The Bactrian ran easily, not even breathing hard despite the weight he bore.

118

It was a long chase, for the temple was on the side of town opposite to the khan. Myron would have been utterly lost in the alleys; but Bessas, having once been over the ground, chose the right turns without hesitation.

Six furlongs from the temple of Ashtarth, the blank fortresslike walls of the khan loomed against the stars. Bessas yelled:

"Let us in!"

The night porter opened the gate. Bessas entered, pushing the man roughly aside. He set the girl on her feet. Then, seeing Myron and Skhâ stumble through the entrance, he slammed and bolted the portal. Instantly came the pounding of sticks and fists against the door and cries of, "Open! Let us in! The man is a robber! He must be brought to justice!"

"Open that gate and it's your last act," snarled Bessas to the porter, who hopped from foot to foot in indecision. To Myron, Bessas said: "Get our gear and saddle up. We'll figure how to draw them away from the gate so we can make a dash."

Myron, gasping, said: "What—what in the name of the Dog *is* this?"

The naked girl screamed something in the Halpine dialect. The proprietor of the khan and a couple of his guests hastened out of the tavern. The pounding on the door increased. Myron cried:

"A pestilence on you, Bessas! If you require a woman, you can purchase——"

"This is no slave, but an oppressed free maiden, whom I am rescuing——"

"Harken, pray!" cried the proprietor. "She says she does not wish to go with you. She did but jest in the temple."

"What?" Bessas whirled on the girl. "Is this true? Speak slowly!"

"It is true," said the girl, beginning to sob. Myron noticed that her arms and thighs were tattooed with flowers and doves. "You s-seemed such a great foolish lout

119

that I thought to have a little fun with you by joking about my hard lot and how I should love to escape it. I never imagined that you would take it all to heart. Then, when you bore me out of the temenos, the jolting so knocked the wind out of me that I could not speak. But I cannot leave home and kinsmen to roam the world with wild adventurers! Cover me, somebody, and let me go back to my temple."

Bessas' pocked face fell; his mighty shoulders drooped. The proprietor opened the door a crack, while Bessas braced his back against it to keep the mob outside from rushing in. By dint of much shouting, the proprietor convinced those outside that there had been a misunderstanding. He let in the chief men, a few at a time, to see that all was now well.

The girl, wrapped in a borrowed cloak, stood with tears furrowing the paint on her face. Bessas stood to one side with hanging head, gnawing his mustache with shame and vexation.

When the girl had been led away, the high priest, backed by temple guards and armed men of the night watch, confronted the Bactrian. The priest's purple robe was disordered and his tall tiara of gilded papyrus awry, and he panted still from unaccustomed exercise.

"My good man," said the priest in his high castrate's voice, "we cannot suffer you with impunity to turn our city upside down and disturb the sanctity of our holy temple by such such ruffianly acts. Either you shall compensate the goddess for the outrage done unto her, or I will turn you over to these men, who will hale you before the magistrate."

"May the Drouth Horse trample you! If you think to squeeze money from me by blackmail and extortion——" began Bessas belligerently, but Myron intervened.

"Let me handle this," he said. "Holy Father, will you accompany me to the tavern?"

Later, Myron found Bessas sitting in a corner of the

quadrangle, drinking in sullen solitude. "I got us off for ten shekels," said the Greek. "He wanted an archer, but I chaffered him down."

"That's robbery! I won't——"

"Oh, yes, you will! Consider your mother. That's better."

Next morning was passed in gloomy silence on the road to Hamath. At the noonday halt, Bessas faced the other two with fists on hips. He gruffed:

"I suppose that, having seen me make a fool of myself, you two have no more respect for me. If that be so, you may leave me; I will release you from your oaths. I'll not lead men who think me nought but blown bladder on legs."

Myron smiled. "On the contrary, old boy, we think more highly of you than before; for now we are aware that you, too, have human weaknesses. Nobody is immune to trouble."

Bessas' brown eyes glared sharply from under his bushy brows. "Do you swear that you speak truth?"

"By Zeus and all the gods I swear it. You, Skhâ?"

The Karian swore also.

"Will you then swear not to mention this matter to others?"

"May I be clawed to ribbons by ten thousand privy-haunting demons if I breathe a word of it!" said Myron. Skhâ also swore.

Bessas broke into a big grin, seized the twain in a double bear hug, and kissed them loudly. "That's better," he said. "I begin to feel like a man and a noble Aryan again." He poetized:

Though thieves and lions in my pathway lie,
And whores and merchants seek to wring me dry,
With iron-hearted friends to guard my back,
I'll stride the dusty road until I die!

121

Myron, biting into a slab of cheese, asked: "What happened at the temple? You were not intoxicated, so what led to that astonishing episode?"

" 'Twas as the wench said," said Bessas, munching mightily. "Know that, for all my prowess, I have never been able to take women lightly, as do most warriors. With women of rank I am shy and tongue-tied, and with the baser sort I am easily disgusted. A wisdom-lover I met in India told me to try abstinence, as did the naked ascetics of his fellowship. But I do not find that easy, either, for my lance is strong and easily couched for the charge. Besides—— Oh, Ahriman smite the whole fornicating sex! Except my mother."

"I sometimes think," said Myron, "that your mother has kept you too close to her for your own good."

"May you be kinless! Leave my mother out of this!" said Bessas, with such a menacing expression that Myron hastily apologized. When the Milesian had calmed the giant, Bessas continued:

"Nor do women look upon me with favor; they are sure that I shall hurt them because of my size. And I daresay I often do, being as clumsy in rut as a horse on a housetop." He grinned. "You should have included a course in practical erotics when you taught me as a boy, O Myron.

"Howsomever, being neither eunuch nor boy-lover, I am ofttimes driven nigh unto madness by unsatisfied lust. If I have sometimes used you two rudely without just cause, that is the reason, and I now beg your pardons.

"When I walked the path of choice in the temenos of Ashtarth, I saw many of the lassies quail at the sight of me. Forsooth, I should have walked out then, but one boldly met my glance. So I chose her. She is Ghulamath, daughter of a building contractor of Halpa. And, indeed, we beat out a fine marching tune in the hut."

"Who was on top?" asked Skhâ.

"None of your affair. When it was over, I asked if I

122

might gallop a second course, if she would spare a few ush for my sword to recover its temper. Whilst we waited, Ghulamath told me a dismal tale of the hardships of temple harlotry: how she has to accept all kinds of strangers, often unwashed and stinking, and eager only for their own pleasure.

"Now, I know that among these folk such temple service is accounted pious and honorable, but to me it seems foul and shameful for a decent woman. So when the lass wrought upon my sympathies, I fell madly in love with her. And when I love, the woman can do aught that she pleases with me.

"Hence, when she sighed the wish that some hero would 'take her away from all this,' as she put it, I did but seek to pleasure her by taking her at her word. Now I see what a fool she made of me." The giant wiped away a tear.

Full is the earth of ills, and full no less are the waters,

quoted Myron. "But we'll help that broken heart of yours to heal. Let us be off."

VI   The Tower of the Snail

SOUTH OF THE CITY of Hemesa, where bright sashes were woven, the blue Lake of Qadesh sparkled in the sun. Once this lake had been but a marsh, where the surly Serpentine paused in its headlong rush to the sea. But, in times of immemorial antiquity, the beings who then dwelt in the land had dammed the fractious flume with massive blocks of stone.

South of the Lake of Qadesh, the ancient city of Qadesh stood on the western bank of the Serpentine. The city shimmered in the soft warm air of the Syrian spring.

123

Orchards and vineyards surrounded the town, while the vivid green of young wheat spread across the plain and up into the foothills of the Libanos.

On the fourth of Ayaru, in his shop off the Street of the Woodworkers, Malko bar-Daniel the wainwright was cutting a tenon in the end of a wheel spoke. Beside his bench was piled a heap of freshly shaven spokes and newly sawn felloes. The hub lay in its wheel pit, waiting for Malko and his son Odainath to hammer the spokes into the mortises spaced around its circumference. Malko had just finished his tenon when one of his grandchildren ran into the yard.

"Grandfather, strangers stand at the gate! They come from Uncle Daniel in Babylon."

Malko, a tall stooped man with a long white beard, unfolded his creaking joints and went to the gate. Three men stood there, sun-bronzed and travel-dusted. One enormous man wore a Persian bashlyk, a Median jacket, and baggy leather breeches tucked into high soft boots. A shorter and older man, of medium height and broad-shouldered build, was similarly clad. The third, young, short, and rolypoly, wore a felt cap pulled over his ears, a tunic down to his bare knees, and stout shoes with the toes curled up.

"Peace," said Malko, touching his heart, lips, and forehead.

"Peace," replied the others, almost in one voice. But their gestures differed according to their origins. The giant thrust out a huge hand to shake. The medium-sized man held up his right hand and flipped it back and forth, with the palm turned inwards towards himself. The short youth crossed his hands on his breast and bowed.

Myron of Miletos introduced himself and his companions and told of their meeting with Daniel bar-Malko in Babylon. Malko said:

"In the name of the blessed gods, my masters, you must stay in my house whilst you stop in Qadesh. Use my humble hut as your own."

124

"Thank you, sir," said Myron, "but your servants were really looking for your other son."

"Mean you my son Odainath? He is in the smithy; I will call——"

"No; I mean your son Kothar, the traveler——"

"El forgive us! Kothar is no longer my son."

"Oh. We are sorry to hear of troubles within your house; but we must find Kothar."

"I do not speak of the doings of apostates and blasphemers, Ramman smite them!"

Malko and his visitors stood silently staring until Malko said: "But come in anyway. By the tongues of Reshap, your mention of this unpleasant matter has made me forget my duty of hospitality."

"But——" began Bessas. Myron jabbed him in the back with his thumb and, with effusive thanks to Malko, led his companions into the court.

An hour later, washed and combed, the travelers, over a skin of the local wine, told Malko of their journey.

"By Hadad and Ashtarth!" exclaimed the wainwright. "You must have set forth on a lucky day, to have escaped so many perils unscathed."

"We anticipate worse," said Myron. "We're on our way to Kush."

"Where is that?"

"Kush lies beyond Egypt to the south. They say it harbors little men less than a cubit tall, called Pygmies, as well as other wonders."

"By the blessed gods, that is indeed a rash project! Beware of deadly foreign demons and the grim gods of strangers."

"Being on the king's business, we must take our chances," said Myron. "So you see, Master Malko, as none of us has been to Egypt, we need a guide who speaks the language and knows his way about that land." As the old man frowned, Myron hurried on: "I'm sure that any member of your family, whatever his shortcomings, would

125

be more trustworthy than the sort of guide we should pick up in the wineshops."

Perhaps the wine had mellowed Malko bar-Daniel. After he had sat in silence for a while, he said: "Well, the last I heard of Kothar he was living in Marath."

"Where is that?"

"On the coast between Arvad and Athar, about a day's journey hence. You must go back to Hemesa and take the road to the coast, which crosses the pass between the mountain ranges and follows the River of Freedom to the sea. Instead of turning south for Palestine and Egypt, you will turn north for about four leagues along the coastal road."

"Do you mean we turn right instead of left?"

"Aye. Thus you will reach Marath. If you poke about among the tombs of the necropolis, you will no doubt find my former son Kothar."

"Is he then deceased?" asked Myron.

"Dead to his family and to the true religion of his forefathers, but not dead in the common sense. Natheless, he dwells in a tomb."

"A curious choice of residence! Is he trying to save rent?"

Malko chuckled. "He says he absorbs magical influences from this ancient monument, which, he avers, goes back before the Flood. And this aura of ancient necromancy, quotha, makes easy the working of his sorceries."

"What is this tomb called?"

"The Tower of the Snail."

Bessas grunted. "A sinister-sounding name. I care not much for sorcery myself. I had my fill of it from that knave in Kabura who enchanted fleas up to the size of dogs and set them on those he disliked."

"Well," said Malko, "say not that I failed to forewarn you. I pray to the holy gods that my information lead you not into destruction."

126

"He who would journey to the rim of the world must expose himself to the shafts of fortune," said Bessas.

During dinner, Myron and Bessas told their host of the quest for the dragon.

"By the tusk that slew Tammuz!" said Malko. "That is a task for a demigod. I regret that we cannot help you out here; but the only Syrian dragon is that which sleeps under Mount Libanos."

"What dragon is this?" said Myron.

"Our legends state that, back in the days of the Flood or thereabouts, a colossal winged serpent with golden scales despoiled the land until Hadad smote it with a thunderbolt. To escape the god, the dragon dove slant-wise into the earth, with such force that it dug the bed of the Serpentine River and finally plunged out of sight altogether. And there it still is. When the earth shakes, we know that the dragon has awakened and is stretching its coils. But I do not advise annoying it."

"I fear that this is not of the same species as the one we seek," said Myron, smiling. "Besides, it sounds too large for even such accomplished dragon hunters as ourselves to subdue."

The sun was sinking in blood and fire into the Syrian Sea when the travelers rode up the coastal road to the city of Marath. South of the town the land, barren and salty, rolled gently away to the sea on the left. On the right it sloped up to the distant ramparts of the Bargylos, on whose shoulders many outcrops of gray limestone, painted pink by the sunset, thrust through the dark-green scrub. Four furlongs to the north rose the massive cyclopean wall of Marath. On the northwestern horizon, the island city of Arvad rode on the purple sea, a jagged sable silhouette against the scarlet sky.

Bessas was lecturing on the iniquity of the knobby bronze bits used by the Immortals. "Certes, you can stop any horse from bolting with that fiendish thing," he fulminated, "but that should never happen to a rider who knows his business and keeps his wits. And a fortnight of such a bit will ruin any horse's mouth for delicate handling. By the beams of Tishtrya, any knave who'd use such a tool of torture on a decent horse should be dipped in dung and hung up by the toes to dry! Now the proper way to——" He broke off to twist in his saddle and peer back. "There's a company on camels behind us."

Myron and Skhâ looked back. Myron said: "I wish I had your eyes. I see some moving specks like insects, but I cannot discern what manner of creatures they are."

Bessas shuddered. "I have an ominous feeling, as if my *fravashi* were trying to warn me."

"Oh, you have been listening too long to Malko's tales of antediluvian magic. Probably this Kothar is merely a man who has learnt to think for himself, so naturally he is regarded as a sorcerer."

" 'Tis those who follow that most concern me. Camels are seldom used along the Canaanitish coast."

"Traders, perhaps?"

"We shall see."

They rode past several tombs, some near to the road and some farther away. No sign of human life did they see around these structures. They caught up with a flock of sheep being driven towards Marath. The shepherd's great fierce dog barked and snarled at them and made their horses shy until the kilted shepherd collared it. Myron asked:

"Do you know of a man named Kothar, who lives in a tomb called the Tower of the Snail?"

"Kothar?" said the shepherd.

"Yes."

The shepherd said something in Canaanitish and pointed northwest. Bessas led the way off the road in the direction indicated. The shepherd scowled after them and urged his flock to greater speed.

The ground was covered with tall yellow-flowered thistles, among which a host of lizards scuttled and rustled. In front of the travelers, standing in a patch of marshy ground, the Tower of the Snail rose stark and black against the sunset.

This edifice was a cube over twenty cubits on a side, built of enormous blocks of rough stone. An opening on the south side and another on the east gave access to the burial chamber. On top, above the cornice, rose the ruins of a pyramidal stone structure, like a small black ziggurat. Some of the blocks from this pile had fallen into the reeds below.

Looking at the tomb, Myron felt a horripilation of awe and fear. The style of the monument was unlike anything that he had seen in his travels. It was as if some intelligent but non-human race, dwelling in this land before the coming of the Canaanites, had built this tower and then vanished utterly, leaving no fragment of their history or legendry behind.

"I must pause to repair my harness," said Skhâ in a terrified squeak. "Go on, gentles; I shall overtake you."

"You'll stay with us if you know what is good for you," said Bessas sharply.

Clutching his amulets, Skhâ obeyed. As the travelers neared the Tower of the Snail, their horses' hooves made wet sounds in the marshy soil. The beasts themselves acted skittish and uneasy. Bessas pulled up in front of the south entrance to the tomb and bellowed:

"Ho there, Kothar bar-Malko!"

The shout died away. Silence reigned, save for the rustle of lizards, the chirp of crickets, the hum of mosquitoes, and the eager munching of the horses and mules on the herbage. The red sun, wreathed in streamers of scarlet and purple, touched the steel edge of the horizon. Bessas repeated his outcry.

"Who calls?" came a voice from the tomb.

Myron felt a stir in the roots of his hair, so much was it like having a ghost answer out of a grave. Rational and skeptical though he was about things supernatural, he would have been happy to be elsewhere at that moment. Beside him, Skhâ jerked his horse around in a moment of panic, but at a bark from Bessas quickly recovered and reined back.

"Come out and see," said Bessas.

A man seated himself cross-legged in the entrance to the tomb. Between the failing light and the man's posture, Myron found it hard to tell much about him. But he got an impression of a lean, pale face. The man wore a long robe and a tall spiral Syrian hat, both of dark blue.

"Hail, mortals!" said Kothar bar-Malko.

"Mortal yourself," responded Bessas. "Why did you not answer the first time?"

"Because I was not here. My body was, but my spirit was far away. And who are you?"

Bessas gave his name and told of the expedition. "Now," he said, "do you want a job as a guide?"

Kothar sat silently for an instant. Then he said: "I must consult certain intelligences known to me ere deciding. Meanwhile, tell me more of your plans. You may come up here to rest yourselves." He lowered a light wooden ladder, which reached from the tomb entrance to the ground. "Have a care, Lord Bessas, as my ladder was not built for one of your poundage."

"Hold the beasts, Skhâ," said Bessas, sliding off his horse.

"Watch your heads," said Kothar as Bessas and Myron came up the ladder.

Myron began exploring like a hound on the scent. Behind him, he heard Bessas order Skhâ to hand up some of their weapons.

In the center of the tower, the passage opened out into the sepulchral chamber. Another low passage led from this chamber to the entrance on the east side of the tower. Carved into the sides of the burial chamber were two tiers of niches for bodies, but all traces of the original occupants had disappeared. Instead, Kothar's gear, including a pile of old manuscripts, was stowed in these niches. Another grave yawned in the center of the floor.

A stairway, running around two of the four walls, led

up to the ruined pyramid on the roof. Darkening blue sky showed through the gaps in the masonry.

When Myron had seen all there was to see of the inside of the tower, he returned to the south entrance, where Kothar and Bessas sat facing each other.

Kothar did not look at all like his brother Daniel. He was a tall man, lean and round-shouldered, with a sallow skin and a long pointed, projecting, and slightly hooked nose. This nose, together with the way he thrust his head forward, gave him the look of a bird of prey. His face was shaven save for a small tuft of a beard on the point of his chin. His large, dark, deepset eyes gazed upon Bessas with a luminous, unwinking stare. He spoke in a low, strangely vibrant voice:

". . . if you think half a shekel a day exorbitant, good Captain Bessas, that is your privilege. But I am not desperate for work. In fact, you come when I am in the midst of my great operation, which I shall have to set aside to guide you."

"What's your great operation?" growled Bessas.

"It is an experiment in the spiritual sciences. I fear you would find an explanation tedious."

"Science or no, I can get plenty of competent guides for threepence a day. So if that is your final word——"

"*Ay!*" came a sudden shout from Skhâ. "We are beset!"

There came a yammer of voices, sounds of animal footfalls, the squeals and gurgles of camels, and the whizz of an arrow. The missile passed between Bessas and Kothar, missed Myron by a digit, and clattered against the walls of the burial chamber.

With a thunderous curse, Bessas leaped up and struck his head on the low roof of the passage. He fell back against the side wall, blinking and gasping. Myron pulled him back to get a clear view of the entrance. Kothar sat with his mouth open.

Myron had a glimpse of Skhâ on his pony, leading the other two horses and two mules away from the tower at a

131

gallop towards Marath. Then they passed out of sight around the corner of the tomb.

Thirty paces away and swiftly approaching were a score of Arabs on dromedaries. Some were stripped down to loin-cloths; others wore voluminous wrap-around skirts, leaving their upper bodies bare. In their midst rode an older man in a robe and head shawl. This man directed the attack, pointing with his crop. Most of the Arabs were archers, though some bore lances or javelins. More arrows struck the stone-work.

Myron hesitated. He had his sword. Two spears lay on the floor of the entrance, and Bessas' bow case lay beside the fallen giant. Bessas sprawled against the wall, still half stunned. Which weapon should Myron use? The Arabs came closer and the arrows flew more thickly; one whistled past Myron's ear.

The ladder! Standing in front of the south entrance to the Tower of the Snail, it was open invitation to the attackers to swarm up. Swiftly Myron reached down and began to haul the ladder up.

"Help me, Kothar!" he cried.

But Kothar did not seem to understand. He gazed vaguely at the scene as if he had gone into another trance. He got in the way, so that when Myron tried to thrust the ladder back into the passage, the upper end struck Kothar.

"To the afterworld with you, god-detested fool!" shouted Myron. "Either help me with this thing or get out of the way!"

When Kothar finally responded, he proved so clumsy and weak in the arms that he was no help. However, they finally got the ladder pulled back into the tower.

Then Myron scrambled for Bessas' bow case. He got the bow out and an arrow nocked just as the Arabs swarmed up to the entrance. On their camels they could look right in. One loosed an arrow at point-blank range; Myron heard a yelp from Kothar as the shot found a mark.

132

Trying to remember all that Bessas had taught him about archery, Myron drew and loosed. He winced as the bowstring lashed his unprotected left wrist, but was pleased to hear a scream from the attackers. *"Eleleleu!"* he shouted, reaching for another arrow.

"Give me the bow, little man," said a familiar growl behind him. "Take a spear and guard the other entrance."

Myron handed the bow to Bessas and brushed past Kothar, who clutched at an arrow wound in his left arm. Myron went around to the other entrance. He arrived as a long-haired Arab, holding a spear, began to climb from the back of his dromedary into the portal.

Myron rushed at the Arab, gripping his spear in both hands. The man saw him coming. Unable, in his awkward position, to defend himself, he threw himself backwards and fell to the ground before Myron reached him.

Outside, more Arabs whirled about on their mounts. All shouted orders and advice at once. Arrows struck the stone-work and whizzed into the entrance; Myron flattened himself against the wall to avoid them. It occurred to him that the archers were loosing blind. In the twilight the entrances would look to those outside like featureless pits of blackness, in which they could not make out the defenders of the tower.

"Out of the way," said Bessas' voice behind him.

Myron squeezed past the giant into the burial chamber. The foe seemed to have been cleared away from around the south entrance, and Myron heard the snap of the powerful Parthian bow and Arab yells from the east entrance.

"Kothar!" he said. "Pick up the other spear and help us!"

"I am wounded," said the Syrian, trying to tie a bandage with his teeth.

"What of it? You still have a sound right arm."

While Kothar continued to struggle with his bandage, Bessas joined them in the burial chamber.

"They have all gone around to the northwest side, where we cannot see them," said the Bactrian. "Now, Myron, if you were the leader of this attack, what would you tell your Arabs to do next?"

Myron glanced upwards. "Those beasts are so tall, I think a couple of Arabs on camels could boost a third one up to the roof."

"And come down through those holes. Kothar, take a spear—for Mithra's sake, will you spend all night fixing that bandage? Here!" Bessas quickly completed the bandaging. "Now take that spear and go up the stairs——"

"I—I have no skill in such matters."

"Then learn, dolt——"

A scrambling noise caused Myron to look up again. Movement showed against the darkening sky.

Myron dashed up the steep stair. As an Arab lowered himself through the gaping roof to the topmost stair, Myron thrust him through the body. The man screamed, clutched the shaft of the spear, and fell off the stairs into the burial chamber below, tearing the spear out of Myron's grasp.

"Look out!" roared Bessas from below.

Myron looked around. Not ten feet away, another Arab, peering down through the same gap, was drawing an arrow to the head. The man was out of Myron's reach, and Myron had no missile weapon. He fumbled for his sword with some idea of throwing it. The arrow was aimed directly at Myron's midriff, and on the narrow stair he had no way to dodge or duck for cover.

A bowstring twanged; an arrow struck home with a meaty sound. The Arab's body jerked and his arrow flew wide. The man groaned and slid out of sight.

"Come down now, Myron," said Bessas.

When Myron returned to the floor of the burial chamber, he found Bessas pulling the spear out of the body of the Arab whom Myron had skewered.

"Good man!" said Bessas. "Yours is the only sure kill

134

yet. I take back anything I may have said against the fighting ability of Hellenes."

"How about those struck by arrows?"

"I made a couple of hits, besides that knave on the roof, but it's too dark to tell if they were kills. Next time I say 'look out,' try to get out of the way of my shot. I must have missed your ear by the breadth of a hair." He grinned. "You should have seen the corpse land on top of Master Kothar here! I used to think you were absent-minded, but compared to him you're as keen as the boar-tusked Verethraghna himself. Now, O thinker, tell me what our foes will try next."

Myron frowned. "They have assaulted each of the three entrances to the tower in turn and been repulsed. If I were their chief, I should divide them into three groups, with orders to attack the three entrances simultaneously. If they can inflict a few more wounds and get inside the tower, they will quickly finish us off."

"Just so. Kothar, push this body to one of the entrances and lay it crosswise as a barricade. It will give us a little cover. If we get out of this alive, by Ahriman's iron yard, I'll see that every man jack of us has a bow and knows how to use it! Now, from this pit I can cover all three entrances, so I shall stay here save when I must help one of you. Take your spears and stand ready to rush to the roof or the lower entrances as I command you."

"But——" began Kothar.

"Shut up! If you be on our side, you shall do as I say. If not, your body will make another useful barricade."

Yelping cries told that the Arabs were renewing the assault. Bessas jumped down into the grave in the center of the burial chamber. There he stood, calmly wheeling from side to side, loosing arrows where targets showed, and bellowing:

"Myron, take the roof, quickly! Kothar, take the east entrance! Myron, come back down and take the south entrance! Kothar, lie down to give me a shot! Kothar, come back and take the roof! Hurry! Get that knave on the stair! Go on, *stick* him! *Kill* him!" bawled the Bactrian, as Kothar made timid, ineffectual jabs at his opponent until Bessas nailed the man with an arrow.

The giant was in his element, running his little battle with the smooth competence of a skilled lapidary cutting a gem. Myron, panting, dashed up and down the stair and in and out the passages, pausing to exchange spear thrusts with the swarming foe.

On one dash, Myron's right leg buckled under him, spilling him to the floor. He sat up, staring stupidly in the deepening gloom. His fingers found the shaft of an arrow that had pierced his leg.

"I'm hit!" he called.

"Plague!" exclaimed Bessas. "Crawl down the east passage and lie behind the dead Arab. If anybody tries to climb over the body, stick him."

Dizzily, Myron obeyed. He had no more than lain down behind the corpse when a hand from outside seized the point of his spear and tried to wrest it away from him.

"*Ea!*" he shouted. "Bessas!" The Arab was strong, and Myron felt the spear sliding out of his sweaty hands.

No help came. Myron strained to pull his spear loose. He could hear the Arab who had hold of the other end talking to a comrade. Then the point of another spear, just visible, came thrusting over the corpse, feeling in the dark for Myron's body.

Myron gave himself up for lost. He could let go the spear and get out his sword. But that weapon was too short to be useful in this extremity, especially as he did not have his shield.

Then a chorus of yells resounded from outside. The Arab released Myron's spear, and the other spear disappeared. Myron raised himself on his elbows to see.

The Arabs were streaming away from the Tower of the Snail. Down the road from Marath ran a crowd of people with torches and spears. At their head rode Skhâ of Barbalissos.

136

The Arabs fled away into the night. Myron, Bessas, and Kothar slid out of the Tower of the Snail into the arms of the kilted townsfolk, whom Skhâ had roused.

"Good lad! I thought you'd bolted," said Bessas to Skhâ. "It is well you got back when you did. Who is the physician of Marath? We are all wounded."

"You, too?" said Myron.

"Just a graze in the ribs." Bessas took his hand away from his side, showing a large dark spot on his jacket. "And a lump on my head the size of a simurgh's egg. How many did we get?"

Besides the two corpses inside the edifice, two Arabs lay dead near the tower. A wounded Arab huddled near the road. Myron would have questioned him, but before he could hobble to the spot the townsfolk had killed the wounded man. There was also a camel dying of an arrow wound. Bessas said:

"Master magician, can you tell who these men were, or why they sought our lives?"

Kothar stepped from one corpse to the other, studying the dead men and the camel, which the Marathites were preparing to cut up for meat. At last he said:

"These are men of one of the nomadic tribes of the Syrian desert. As to which tribe, or the cause of their attack, I shall have to consult the higher powers."

"Consult away."

"Do you still wish me to guide you?"

"Perhaps—for fourpence a day, no more. If you guide as you fight, by the fangs of Azi Dahaka, we are likely to find ourselves in Scythia when we aimed for Kush!"

A disturbance attracted Myron's attention. An Arab had halted a dromedary at the edge of the ruddy torchlight. Like the leader of the attack, he wore a long robe and, on his head, a square of cloth folded diagonally and held in place by a headband of rope. Although he held up a hand in greeting, some of the Marathites began to shout threats and insults and to throw stones.

"Stop!" cried Myron. "He wishes to speak."

The hostility of the Phoenicians only became louder, until Bessas shouldered his way to the front and cuffed a couple of the more violent townsfolk.

"Shut up!" he thundered. "What do you want, Arab?"

"I have a letter for Kothar bar-Malko."

"Who are you?"

"Adi ibn-Thabit, of the Banu Hassan."

"Are you one of those who just now attacked us?"

"Attack? The gods forbid! I am but a peaceful messenger."

"Know you aught of this attack?"

"I know only that I passed, on the road, a troop of the Banu Tarafa, having wounded men among them."

"They are not the same as your tribe?"

The Arab spat. "Those desert vermin? Nay! The Banu Hassan are civilized folk, who dwell in Thadamora and protect the caravans passing through. These others are but sand thieves."

"How did you know who they were?"

"By their garments, their harness, and their speech."

"Did you speak with them?"

"Not I! They would have known me for a Hassani and slain me, as their Shaykh Waliq is at feud with our Shaykh Alman."

Kothar came forward, took his letter, and handed a small piece of silver to the Arab, who faded into the darkness. Kothar unrolled the letter in the light of a townsman's torch. He frowned over the spidery writing, then rolled the missive up and slipped it into his girdle. He looked at Myron and Bessas with a thoughtful expression.

"As soon as our wounds be healed, I shall be ready to guide you, at the last fee you named," he said.

As it fell out, Myron and Kothar became feverish from their wounds. Although Myron recovered quickly, the Syrian languished for several days. While waiting for Kothar to mend, Myron, who could not see any young person without an urge to teach him something, drilled

138

his landlord's small son in the multiplication table. He also inquired about the origin of the Tower of the Snail, but of this the Marathites professed an ignorance as deep as his own.

At last, on the ninth of Ayaru, the company, now increased to four, set out for Athar. A day's ride brought them to this triple city, where the settlements of the Arvadites, the Sidonians, and the Tyrians formed separate walled inclosures within the outer wall.

The travelers put up at an inn in the Arvadite quarter. Bessas, Myron, and Skhâ sat down after their dinner to enjoy a *qa** of wine apiece, while Kothar who did not drink, engaged in low-voiced converse with the proprietor. Presently these two came to where the others sat.

"Gentlemen," said Kothar, "my familiar spirits have guided me to news that should interest you. Speak, good Master Ithobaal."

The innkeeper said: "A man was here two days ago, asking after Captain Bessas and Master Myron."

The two travelers named sat up so suddenly that Myron spilt his wine. Both burst into questions.

"Nay, nay," said Ithobaal. "The rogue did not give his name, and he was such an ordinary-looking little fellow that your servant would find it hard to describe him. A Persian, I should say from the cut of his trousers and the accent of his speech. He would not say what he wanted, and when I wist nought of those whom he sought he rode away."

Bessas asked: "On an ass?"

"Nay, on a fine riding camel."

Myron said: "When he found he couldn't keep pace with us, he must have changed his mount and cut across the desert by way of Thadamora."

"He must have ridden as if the Corpse Fiend were after him," said Bessas, "to get here so soon."

"True," said Myron. "He no doubt traced us as far as

* 1 *qa* = 1½ pints.

Qadesh. Knowing our destination, but not knowing about our side journey to find Master Kothar, he inferred that we should turn south upon reaching the coast. Have you any idea whither he went, O Ithobaal?"

"Ere he departed, he said something about asking in Damascus."

"That," said Myron, "means that he is making a cast inland. If we remain on the coastal road, we shall keep clear of him."

"Unless," said Bessas thoughtfully, "he threw out that remark to deceive inquirers, like us." He smote the table. "By the four teats of Ishtar, but for those damned arrow pricks, we had been ahead of him yet! Hereafter we shall all wear our jacks whilst on the road, no matter how they irk us!"

Myron thought of replying that, as he and Kothar had been wounded in the limbs, their leathern cuirasses would not have saved them. But he knew Bessas too well to start an argument. Instead he said:

"I thought things had quieted down for the nonce, but it seems not. What with temples full of harlots, tombs full of antediluvian magic, and Persian spies, at least we are not finding our journey dull!"

VII   The Valley of Thieves

THE FERTILE PLAINS of Samaria gave way to the mountains of Judaea. The road—a mere track, unsuited to wheeled traffic—wound among long, sweeping slopes patchily covered with coarse, prickly scrub. Great flocks of northbound birds, from swifts to storks and steppe eagles, flew overhead. As the sun sank over the dusty gray-green hills of Ephraim, Myron said:

"O Bessas, we shall never reach Jerusalem tonight."

Bessas grunted. "I knew not that the roads of Judaea

140

wound and writhed like serpents in pain. Kothar, how much farther to Jerusalem? . . . *Kothar!*"

The Syrian awoke with a start. "Your pardon, mortal; I was communing with a distant colleague. What said you?"

"How far to Jerusalem?"

"Perhaps six or seven leagues."

The road had risen from a wide valley along a winding ridge. Now it dipped again, this time into a narrow, steep-sided valley whose slopes were thick with dusty-looking olive trees. A large yellow fox with black-rimmed ears barked at the travelers and ran for cover, dodging from one thorny apple-of-Sodom bush to another. Myron said:

"In an hour it will too dim to find our way. The moon is dark and the roads are rough."

"We'll camp here, then," said Bessas. "Our friends have been sleeping in beds long enough. It is time that we learnt if they be boys or men, for there will be a plenty of camping in Kush."

"I have camped in the desert near Barbalissos," said Skhâ. "What would you that I did?"

"You shall unharness the beasts, whilst Kothar gets a fire going and Myron and I assemble the tent. That knave who sold it to us in Babylon said it was so simple a child could put it up, but it looks as complicated as the Great King's pavilion."

Bessas unloaded the mass of poles, ropes, and tightly woven camel's hair canvas from the mule that bore it, while Kothar struggled with flint and steel and tinder. Skhâ, removing horses' bits and pack saddles, chattered on:

"Once my great-uncle Mizai, fighting for the last King Psamatik of Egypt, camped in the Desert of Shos whilst scouting the Persian bourn at the start of the war with Cambyses. The scouts were Arabs on camels, but the Karian battalion were sent to keep an eye on the Arabs lest

141

they change sides or fade away into the desert without the king's knowledge.

"Around the campfire, the Arabs told tales of their national spirits and demons. So Mizai was not much astonished when, during his watch, he found before him a woman of strange and unearthly beauty. She was tall and slender, with long black hair and skin that shone white in the moonlight. The desert breeze fluttered a gown as sheer as cobwebs.

" 'Good evening, madam,' said Mizai.

" 'Hail, mortal,' said she. 'Know that I am Lailat, the spirit of the waste.'

" 'Forsooth?' said my great-uncle. 'Know that I am Mizai son of Avetho, a Karian. What would you?'

" 'I seek a new lover,' said she. 'For days I have watched this encampment in my other form, and you are the man I have chosen.'

" 'Well now,' said Mizai, 'that is most kind of you. Was that big owlish bird, which has been flapping about, you?'

" 'Aye. Now you shall come with me to the ruins of Balad al-Jann. There we shall revel amongst the tombs, served by my horde of lesser demons——'

" 'Excuse me, madam,' said Mizai, for he had heard many tales of men who went off into the sea to live with mermaids, or into the woods to live with nymphs, and somehow these tales always ended badly. 'What befell your last lover?'

" 'Oh, that is no matter. His powers began to fail, so I turned him into a scorpion. But think not to escape me! Your comrades are sunk in enchanted slumber; they will not aid——'

" 'That was not what I had in mind, my lady,' said Mizai. 'I did but think it behooved us to make trial of each other or ever we set up housekeeping in your City of Spirits. I could not bear to have you disappointed after you had gone to so much trouble; and, moreover, I doubt I should make a good scorpion.'

"Lailat agreed to Mizai's proposal. Now, my great-

142

uncle may not have been wise, strong, or brave beyond the wont of most men, but in one regard he surpassed all mortals. And so it happened that presently Lailat sighed and said: 'My dear Mizai, you are perfect. I foresee a long and happy companionship——'

" 'Oh, but the trial has only begun,' quoth Mizai. 'Wait but an ush or two and you shall see.'

"So more time passed, and Lailat said: 'O Mizai, you are a lover beyond my wildest hopes. Let us forth——'

"But my great-uncle only replied as before: 'The test is by no means completed. Bide a few ush in patience.' And when more time had passed, Lailat said: 'Truly, now we must go; for even in love there can be too much of a good thing.'

"But my great-uncle only answered as before. And when she became insistent, so did he. The dispute waxed warm, and of a sudden Mizai felt his face buffeted by mighty wings and his shoulder gashed by a sharp talon; for he held in his arms a great gray eagle-owl, which struggled to escape. He tossed the bird into the air, watched it flap away over the moonlit waste, and returned to the camp, laughing like one bereft of his senses."

Bessas' laugh rumbled. "A capital tale, boy; but now help to gather sticks for the fire."

Myron and Bessas solved the problem of the tent, but Bessas tugged too hard on the ropes on his side and pulled out the pegs on Myron's side. The structure collapsed. Skhâ snickered.

"You don't know your own strength, Bessas," said Myron mildly.

"Better to have it fall down now than later, when we're sleeping in it," said Bessas.

At last the tent was up. As he staked out the horses and mules in patches of grass, Myron reviewed in his mind the travels of recent days.

From Athar the four had ridden down the Phoenician coast, past the great precipitous promontory called Penuel, the Face of God; past Gubla with its warehouses full of papyrus from Egypt, awaiting transshipment to all parts of the Inner Sea; past Dog River with its guardian stone wolf and its inscriptions of ancient invading kings. They had seen the flowers and grottoes of Beroth under the towering snowcapped mass of Mount Libanos.

At Beroth they witnessed a sacrifice to the local Baal. The purple veil of the temple was drawn aside, revealing a huge squat bronzen statue of the god, horned and winged and gleaming with unguents. A fire crackled in Baal's potbelly.

Six matrons of the city's leading families stepped proudly forward to hand their first-born sons—children less than a year old, swaddled and bound—to shaven, skull-capped priests in gauzy purple robes. The priests paraded up the steps to the platform beside the god's outstretched hands and placed the children on these hands of hot metal. The screaming victims flopped like fish, rolled down the slope of the divine forearms, and fell through the gap between the god's elbows into the fire below. The twang of the harp, the clang of the sistrum, and the swelling sound of the hymn half drowned their shrieks; the stench of burning flesh mingled with the heavy odors of perfume and incense. Priests and priestesses, with their skirts hiked up to their waists and their eyelids painted green, pranced in the measures of a sacred dance.

When Myron and Bessas expressed their horror, Kothar snapped: "Hold your tongues, mortals, if you would not be torn to pieces! These folk take their religion to heart and will suffer no gibes from unclean outlanders."

After Beroth, they had passed through Sidon with its crowded, bustling harbor behind a meager breakwater, where fishermen's nets, dying in the sun, stretched from house to house like gigantic cobwebs. They paused at Old Tyre with its stinking dye works, filling the narrow streets with their reek, while New Tyre frowned across the water at them from its fortified island.

144

Myron had fraternized in the taverns with many Phoenician men of business. These were portly, full-bearded, hook-nosed men in robes and conical caps. Golden rings gleamed on their fingers and in their ears, and the dwarfish images of the Pataecian gods, in gold and crystal, hung round their necks.

The Punic merchants were men of a breed quite different from an adventurous pedant like Myron, or a bluff and brutal warrior like Bessas, or a mystical seer like Kothar. Despite a certain somber austerity of manner, they were often affable and sometimes even kindly, but in an abstracted way, because all the time they were really thinking of trade and profits. . . .

"Should you learn the shape of the earth, Master Myron, how would that affect our trade routes in the Western Ocean? Could our ships range on forever without fear of falling over the edge?"

"Aye, Master Myron, your servant has heard of your Greek *Iliad*. Can you purpose a plan whereby we could have it copied and sold at a profit?"

"The land of Kush? We know little of it here. But I will make it worth your while, friend Myron, to submit a confidential report on the openings in that land for imports and exports. . . ."

Yet these Phoenicians were no weaklings. They would fight like fiends in defense of their cities and their trade routes. They would defy stormy seas, man-eating savages, and strange gods in their eagerness to open up new lands to trade. But they looked upon Bessas' Aryan notions of honor as childish. Insult or rail at one and, instead of losing his temper in turn, he would merely say, well, do you wish to make a deal or do you not?

At length Myron wearied of their implacable commercialism. He was glad to reach Akko, the southernmost large Phoenician city.

In Akko the commander of the Persian garrison, to whom they applied for fodder, had warned them of a plague at Yapho, farther down the coast. They therefore

145

turned inland, leaving behind them the white beaches around the mouth of the Belos, where men shoveled the gleaming sand into sacks to sell to the glassmakers. In Shechem, a Samaritan with his face tattooed blue had told them of a valley of ill fame. . . .

"Bessas!" exclaimed Myron. "This must be that Valley of Thieves whereof the man in Shechem warned us. He said that we should traverse it just before we reached Eshkol, and that it has an evil repute."

"*Vaush!* 'Twill prove the boys' mettle as well as their camping skill. We'll keep a double watch; the tent is small for three anyway."

"You mean, it's small for four. You occupy the room of two."

"I should say, it were small for two: one normal man like me and two half-sized Pygmies like you." Bessas continued:

> *When lions roar upon a moonless night,*
> *And ghastly specters mortals do affright,*
> *'Tis then our metal shows its temper true,*
> *And quaking cravens scuttle into flight!*

"There is yet enough light for a few flights of arrows; so hang up the butt, Skhâ—on that tree yonder, so that shafts that miss shall strike the hillside and easily be found again."

Myron and Skhâ groaned, but Bessas was inexorable. "Worms breed in soft flesh. Besides, this is my revenge for your making me learn to swim in that accursed cold Serpentine."

"You have already had your revenge, old boy," said Myron, "by nearly drowning me when you caught me round the neck. I thought the grandfather of all octopodes had me in its tentacles."

"You, too, Kothar," said Bessas. "I care not if you be the greatest wizard unburnt. It is well to have a sharp shaft to fall back on, in case your spells get wet."

"Not him!" said Skhâ. "If he shoots one arrow, I shall wrap myself in horse cloths and hide in the tent. Else there were no safety in any direction. . . ."

In the narrow valley the sun had already set, and darkness soon ended the archery. The travelers took down the straw-stuffed bag that had served that as a target and gathered up stray arrows from the earth of the slope beyond.

As they ate their Spartan supper of bread, cheese, dried beef, onions, and cheap local wine, the scrub and the olive groves wakened to nocturnal life. Insects chirped and buzzed; bats whirred; jackals yelped; serpents hissed; lizards rustled; and a large white owl uttered curious panting sounds from a nearby tree. The howl of a wolf came faintly from the heights of Mount Ephraim, to be answered by the eerie laugh of a hyena. Myron wished for the hundredth time that he could tarry long enough to investigate every natural phenomenon and write notes about it, to be used some day in a great all-embracing explanation of the universe.

"Kothar," said Bessas with his mouth full, "that blue-faced lad in Shechem said that this valley is notorious as a haunt of robbers, whence the name. What says your magic about our chances of getting through unscathed?"

"My familiars report no perils imminent, though many distant," said the Syrian. "It is as if we were sheep in a fold, and wolves did sniff about the walls of the fold but had not yet found entrance. For a deeper study I should need more time and gear, or else the True Anthrax."

"What is that?"

"A fabled red gem, of the ruby kind, which darkens whenever danger threatens its owner."

"Hmm. I see how such a bauble might be useful, though one could hardly take time in the midst of a battle to haul out the gem to see."

Myron said: "One might have it mounted in an armlet, so that one could snatch a quick look from time to time."

"And whilst the warrior gazes into the mystic depths of

this marvelous gem—whisht!—off goes his head." Bessas laughed like distant thunder. "What are the other properties of gems?"

Kothar told of the diamond, which confers fortitude and makes the wearer proof against spells and spirits; of the sapphire, which strengthens the sight; of the emerald, which gives foreknowledge of the future; of the topaz, which conveys calm courage; of the green jasper, which strengthens the bowels; of the amethyst, which averts drunkenness. . . .

Kothar stopped, raising his head to listen. "A mortal draws nigh," he said.

A scrambling noise was followed by sounds of running and heavy breathing. A man burst out of a patch of scrub. While the others sat and stared, Bessas stuffed the rest of his loaf in his mouth, rose, and drew his sword, all in one smooth blur of motion.

The newcomer was young, wearing a knee-length black tunic and a round felt cap of the Phoenician type. His clothes were torn and stained. He was tall and well-built, with a jutting nose, a receding forehead and chin, and prominent eyes.

"S-s-save me!" he gasped.

"From what?" mumbled Bessas, spraying crumbs.

The man clutched Bessas' forearm and tried to speak but failed at first for want of breath. At last he said: "The S-Scribes of Jerusalem are after me. They will slay me if they catch me."

"Why should they do that?"

"Because I slew one of their men."

"Why?"

"They captured me when I—when I entered the city this morning on an errand for my temple—but here they come. It is a long—ah—story, which I will tell you later. But hide me now, in the name of the blessed gods! I can run no farther."

"Wrap him up," said Bessas.

Sounds of movement came from the southern end of

the valley, and the tethered mules and horses stirred uneasily. Myron and Skhâ wound the fugitive in cloaks and horse cloths, tied him up, and laid him on the ground near the campfire as if he were but one more bundle of gear.

A man on an ass rode into view. Behind him came several others afoot. More men emerged from the olive groves at the sides of the valley. The mounted man was plump, snub-nosed, and well-dressed in the Judaean fashion, wearing a tall hat wound with a low turban in Syrian style. The rest were a rough-looking lot, girt with long knives. Several carried spears or bows. Strips of cloth knotted around their heads kept their long unkempt hair in place.

"Get your bows ready, boys," said Bessas, slinging his bow case over his shoulder and picking up his buckler. He faced the mounted man as the latter pulled up. "Peace!" he said.

"Peace be with you," said the newcomer. "Have you seen a fugitive? A man about six feet in height, in a black tunic, with a shaven face?"

"Nay; not here."

"If he be not here, you will not mind our searching your tent and gear to make sure that he be not hidden."

Bessas' voice rumbled like a distant storm. "On the contrary, I should very much mind. Who are you?"

"I am Ira ben-Shaul, a Scribe. We seek Shimri ben-Hanun of Gaza, a murderer and idolater."

"Well, I am Bessas of Zariaspa, a Bactrian nobleman, and I let nobody search my gear. So seek your idol fancier elsewhere. Who licensed you to hunt men through the countryside?"

Ira's eyes seemed to blaze in the twilight. "The Lord God of Israel, the only true god, authorizes us! We know the man is around here somewhere. We traced him to Eshkol and have searched the land on both sides of this vale. Stand aside, or it will go hard with you."

"Nock your shafts," said Bessas over his shoulder. His

149

sword hissed out of its scabbard. "Know, pig face, that I am on a mission of the King of All Kings, and any man hinders me at his peril. Whoever touches me, or my men, or my gear, will greet his forebears in the Judaean hell!"

The Scribe drew in his breath sharply. There was a concerted movement as his men—now swollen to more than a score—closed in around him and edged forward, gripping their weapons.

Myron, standing with an arrow nocked, felt his heart pounding painfully. If the Judaeans rushed them, Bessas, with his superhuman size and strength, might cut his way out, leap to the back of a horse, and escape. But the rest were surely doomed. Even with bucklers and leathern corselets, he and Skhâ could hardly defeat such a force by themselves. They had no redoubt like the Tower of the Snail to make up for the difference in numbers. The best they could hope for would be to take a few of their enemies with them to the land of the shades.

Kothar had not even armed himself. The Syrian sat calmly on the bundle containing the fugitive. Now he spoke in his curious low voice, whose vibrancy carried his words as far as most men's shouts.

However, instead of using Aramaic, the common speech of the Empire, Kothar spoke in the Hebrew dialect of the Canaanitish tongue. As Kothar talked, Myron saw the eyes of the Judaeans widen, so that their whites gleamed in the firelight. The ruffianly men edged back. Even Ira the Scribe pulled on his bridle, so that the ass backed away from Bessas.

At last Ira spoke a curt sentence and rode off on the road to northward, followed by his men.

Bessas turned on Kothar with a puzzled frown. "What said you?"

Kothar gave a rare smile. "First, I told them that a man had passed us on horseback, riding hard, an hour ago, and that this was perhaps he whom they sought. Then I told them that you were a leper."

"*Me a leper?* By Mithra——"

"Why, yes. I said that you had come down with the dread disease and, all else having failed, were on your way to Jerusalem to pray to Yahveh for a cure. It seemed reasonable enough to them."

Bessas rocked back on his heels with a roar of laughter. Kothar said: "Not so loud, or they will hear you and know they have been tricked!"

Bessas moderated his mirth, though for some minutes he kept bursting into rumbles and sputters. "At last Master Kothar has shown his worth! I could never carry off such a deception, for we are drilled as children in the virtue of truthfulness. But at times even truthfulness can be too much of a good thing."

Myron: "Had we not better unwrap Master Shimri, before he suffocates?"

"Not so fast," said Bessas. "They might wait out of earshot and then rush back to surprise us, thinking that we had done just what we have done. Are you all right, O Shimri?"

A mumble came from the roll of cloths. Bessas told Skhâ to bridle his pony and sent him along the road to scout. The Karian reported back that the Judaeans were indeed on their way north, moving swiftly. So they untied Shimri ben-Hanun.

"Now," said Bessas, "let us have your story. It had better be good, or we'll tie you up again and take you to Jerusalem to give to these Scribes. I acted on impulse in giving you shelter, and having done so I could not betray you; but he who meddles in strife that concerns him not is like one who seizes a wolf by the ears. Speak, man."

Shimri's face worked, and presently he began to speak. Myron perceived that the youth had a disagreeable voice: loud and high-pitched, with a slight stammer. He sprayed spittle as he spoke, while thrusting his head close to his hearer and waving his forefinger under the victim's nose.

"Know, Lord Bessas," he said, "that—that in former times—ah—many peoples dwelt in Judaea: Philistines,

151

Israelites, Moabites, Edomites, Midianites, Ammonites, and others. And each had its own gods, and if a man liked not the gods of his fathers, he could worship those of a neighboring people, and none gainsaid him.

"And later we all came to be called Judaeans and to speak the same speech. Your servant, for example, is descended from the Philistines. And then the king of Babylon conquered the land and carried off thousands of our folk to Babylonia. But still, in Judaea, every man worshiped what gods he saw fit.

"But—ah—when the Persians overthrew the kingdom of Babylonia, the exiled Judaeans began to return to Judaea. During their exile, the priests of Yahveh, the storm god, had attained to power amongst them.

"And now—ah—now the returned exiles have become powerful in Judaea. And many of these men say that Yahveh is the only god, all others being mere lumps of wood or stone. Calling the old cults false, they say that these must be destroyed and all Judaeans compelled to worship Yahveh. This would, of course, greatly profit these godless priests of Yahveh."

Bessas said: "I understand, because we Aryans have had like troubles with the so-called reformed religion of Zoroaster. Go on."

"The priests of Yahveh do not attack the other religions openly. Instead they employ fanatical laymen called Scribes to do their dirty work. While the Scribes claim to be learned students of Yahvistic law, it is they who lead mobs to the destruction of the temples and the murder of the leaders of other religions. They have made it almost as much as a man's life is worth, if he be a follower of another god, to enter Jerusalem.

"Now, your slave adores the great god of Gaza. This is Marna Maiuma—the Lord of the Waters—the mighty and kindly and bountiful Dagon. And I also worship Dagon's divine spouse Ashtoreth."

"Another name for Ishtar," murmured Myron. "I must make a note."

152

Shimri continued: "Although your servant is a smith by trade, I am active in the affairs of my temple, being a member of the Board of Sacrificers. Now—now we have —or had—a congregation of Dagon-worshipers in Jerusalem. But the Yahvists have destroyed the poor little temple of these folk and have driven them into hiding by cruel persecution. When no word of our co-religionists in Jerusalem had reached Gaza for a year, the high priest sent me to Jerusalem, to seek out our people and see how they fared. I was also given silver for them, in case they were hard pressed.

"B-but some spy must have warned the Yahvists. For no sooner had I entered Jerusalem by the Valley Gate than a band of Yahvists, under this same Ira ben-Shaul, seized me. They took my ass and money and dragged me across the city towards Mount Sion, where the Yahvist temple once stood and where the Yahvists still have their headquarters.

"Ah—now, I knew that once these knaves got me within walls, I were a dead man. So, as they marched me along the Valley of Cheesemongers, I snatched a dagger from one of my captors, stabbed him, and fled out the Fish Gate. And I have been on the run ever since. Luckily for me, the Yahvists had no horses ready to hand. I should have gotten away, but hunger forced me to stop in Eshkol to beg a loaf, and thus the Yahvists picked up my trail. And now again I am famished—famished! Could you gentlemen spare a few bites?"

Watching Shimri wolf down a meal that would have done credit to a lion, Bessas said: "Your tale satisfies me. But now that we have you, what shall we do with you?"

"Whither are you bound, my masters?"

"To Egypt."

"What is your purpose?"

Bessas told briefly of his plans.

"Well," said Shimri, "ah—could—could you not use another man? I am a good man of my hands; I can wield a weapon or repair broken metalwork. I cannot tarry in

153

Judaea; for, now that I have shed the blood of a Yahvist, they will hunt me down, even in Gaza."

"Grip my hand," said Bessas. "Now squeeze."

This time Bessas had to put forth nearly all his vast strength to force Shimri to own himself beaten. As they unclasped and wrung their hands, Bessas said:

"Smithing has given you a fine grip. Can you shoot?"

"I am the champion archer of the civic guard of Gaza."

"Very well, we'll give you a chance to prove it when the sun rises. Know, besides, that I expect those of my company to obey my commands without pause or cavil. If they do not, I saw them in two as the wicked Spityura did his brother King Yima!"

"I understand."

"Very well. When we get to Jerusalem——"

"*Oyah!* Ask me not to go back to—to Jerusalem! Not when I have only now escaped! By Dagon's scaly tail, you might as well cut off my head with that great long sword and have done with me. But there is no reason why you should—ah—go through Jerusalem anyway. The town has little for sale save wool.

"Now Gaza, being a caravan center, has splendid marts. We can also get to Gaza in time for the spring festival, which I feared I should miss. You will like it." Shimri burst into a loud, braying laugh. "Is there anything more to eat? I still hunger."

VIII The Fish-Tailed God

BEYOND YABNE-EL they reached the sea once more and rode down the coast of Philistaea among sand dunes and low hills dotted with palms and tamarisks. They passed caravans, single wayfarers, and once in a while a Persian post rider.

Some traveler was always in sight: a family group, trudging through the sand in search of opportunity; a private letter carrier, ambling along on his ass with his leathern letter bags; a pair of young nomads from some shaykh's family, with bright sashes and jeweled daggers, galloping recklessly down the middle of the road and shouting to make way; a gang of manacled slaves shambling sadly ahead of a whip-wielding overseer; a local magnate, borne in a gilded litter with guards and whifflers tramping behind and before.

Shimri ben-Hanun, for whom room had been made on a baggage mule by shifting loads, proved himself as able an archer as he had said. He was certainly strong, athletic, and handy.

But Myron still looked at the young man with reserved speculation. There was something odd about him. His face twitched and grimaced nervously, and he sometimes grinned or laughed without apparent cause. He wanted to stop at every village to buy a snack of food. As they neared Ashdod, Shimri said:

"It were better not to speak my name in Ashdod, or in Ashqelon."

"Why?" asked Myron.

"Be-because there are rival temples of Dagon in these cities—rivals to ours, I mean—and while I do not think that their people would attack us, there might be some unpleasantness."

Myron said: "If these three temples all worship the same god, and if all are threatened by the Yahvists, I should think you would find it expedient to unite your forces."

"What, our people take orders from lousy Ashdodites and Ashqelonites?" Shimri guffawed. "As our cult is the oldest, going back to the Flood, they ought to take orders from us! Besides, we are the only ones that perform the correct ritual of baptism, with total immersion."

"Perhaps; but we Hellenes have learnt some costly lessons from the Persians about the value of unity."

They passed through Ashdod and Ashqelon without incident and in mid-afternoon reached Gaza, set amid

155

yellow sandstone hills half a league from the sea. The citadel stood on a hill surrounded by hundred-foot bluffs, while the town sprawled untidily about the base of the hill. The streets were crowded with trains of dromedaries and other beasts of burden, for here met the caravan routes to Egypt, to Elath on the Red Sea, and to the great Phoenician and Syrian cities.

The temple of Dagon stood on a seaward slope. Within the temenos, at a lower level than the temple, was a structure like a Greek theater, with many tiers of stone seats. Instead of a stage, however, the seats faced a large tank of water. The pool was filled from a fountain, which sprayed from a vase in the hands of a sculptured Dagon: a long-bearded, benign-looking god whose lower half took the form of a fish's tail.

Beyond the upper tiers of seats spread the broad temenos, planted with palms and pomegranate trees. Amid the greenery rose a many-columned temple. In front of this temple, Shimri ben-Hanun presented his fellow travelers to the high priest of Dagon, the most holy and reverend Meremoth ben-Achish.

"Peace to you, my sons," said Meremoth, a short man with a paunch and a pleasant smile. "Certes you shall be quartered on the temple grounds, without cost to you, as a small return for your charity to Shimri. Dinner shall be sent to your quarters within the hour." (Shimri burst into a wide and foolish grin, so that to Myron he looked more than ever like some stalk-eyed sea creature.) "After you have eaten and rested, perhaps you were fain to witness our vernal ceremony of baptism. Who knows? You might be converted to the worship of the merciful Lord of the Waters."

"What happens, sir?" said Bessas.

"There are hymns and prayers and a sacred dance, thanking the god for the bountiful crops and fisheries of the season past. Then all the initiates enter the tank, one at a time, and there their sins of the year are washed away."

156

Shimri laughed, spraying saliva. "That is what the accursed Yahvists most object to. They—ah—they have some silly idea that we ought to go swimming in our shirts!"

Meremoth cast a sidelong glance at Shimri. "Do I understand that your purpose to take this lion of the faith with you to Kush?"

"Aye," said Bessas. "Think you he will do? If he fights as he eats, he were an army in himself."

"I think it a noble conceit; Philistaea will not be safe for him for many moons to come. Kalev! Conduct these gentlemen to the quarters reserved for pilgrims of rank. . . ."

Bessas swallowed the last of his dinner and rose. "We cannot idle away the afternoon if we wish to see that ceremony Father Meremoth promised us. I must buy a horse and some gear for Master Shimri. Remain here to guard our possessions, Skhâ."

Kothar, who ate little, had already excused himself, saying that he wished to speak of spiritual matters with one of the priests of Dagon. When Bessas, Myron, and Shimri returned from their shopping, Skhâ had disappeared, too. The temple servants disclosed that the Karian had gone out shortly before, after asking the way to the best tavern.

"We sent him to Baruch's," they said. "He carries a good line of Judaean and imported wines and Egyptian beer, and he robs not the stranger. Three streets north. . . ."

Because of the hour, Baruch's tavern was not yet crowded. A low sun beat in through the small window; flies buzzed gently in the dusty heat. In one corner sat three long-haired Persians in low-voiced converse. In another, a clean-shaven Egyptian pored over the cryptic picture writing on a long strip of papyrus. An Arab and a Judaean played tjau, or Egyptian checkers.

Skhâ son of Thuvlo had backed Baruch himself

against the wine counter and was talking a stream of chatter in a high, excited voice, waving his pottery mug until the beer slopped over.

". . . so here we were, in this accursed Tower of the Snail, with a hundred wild nomads swirling about and thirsting for our blood, their arrows flying thick as hail. . . ."

Skhâ's voice died as he became aware of Bessas, looming over him with a dangerously ruddy face. "Oh, greetings, Lord Bessas! I hoped you would come along because I came in here forgetting that I had no money, and was that not stupid of me? I was just telling Master Baruch——"

"Shut up and put down that mug!"

"Why?" said Skhâ. "Is it that——"

Bessas' hamlike hand came around and dealt the Karian a terrific buffet, sending him clear across a table to sprawl on the floor. Myron ran to pick up the unconscious man, saying:

"I hope you haven't broken his neck!"

"I think not; it takes a harder blow than that." Bessas threw the remains of Skhâ's beer in the young man's face. "He revives. Drag him back to the temple. How much is the scot, taverner?"

On their way back, Skhâ stumbled along in a daze, with one side of his face reddened and swollen. "You loosened my teeth," he mumbled at last.

"Chew on the other side of your face for a few days, and they'll tighten up again," said Bessas. "That is nought to what will happen the next time you desert your post. A whip for the horse, a bridle for the ass, and a rod for the fool's back."

"I will not follow a leader who uses his men so cruelly! I am no slave! I will go home!"

"Go ahead. But you will find it a long walk."

"How dare you! That piebald pony is mine!"

"Horse dung! You have just as much right to it as I have, which is right of possession. And who gave you

158

leave to blab our affairs in public, so that the whole city shall know our plans? You know that we have ill-wishers, and our safety demands discretion. Better to stumble with the foot than with the tongue. Well, what are you waiting for? Yonder lies the Ashqelon Gate and the road to northward."

Skhâ trudged a few steps in silence. Then a voice spoke behind them in Persian:

"Are you not Bessas of Zariaspa?"

Bessas whirled. Myron could not be sure, but he thought this might be one of the Persians whom he had seen in Baruch's tavern. The man wore a short-sleeved shirt, embroidered trousers, and a bucket-shaped leathern hat.

"Who are you?" demanded Bessas.

"May God befriend you; call your slave Cyaxares. I have that to say which will interest you."

"What is it?"

"Not in the street, sir. Will you excuse your friends and step this way?"

"Myron here is my lieutenant. What is news for me is news for him, too."

"We prefer to talk to you alone."

"No Myron, no talk."

"Be it as you wish. Hither, pray."

"Skhâ!" said Bessas. "Hasten back to the temple and tell Shimri and Kothar that we have gone with this man. If we be not back by dark, arm yourselves and look for us."

As Bessas and Myron followed Cyaxares, Myron muttered in Greek: "Suppose that, instead of reporting to the temple, Skhâ carries out his threat to desert? It will be some time before he ceases to resent that blow, which would have staggered an elephant. You are so hasty!"

Bessas shrugged. "We must needs take some chances."

Cyaxares led them into a winding alley, through a door, down a short hall, and into a room. A pair of rush-

159

lights on a small table dimly illumined this room; a curtain was fastened across the one small window.

Four men sat in the room. As Bessas and Myron entered, they rose and bowed with hands crossed on their bosoms in formal Persian style. All four wore bashlyks pulled up to their eyes, so that Myron could not tell whether they were already known to him.

Bessas and Myron seated themselves. After a short silence, one of the masked men said:

"Hail, Bessas son of Phraates! We heard that you were bound hither and hoped to intercept you. The loquacity of your Karian made our task easier than it would otherwise have been."

"Some day," growled Bessas, "I shall wring that young rattlepate's neck. But what do you wish of me?"

Again a short silence. Then: "We know the cause of your journey to Kush. Would you say that the king had used you justly?"

Bessas narrowed his eyes. "On that, men's opinions might honestly differ. But you brought me here to tell me something, not to ask me questions."

"Your slave begs your pardon. What I mean is: since King Xerxes has dealt so rudely with you, would you——"

The sound of scuffle interrupted. Cyaxares and another Persian burst in the door, dragging by the arms a small nondescript man, also in Persian dress. Cyaxares said:

"We found this knave lurking in the alley, trying to listen in at yonder window."

A masked man thrust a rushlight close to the prisoner's face. "I know this rogue. He is Datas son of Zamaspes, King's Eye of the third class. Hold him tightly." The masked man drew his dagger.

The prisoner began to struggle frantically. He shouted: "Help! Murd——"

The dagger found the heart of Datas, who jerked and went limp.

160

"Dispose of him after dark," said the killer. He turned back to Bessas, wiping his blade. "As my unworthy self was saying, would you list to place upon the imperial throne a legitimate prince, in room of the lecherous, bungling son of the usurper?"

Bessas gave a non-committal grunt. "And how know I that you are not more agents of Xerxes, striving to trap me in treason?"

"You have just seen what we do to Xerxes' spies when we catch them."

"But I still have only your word that things are as they seem, and that the dead man was in sooth an agent of the king."

The masked speaker turned. "My lord, this fellow is stubborn. Shall we discover all to him?"

"We might as well," said the seated man thus addressed. "Usually we sound a man out, little by little; but time is lacking for that approach." He rose and pulled off his bashlyk, revealing a shock of graying hair. The man, thought Myron, was elderly but vigorous. "O Bessas, you look upon Orontes son of Cambyses, rightful heir to the throne of Persia. How long will you supinely endure the misdeeds of the usurper's son, who throws away the glorious Persian armies in reckless and blundering forays against the barbarous Hellenes; who destroys his most faithful and virtuous follower, his brother Masistes; who. . . ."

Orontes declaimed an impassioned oration, reciting King Xerxes' faults, real or fancied, and promising to do better in every respect. He concluded:

". . . and when I am king, the Empire shall be a paradise on earth. Taxes shall be lowered; the army shall be modernized and its pay increased; trade shall be fostered; the poor shall wax prosperous and the prosperous become rich. Honor and justice shall reign from Hind to Thrace, and from Scythia to Kush. By the sacred Mount Hukairya I swear it! Already I have hundreds of partisans among the Aryan nobility. Next year it will be thousands. I need

161

such a mighty and valorous man as you. For years I have watched your career and planned how best to draw you into my following. In dealing with Xerxes you will earn nought but suspicion and ingratitude, whereas my supporters shall be greater than kings! And those who join before the victory shall have precedence over those who come later. How say you, Bessas son of Phraates?"

Bessas gave a small sigh. "Your proposal might beguile your slave another time, Lord Orontes. But now, gentlemen, I must needs carry out my mission and obtain the release of my mother."

"You know not that the false king will in sooth release your mother. He is as likely to slay the twain of you for some fancied grudge."

Bessas muttered to Myron in Greek: "Stand by for trouble." His mouth was set in hard lines as he turned back to Orontes. "I am sorry, gentlemen, but I am not to be had. If I succeed in my mission, approach me afterwards and we shall see. Meanwhile you may trust me to keep silent——"

"I fear it is not so simple," said the man who had stabbed Datas, blocking the door. "We urged you to join us; very well, you refuse. But we cannot then let you go——"

In a flash, Bessas whipped out his sword and struck, not at the man facing him, but at two rushlights. Their bronzen holders flew against the wall with a double clank, and both yellow flames went out. Now the room was lit only by the little daylight that could pierce the curtain over the window.

"Come on, Myron!" roared Bessas.

Myron leaped up and threw the stool, on which he had been sitting, towards the other masked men. In the momentary darkness, before his eyes adjusted themselves, he heard the sound of a heavy blow and the fall of a body. With a loud rending of wood, the door flew open, tearing out its socket pins.

For an instant Myron saw the doorway blocked by the

162

huge silhouette of Bessas. The augmented light also revealed the man who had killed Datas lying across the door sill. Of the other men in the room, some were rising, some drawing daggers, and one was picking himself up off the floor after having been struck by Myron's stool. So lightning fast had Bessas' action been that the conspirators had not yet been able to gather themselves for a rush.

Myron sprang through the doorway, hurdling the fallen man, and pounded down the hall after Bessas, who had already reached the outer door. The giant paused long enough to sheathe his sword and assure himself that Myron was with him.

They ran out into the alley as the Persians poured out of the room behind them, crying pursuit. Someone blew a whistle; shouts and tramplings came from other parts of the house.

At the end of the alley, Myron and Bessas came to the wall surrounding the temenos of the temple of Dragon. The alleys were deserted, as most of the people of Gaza were at dinner. Bessas took a few steps along the alley that followed the wall, then paused to listen.

"They come from both directions," he said. "Over the wall with us!"

Although the wall was higher than Bessas' head, he placed his huge hands on Myron's waist and effortlessly boosted the Greek up to the top of the wall. Then he caught the rim and swung himself up, straddled the wall, and dropped down inside. They crouched in a dense grove of palms.

Myron groaned. "Herakles! I turned my ankle when I fell in here. If I survive this frightful journey, I'll stick to school-teaching the rest of my life."

"A pox on your ankle!" muttered Bessas. "Listen!"

A clatter of feet and a rush of Persian speech revealed that their pursuers had reached the point outside the wall that was nearest to the fugitives. Orontes' voice sounded:

"Less noise, you! We would not rouse the city. Where

163

could they have gone, since we came out both alleys? We should have trapped them here."

"Belike they climbed the wall," said another voice.

"That must be it!" said Orontes. "That Bessas has the thews of a lion. Cyaxares, take your six men down that way to the small gate, break it open, enter the temenos, and beat up the bushes towards this place. Izates, make your men kneel to form a pyramid against the wall, so that we can scale it. Fear not the temple guards; they will not interfere when they see our steel. For our own safety, these men must be slain."

"The fellow has some ability as a captain," said Bessas. "Let's get out of here. Beware of snakes."

Bessas led the way, with Myron limping behind. Beyond the palms lay a band of ornamental shrubs and flowers, planted in rows in the Persian style. Beyond these loomed the temple, tinted pink by the setting sun. On their right they could see the corner of the theater, below which, out of sight, lay the tank of water.

"Merciful gods!" said Bessas.

Issuing from the temple, and winding past the theater and down towards the pool, came a procession of naked men and women. They came in no special order of sex or age: male and female, old and young, lithe and paunchy, all were intermingled.

"This must be Father Meremoth's baptismal procession," said Myron.

From the palm grove behind them came sounds of Orontes' men and snatches of speech: "Look into that dark clump. . . ." "No, they are not here." "Perhaps they have run into the temple. . . ."

The nude procession wound down out of sight to the right. The tail end of the line passed in front of Myron and Bessas, not over twenty paces distant, but driblets of tardy worshipers continued to issue from the side door of the temple, running to take their places at the end of the line.

Behind Myron, sounds of pursuit came closer. Myron said: "We cannot remain here. But I cannot run, alas!"

"What in the name of Ghu can we do?" said Bessas. "I cannot abandon my comrade!"

"Thanks, old man," said Myron. "Let me think. . . . By the Dog of Egypt, I have it! Do you see this big shrub? If we conceal our garments beneath it, we can dash out and join the end of the procession without anyone's being the wiser. The Persians would not recognize us without our bashlyks."

"Mithra! *Me* expose myself in that shameless fashion? I had liefer die!"

"Well, you will soon have an opportunity." Myron began to disrobe. "Those fellows behind us are coming closer. Think of your mother! Besides, we need baths, and these will be free."

With the look of a man led to execution, Bessas imitated Myron. Choosing a moment when no more latecomers were running from the temple, and those already in line were looking towards the pool, Myron limpingly led his huge comrade out of the shrubbery and up to the tail of the line.

They had no sooner joined than one more initiate, a beautiful, copper-haired, superbly formed young woman, fell in behind them. She at once began to chatter:

"Is the ceremony not thrilling? Does not Father Meremoth stage it beautifully? I am sure the gods are pleased. I have not seen you at these rites before; are you but lately initiated?"

Bessas, next to this beauty in line, answered with inarticulate grunts. He kept his head averted, blushing a rosy pink. Fearing that his comrade would arouse suspicion by this churlish conduct, Myron changed places with Bessas and gravely answered the girl's questions.

They were descending the slope to the pool when an altercation broke out behind them. Evidently the temple guards and the followers of Orontes were having it out. A

165

priest, resplendent in a robe embroidered with golden thread, hurried up the steps of the pool, frowning portentously. Snatches of talk wafted down:

". . . murderers hid in here. . . ." "How dare you disturb our divine services?" "Stand aside, or it will be worse for you!" "We will appeal to the governor. . . ."

"What is the matter?" said the girl. "Have strangers invaded our holy precinct?"

"If they are unauthorized, no doubt the Lord of the Waters will deal with them in his own fashion," said Myron blandly.

A Persian and a temple guard walked past them, arguing furiously in an undertone. Myron whispered in Greek: "Do not look around or display any interest!"

Bessas held up a skinned knuckle and replied in the same tongue: "I fear I broke that fellow's jaw."

The Persian and the Judaean passed on. Bessas and Myron found themselves at the edge of the pool.

The bald, wrinkled oldster who preceded them stepped down the marble stair into the pool. There a pair of naked priests awaited him, standing chest-deep in water. As the man submitted to being ducked by the priests, cymbals clashed, a drum rolled, trumpets called, and the audience on the theater benches burst into a song in an archaic tongue that Myron did not recognize, but which he supposed to be the dead Philistine language.

"Go ahead," he said to Bessas. "You are expected to swim the length of the tank."

Bessas cast a stricken glance back at his lieutenant and strode down into the pool. The priests pushed him under, and he came up coughing and spluttering. When he got his breath he began to swim slowly and clumsily.

A high, piercing voice, that of Shimri ben-Hanun, called out in Aramaic over the song of the worshipers: "Hail Bessas, the Bactrian hero!" A shriek of laughter in Skhâ's voice followed.

Bessas cast a ferocious glower towards the grandstand.

166

At once he missed his stroke and went under. He came up, coughing and spitting, and waded the rest of the way. Attendants with towels awaited him at the exit stairway. The scarlet sun sank below the edge of the Syrian Sea.

Back in the pilgrim's quarters, Bessas said: "You damned fool, Shimri, you might have gotten us slain by your folly! I ought to leave you here for that reason alone."

"Oh, master, it was not so bad as that!" said Shimri, giggling. "Nought went amiss. And we were so astonished, seeing you and Myron in the procession, that I could not help speaking out."

Bessas glared round the circle. Skhâ, sitting on his pallet, held his hands over his mouth in a futile effort to bridle his mirth. Even Kothar, who best maintained his usual gravity, allowed the corners of his mouth to twitch a trifle.

Myron said: "What I don't understand, O Bessas, is why you acted so standoffish with that girl behind us. She was a handsome wench and very friendly."

"Would you know, forsooth? The reason was that I have not exercised my lance since Halpa, and I feared that the sight of the filly would rouse my lusts, with results for all to see. Would that not be a fine addition to the cerem——"

A knock sounded, and there stood Meremoth. He came in gravely, exchanged pleasantries, sat down, and then burst into laughter.

"So you are now fully baptized Dagonites, without having been initiated! It is most irregular, but under the circumstances your servant blames you not. At least your sins are now cleansed from you. I have learnt of that gang who pursued you hither." He wiped his eyes. "All I can say is, lucky the lord who has such abandoned rogues as you on his side!"

Bessas managed a wry grin. "Next time I am to be shown to the world in this outlandish fashion, I will try to have my whiskers curled and my visage painted like a proper Aryan gentleman."

"I fear the paint would wash off; nor would the curls fare better." The priest became serious. "But I cannot advise you to tarry. We can afford you but little protection. The Persian governor at Ashqelon has only a few armed men. In the sight of our local magistrates, if one Persian cut the throat of another, that is all to the good and no concern of theirs."

"In other words," said Bessas, "we had better get out whilst our heads still adorn our shoulders."

Kothar said: "The omens are dire for leaving now."

"The omens are a lot worse for staying," replied Bessas. "Can you send a man to rouse us at the beginning of the second watch, Father Meremoth? We shall lie down and go to sleep at once, to strengthen us for the journey!"

Having bid the priest good-night, Bessas proceeded to do just this.

Before false morning raised its misty spear above the deserts of Shos, Bessas' company reached the frontier post of Rapih. Here they crossed from the satrapy of Syria into that of Egypt. Bessas' five mules were heavily laden with leathern water bottles against the hard march along the Sinaitic coast.

Bessas and Myron turned in their saddles to look back along the dark undulations of the dunes, cast into sharp shadows by the rising of the bisected moon behind them.

"Well!" said Myron. "Praise the gods and goddesses, at least we shan't have to worry henceforth about spies and assassins sent after us by kings, nobles, and pretenders. Although I bow to Adrasteia, they can hardly reach us in Egypt."

"If they come, we shall be ready," said Bessas. "In vain the net is spread in the sight of the bird."

"Let's hope so. They have made the journey a nightmare hitherto, but now we need fear only being gulped down by the great Serbonian bog."

168

Kothar looked from one to the other with a speculative expression. Off in the tamarisk clumps, a hyena laughed. At least, Myron hoped it was a hyena.

King Xerxes sat in the chamber of his wizard Ostanas. The king handed the seer a roll of crackly yellow papyrus, which the latter unrolled.

"What make you of that?" said the king.

Ostanas moved a lamp closer and squinted in the yellow light. He read slowly aloud:

DAURISES, SUBGOVERNOR OF PHILISTAEA, PROSTRATES HIMSELF BEFORE THE GREAT KING, THE KING OF KINGS, THE KING OF THE WORLD, XERXES SON OF DARIUS, THE ARYAN, THE ACHAEMENID.

Know, O King, that two days past, word came to your slave that a Persian had been slain in Gaza. Knowing how little the Judaeans care for sacred Aryan blood, your slave at once rode forth to look into this crime in person.

The man had been knifed and buried in the sand of the beach. His body was discovered when dogs were seen digging at the spot. Your slave brought the body back to Ashqelon, where a King's Eye, Rhambacas by name, identified the dead man as King's Eye third class Datas son of Zamaspes.

It may be more than happenstance that, the day before this discovery, the man Bessas of Zariaspa, concerning whom the Great King wrote his slave, left Gaza bound for Egypt. However, Meremoth ben-Achish, high priest of Dagon of Gaza, informs my unworthy self that Bessas and his followers lodged at the temple of Dagon during their sojourn in Gaza, and that as far as Meremoth knows they took no part in any stabbing affray. Your slave will continue to investigate this deplorable crime with the utmost energy and diligence whereof he is capable.

169

"Well?" said the king.

"Let us consult those wiser than we, sire," said Ostanas, blowing up his brazier and feeding it jasmine seeds.

As the seeds popped and the writhing thread of blue smoke arose, Ostanas stared at it, resting his white-bearded chin upon his knobby old hand. At last he said:

"Methinks the pretender Orontes is involved in this. The smoke tells your slave that Bessas sought out the pretender in Gaza to assure Orontes of his loyalty—to Orontes, that is—and that, when Datas espied them at their tryst, Bessas slew him."

Xerxes slowly closed his fist. "Datas was a good man; I shall miss him. We must make certain that, when Bessas returns, he slip not through our fingers. My Majesty has plans for that villain!"

Ostanas smiled a snag-toothed grin. "And so, my lord, have I."

IX The White Castle

IN THE DIRTY LITTLE INN at Tahapanes, on the Pelusiac branch of the Nile, flies buzzed and circled languidly as the afternoon declined. The sun slanted through the window and gleamed on a copper statue of a cat, which sat on the counter and stared haughtily at the mere mortals who shared the room with it.

Myron sat at a table, writing in his journal. From time to time he sipped at a mug of beer, for he was determined to accustom himself to the stuff. Bessas sat at the same table, swilling beer in great gulps and honing his sword. At the other table, Kothar threw dice with Pnon the innkeeper. Bessas finally jerked a hair from his black mane and tried his blade on it. Satisfied, he spoke:

"Boys, I'll throw a round of dice with you. Low man goes out to buy food for our dinner and fuel for Master Pnon to cook it with."

Pnon, fat and greasy, said in broken Aramaic: "If you use these magical dice, you surely lose. Already your Syrian friend win cost of your dinner from me."

Kothar swept up the three dice and blew on them. "It is simply that my gods take better care of me than yours do of you—or perchance I take better care of them, by prayer and sacrifice. But I shall have to go anyway, as neither of you can converse with the folk here. Where are those two scatterwitted youths?"

"They went for a stroll in the market place," said Myron. "By rights it is they—watch out!"

Kothar, rising, had knocked against the copper cat, which swayed as he clutched it and settled back on its base. Myron passed a hand across his forehead and said:

"Did you work a spell on that cat? I thought surely it would fall, and we should have to buy it of Master Pnon."

Pnon laughed and picked up the statue. "Heavy weight in base, see? Not fall—*ha*, what that?"

A rising noise of running and shouting came to Myron's ears. The door flew open; in rushed Shimri and Skhâ. The former slammed the door and shot the bolt, while the latter panted:

"They—they are after us! Save us!"

"What are they and what would they of you?" said Bessas.

"Shimri kicked a cat in the market place——"

"I meant no harm!" wailed Shimri. "May I eat pork if I lie! This abandoned beast kept rubbing against my legs, and I did but push it away. Then a man began shouting and pushed me, and I thought he was fooling and pushed him back, and they all began screaming and throwing clods——"

The door boomed as men hurled themselves against it. A wild-eyed face glared in through the small window. A skinny arm thrust into the room, pointing at Shimri, while foaming lips screamed threats and imprecations at the foreigner.

"Gentlemen!" cried Pnon. "You must go away now al-

171

ready! This man do terrible sacrilege! These people tear down my inn, kill me, if you not go! Get out!"

"Where in demon land are our other arms?" roared Bessas. "In the stable? Myron, go fetch——"

"Get Shimri out the back door," said Kothar. "I will deal with these folk. Pnon, light me an oil lamp, quickly. And fetch me a couple of fresh eggs."

"Are you mad, man?" cried the taverner, but he lit a small clay lamp from the embers of the hearth fire.

A louder bang on the door told that some sort of beam or log had been brought into play as a ram. Kothar said:

"Sit down, mortals, and act as if you were enjoying yourselves. On your lives, smile!"

Kothar did something with the lamp, and with his free hand pulled back the bolt and opened the door. The crowd outside, about to make another rush with their log, stood stupidly staring. Kothar stepped into the doorway, opened his mouth, and blew out a blast of yellow flame.

The Egyptians in front screamed and tried to back away but were prevented by those behind. Kothar spoke in that strange, low voice. At once the yammering died. Although Myron could not follow the crackle of the Egyptian sentences, he caught the name "Kothar of Qadesh." Kothar was introducing himself. Then he invited the multitude into the tavern.

Although there was room for only a few inside, others crowded at the door and the window to see. Keeping up his soothing spate of talk, Kothar waved his delicate hands to prove them empty, then pulled a die from one man's nose, a duck's egg from the ear of another, and a kerchief from the mouth of another. He juggled a ring, a cup, and a dagger. He placed three cups upside down and invited the audience to guess under which a large ivory bead lay hidden.

An hour later the crowd straggled out, chattering cheerfully and profusely thanking Kothar. Myron gave a long whistle and asked:

"What did you tell them about Shimri, Kothar?"

"Nought. I had planned, at need, to say that he was insane, and we were taking him to a temple to pray for his cure. But the rabble became so bemused by my little tricks—which must not be confounded with the true higher magic—that they forgot about him."

Pnon had gone to the stable to fetch back the wretched Shimri. Myron looked sharply at the guide. "Let me see those dice for a moment." When Kothar wordlessly handed Myron three dice, Myron looked them over and said: "Now the other set, pray."

"What other set?"

"You know what I mean. Come on; hand them over."

"Do as he says," rumbled Bessas.

Kothar produced another triad of dice. Myron squinted and said: "I thought so; flats. Some day you will employ these on a man with the wit to test them for true square-ness, and the results will be unfortunate for you."

Kothar shrugged. "I know my business, and I have not used my little lucky gems on you."

Myron and Bessas burst into laughter. The latter said: "By the boar tusks of Verethraghna, Kothar, you are a rascal, but too useful a rascal to be discarded."

Kothar smiled faintly. "If that opinion pleases you, cherish it. You know not to whom you speak."

Myron suggested: "Why don't you take a perfect set of dice and have weights inlaid in one side, as with that copper cat? You would achieve the same result with less risk."

Kothar raised his eyebrows and put away his baubles.

On the evening of the last day of Ayaru, Bessas of Za-riaspa and his following crossed the Nile from Troyu to Memphis. As the ferry could carry but one horse or mule at a time, the crossing took more than two hours, while the sun sank behind the colossal walls of Memphis—the City of the White Wall, the Abode of the Soul of Ptah.

Over the towering walls of pearly limestone appeared

173

the upper parts of a host of colossal statues erected about the temples by the kings of yore: the Senuserts and the Rameseses. The citadel, called the White Castle, also loomed above the wall. This was an artificial hill, surrounded by forty-foot limestone walls. It rose in the midst of the city, bearing barracks and palaces on its top. Beyond the city, the points of a score of pyramids, great and small, rising from the edge of the desert, pierced the darkening sky with black triangular teeth. Behind the travelers to eastward, a long, ragged rank of purple hills dissolved into the oncoming dark.

The travelers put up in the foreign quarter, around the temple of Hat-hor in the southeastern part of the city. Kothar led them past spicy-smelling markets and stinking alleys to the inn of Hazael of Damascus. Here, in the tavern on the ground floor, pale men with yellow hair in long braids, and brown men in turbans, with beards dyed orange, blue, and green, and men with black skins marked by tribal scars gorged and guzzled, while thunderous snores wafted down from the dormitory overhead.

On the first of Simanu, they climbed the long stair of the White Castle to present the documents entitling them to food and fodder from the royal stores. The official who indorsed their applications said:

"You should present your respects to the satrap. He holds audience this morning."

"Where?" asked Bessas.

"In the audience room of the east wing of the palace. Hand your letter of introduction to the usher, who will throw it through the audience chamber window."

As he turned away, Bessas said: "By Ahriman's arse, that is the most outlandish way of conducting an audience I ever heard of. Let us see how it works."

They easily found the jostling, chattering crowd around the east wing of the ancient palace of King Wahabra. Most of the crowd were shaven Egyptians in white linen, though here and there were seen the flapping trousers of Aryans, the knitted caps with dangling tails of Babylonians, the tall spiral hats of Syrians, the ostrich-plumed headdresses of Libyans, and garb from other parts of the Persian Empire.

They crowded around a wall of dun-colored brick, pierced only by one small door and one small window. Before the door stood a pair of trousered Persian soldiers, bearing shields with bosses of gilded bronze, which blazed with the light of the fierce morning sun.

A eunuch in a gauzy robe stood by the window. People thronged around, trying to press sheets and rolls of papyrus into the eunuch's hands. All shouted about the urgency of their respective petitions. The eunuch shouted back:

"Easy, pray! Get in line! Do not push! All shall be taken care of! Quiet, good people! Slowly! Get in line! One at a time!"

Paying no heed to the eunuch's demands, the crowd pushed harder and shouted more loudly. Bessas shouldered his way through the throng, which gave back before him with scowls and muttered curses. The eunuch picked him out by his towering stature and called:

"You there! Have you aught to present?"

"My respects to the satrap. Here is a letter from the Great King signed by the *hazarapat* Artabanus, commending me to all satraps and subgovernors. They told me to hand it to you, but I shall want it back."

The eunuch glanced at the sheet of parchment, rolled it up, and tossed it through the window. "Wait," he said, and turned back to the importunate horde.

Presently a voice from the audience room called: "Send them in!" The eunuch pushed aside the crowd and ushered Bessas, whose followers trailed in his wake, to the door.

Myron found himself in a room whose plastered walls were decorated with colored pictures in the old Egyptian style, depicting the deeds of animal-headed gods. Captions in Egyptian priestly writing, made up of little processions of men, animals, plants, and other objects, ran along the

175

wall above and below the pictures. Costly Persian rugs lay on the floor, golden lamps gave off a reek of castor oil, and the satrap sat at a papyrus-littered table of ivory and ebony.

Achaemenes son of Darius, brother of King Xerxes and governor of the satrapy of Mudraya, was a tall, well-built, handsome man, with glossy black hair and the long hooked Achaemenid nose. He was younger than Xerxes, whom he otherwise much resembled. His robe was sewn with pearls; jewels winked red and green and purple from his narrow diadem of yellow gold. His expression was weary, sleepy, and bored.

There were six other persons in the room: a pair of bodyguards, a secretary, an interpreter, and two clerks. One of the clerks stood close to the small window. When he received a signal from the secretary, he called through the narrow opening: "Next!"

A piece of papyrus whizzed through the window. The clerk caught it with the skill of a seasoned ball player, glanced at it, and passed it to the other clerk, who sorted the missives into piles: those to be routinely dealt with by underlings, those to be brought to the satrap's attention, and those to be rejected out of hand.

The secretary took those for the satrap's personal attention and read them to Achaemenes in Persian, while the translator stood by to help with petitions in unusual languages. After each letter was read to Achaemenes, he dictated a reply. This, if short enough, was written on the original petition; otherwise the secretary wrote a separate letter and fastened the two together with a dab of gum. A murmur of talk between the secretary and the governor floated in the air:

"Another of these heirs despoiled by his wicked guardian. . . ." ". . . complaint of corruption in the Province of the Catfish. . . ." ". . . should be looked into; send the detective Sebek-hotep. . . ." ". . . tax gatherer slain by a mob in Duqau. . . ." ". . . has been in prison six months without action. . . ." ". . . theft of arms from arsenal. . . ." ". . . brother-in-law threatens to slay him; he wishes governmental protection. . . ." "The villagers of Kaïs complain of a demon that haunts their fields; can we send an exorcist? . . ."

At last Achaemenes looked up, yawned prodigiously, and asked: "Which is Bessas of Zariaspa?"

Bessas crossed his hands on his breast and bowed low "I am he, my lord. The gods give Your Highness long life and wealth."

"Auramazda, and whatever other gods there be, befriend all of you," said Achaemenes. "What think you of Egypt?"

Bessas smiled grimly. "Shall your slave be polite, my lord, or shall I say what I think?"

"The latter."

"By your leave, sir, I like it not at all."

"Why not? The flies and the heat?"

"Nay; I have seen worse in the East. It is something hard to describe exactly—something in the atmosphere. I have the feeling that the people are fain to tear me limb from limb, being restrained only by fear of the government and of me personally."

"Your feelings deceive you not," said the satrap. "Have there been any outright attacks upon you?"

"Nay; except——" and he told of the broil at Tahapanes. "Aside from that, it is well that of us five only Kothar speaks Egyptian. I am sure that some of the words addressed to me in the last few days have been mortal insults. Had I understood them, honor would have compelled me to wipe them out in blood."

"You must restrain yourself, Captain Bessas. We sit on the lid of a boiling cauldron here. A rash act could cause trouble far beyond the scathe to your feelings from a native's gibe."

"Be it as you wish. But, my lord, a noble Aryan cannot brook insolence. What can one do?"

"I suggest that you and Master Myron abandon your Persian dress—at least as to the trews and bashlyks."

177

Bessas grunted. "Very well, Your Highness. But your slave makes no rash promises as to what he will do the next time dung is thrown at him. What is the cause of this hostility?"

"As you no doubt know, Egypt was a mighty kingdom for thousands of years or ever Cambyses conquered it, and the Egyptians—those above the lowest classes, at least— have not forgotten. They are the most self-conceited of men, deeming themselves the bravest, truest, and noblest of mankind. This is of course ridiculous, since everyone knows that the Aryans are the noblest of men, and the Persians the noblest of the Aryans. But that is how these wretched Egyptians think, and nought will persuade them otherwise. Hence it galls them beyond endurance to be ruled by those they regard as unwashed barbarians.

"In addition, the priesthood hate us because we have forced them to pay their fair share of the costs of govern- ment, and the superstitious masses follow the lead of the priests, heedless of the fact that these priests have battened on them for centuries, like a horde of blood-sucking para- sites. And they all hate us because twenty years ago we put down their revolt against the Great King's god-established rule. Now tell me somewhat of the quest whereon my noble brother—whose rule God strengthen—has sent you."

When he had heard, Achaemenes sighed. "Betimes I wish I could leave my grinding task here and set out on such a venture. But empery is a demanding mistress. I will give you a letter to Astes, who rules the satrapy of Kushia from the island of Yeb. You may have trouble get- ting from Kushia into independent Kush, because fight- ing has lately broken out along the border. The barba- rous black Kushites appreciate the benefits of Persian rule as little as do the Egyptians.

"If you return this way, bearing the banners of victory, send me word; for I, too, am fain to see this dragon. One more thing: have you come upon any signs of treasonable

178

plots against the Awful Royal Glory? As, say, by pretenders to the throne?"

"Well—ah—no, my lord."

"Why did you pause, Master Bessas? Come, sir, if you know aught of such cabals, it is your duty to warn your natural lords." Achaemenes' indolent air had vanished.

Bessas shook his head. "It is nothing, Your Highness; nought but a few words, half remembered, spoken in a tavern in Phoenicia."

"What tavern, and what words?"

"I remember not, sir; some remark about kicking the lousy Persian dogs into the sea. But I had drunk too deeply, so I cannot firmly grasp the memory."

Achaemenes looked sharply at the Bactrian, who flushed with patent embarrassment. "Did you hear any names?"

"I cannot tell, my lord."

"Such as Orontes, perhaps?"

"It could have been so, sir; but I truly know not."

"Why have you not reported this before?"

"Your slave heard nothing clearly enough to make an accusation, my lord. And now all is hazy, like fragments of a forgotten dream. After all, if ever rash words spoken in a tavern, damning the government, were reported to you, there would not be enough secretaries in the Empire to record them, nor would you have time to hear them, though you listened night and day."

"It is wrong that men should utter such treasonous words with impunity," said Achaemenes.

"Perhaps, but, like fornication, it will never be stopped, be a ruler never so mighty and never so just. As an old haunter of taverns, your slave can perchance claim knowledge of this matter denied to Your Highness."

Myron added: "The only sure defense against reproach, sir, is obscurity."

For a time Achaemenes sat staring somberly at Bessas and drumming on the table with his fingers. At last he said: "Well, next time, bear your duties to your lawful

179

sovran more keenly in mind. Auramazda further your enterprise!"

Next day, the travelers rode southward through the endless green corridor that is Upper Egypt. Sometimes the steep walls of the valley pressed close on either hand. Sometimes they receded until they could no longer be seen from the river road.

Big white asses bearing kilted Egyptians and their burdens trotted past, their bells jingling. Along the blue river and the many canals, muscular naked brown peasants hoisted water by creaking swapes, with posts of sundried mud and booms made from roughly trimmed tree trunks. Black-and-white ibises soared over the shallows, while kites and falcons screamed in the deep blue sky. Every few furlongs brought the travelers to a village: a squalid cluster of tiny huts of deep-brown clay, noisy with the chatter of peasants. From these hovels, swarms of naked children of the same muddy hue scampered out to beg with shrill voices and outstretched hands and to hurl curses and clods when refused.

Once Skhâ burst out: "What will they say back in Barbalissos when I tell them that I, the son of Thuvlo the dyer, have been presented to a satrap, the Great King's brother and one of the greatest lords of the realm? Truly this Achaemenes seemed a man of kingly qualities!"

"It takes more than fine feathers to make fine birds," said Myron.

Bessas grunted. "He's no fool, at least. He had me sweating over that matter of Orontes."

Shimri gave one of his jarring laughs. "Why told you not the entire tale?"

"It is foolish to entangle oneself, any more deeply than can be helped, in the struggles of the great. The man who is down today may be up tomorrow, and rancor outlasts gratitude as stone outlasts wood."

"Quite right," said Myron. "Besides, if Achaemenes disapproved our not reporting a chance word in a tavern,

180

you can imagine how he would have felt over our not divulging our meeting with the pretender himself. My dear Bessas, you are absolutely the world's most unconvincing liar! I shall have to give you lessons in that art as well as in swimming."

"That won't be needed," replied Bessas. "I hereby appoint you official liar of our expedition; your people naturally excel at the art. Hereafter you shall deal with Achaemenes and his ilk."

"Is Achaemenes as good as he is splendid to look at?" asked Skhâ.

"Who can tell?" said Myron. "Men hide their true natures behind a mask of benevolence, and men change with time and the pressure of circumstance. In the early years of his reign, everyone praised you-know-who to the skies. And indeed he did well at the outset. But I suppose the responsibilities and the temptations of kingship, acting together, in time break down the strongest character. Cambyses, who also started out well, fell into fits of madness at the end of his reign and thought he saw little red snakes in his wine."

"Maybe so," said Bessas. "But Cyrus and Darius continued to rule ably into eld. And Masistes would have done the like, had he gained the throne. Withal my father, who knew Cambyses, averred that those tales of Cambyses' madness were but lies sent abroad by Egyptian scribes, in revenge for his conquest of their country."

"Ah, but how can one determine in advance how the king will turn out? That's why in Hellenic cities we elect our chief men to office for limited times only."

"All very well for those lousy little walled villages you call cities, but it were absurd to apply such methods to a great empire."

Myron smiled wryly. "As the wise Solon wrote":

The people in their ignorance have bowed
In slavery to a monarch's single rule.

181

Bessas continued: "Masistes, now—ah, there was a man for you! Had the gods willed otherwise. . . ." The giant sighed and wiped away a tear.

"What about Masistes?" asked Skhâ. "Was that not a brother of the king, who died when I was a boy?"

"Aye," said Bessas somberly. "As I know the story better than most, since my father was a follower of Masistes, I shall tell the tale.

"Masistes was a brother of King Xerxes, satrap of Bactria, and commander of one of the six army corps. He had a wife, with whom he lived in such happiness as is possible to those in the married state, and several sons and daughters.

"After failure of the expedition against Hellas, Xerxes returned to Shushan. There he fell in love with Maisistes' wife, who however refused his suit. Not wishing to drag her to his couch by force, because of the standing of his brother, Xerxes thought to bring suasion to bear upon Masistes' wife by marrying her daughter Artaynta to his son Darius. Then, losing his passion for Masistes' wife, he conceived one equally hot for his daughter-in-law Artaynta, who did not deny him.

"You may judge the wisdom of promising to any mortal, let alone a woman, that one will give her anything she asks. Yet Xerxes, assotted with Artaynta, made this promise. And she demanded, of all things, the royal robe that Queen Amestris herself had woven for her husband the king.

"Fearing that his intrigue would be discovered, Xerxes tried by extravagant offers to persuade the foolish and reckless girl to change her demand. He offered her cities, treasures, and even a private army; but no, she would have the robe and nought else. At length Xerxes yielded and gave her the garment, which she wore. And, of course, Amestris heard of this gift.

"Now, whatever the virtues and faults of the Achaemenids, I had ten times rather be in the bad graces of one of them than of their women. This bloodthirty bitch of a queen decided, by some strange womanish process of thought, that Masistes' wife was the cause of Xerxes' intrigue with Artaynta. So, at the king's birthday party, she demanded Masistes' wife to do with as she listed. Custom requires that the king deny no request made to him at this banquet. Again the king sought to refuse. But Amestris persisted until, wearied of her demands and loath to break the law of the feast, he again gave in.

"Xerxes summoned his brother Masistes and ordered him to divorce his wife and wed one of Xerxes' daughters. But Masistes, who loved his wife, refused with such firmness as he dared to show. Meanwhile Amestris had sent soldiers to Masistes' quarters to mutilate Masistes' wife. They cut off her breasts, nose, ears, and lips, and they tore out her tongue.

"When Masistes returned to his house and found his wife so horribly used, he gathered his sons and partisans. Mad with fury, all set out for Bactria, where Masistes was much beloved and where he meant to raise a revolt against Xerxes. But Xerxes sent cavalry after them, and these overtook them on the road and slew them all."

"How t-terrible!" said Shimri, who was changing the padding inside Skhâ's helmet to make it fit better. "Had I been there, I should have saved Masistes."

"Forsooth? I think not. Anyway, it is said that Xerxes moaned and wept over the loss of his brother, who had been his ablest and most loyal supporter. And it is whispered that Xerxes has not slept with Amestris from that day to this. But of course all that did not bring back the noble Masistes."

"Ha!" said Shimri. "If—if the king's women misbehave, why does he not have them simply drowned or strangled?"

Myron: "With a mere slave or concubine he could, but not with his official wives. Know that Darius, when he acceded to the throne, agreed to take wives only from the families of the six conspirators who assisted him, and Xerxes follows the precedent. These families, the Daduchids and the rest, are the mightiest lords in the Empire. While they hold together and support the king, his throne is secure; but let him antagonize them and it would soon be rocking under his fundament. Oh, well, that's monarchy for you."

"It is not merely monarchy," said Kothar. "All government by common mortals falls into such disorder. Men will never be governed justly until they give all power into the hands of those who possess true occult wisdom— that is, persons like my unworthy self."

At Siout, Myron and Bessas quarreled. The cause of their quarrel was this: At Memphis, Bessas, claiming the need for haste, refused to grant Myron an extra day in which to visit the Sphinx and the pyramids of kings Khufu and Khafra three leagues north of the city. Then, when Bessas learnt that the men of Siout practiced a peculiar technique of fighting with quarterstaves, he took a day off to seek out experts at this form of combat and hire these men to teach him their tricks. At this, Myron bitterly complained of the loss of his chance to add to his store of knowledge.

"You may sneer at my mastery of different kinds of fighting," growled Bessas, "but 'twere better if you spent more time in weapon practice yourself. Whither we are going, such skills are all that will stand between us and the Bridge of Judgment."

"All I said," snapped Myron, "was that knowledge of other kinds is equally important——"

"Plague take you!" roared Bessas, his pock-marked face dark with rage. "If you like not how I run this venture, take yourself off! I release you from your oath! Get out of my sight, you lying, cowardly, boy-loving Greekling!"

Myron rose, pale. "For that I'll fight you. Get your weapons—anything but your bow—and I will get mine."

"Do you mean that?"

"You shall see when you feel my steel." Myron undid

184

his baggage and pulled on his helmet. Bessas began to arm himself likewise.

"Mortals!" said a low but penetrating voice. It was Kothar, sitting quietly on a palm log. "Ere you shed each other's blood, I have that to say which may interest you."

"Forsooth?" said Bessas.

"Knowing the dangers of our journey, I have sought advice from the higher powers. I have watched the flight of birds; I have observed the wheeling stars; I have listened in the stillness of the night to the voices of my familiars. And I tell you this: disembodied spirits of evil, sent by your ill-wishers, menace you at this very moment. Unable to strike directly at you, because of my counterspells, they seek by sowing discord to incite you to destroy yourselves.

"Perils encompass you round, which united you may overcome. But, if you break up in a quarrel now, or ever the course be run, disaster will surely strike you all—those who go on and those who go back. So say the divine powers."

"Well——" said Bessas.

"Well——" said Myron.

"Oh, to demon land with it!" growled Bessas. He threw down his sword and buckler, caught Myron in a bear hug, and loudly kissed the smaller man on both cheeks. "Will you forgive my insult to your courage, old friend? By the Seven Guardian Stars, had you been a craven, you would never have stood up to me."

Myron had been, a moment before, fully expecting to die. Hence he was vastly relieved by the reconciliation, although he did not think it prudent to make much of this. He said:

"Really, old boy, I am no braver than most."

Bessas said: "You are brave enough for me. Belike the shortness of our tempers is the result of too much virtue for the past fortnight. Let's celebrate!"

"Celebrate what?" said Kothar.

"Just celebrate. I make merry when I feel like it, not

when some priestly calendar says I should. We'll make a night of it!"

> *Our throats are dry, our lances stiff and keen;*
> *For many a dusty furlong have we seen.*
> *Break out the wine and tune the twanging lyre;*
> *We'll sing, and dance, and futter every quean!*

That evening, while Bessas, Myron, Shimri, and Skhâ reveled at the inn, Kothar bar-Malko sat quietly in an anteroom of the temple of Wepwawet, the wolf god of Siout. He wrote:

KOTHAR OF QADESH GREETS THE HOLY BELKISHIR, HIGH PRIEST OF MARDUK OF BABYLON

Mindful of your charge, your servant has guided those mortals committed to his care as far as this city of Siout in Egypt. Deadly perils have threatened us, and more than once we have been saved only by my occult insight and presence of mind. Today I averted a breakup of the company resulting from a quarrel between the leaders, Bessas of Zariaspa and his lieutenant, Myron of Miletos. For I agree with Your Holiness that the expedition must come to its appointed end, not in this teeming land where Persian officials watch the fall of every sparrow, but in the unknown territories beyond Kush where their fate can never be traced. Tomorrow, if my fellow travelers be not palsied from the effects of their disgusting dissipation, we shall resume our journey.

Kothar long studied the letter. Then he knelt and raised his arms in prayer. Long and fervently he prayed, with sweat bedewing his brow. He muttered:

"Seteh, patron of wizards and guardian of foreigners in the land of Khem, help me to decide!"

186

Fifty leagues south of Siout lay the second city of Egypt, a city of many names. To the most ancient Egyptians it was Weset; to those of more recent date, Opet. Those who now dwelt there more often called it the City of Amon, or simply the City. To the Greeks it was the City of Zeus, or Thebes of the Hundred Gates.

"I see no hundred gates," said Myron, as they neared the sprawling suburbs on the east bank of the Nile. "In fact, I see no wall at all. What sort of city is this, to have no wall?"

Kothar said: "There is none; or, if there ever was, it was outgrown in ancient times, and demolished and never rebuilt. For sieges, the temple inclosures provide space and security for the people. I believe the term 'hundred gates' refers to the pylons of these temples, of which there are ten pairs in the temple of Amon alone."

"I see what you mean," said Myron, staring in amazement at the vast lion-colored brick wall that inclosed the temenos of this temple, ahead and to their left.

Farther away on the left stood the smaller inclosure of the temple of Mont. Other temple walls, thirty to forty cubits high, could be seen across the river, in the City of the Dead on the west bank. Over the tops of these walls Myron glimpsed the roofs of temples, upheld by lotus-topped columns of enormous girth.

Nowhere in all his travels, not even in mighty Babylon, had Myron seen anything to compare with this amazing mass of sacerdotal stonework. Although Opet was a large and flourishing city, the private houses and the people seemed dwarfed. The sheer size and number of the temples rendered ordinary folk insignificant.

"If this be the Great Temple of Amon," said Myron, "It is our present destination. I have a letter of introduction to"—he fumbled in his scrip—"the priest Jedhor, Second Prophet of Amon."

They dismounted and walked along an avenue, flanked by two rows of stone rams, to the gate in the outer wall. Kothar spoke to a temple guard, who bore a large wicker shield and a copper-headed spear and wore a helmet of crocodile skin. Kothar turned back to Myron.

"Our luck holds," he said. "Your man is now First Prophet of Amon. This means that he is the most powerful Egyptian in the land of Khem."

The guard whistled up another guard, who led the party through the gate. The outer wall of the temenos was a rough square, more than six hundred paces on a side. Inside lay the main temple. This was in the form of a long rectangle, four hundred and fifty by one hundred and fifty paces.

However, the symmetry of this rectangle had long ago been spoilt by kings who haphazardly added more buildings and monuments, until the vast temenos had become a chaos of walls, columns, pylons, courts, temples, statues, obelisks, and shrines. The temple compound was like a city in itself. Small detached temples stood here and there outside the main mass and in the courts of the larger temples. Most of the walls were covered with painted carvings, which showed forgotten kings dispatching their foes and adoring their gods.

The soldier led them through a vast unfinished pylon inside the wall, through a colonnaded court above a hundred paces on a side, and into an immense roofed hall. At the entrance they gave up their cloaks, boots, and other garments of animal origin to the doorkeeper.

Here a forest of more than a hundred carven columns upheld the roof. The twelve central columns were so huge that six tall men, with arms outstretched, could scarcely close a ring about one of them. Bessas remarked:

"No artist, I, but I like the audience halls at Persepolis better. There the columns are not so thick that a man can see nought."

Myron said to Kothar: "I wonder they let us in here; we are not purified initiates."

"Fear not; this part is open to the public. It is a long way yet to the sacred areas."

They passed through a bewildering series of pylons, courts, and passages. Bessas said: "It must take a new priest a year just to learn his way around this barrack."

They were made to sit in an open court on a bench of tawny brick while the First Prophet, the high priest of Amon, completed his devotions. Shaven-headed priests hurried by. Egyptian laymen wandered past in low-voiced groups, sometimes staring at the travelers. There was no open hostility, because Myron and Bessas now wore kilts instead of their telltale Persian trousers. They were obviously foreigners, but in their nondescript garb they might have been from anywhere.

Myron waited with keen anticipation, his heart pounding. All his life he had heard of the ancient wisdom of Egyptian priests. Having, by this unexpected stroke of luck, gained access to the highest priest in Egypt, Myron thought that surely he should be able to pry out some of this hoarded wisdom. If anyone knew the answers to the riddles of the cosmos, it should be the First Prophet of Amon.

As the sun sank, they were led through more passages into a room in a subsidiary building, where a small, slight, shaven-headed man in a voluminous and elaborately pleated white linen vestment sat on an ivory chair. Myron first guessed the man to be about his own age. But when the man smiled, his face, previously smooth, sprang into a multitude of wrinkles that showed him to be much older.

"Peace," said the small man in good Aramaic. "I am pleased to welcome friends of my old friend Uni, whose career I have long followed. I was a mere officiant when he entered the priesthood. Had he remained here he might have risen far in the hierarchy, but duty called him to the foreign field. I hope some day he will come back; who drinks the water of the Nile will surely return thereto. Tell me more about him."

Myron told about Uni. Then Jed-hor said: "I thank you, my son. As one ages, the doings of friends of one's youth become of increasing interest. When did you leave Persepolis?"

"On the fourth of Nisanu, Your Holiness."

Jed-hor frowned in the effort to translate the date into the Eygptian calendar. "By the horns of Hat-hor, that is good time! Two months and a few days over."

Shimri said: "That is—that is the doing of Lord B-Bessas, who has driven us as Yehu drove his chariots."

Jed-hor continued: "You cannot maintain such a pace in the roadless south. But doubtless you have much to tell of your journey so far. We hold a small feast in honor of Bes within the hour; will you company with us?"

X   *The City of the Dead*

THE FEAST was held in the court of the small temple built by Rameses the Third to Mut, Amon, and Khons. Myron found himself next to a withered lady wearing a great golden gorget set with gems, which flashed crimson and green and purple. Introduced as the First Concubine of Amon, she turned out to be Jed-hor's wife. As she spoke nothing but Egyptian, Myron could not make small talk with her beyond the few words of that tongue that he had picked up. But the First Prophet, on the other side of the woman, conversed with Myron from time to time.

Several things about this banquet startled Myron. The first was the fact that the serving maids were nude, save for an unconcealing string of beads about the hips.

His next surprise occurred when one of the girls appeared with a silver tray. On this tray stood a number of conical objects, white with red tips, four or five digits high. The maiden, smiling prettily, confronted the First Prophet and planted one of the cones firmly on top of the high priest's head. She placed the second cone on the head of Jed-hor's wife, the third on the head of Bessas, the fourth on that of the Second Prophet of Amon, and the fifth on the head of Myron son of Perseus.

As the girl balanced the tray before Myron, he became aware of a strong perfume, which waxed even heavier when the cone was mashed down upon his hair. Rolling up his eyes, he asked Jed-hor:

"What *is* this, Your Holiness?"

"Perfumed fat," said the high priest. "Tip not your head, lest it fall off. It will soon melt and run down over your garments imparting heavenly odors unto them."

Although the idea of soaking his clothes with melted grease did not appeal to Myron, there was nothing he could do. The remaining diners received cones. Wine was passed and drunk to Bes. The diners sang a hymn as an orchestra of gauze-clad girls played the harp, the lyre, the lute, and the double pipe. Food appeared. The party became boisterously jolly.

Jed-hor drank wine from a golden cup set with beryls, sardonyxes, carbuncles, and smaragdi. He leaned around his wife to say to Myron: "Your Syrian guide, that what-is-his-name—Kothar—seems not to enjoy himself."

Myron, toying with his own plain pottery cup, glanced to where Kothar sat, eating little and watching the flitting forms of the naked maidens with glum disapproval. "He is a man of austere, ascetic nature, who hopes that his abstinence will gain him great magical powers. I think he is shocked by your conviviality."

"Bes is the god of mirth and merriment," said Jed-hor, "so it is only meet that we honor him with a gleesome party. When a man controls his lusts as strictly as your friend appears to do, the reason is not that he is strong, but that they are weak. He has not touched his fish, poor abject! We serve it to laymen and foreigners, albeit the rules of the priesthood do not let us eat it ourselves."

"Syrians do not eat fish either," said Myron. "As the five of us all come of different stock, each of us has some-

191

thing different that he cannot eat. Kothar will not eat fish or pigeon; Shimri will not consume pork."

"We eat no pork here," said Jed-hor, "save at the feast of Osiris and Khons."

"And *you*, sirrah," said Bessas, looking around past the priest at Myron, "won't drink healthy and delicious milk! So scoff not at others' foibles."

"Nor would you eat that savory octopus they served us in Marath," retorted Myron.

"I, eat that hideous sea monster? Ugh! It reminded me of that demon they kept in the pool in the temple in Takshasila."

Jed-hor commented: "That which seems but meet and proper to us may appear odd to our friends, eccentric to strangers, and barbarous to foreigners. Will you spend a few days in seeing the sights of Opet ere you proceed?"

Myron gave the priest a smile that was somewhat forced, because the scented grease, trickling down his face and neck, had begun to spot his only decent shirt. "What sights do you suggest, sir? This temple seems to me as wonderful as anything I have seen, from Persia to Egypt."

"Right and true a million times! No land surpasses Khem for monuments of antiquity. Ere you depart you must see our Hall of Priestly Statues. About twenty-five years ago, one of your clever Milesians—what was his name? Hek something."

"Hekataios the geographer?"

"I believe so. Thinking to impress us with the ancience of his tribal traditions and the splendor of his ancestry, he began to boast of his genealogy, asserting that his sixteenth ancestor in the direct line had been a god. So my father, who was then First Prophet, led this man into the hall and showed him three hundred and forty-five wooden statues of First Prophets, every one the son of his predecessor."

"What did Hekataios say to that?"

192

"Nought. What could he say? However, for the greatest sights—after this temple—you must cross the river to the City of the Dead, where stand many temples and palaces from the great days of Egypt. There the kings of yore lie buried—or rather, there they did lie buried until the villainous grave robbers plundered them." Jed-hor's beady eyes glared at Myron, like those of an angry snake. "If you would fain lay up credit with the gods and with all men of decent feelings, use your influence at the Persian court to have these tombs properly guarded. Now the satrap sends a couple of lazy spearmen to patrol, and these knaves find a sheltered spot and pass the night in drinking, gaming, and sleeping, allowing the accursed gangs to commit their vile depredations with impunity. May Mertseger sink her fangs into them! But I must not spoil your feast by ill-timed complaints, my friend. Whither are you bound?"

"Your Holiness, our destination is the sources of the Nile. Now, I am familiar with the tale of the two conical mountains, each with a fountain on top. But what more can you tell me about Kush and the unknown lands beyond?"

"Only that the pious priests of Amon of Meroê guide the government of Kush in its courses. Every century or so they send a legate hither to make certain that they still perform the immemorial rituals aright. I understand that they keep an admirable custom there. When the king begins to lose his powers, or if he turns out to be a bad man, the priests command him to slay himself, and this he invariably does. Who shall say that the Kushites are less enlightened than we? Now, man of Miletos, devise me of the court of King Xerxes. How fares the king in health and spirits?"

"That were difficult to say. The king leads a secluded life, rarely seen by such as me save at reviews and ceremonies. . . ."

Myron went on at some length about Xerxes. Although he was careful not to say anything that might be held against him, Jed-hor wrinkled up his aged face and said:

"Given time, pride and self-love can turn all the virtues into vices, as water dissolves a lump of salt."

Myron tried to drag the conversation back to things that concerned the expedition. He asked about the dragon of the Ishtar Gate, taking one of his sketches from his scrip to show Jed-hor. But the priest replied:

"Those lands harbor many strange beasts, surely. But for the details I answer not. Animals are out of my ken. Now, Master Myron, tell me of the king's sons Darius and Artaxerxes. Live they in amity or in enmity with each other and with their royal sire?"

Myron told of the characters of the princes, and Jed-hor commented: "Self-interest, acting in divergent directions, can in time make the bitterest foes of the firmest friends and the closest kinsmen."

"How about the people of Kush? Are they as faultless and virtuous as Homer asserts of the Ethiopians, which I take to be the same folk?"

"I have not read your Homer. But, from all I hear, the Kushites are but mortal men, and you know what they are. Besides, does not every virtue, carried to excess, become a vice? May the Hidden One preserve me from faultless men!"

"Another thing, sir. The problem of the shape of the earth has long beguiled your servant. Now, in traveling hither from Syria, I have observed that the constellation we call the Lesser Bear, which wheels about the celestial pole, circles lower and lower in the sky, the farther south we proceed. So the pole itself must be lower. And I have striven to imagine what form the earth could have to cause this change. If the earth were curved convexly, like a section of a sphere, this effect would ensue. But then we should find ourselves walking down a slope that becomes ever steeper, and the Nile would flow south instead of north."

194

"That were as impossible as that the sun should rise in the west!"

"No doubt; but what says the wisdom of the priests of Amon about these astronomical matters?"

"I know not; some effect of increasing distance from the pole, I suppose. You make me feel very ignorant, my Greek friend."

"I am sorry——"

The First Prophet cackled. "*Tsk, tsk;* apologize not. I, like other men, own up to minor failings in hope of convincing others that I have no major ones. Continue."

"Well then, what say the priestly archives about the shape of the earth?"

Jed-hor: "That the earth is a hollow oblong box, with mortals creeping about like ants on the floor thereof. However, I am not qualified to dispute such a matter. The exigencies of trying to please the gods, placate the Persian government, and guide the masses absorb what effort I have to give. Now tell me of Artabanus the minister. . . ."

Myron gave up, as it was plain that Jed-hor was not in the least interested in the shape of the earth, or the fauna of Africa, or any other general question, any more than the Phoenician merchants had been. Myron realized that the old man was no superhuman sage after all. Instead, Jed-hor was a shrewd and cynical politician, determined to wring from his guests every scrap of court gossip and rumor that could possibly help him in his bloodless but unending struggle with the Persian government.

So Myron cautiously talked of Persian politics with Jed-hor, while jugglers, singers, and naked dancers performed. Jed-hor spoke of many matters, and thus Myron learnt of the smashing victory which Kimon the Athenian had lately won over the forces of the Great King at the mouth of the Eurymedon, in Asia Minor.

Skhâ drank deeply, tried in vain to make an assignation with a dancer, and finally went to sleep in a corner. Bessas followed the dancers with burning gaze, while

195

Kothar ignored the entertainment to speak to his neighbors of spiritual matters.

The only untoward incident occurred when a young priest sitting opposite Shimri suddenly sprang to his feet, shook his fist at the Judaean, and poured out a flood of abusive Egyptian. Shimri sat in popeyed, open-mouthed astonishment. Jed-hor called out an order, and two other priests hustled the angry man out.

"Our humble apologies to our guests," said Jed-hor. "The young man drank his wine faster than was good for him. This deplorable conduct will be remembered when the time comes for his promotion. Now, Master Myron, tell me more of the affairs of court. If that of Xerxes be like others, there is usually a knot of the discontented who rally round an opponent of the minister or favorite of the moment; for hatred of favorites is nought but hope of favor. . . ."

After the party had broken up and the travelers had been led to pilgrims' quarters, Myron said: "Kothar, what happened between the priest and Shimri?"

"You know how Shimri spits as he speaks. He insisted upon talking to this priest, though neither could understand the other. And a tiny drop of spittle flew from the mouth of Shimri to the robe of the priest. To be touched by a foreigner, and worse yet by the spittle of a foreigner, rendered the priest unclean, so he must needs undertake a tedious ritual of purification. Hence the fellow was wroth."

"I can see how he might be. But what did the priest say?"

"I believe he called Shimri a flea-bitten sand dweller, a god-detested son of Seteh, and a spy of that dung-eating tomb robber Achaemenes, if you will pardon the expressions."

Bessas, who had overheard, gave a low rumble of laughter. "Demon land has no fury like that of a priest who is asked to pay taxes as ordinary folk must." He followed Myron into the cell set aside for the twain of them.

196

"How did you make out with old Jed-hor? He talked to you much more than to me, you garrulous Greek!"

Myron told of his bitter disappointment in the prophet's wisdom. Bessas clapped him on the back in a rough but not unkindly way. "It is even as I told you, man."

Some seek for truth in ancient, crumbling screeds,
While others would unravel priestly creeds;
But as for me, I look for wisdom true
In wine, in women, and on noble steeds!

"However," said Myron, "a useful thought occurred to me during our conversation." He repeated what Jed-hor had told him about the tombs of the kings across the river and the gangs of grave robbers that plundered them.

"Now," he said, "there may be a more hazardous pursuit than cutting off the ears of living kings, but if so I haven't heard of it. Could we not, however, get in touch with these grave robbers and arrange to buy an ear from the mummy of one of these long-dead kings? Thus we shall obtain at least one of the objectives of our quest."

Bessas' mouth fell open. "You have the wisdom of the lawgiver Oroxaeus, little man. Kothar!"

The Syrian put his head in the door. "Aye, Lord Bessas?"

"Come hither; I have a job for you. . . ."

As Bessas explained, Kothar's mouth turned down. "Ah, me! I forelooked an evening of quiet communion by spirit with a colleague in Hind. Instead, I must prowl through reeking dives and consort with unwashed ruffians."

"There is no help for it," said Bessas. "You speak fluent Egyptian, whereas we know only a few phrases like 'where is the latrine?' Withal, I suspect that, despite your fastidious pose, you have had more to do with the underworld than either of us. So be on your way!"

197

Next morning a red-eyed Kothar reported: "By the grace of the invisible spirits, I found the man you seek. His name is Tjay, and he plans to lead his gang tonight to the robbery of a tomb at the southern end of the Valley of Kings, as yet unplundered. When I told him what you sought, he demanded fantastic prices, but I chaffered him down to ten shekels for the royal ear. He does impose but one condition: that you and Myron accompany him on the raid."

Bessas frowned. "Why? It seems not in character, for any thief to discover to outsiders the source of his loot. I sense a hidden gin in this jungle."

"The reason Tjay gives is that he would have you satisfied that the ear is forsooth that of an authentic king and not of some royal cook or second butler. Myself, I suspect that he wishes your strong arms in case of conflict. These gangs parcel out the City of the Dead among themselves, assigning plundering grounds by treaty, with metes and bounds like sovran nations. But, like sovran nations, any gang will poach on the territories of another if it thinks it can do so without scathe. Tjay's band, being small, needs reinforcement for such a razzia."

Bessas drew his sword and tested the edge with his thumb. "O Myron, is your blade good and keen?"

"Sharp enough to shave with, did I wish to adopt the Egyptian fashion," said Myron lugubriously. "Had I known what I was getting into, I should have been less ready with suggestions."

Kothar smiled maliciously. "Even a fool, when he keeps his peace, is accounted wise, and he who shuts his mouth is esteemed a man of sound judgment."

"Take a look at your sword, too, Kothar," said Bessas.

The Syrian's smile vanished. "Oh, but good my lord! I had no intention of going on this foray. I am quite unsuited to such nocturnal desperatisms."

"Natheless, you shall come, if only for your command of the Khemite speech. I would not have us fall into

198

some ambush and then try to work out tactics with friend Tjay by sign language."

Kothar paled, sank to his knees, and kissed the hem of Bessas' tunic. "Spare your slave! I will do whatever you command, but not this! You know not what you ask!"

"What do I ask of you?"

"It is not the knives of rival robbers, or the spears of the guardians, or the staves of the priests that I fear, but the sinister supernatural influences that hover over the City of the Dead. You cannot sense them, but to my occult insight they appear as plain as if they were a vast black cloud of bats, sweeping back and forth over that fell necropolis. I feel them; they call to my soul: Come, Kothar bar-Malko, come within reach of our claws!"

The man seemed so genuinely terrified that Myron, whose sympathies were easily touched, might have let him off. Besides, despite his skepticism about spooks, he felt his own viscera crawl with fear at the Syrian's words. But Bessas was inexorable.

"You care not if these demons bear off my soul and Myron's to some unknown hell!" he growled. "My *fravashi* likes this enterprise neither, but I know my duty. Well, useless though you be with a sword, you still know more spells and other magical antics than the rest of us. So you shall come along and recite manthras to hold your fiendly hosts at bay, whilst Myron and I cope with mundane threats from the material plane."

A swarm of small boats, each flying a single papyrus sail, ferried passengers from Opet to the City of the Dead. As the Nile was at ebb, Bessas, Myron, and Kothar had to jump out into ankle-deep water, wade ashore, and walk over a long stretch of half-dried mud before reaching the bank of the river. After scrambling up a low bluff by a narrow sandy path, they found themselves above the high-water mark of the river.

Ahead, a broad plain spread out before them, dotted

with temples, shrines, palaces, and hundreds of huts of temple servants. Plots of cultivation lay amidst the buildings, but the winter's crops had long since been harvested, leaving brown stubble. About a league away, black against a sky still banded with vermilion and gold and emerald from the departed sun, rose the ramparts of the Libyan desert.

Other visitors also came and went. Egyptians, most of them boys, swarmed around with torches to sell and asses to rent. Kothar, snapping: *"Ennen! Ruek!"* at them, strode through and on across the plain.

The sky darkened; bats whirred overhead. The buffs and browns of daylight darkened to purples and grays. Pilgrims lighted their torches, making orange splashes in the twilight. The Bactrian and his companions crossed a rickety bridge that spanned a small arm of the Nile, now but a dried-up moat lined with black mud cracked into polygonal patterns. The two colossal seated statues of the third Amenhotep, faintly washed with the silvery sheen of the rising moon, towered up on their left against the awakening stars.

"The priests inform me," said Kothar, "that to see the City of the Dead in its greatest glory we should have come here a few centuries back, when wealth was to hand for the upkeep of all these establishments. Now, because of the rapacity of the Persian officials—so they say —some of the temples are reduced to a mere handful of priests, and some have been abandoned to the lizard, the jackal, and the stone-stealing peasant. This distresses the priests full sore."

Myron murmured: "While I love great art of whatever nation, I imagine that the common people whose substance was squeezed out of them to build these fine god-houses might feel a bit differently."

Kothar: "Of course, to a scoffing unbeliev—— *Yai!*" A bat, swooping close past his head, caused him to leap and yelp. "Being doomed to this rash undertaking, I strive to pass it off bravely. But this is hard, because only

200

I understand the full depth of the peril into which we are rushing. You, who comprehend such matters not, can afford to be fearless."

They walked along the path that led to the great mortuary temple of Queen Hatshepsut, a vast, severely symmetrical pile of monumental stairways and endless colonnades. Behind the temple towered a jagged cliff, whose sharp spires soared a hundred cubits above the plain. People, cloaked against the chill of the desert night, passed them coming and going. Egyptian pilgrims, foreign sightseers, and shaven priests flitted by like ghosts. Voices were hushed as the darkness deepened. The torches looked like a surging swarm of orange fireflies.

"By the time we reach this tomb," said Myron, "my feet will be so sore that I could not flee from a toddling babe, let alone from a man or a demon."

"Keep your voice down," said Bessas. "Some know the Syrian speech. 'Tis but a furlong farther."

The temple of Hatshepsut no longer boasted a corps of resident priests. The properties on which the temple relied for support had disappeared by alienation and confiscation centuries before. Sightseers prowled about the deserted fane, which still stood in good repair. A pair of voluble Hellenes were energetically scratching their names in the limestone of one of the square pillars. One scratched with the point of a dagger while the other held a torch.

"That is the sort of thing that incenses the priests," said Kothar. "If those saucy knaves do not live to rue their insolence towards the great queen's ghost, I shall be much astonished."

He led his companions to the right. At the northern extremity of the mortuary temple, where the sides of the half bowl in which the temple stood began to slope up sharply, a voice hissed out of the darkness.

Kothar whispered introductions. "This is Tjay," he said. "He will lead us to the top of the cliff, where his men await."

201

"Do you mean we shall scale *that?*" said Myron, almost in a squeak, as he pointed to the cliff.

"Certes; it would not do to take the well-traveled road to the Valley of Kings. This is a mountain path, known to few. Let us be on our way."

Bessas spoke quietly to Myron: "If you are not used to mountaineering, keep behind me, watch what I do, and don't look down. I have done enough climbing in the mountains of Gandara to have the hang of it."

The climb, though not quite so dreadful as Myron had feared, was bad enough for one not used to it. At the top he panted: "Let me—let me catch my breath. Now I know what Pindaros means by the term 'age always hateful.' "

Four more shadows shimmered into view in the moonlight. Kothar explained: "These are Tjay's men. Two others have gone to the temple of Seti to raise a disturbance and draw the guards thither. Come along."

"You mean—you mean we are not there yet?"

"Gods, no! The tomb is another half-league."

The Valley of Kings was a wide-spreading complex of troughs, ravines, and bays. Myron panted, slipped, and stumbled behind his companions over knife-edged ridges and up and down slopes fit only for goats. Kothar, walking in front of him, stopped so suddenly that Myron bumped into him. The Syrian squealed and seized Myron's arm with frenetic force. The guide was trembling.

"What is it?" said Myron.

"Do you see?" Kothar pointed across the rock hills. "It is the cobra goddess Mertseger, who guards the tombs of the dead. She lies in wait for us!"

Myron peered. Was it a trick of the moonlight, or did a long, dark, serpentine shape indeed sprawl across the landscape? Were those a pair of low-hanging stars, or the eyes of the divine serpent?

For an instant Myron almost screamed and ran. Then, by a colossal effort of will, he blinked and shook his

202

head. The vast ophidian form vanished—or did it whip out of sight?

"There's n-nothing there," he chattered. "It is all your im-imagination. And why does she not assail these other miscreants——"

"Blast you two, hasten!" hissed Bessas.

The moon was almost overhead when they came to a pile of tailings, which had been dug away to reveal the entrance to a tomb. This tomb opened into the side of a ravine.

Myron's scalp tingled as he looked into the black aperture. The thieves murmured. Two of them fastened their mantles over the entrance to make a curtain. The others slipped in, motioning Bessas and his companions to follow.

Inside, inky blackness engulfed them until it was shattered by the sparks of flint on steel. Presently the grave robbers had a couple of tiny pottery lampions burning and filling the tomb with the stench of castor oil.

The flickering yellow light revealed that they stood at the head of a shallow flight of steps—or rather, two parallel flights of steps with a sloping plane between. White stucco covered the side walls. At the foot of this double stairway was the main entrance to the tomb. A heavy stone door, already forced, now lay at an angle against one side of the tomb corridor.

Kothar whispered: "It seems that this tomb lies in the territory claimed by Imisib, a rival gangster. Imisib discovered the tomb and planned to loot it at leisure, but one of his henchmen blabbed. So Tjay hopes to clean out as much as he can by one quick raid. Naturally, he is queasy lest Imisib's gang trap us here and cut us all off."

"Now he tells us!" muttered Bessas. "I do not suppppose these things have back doors?"

"Nay. Now must I perform my part, for you stand in danger of other than earthly origins. The gods have mercy upon us!"

From under his cloak, Kothar produced a small censer and a bronzen sistrum. He lit the censer from one of the lamps, and a horrid sulphurous stench commingled with the smells of castor oil and of musty antiquity. He swung the censer and shook the sistrum, which gave a shrill unmusical clank. Again and again he sounded the instrument, uttering exorcisms in a low vibrant voice. At last he spoke in Egyptian to the grave robbers, who filed down the steps.

Over the main doorway was painted a scene showing two goddesses worshiping the divine sun. Inside the doorway were other painted scenes: a winged goddess and a god investing the king with divine powers. Masses of picture writing ran along the wall above and below these scenes. Bright-hued serpent-headed vultures flew along the ceiling. Kothar made one of the thieves hold a lamp still, near the writing, while he scanned the little processions of men, beasts, and plants.

"This man was truly a king, albeit a king of small importance," said the Syrian. "There is his name: Siptah."

Myron trailed the others along the silent corridor, which sloped down for a few reeds,* then ran level, then descended again. A plethron** and a half from the entrance, the corridor opened out into a broad square chamber, over sixteen cubits on a side. Four square pillars supported the ceiling. Except for the central aisle between the pillars, the chamber was packed and stacked with the dead king's personal effects. The lamplight shone upon an incredible treasure.

There were bedsteads of ivory and ebony; gilded couches; whole chariots of gilded wood; chariot wheels and poles trimmed with gold; cedar-wood chests; bronzen coffers inlaid with fayence; chairs of gold and ebony; alabaster lamps and vases; cups and dishes of gold and silver; swords and daggers with inlaid sheaths, golden hilts, and crystal pommels; gold-headed, jeweled walk-

* 1 reed = 10½ feet.
** 1 plethron = 100 feet.

204

ing sticks; lapis-lazuli cosmetic jars; an ebony shrine on which was coiled a jewel-eyed golden cobra; bows and staves bedight with golden filigree; statuettes of gold and copper and malachite; scepters, riding crops, footstools, headrests, crowns, gorgets, necklaces, amulets, pendants, bracelets, pectorals, fans, rings, chains, embroidered robes, gilded sandals, inlaid gaming boards. . . .

The gleam of gold and silver, the sparkle of jewels, crystal, and colored glass, and the glow of ivory, fine stone, and rare woods made Myron's head swim. He muttered:

"By Herakles, if this be the hoard of a minor king, I can hardly imagine the tomb of a Rameses or an Amenhotep! A man could buy a kingdom with a tithe of this stuff."

"Not so easy," grunted Bessas. "Remember, these rogues must dispose of their plunder through fences, who'll mulct them of most of their gains. And the fences in turn must deal with other shady characters who won't give them full price. So, when all is done, the wealth thus liberated will be spread about quite widely."

"The spirits have smiled upon us," said Kothar, "for only rarely do the robbers come upon such a hoard as this. Most of the tombs were plundered long ago, during the ages when the land of Khem was sunken in anarchy. Now Tjay wants us in the burial chamber."

From the pillared hall, the corridor sloped down again and then ran level for nearly a plethron more before it reached the burial chamber, almost as large as the pillared hall and, like it, stacked with royal possessions. Here, the lid of the alabaster sarcophagus had already been pried off by earlier burglars, and Tjay's thieves were now lifting out the painted wooden mummy case. The lid came up with a creak of ancient, bone-dry wood, and there lay the mummy of King Siptah.

Next they pried out the mummy, which, over its wrappings of linen, was bound with bands of gold. These the thieves stripped off with practiced adroitness.

205

Kothar said: "Tjay says, if we want the king's ear, we must unwrap the mummy cloths. They will be otherwise occupied."

The tomb robbers were expertly going through the chambers. Two held a cloak by its corners while the others tossed into it the objects combining the most value with the least bulk.

"Hold the mummy crosswise on the mummy case," said Kothar, "whilst I unwrap the head."

Round and round went Kothar's hands, unwinding the crumbling yellowed cerements. The little oil lamp, flickering from the floor, cast weird shadows against the walls. These shadows reminded Myron unpleasantly of the beast-headed gods of ancient Khem. He had to clench his jaw to keep his teeth from chattering. When he should have been observing every detail of the surroundings for future reference, he found that his mind could focus on nothing save an intense desire to be gone.

"Behold King Siptah!" said Kothar, unwrapping the last layer of linen strips. Beneath them transpired the sunken brown face of Siptah, the lips drawn slightly back to expose the teeth in a faint, sardonic grin. On the king's shaven head rested a close-fitting golden headdress, with a cobra rearing its head in front and a vulture's wings coming down over the ears at the sides.

Kothar gingerly pulled off the headgear, whose thin gold gave out faint creaking and rattling sounds. He took out his knife, looked about uneasily, uttered a cantrip, and began to cut.

"This stuff cuts like wood," he muttered.

The robbers completed their work in the burial chamber and left. From the pillared chamber came faintly the clank of metallic objects tossed into the grave robbers' cloak. The three in the burial chamber were alone, save for the mummy.

"There you are," said Kothar at last. He handed the hard, shriveled, dark-brown ear to Bessas, who turned it over and dropped it into his scrip.

"What do you now?" rumbled the giant.

"I am cutting off his other ear," said Kothar. "If one ear will make a mighty magic for Ostanas, I see not why the other should not do the like for me."

"Well, hurry!" said Bessas. "I am fain to leave this accursed place."

The robbers had moved away from the treasure chambers and towards the entrance to the tomb. The sounds of their movements came more faintly to the travelers' ears.

A shout echoed down the corridor. Then came a chorus of outcries, a trampling of feet, and a clash of steel. Torchlight flickered far up the passageway.

Kothar leaped up from his task. He dashed out the door and up the corridor. Bessas and Myron, drawing their swords, started after but met him coming back, his visage working and his eyes large and luminous in the gloom.

"It is Imisib's gang!" he hissed. "They have trapped us! Mertseger has had her revenge!"

"How many?" said Bessas.

"I know not; perhaps a score."

"We'll pile furniture across the corridor——"

"Nay! That were but to defer our doom. Come back to the burial chamber with me. Do as I say!"

The Syrian's voice rang with an authority that Myron had never heard in it before. Wondering what scheme Kothar had in mind, Myron followed the others back to the burial chamber, on whose floor the little lamp still burnt.

"Help me to drop the mummy case back into the sarcophagus," said Kothar. "That is right. Now place King Siptah on the floor behind it, so."

Kothar took the golden headdress and put it on his own head. Sounds of combat rolled closer; a man uttered a long, high scream.

Kothar picked up a bunch of mummy wrappings from the floor and wrapped them about his own head, beginning just below the eyes. When his face was unrecognizable, he secured the strip in place. He wrapped his cloak about his body below the armpits and lowered himself into the mummy case.

"Get down behind the sarcophagus!" he whispered. "If I say 'run,' that means that the others will have fled; run after them and mingle with the fugitives outside. If I say 'fight,' sell your lives as dearly as you can. Now crouch down out of sight and hold your tongues."

Sounds of combat from the corridor died away. Soon there were no more noises of scuffling, no more yells of stricken men. Footsteps approached; heavy breathing sounded from the entrance to the burial chamber. Myron, not daring to look up, could imagine a group of ragged tomb robbers, panting and sweating and holding bloody knives, clustered in the entrance, while those behind peered over the shoulders of those in front.

From the sarcophagus came a sound of motion. Kothar sat slowly up and pointed a skinny hand towards the entrance to the chamber. His voice, unnaturally deep and hollow, boomed out in the syllables of the Egyptian tongue:

"Who dares to disturb the rest of King Siptah?"

For the length of three heartbeats there was utter silence. Then piercing shrieks broke from the thieves. With a wild scramble, they bolted back up the corridor.

"Run!" said Kothar, leaping out of the sarcophagus.

Myron ran. On the floor of the corridor lay a couple of knives dropped by the thieves in their flight. Beyond them lay the bodies of two of Tjay's men.

One of the cloaks in which they had been gathering loot lay near them, its precious load scattered across the floor and gleaming faintly in the light reflected from the burial chamber. Myron felt precious relics of antiquity crunch beneath his boots. He raced through the pillared hall, on whose floor an abandoned torch still glowed. He ran up the long passage and bounded up the steps.

The three tumbled out of the entrance into the moonlight that bathed the ravine, and into the milling, gibbering crowd of tomb robbers. One of these addressed a question in Egyptian to Myron, then looked past the Milesian with wide-eyed astonishment. The man pointed and cried out.

Myron, turning, saw what was amiss. Kothar still wore the golden headdress of King Siptah. In an instant he, Kothar, and Bessas formed a knot at the entrance to the tomb, swords out, while the thieves ringed them with drawn knives.

"We shall attack," growled Bessas. "I can cut our way through these curs, if you two will guard my back. Follow me! Verethraghna aid us!"

Bessas leaped with the speed of a charging leopard, his sword a silvery blur in the moonlight. One thief went down, slashed to death. The others tried to close around the Bactrian but were driven back by the thrusts and slashes of Myron and Kothar. Myron caught one stab in the folds of the cloak wrapped around his left arm. As his leathern corselet stopped another, he felt his sword cut meat.

Cursing his age, Myron found he was panting and falling behind the other two. His heart pounding painfully, he whirled and slashed in a frenzy of effort.

Then came a distraction. A band of white-clad men came running up the ravine, pointing and shouting. In a twinkling the fight at the head of the ravine broke up. The steep stony landscape was dotted with fleeing figures, pursued by shaven-headed, linen-clad men with swords.

"This way!" cried Bessas, leading his companions with long bounds up the mountain trail by which they had come.

The Bactrian set a fearful pace. Myron stumbled gasping after his leader, never quite losing sight of him but never catching up. Behind, the sounds of flight and pursuit died away. When silence and solitude once more reigned in the Valley of Kings, Bessas halted, dragging his forearm across his forehead. Myron gasped:

"Who—who were those men—who arrived—at the end?"

"A patrol of priests, trying to put down grave robbery," said Kothar.

Myron said: "O Bessas, however did you remember the way? I was hopelessly lost before I had followed this trail for a bowshot."

Bessas' white teeth gleamed in the moonlight. "My mind may not be up to such flights of the spirit as Kothar's nor yet such feats of intellect as yours, but I have enough wit to pay heed to where I put my feet! Kothar, in the name of the Sleepless One, take off that crown ere we meet another body!"

Kothar doffed the object and hid it under his cloak. "You are right. If I walked into the temple of Amon wearing this, it might give rise to questions. It might even be deemed in bad taste!"

XI The Isle of the Elephant

SOUTHWARD, league upon league, stretched the dusty road to Kush. It followed the broad blue rippling ribbon of the Nile, with its verdant margins of palm and papyrus, its strips and plots of farmland, and beyond these the tawny bluffs that marked the metes of the desert.

South of Opet, the valley opened out for a space. The air became hotter. At night, unknown constellations wheeled across the southern sky, and from the river came the grunting of the hippopotamus and the bellowing of the bull crocodile. The people became darker of hue and blunter of feature.

The road worsened. Myron and his companions showed a nervous awareness of the fact that the hardest part of their journey would soon be upon them. Back in Asia, time, money, and possibilities had seemed unlimited.

Now the journey had taken substantial bites out of time and resources.

The thought came into conversation again and again: Suppose the dragon proved uncatchable? Or suppose it lived somewhere other than at the headwaters of the Nile? Or suppose it did not exist?

"In that case," said Bessas firmly, "we have come on a sleeveless errand. We shall find out in due time, and meanwhile the next man who brings up the subject shall be ducked in the Nile!"

"B-b-but Chief!" sputtered Shimri. "If there be no—if there be no sirrush, what shall we do? Trick out a crocodile with false ears? Or——"

"Throw him in!" said Bessas. And it was done.

While the beasts of burden renewed their strength by eating, Bessas spent hours in practicing sword strokes and archery and in bullying the others into doing likewise.

Myron worked on his journal. He had bought a roll of papyrus, but he found that he soon had covered all of one side of the roll with writing and had to start on the back.

When not eating, Shimri asked foolish questions, told pointless jokes, and uttered loud meaningless laughs. On the other hand, being dexterous, he mended not only harness but also personal gear and garments.

Skhâ cheerfully fetched and carried. The rigors of the journey had banished some of the fat from his tubby form. He told more tales of the amatory exploits of his great-uncle Mizai, who, if the Karian was to be believed, must have left descendants in half a hundred countries.

Kothar, during this time, withdrew into lengthy silences. Sometimes his companions overheard him at night, praying to unknown gods or conversing with unseen presences. He questioned his fellow travelers about their dreams, which were many and vivid.

Bessas, for instance, dreamt that he was impaled on a stake, while a dragon tore at him, all the while uttering endearments in his mother's voice. But whatever the dream, Kothar's interpretation was the same.

211

"The gods are trying to warn us," he would say. "Supernatural beings from the world of spirits menace us. You must put your trust in me."

Dust devils appeared over sandy stretches beside the endless river, as if pursuing the travelers. After Kothar wrought a mighty incantation against them, they went away for a while.

The local Egyptian dialects began to give Kothar trouble. When Bessas asked him if he had ever been this far south before, he gave evasive replies until Bessas caught him by the front of his robe and roared:

"May the Corpse Fiend crunch you up! I want the truth, by Mithra!"

"I have in sooth been here," murmured the Syrian, "but in previous lives, not in this one."

This led to an argument on reincarnation. Bessas had heard much of it in India; and Myron said: "I am told that a philosopher of Samos, one Pythagoras, held such a doctrine."

"It's an idea," said Bessas, "but I see not what good it does you to have lived before if you cannot remember your previous lives. You would only make all the same stupid mistakes over again."

"Perchance you mortals cannot remember your previous lives," said Kothar.

"Meaning that you can, eh?"

The guide smiled enigmatically.

On the sixteenth of Simanu, the bluffs closed in until there were only narrow strips of verdure along the river. The Nile widened. Islands, large and small, rose from its placid surface and split it into many channels.

The town of Swenet appeared, hemmed in between the river and the bare buff-colored cliffs. In the market place they saw burly, shaven, linen-clad Egyptians; black-brown, leather-capped Nubians; mop-haired, surly black Bugaitae and Ophirites from the Red Sea; slender and voluble Dankalas from the Cataracts; and Kushites who

212

had brought hides, tusks, and plumes up from the South to trade.

The Kushites were slight, black-skinned men in kilts of cloth or leather. Some had a strip of the skin of a yellow wildcat or other beast wound turbanwise around a mass of curly black hair. Every one had a set of tribal scars cut in his cheeks.

Kothar learnt in the market place that the satrap held court in his palace on the island of Yeb, a bowshot from the waterfront. Thither they took their way. At the ferry landing, Myron grasped Bessas' arm, saying:

"Well, grind me to sausage and feed me to Kerberos; look at those! We haven't seen them since we left Memphis."

He referred to a number of dromedaries, which lay in the sun and rhythmically moved their jaws. Among them squatted or lay a dozen skirted Arabs. These were easily distinguished from the Egyptians and Nubians by their slender build, sharp birdlike features, hawk noses, and pointed beards. They stank of rancid fat, which glistened on their long black hair. Some conversed in low tones; some stared blankly; some of them knitted caps or socks; some slept in patches of shade.

As Kothar approached the group, the Arabs raised their heads with a motion that made Myron think of snakes. Their expressions were sullen and wary; their dark eyes glittered. Hands strayed towards the hilts of daggers. But when the Syrian spoke to them in their own tongue, teeth flashed in sudden smiles.

"They say," said Kothar, "that they think the satrap has lured their shaykh to Yeb and treacherously seized him there. Short of causing the waters to part, as a Judean magician is once said to have done, they cannot think how to rescue him. They beg that the great rich lord"—he nodded at Bessas—"put in a word for their chief when he gets to the island."

"Who is this chief?" asked Bessas.

"Zayd ibn-Harith, shaykh of the Banu Khalaf."

213

"Tell them we'll do what we can. This boat looks fairly sound; make me a bargain with the boatman, Kothar. Skhâ and Shimri, stay here."

While they waited for Kothar to complete his haggle with the boatman, they were startled by unearthly shrieks from a nearby house. When they asked about this, they were told the noise was made by black boys captured by slave raiders, who were being castrated before being sent north to serve as eunuchs in the harems of Persian lords.

Myron winced as this explanation unfolded. "I always thought a eunuch a figure of fun, but I suppose that to the victim it is quite as dreadful a tragedy as the tale of Xerxes' brother Masistes."

"My dear old friend," said Bessas, "you are really too kindhearted for this rough, rude world, one of whose laws is that the strong shall rule and exploit the weak. Since we cannot change the world, let us make sure that we be counted amongst the strong."

The satrap's palace and other houses and temples lay on the isle, half hidden by a jungly growth of palm trees. Before the palace stood a pair of soldiers from Yeb's Judaean garrison: burly, black-bearded men in corselets of lizard mail.

Inside the palace was noise and turmoil. A pair of Judaean guards held by the arms a tall, thin old man with a long gray beard, wearing an Arabian robe and head shawl and silver hoops in his ears. Two more held a slender veiled woman. Both captives struggled and shouted. Several others in the room, including a trio of Nubians and the heavily rouged little man on the satrapal throne, were also shouting.

The small man at last leaped up, shaking his fists above his head, and screamed, "Quiet!" in Persian. Another man, an Egyptian from his appearance, yelled, "Silence!" in Egyptian and Aramaic.

The noise continued, however, until an accident inter-

214

rupted it. The small painted man, in his agitation, stood on the seat of his throne. While hopping and shouting from this point of vantage, he caught his foot in his cloth-of-gold embroidered robe and fell to the dais on which the throne stood.

An awful silence descended upon the chamber. Soldiers and litigants looked uneasily at one another, as if momentarily fearing a massacre of all so unfortunate as to have witnessed the downfall of the satrap's dignity. The Egyptian leaped to help the small man up and dust him off. The latter, cherry-red of face, glared for half an ush about the room. At last, in a strangled voice, he said:

"Can anybody here speak both Arabic and Persian?" The Egyptian repeated the question in Aramaic.

"I can," said Kothar.

"Then," said the Egyptian, "in the name of the First Ennead, do! Be our interpreter. Our regular interpreter has been devoured by the crocodiles; His Lordship speaks nought but Persian; and our prisoners know neither Aramaic nor Egyptian to speak of."

"Who are you, anyway?" said the satrap.

Kothar introduced himself and his fellow travelers.

"Oh," said Astes, satrap of Kushia. "You should not have come in unannounced. But my usher had to leave his post to help out with this devil's dance. So My Excellency will pardon the affront. Ask this old sand thief what became of the young man who spoke some civilized languages."

Kothar repeated the question. After Shaykh Zayd had spoken, the Syrian explained:

"He says the clan held an all-night dance the night before last to celebrate the fullness of the moon. And this youth became so overwrought with the joy of the dance that he sought to lay lustful hands upon the shaykh's daughter——"

"This hussy here?"

"Aye, my lord. So, says the shaykh, there was nought to do but cut his throat."

215

"Ha!" snarled Astes. "Nought to do but cut his throat, eh? Who does he think he is, to go cutting people's throats? The satrap? But let us get on with the current case. Say unto him: These Nubians, from the Fifty-League Oasis west of the Second Cataract, aver that, two moons ago, the Banu Khalaf rode out of the desert and fell upon the Nubians who dwelt in the oasis. Many they slew, for the Nubians were taken unawares and adread at the sight of the camels, which they had never seen before. Hence they could not fight so stoutly as is their wont. Of those who failed to escape, the Arabs put all the men to the sword and made slaves of the women and children. How answers he?"

There ensued a long dialogue between Kothar and Shaykh Zayd. At last the Syrian said:

"Skaykh Zayd replies as follows: O great governor, protector of the poor, lion of righteousness, camel of the province——"

"Yes, yes, omit all that. Get to the answer."

"Well, sir, he says that he did but carry out Your Highness' commands."

"What! By the beams of Mah, is he mad? I never commanded him to go about enslaving and murdering the Great King's subjects."

"The shaykh explains thus: Last year he was driven out of his grazing grounds in the land of Midian by a band of treacherous, murderous, bloodthirsty villains called Lihyanites. So, finding no other neighbors weak enough to overcome and despoil of their lands, he led the Banu Khalaf into Egypt.

"In Midian the tribe had eked out its living by hiring out to merchants, to carry their goods on its camels. Since he found that the camel was almost unknown in Egypt, the shaykh has sought for some part of the land of Khem where he could use his beasts to advantage. His gods, he says, revealed to him that the trade routes running south from Swenet offered the best possibilities, as they pass

216

through difficult desert country and are now plied only by a few hardy farers on asses or afoot.

"During his travels he learnt that, ere he began to ply these routes, he must needs get leave from the satrap. Wherefore he waited upon Your Excellency."

"All true," said Astes. "But what has it to do with his seizure of the Fifty-League Oasis?"

"We are coming to that, sir. Receiving Your Highness' gracious permission, he sought out oases along the routes in question. As a successful caravan business depends upon control of the oases, he says that you must have meant him to seize these oases, else why would you have sent him forth? To perish in the desert?"

Astes again turned dangerously red but merely said: "Continue."

"Discovering that the Fifty-League Oasis was inhabited by a handful of wretched, stinking, cowardly Nubian peasants——"

"Liar! Thief! Murderer!" howled the Nubians until quieted by shouts from the satrap.

"——the Banu Khalaf naturally took control of the oasis, as the gods plainly meant such a natural feature to be under the rule of those best fitted to use it. As for enslaving the surviving Nubae, that is but just, as they lost the battle; whereas, had they been as good men as the Banu Khalaf, they would either have defeated them or died fighting. And now, says Shaykh Zayd, how can Your Excellency eat bread and salt with a man, and entice him to this isle with promises of rewards, and then treacherously seize him and try him, as if he were a mere slave or peasant?"

"*He* accuses *me?*" screamed Astes. "To the House of the Lie with him! Throw the insolent scoundrel into a cell, and his daughter, too! I will dispose of this case later, when I have thought up a fitting punishment for their villainy." Still fuming, he turned to Bessas' company. "Now, you other people. What do you want, you great lout?"

217

"Did you speak to me, sir?" said Bessas, raising his bushy brows.

"Certes! Whom thought you that I spoke to?"

Bessas bit his lips with anger but, calmly enough, told of his mission. "I have here a letter from the Great King, signed by Artabanus, asking the help of all satraps. I also have a letter to Your Highness from the lord Achaemenes, asking that we be sped on our way to Meroê——"

"Bugger Achaemenes!" cried Astes. "You may not go."

"Not go to Meroê, my lord?"

"No, not go to Meroê. You would have to reach the Kushite outpost of Napata, and there have been raids and forays all along the bend of the Nile around Napata. It is a virtual undeclared war. If you go blundering about there, you will be slain either by mistake by our own troops or as Persian spies by the wild Kushites, and I shall be blamed."

"But, sir, the Great King commanded me——"

"The Great King knows not how things are in Kushia. You may either settle down here until order is restored, or return whence you came."

"But, my lord, I have another letter from the Great King to the king of Kush——"

"It is I who decide here, and I have decided that you shall not go. Dare you to question my decision, sirrah?"

"Nay, but——"

"No buts or ifs, you hairy barbarian! What My Lordship asserts, so shall it be! The audience is ended; you may go."

Astes swept out, leaving Bessas and his fellow travelers gaping.

Myron was sitting with Kothar in the tavern of Yeb, sipping a cup of heavy wine sweetened with date sirup and playing tjau. Bessas came in with one of the Judaean soldiers, whom he presented to the players:

"This is my friend, Deputy Captain Yehosha, whom I asked to have a drink with us."

218

The Judaean was a man of Bessas' age, shorter by half a head but fully as broad and brawny, with a large hooked nose and a flowing black beard. Both he and Bessas had evidently been drinking for some time already. Yehosha clapped Myron heavily on the back, saying:

"Who wins? Oh, I see, you do. You will have no chance, Master Kothar, so long as you leave your dogs scattered about the board in irregular groups, whilst your foe gathers his into a solid phalanx." He spoke fluent Aramaic, though with an odd accent.

"I resign," said Kothar glumly. "The spiritual forces fight against me today."

Myron drank. "I merely apply the lesson I learnt when I was trained as a *hoplites* in Miletos, long ago, namely: that a force of well-armored spearmen can repel any other troops in the world while they keep their formation—as the Athenians proved at Marathon."

"You Hellenes never cease boasting of that little border skirmish," said Bessas. "At that, the Athenians would have been smashed like a plover's egg beneath a horse's hoof if Darius' silly generals had not misused the world's best cavalry by making them fight on foot."

Myron said: "Why not tell Xerxes to challenge the Athenians to a return match, with everybody mounted this time? I can just hear the clatter of armored Athenians falling off their nags." He turned to Yehosha. "Didn't I see you at the palace this morning?"

"Aye; your servant had charge of the Nubae." The Judaean grinned. "How like you our little wasp of a satrap?"

"My dear sir, I have encountered many governors and other officials, but never one like this. Is he always in such a rage?"

"Usually." Yehosha lowered his voice. "Astes has three reasons for being wroth just now. One: he is fain to be a hero, so he tried to lead a squadron in person on the Kushite frontier, a fortnight ago; got ambushed and lost half his force. Two: he especially hates all large, tall men

219

like Master Bessas. And three: he is exasperated by the case of the Fifty-League Oasis, because neither plaintiff nor defendant has any wealth that the satrap can extort in return for a favorable judgment. These poor Nubians own nought but a few iron hoes, while the Arabs have only a few hundred mangy camels, which have no value here because the Egyptians fear the beasts."

With a faraway look, Bessas muttered: "On the northern frontiers, if a man spoke to me as has this unmannerly little knave, I'd break his neck."

"Many feel as you do." The Judaean smote his broad chest, so that the bronzen scales jangled. "*Hoy!* The great Yahveh must be wroth with us, to send us such governors. The one before this was drunk all the time, and the one before him slept all the time. This one is not only arrogant and ill-tempered, but also has his hand in everybody's purse. Truly we get the dregs of the Persian Court."

Bessas said: "I suppose the king cannot find good men who will take such an out-of-the-way post. This rascal is doubtless the brother-in-law of some member of the Council of Seven, who must be taken care of somehow—preferably far from Persepolis."

"Tell me," said Myron, "how came a garrison of Judaeans to be stationed here, so far from their native land?"

Yehosha replied: "It started long ago, when a king named Psamatik ruled Egypt. Some say he invaded Judaea, seized thousands of our folk, and settled them here as a shield against the Kushites. But we have been here for generations, so that the Isle of the Elephant is home to us."

"Is that what Yeb means?"

"Aye; though whether because the beast once roamed hereabouts, or because the Kushites fetch ivory hither to trade, I know not."

Myron asked about the sirrush, showing his sketches. Yehosha stroked his beard and said:

220

"I cannot aver that such a beast has come within our ken. True, many strange creatures are said to dwell in the south. There is the man-eating bull, whose eyes flash fire and whose horns move like the ears of a dog. There are serpents so vast that they coil about elephants, crush them to death, and swallow them whole. One must approach hills warily, lest a hill turn out to be one of these reptiles coiled up and sleeping off its last repast of elephants and hippopotami.

"To the southwest, in the land of the Eaters, live men with dogs' heads——"

"The land of whom?" interrupted Bessas.

"The Eaters, they call them; cannibals. Along the shores of the Red Sea, at certain times of year, swarms of winged serpents fly up the dry river valleys and would overrun Egypt, were it not for the ibises that gather there to devour these vermin. But I cannot truthfully say that I know your Babylonian cat-lizard."

"We must go on, natheless," said Bessas. "The Great King has so commanded. If Astes gainsays us, we shall have to evade him."

"Easier said than done," said Yehosha. "Astes, for all the paint on his face, is a shrewd and energetic man. His patrols scour the roads, inquiring into everything. The satrap ofttimes rides out with them to keep them up to the mark."

Myron said: "When will these border disturbances subside?"

"Not soon, if ever. No fixed border has ever been drawn. The region of the Nile bend forms a zone of raiding and counterraiding, to the ruin and destruction of the folk who dwell there. We raid as far as the Napatan reach of the Nile, whilst their war parties have pierced as far north as Buhen. Two years ago they overran that fortress and slew or carried off every mortal therein."

"Why don't the Persians and Kushites draw up a boundary, marked by monuments as in Hellas?"

"Because the Kushites will not admit our—that is,

221

the Persians'—right to rule Egypt, let alone the satrapy of Kushia. Because their kings once ruled the land of Khem, they assert they still should righteously do so. Even less will they acknowledge Persian rule over northern Kush, which their kings ruled until Darius' soldiers drove them out—or the gold mines of Kush, after which the Persians lust as a sailor home from the sea lusts after a wench.

"So, you see, you are not likely to get to Napata now, especially as you are not after booty of the sort that the satrap could get his claws into. Your chances were better if you were outfitting a slave-catching foray, or seeking the treasure of Takarta."

"What treasure?" asked Myron.

"Takarta, the last king to rule Kush from Napata. When the Persians captured his palace, their general was furious—my father, who fought in that campaign, told me how he raved—at failing to find the private hoard of the king. So the tale has grown up that Takarta, for all the haste of his flight, bore off his nest egg. It is fabled to have included the True Anthrax."

"Eh? What is that?" said Kothar suddenly, coming out of his meditations.

"You know, the gem that darkens when danger——"

"Yes, yes, I know the jewel's mystic properties. But how came the Kushite kings to possess it?"

"It is said that the Anthrax belonged to Egyptian kings who reigned before the Kushites conquered Khem. The Kushite kings seized it and, when driven out by the Assyrians, took it with them. But I think these are all mere fables. Belike some Persian rankers got to Takarta's treasure chest first, stuffed the baubles into their pantaloons, and held their tongues."

Kothar said: "Could we now go to the satrap and change our story, saying that we were really in pursuit of slaves or treasure?"

"Not with Astes! Being a very suspicious man, he

would probably sentence the lot of you to the granite quarries."

Myron unfolded the sheet of parchment on which he had drawn a map of Egypt, saying: "If *this* be the disturbed frontier zone, why could we not go around it, to east or west? Neither Kush nor Kushia extends indefinitely into the desert."

Yehosha frowned at the sketch. "*He'akh!* There is, forsooth, the western route that passes through the Fifty-League Oasis, over which the Banu Khalaf and the Nubae quarrel. But that route is a horse killer, so widely spaced are the water holes. And if you miss one well, you are dead."

Myron burst out: "I have it! We'll hire Zayd to get us to Meroê with his camels. The money we pay him will enable him in turn to pay off Astes and the Nubae, so they should not object, and we shall avoid the fighting zone."

Bessas: "The very thing! See, Yehosha, what a wise lieutenant I have?"

Yehosha said: "A clever scheme. Be sure to take with you not only the shaykh but also his daughter Salîmat."

"What's this? On such a hurried enterprise as ours, women are an encumbrance. They cause strife amongst the men, who vie for their favor. Why should we be burdened with one?"

"Because she is the real head of the clan, having wit for two. Zayd is a fine old fellow in his way, aside from the fact that he has never learnt that it is wrong to rob and murder. He has good friends amongst the Judaeans of Yeb, for we children of Shem must stick together in far lands. But the daughter is the real force of the twain."

Bessas shook his head. "I still like not that plan. But let's have a song. Know you *The Lousy King of Lydia?*"

"Aye, though I cannot remember all the words. How goes it?" The two deep bass voices rolled out:

223

Have you ever heard of the Lydian king who reigned in
the days of yore?
He lost his taste for his concubines and found his wives
a bore. . . .

The next day, they persuaded Astes to let them see
the prisoners. The old shaykh listened with grave courtesy to Bessas' proposal and looked at his daughter.
"What think you, my dear?"

Salîmat was a rather small, slight girl, quick as a cat
and lithe as an eel. Although nearly as swart as a Nubian,
she had delicately aquiline features that would have
graced a Greek vase. In the courtroom, these features
had been hidden by a blue veil, but one end of this veil
had now been unfastened so that it hung down to one
side.

Besides the veil, Salîmat wore a robe consisting of two
long strips of cloth, fastened at shoulders and ankles but
otherwise loose. Thus, whereas Salîmat appeared fully
clad from the front or the back, she was virtually nude
from the side.

"How many men and beasts now comprise your company, Captain Bessas?" she asked. When Kothar had
translated the question and the reply, she thought briefly
and said: "A score of camels should carry fodder and water enough to get you all to Meroê. For that, we shall need
five or six of our men."

Shaykh Zayd said: "Let us take Zuhayr and Amr and
Shaddad——"

"Not Zuhayr!" cried Salîmat. "He is a trouble-making
loafer."

"Very well, my dear. You may choose the men. But
someone must also go to command them. Naamil——"

"Uncle Naamil is too fat and sleepy, and you are too
easy-going. I shall have to go, as I am the only one they
really fear."

"Salîmat! I am shocked by such an unladylike suggestion!"

224

"It is the only way, Father, and well you know it. No one else in the clan could do it."

"Then it were better not to undertake this rash journey, and to eat the bitter bread of poverty with the best grace we can muster."

"But Father! Think of the chance you will have of opening new trade routes!"

After a brisk dispute in guttural Arabic, Zayd gave in. He sighed: "But I cannot send you off alone, amid all these lustful men. I shall have to chaperone you, leaving Naamil to rule in my absence." He explained to the others: "You see, sirs, we Arabs are jealous beyond all other men of our women's virtue. Amongst other nations, women leave their proper place in the tent and engage in all kinds of lewd behavior. But not amongst us! With us, the man commands and the woman obeys, as the gods intended!"

"So I see," said Bessas, suppressing a smile.

The old man looked sharply at the Bactrian. "You are not, my young friend, having a quiet laugh at my cost? I will tell you a tale to show you how gravely we *badawîn* take these matters.

"When I was a stripling, I visited a clan allied with ours, the Banu Aqil. The shaykh of this clan was Hira ibn-Kulthûm, a man of firm principles. So strict with his wives was he that he would not let either of them leave the tent by daylight, even for their most imperative needs, lest other men cast lustful eyes upon them.

"Now it happened that one morning I, being a poor nobody, had had no breakfast. As I strolled past the shaykh's tent, there wafted to my nostrils the most heavenly odors of cookery that I had ever known.

"Know that in a desert-dwelling clan, things are more or less owned in common. If a man need food or clothing, he may ask any fellow clansman, and his kinsman will deny him nought in reason. The same applies to guests from allied clans.

"So, thinking only of my ravening appetite, I thrust my
225

head into Shaykh Hira's tent to beg a bite from him. And there he sat, with his wives on either side of him, eating. Then, too late, I remembered his strictness concerning his women.

"The shaykh looked up and uttered a greeting. Amongst us there are many greetings, and to each a certain reply must be given if one would not be known as a mannerless oaf. But so overcome with terror was I that, instead of returning Hira's greeting, I could only cast myself down upon my face and stammer a plea for mercy.

"Ere my heart had given three beats, the men of the Banu Aqil seized me, bound me, and dragged me to another tent, where they mounted guard over me. There I lay all day, commending my soul to Ilâh and Ilât and expecting every instant to be my last.

"But, as the sun was setting, in came the shaykh with orders to loose me. 'O Zayd ibn-Harith,' quoth he, 'long have I pondered this matter. At first I meant to have you slain, as I should have done to one of my own clan for taking such a monstrous liberty. But then, thought I, the fact that you returned not my greeting—albeit I have always known you for a well-mannered youth—gave me to believe that the gods must have taken away your wits. Since it were unjust to hold a madman to account for the deeds of his madness, I pardon you. But, lest another such seizure come upon you, it were better that you return to your own clan.' Needless to say, I acted upon this advice instanter."

They jounced along the desert road to the Fifty-League Oasis. Bessas, his money belt lightened and his temper soured by the bribe extorted from him by Astes, treated Salîmat with circumspection. When he spoke to her, it was with all the formal courtesy of an Aryan gentleman; but he saw to it that he seldom had occasion to speak to her.

Myron, wishing to learn Arabic, conversed with the

girl at length. As he was already fluent in Aramaic, the related Arabic tongue posed no great difficulty. He found Salîmat a ruthlessly practical young woman, brilliantly skilled in the arts of managing a camel caravan. He wondered how many such strong natures the company could acquire before it flew apart from internal dissension.

At last the Fifty-League Oasis rose out of the desert. As Bessas' company neared it, Arabs of the Banu Khalaf ran out of their camel's hair tents and rode in from the desert on their camels to welcome their shaykh. A score of naked Nubian women and children, watched by whip-wielding Arabs, were hewing wood and drawing water. One of these women looked dully up at the company and sighted the Nubian chief, who had come along, riding an ass, to see that all his folk were freed. The woman burst into shrieks. Soon, despite the cracks of Arab whips on their bare black hides, all were screaming.

Shaykh Zayd made his camel kneel. As he got off, his clansmen crowded round to kiss his hand. The din became such that Myron could make out nothing until the shaykh creakily mounted a palm log and cried:

"*Ya jamaʻaya!* My good people, I pray you! A little quiet! Now I will tell you what has befallen. . . ."

The Arabs listened quietly until they learnt that, as part of the deal with Bessas, the satrap, and the Nubian chief, they would have to free their newly acquired slaves. Then an angry murmur ran through the crowd. They turned to one another, gesturing and expostulating. The shaykh called again for quiet, but none heeded him.

Soon fists were shaken and knives were flourished. Burning with indignation, the Banu Khalaf began to scream threats to slay all the Nubae and the foreign dogs as well. The shaykh's tearful protests were drowned out. Myron and Bessas looked at one another, loosened the swords in their scabbards, and gathered their company into a compact knot.

227

Then Salîmat leaped to the log beside her father and cried, in a screech that cut through the hubbub: "Be silent, dogs!"

The noise died.

"What sort of behavior is this?" continued the girl. "Are you a mannerless mob of townsfolk, or true *badawîn*? Why do you welcome us and then act so as to destroy us, and yourselves as well? Listen whilst I tell you how we stand. . . ."

An hour's shrill harangue turned the Arabs from their purpose. The wretched captives were suffered to depart with their chief. The clansmen came shamefacedly up to Bessas to assure him of the hospitality of the desert and to kiss his hands in gratitude for the liberation of their shaykh. Myron said to Bessas in Greek:

"Isn't it wonderful, old boy, how among these folk the men command and the women obey?"

From the Fifty-League Oasis, Bessas' expedition forged southward. The original company of five men and ten animals was now augmented by the shaykh, his daughter, and six more Arabs of the Banu Khalaf. The Arabs rode and led a force of twenty-two camels bearing fodder and water for the less hardy horses and mules.

They swung back to the Nile only to pick up water at the southernmost point of the southerly bend, near Karutjet. Then they struck southeastward across the desert again. Coming to the Nile twenty leagues above Meroê, they followed the track along the northern side of the river downstream for three days.

Sometimes they jogged along a narrow strip between the river and towering brown cliffs. At other times they looked across wide flat plains, sparsely speckled with shrubbery. A fine dust blew in from the desert and got into everything. As they followed the river northwest, the country became more of a desert, the barren soil being covered by shiny round red and black stones.

228

"Beshrew me if this be not iron-bearing country!" said Shimri.

The first afternoon along the river, Shimri's horse acted sick, hanging its head and moaning through its nose. One of the Arabs told Myron:

"I tried to warn that man not to let his horse eat of the *ushar*, but he heeded me not. So I thought he must have some charm against the poison of this shrub."

Myron asked Shimri about this. The Judaean gave a nervous laugh and said:

"Oh, he came up shouting some gibberish, whilst I was looking at the iron ore, but I never heed what these barbarians say. All they want is a chance to rob one."

By nightfall the horse was dead and Bessas in a fury. Shimri hid in a gully until the Bactrian's wrath was softened. By the most tender care, Bessas had so far avoided losing a single horse or mule. He was, however, far less solicitous with his human companions. It was as if, being himself impervious to heat, cold, thirst, hunger, and fatigue, he took it for granted that all other men were equally hardy.

The Arabs skinned and ate the horse. Bessas warned his followers thereafter to keep their beasts away from the thick, fleshy, bright-green leaves of the poisonous shrub.

On the seventh of Duuzu they arrived at the mud-hut village of Epis, opposite Meroê, capital of independent Kush. Here a ferry ran. Bessas and Zayd crossed on the ramshackle flatboat while Myron and Salîmat, as the two leaders' lieutenants, remained to the last to make sure that all the other men and beasts got across in good order.

"Master Myron!" said Salîmat, looking gravely with dark eyes over the top of the veil. In the desert and at the oasis, she had laid aside the veil, but now that they were traveling through settled parts of Kush she resumed it. "Pray tell your man Skhâ that, if he make another advance towards me, I shall slay him." Quick as a serpent's

229

stroke, she whisked a curved dagger from under her robe.

"I certainly will," said Myron.

He did not doubt that Salîmat would indeed kill Skhâ or anyone else who molested her. Perhaps old Zayd thought he had to come along to protect his daughter, but any protecting was likely to be the other way round. The shaykh presided benignly over his little caravan and exchanged elaborate courtesies with Bessas and his people. But it was Salîmat who routed the Arabs out before dawn, bullied them into motion, inspected the lading of the camels, settled disputes, and decided when and where the company should stop for the night.

XII   The Courts of Kush

UNDER A BLINDING SUN, blazing high overhead in a brassy sky, the city of Meroê shimmered in merciless heat. Within its wall of sun-dried mud stretched a jumble of mud-brick houses. Little motion was visible, for in the heat of the day most Kushites disappeared within their walls. Here and there one might be seen, curled up asleep in a patch of shade. Somewhere a blacksmith's hammer clanged.

Outside the wall, the ground stretched away westward in a barren plain towards the Nile, invisible below its bluffs in the middle distance. To the east the country rose in a range of small, stony hills. On the south side, in the precarious shade of a giant sacred sycamore, huddled the tents of Bessas' company. They were camped outside the walls because Meroê had no inn.

Past these tents ran the road to Soba and the south. This road was merely a track in the sand, beaten by the feet of slave hunters and their victims, which ended at the Soba Gate, a large wooden door in the mud wall.

A pair of Kushite soldiers guarded this gate. The pair sat on the ground against the wall, with lean black arms encircling their legs and bushy black heads pillowed on their knees, sound asleep. Their iron-headed spears and cowhide shields, painted in gaudy patterns of red, white, and black, leaned against the wall. A bowshot away, down the road, a score of huge brown vultures tore at the carcass of an ass.

Bessas' remaining horses and mules stood under the trees in pairs, head to tail, flicking flies. The camels, their long legs folded beneath them, chewed their cuds.

Within the encampment, hardly more motion was seen than in the sleeping city. Zayd's Arabs slept or stared blankly into the distance, not bothering to brush away the flies. Shimri, having just returned from a visit to the local smiths, hummed tunelessly while he mended a harness strap. Myron searched his garments for fleas and lice.

Bessas and Kothar emerged from the gate and strode towards the camp. "Myron!" called Bessas. Then, placing his face close to Zayd's tent, he cried: *"Ya Shaykh!"*

Zayd appeared blinking and yawning. *"'Ahlan wa sahlan,"* he muttered. After the shaykh came his daughter. Bessas snarled:

"Know you what that little son of Ahriman, Barga, has been doing these ten days past?"

"What?" said Myron.

"He has been playing us like fish on a line, taking our bribes every day for promises to get us an audience on the morrow. But it turns out that Barga has no authority to arrange an audience with the king at all! This king does not *give* audiences. He is far too sacred for such defiling intercourse with mortals. By the Sleepless One, if Kothar had not restrained me, I had torn the rascal to pieces, as boys pull insects apart!"

"Isn't he the Royal Usher?" said Myron.

"He is, but the person with whom he should arrange audiences is the minister, General Puerma."

"Who is on campaign," said Myron.

"But who is due back today or tomorrow. He sent a

231

runner ahead. Now Barga assures us that we shall have an audience with Puerma tomorrow."

"Let's hope it be not another chicane," said Myron.

"It had better not be," said Bessas, glowering, "or I'll lure the scoundrel outside——"

"He'll only protest that it is all a misunderstanding; that he did not fully comprehend Kothar's Egyptian," said Myron.

"I suppose so," said Bessas. "Where's Skhâ? It is time that he and Shimri took the beasts to graze."

Shimri looked up. "In this g-god-forsaken land, the grass is so sparse that the animals have to gallop from one tuft to the next."

"Skhâ went into the town," said Myron. "Here he comes now."

The short Karian trotted out the gate. "Ho, comrades! Guess what! I have found us a willing woman! Or rather," he amended, "one whose owner is willing."

Myron smiled. "At my age, my boy," said the Greek, "I find that black skins and flapping breasts fail to arouse what little lust I still have."

"Oh, but this one is young and well-formed."

"Then she will have that female circumcision that they practice here and in Egypt, which closes up their——"

"Nay; she comes of the Megabarri, who live up the Astabara and do not——"

Bessas cleared his throat, and the Karian fell silent. Bessas said: "Methinks this conversation is unfit for the ears of the young lady." He nodded toward Salîmat.

"Oh, but she understands not—"

"I think she understands more Aramaic than she admits. Eh, my lady?"

A peal of laughter came from behind the blue veil. Salîmat replied in broken Aramaic: "I go back in tent; leave men to talk as like."

Salîmat returned to the tent, followed by Bessas' burning gaze. Bessas murmured in Greek:

"Do you know, O Myron, that next to a good horse, a

good woman is the most precious possession one can have?"

Then the Bactrian shook himself, like a man coming out of a dream. His deep voice boomed out harshly in guttural Aramaic:

"The damnedest thing is that I cannot find anybody in Meroê to talk about the road to the south and the sources of the Nile. They call the Upper Nile the Astasobas, meaning 'River of Darkness,' and feign that they never heard of the course of this fell flume."

Shaykh Zayd, using Kothar as interpreter, said: "I know the reason, father of a sword. The established traders and slave hunters fear lest you invade their territories and compete with them. So they have spread the word that you are not to be helped. Count yourselves lucky if they stir not up the mob against you, saying you are foul foreign fiends and witches who would steal their children to devour. We have encountered much of that in Egypt."

Bessas slapped his thigh. "As I feel now, I should welcome a battle with the whole of Meroê. When——"

He wheeled, staring down the road. Along the track came faintly the sound of drums. "Puerma!" he exclaimed.

Meroê came to languid life. The sleeping soldiers awoke, yawned, and picked up their spears and shields. Others joined them. People issued from the gate, first in a trickle and then in a stream.

The guardsmen cleared the road for the approaching army. They ran up and down the sandy track, screaming at the citizens and beating them back with the shafts of their spears. Once the quick tempers of the Kushites erupted into a brawl. There was an instant of yelling. Spearheads flashed in the glare, and a dead man was dragged out of the press for his family to wail over.

The other Kushites lined up on both sides of the road. There were mop-headed men and women with tribal scars on cheeks and the kilt of Kush about their loins. There were swarms of naked black children. Bessas and

233

his party elbowed their way to the front, ignoring the scowls of the Kushites and the movement of the men's hands towards the daggers strapped to their upper arms.

The drumming became louder. A cloud of dust appeared down the road. Out of it issued a group of whifflers with staves to clear the way. Then came a squad of drummers, madly beating complex rhythms on deep, narrow drums. The vultures flew up from their feast and flapped in circles, croaking indignantly.

After the drummers ambled General Puerma on an ass. Although the ass was one of the big white Egyptian breed, it was hardly large enough to carry the general, whose bare feet scarcely cleared the road. For Puerma was a large man, tall and rather fat, so that he must have come close to Bessas' weight. He wore a towering headdress made of a lion's mane, a cuirass of silver scales, and a kilt embroidered with gold thread. One man led the ass while another trotted alongside, holding a parasol over the general's head.

The Meroites screamed "Puerma! Puerma!" The general smiled blandly, but his smile vanished as he stared hard at Bessas and his companions before riding on.

After the general came men carrying loot. There were bags of gold dust. There were tusks, hides, horns, and plumes. A man carried a basket full of dubious brown objects.

Then came captives. Each bore a forked wooden pole about four feet long. The captive's neck was clasped in the fork of the pole and held in place by rawhide lashings, while his wrists were lashed to the long end of the fork. To avoid exhaustion, each prisoner rested the end of his pole on the shoulder of the captive in front of him.

The captives were mostly men, although there were some women and children. They were of many types. There were slender, bearded, hook-nosed, light-brown highlanders; there were squat, thick-thewed, inky-black men with full lips and slanting eyes. Some were as tall as Bessas, but thin as storks; others were equally tall but mightily muscled. Some had the lower middle front teeth missing, while some bore tribal cicatrice patterns on shoulders or buttocks. Most were completely naked, and many bore partly healed wounds. Kushites with whips and bludgeons hustled them along.

After several hundred captives had passed, the soldiers appeared. These were a column of lean, raisin-colored men, wearing the skins of lions, leopards, and other beasts, with bunches of ostrich plumes nodding from their topknots. Many had their bodies painted with vermilion and chalk. In some, the right half of the body bore one pigment and the left the other; others flaunted gaudier patterns.

Each bore a spear—sometimes with an iron head and sometimes with a head of sharpened antelope horn—and a shield of elephant, rhinoceros, or hippopotamus hide. In addition, most carried additional weapons, such as a longbow made of a palm rib, a knobbed wooden club, or a bundle of javelins. There was no uniformity in their equipment.

Gold abounded among them. It gleamed from rings, earrings, armlets, torques, and anklets. It jingled in chains and in strings of amulets. Myron remembered Yehosha's remark about the gold mines of Kush.

Puerma's soldiers did not march. They straggled, shaking their weapons and uttering boastful shouts. Whenever one sighted a woman he knew, he shouted a few words and made sexual motions, raising raucous laughs.

Sweat ran down the soldiers' bare chests. Choking clouds of dust arose. Myron, though not finicky, found the massed odor overpowering.

Following several thousand soldiers came slaves bearing food and equipment, though this was scanty by the standards of more northerly lands. Beside Myron, Bessas remarked:

"Do not make the mistake of thinking these fellows, even if they look primitive and disorderly, are not war-like. Many times they have held their own in battle with the Persians. Some of my military friends who have faced their screaming charges are not eager to do so again."

In the main square of Meroê, officers strove to beat and kick their men into some semblance of a hollow square, while outside the mass of soldiers others rushed about beating back the common people, trying to keep them from mingling with the warriors. But their struggle was hopeless. As soon as the officials had passed, the masses began to stir, chatter, and mingle like any crowds. Every soldier had a tale of deeds of dought that he wanted to tell.

Myron, standing on tiptoe, could barely see over the mop heads before him. Bessas and Zayd, towering over the throng, watched impassively, while the stumpy Skhâ danced and wriggled about, seeking a view. Kothar, unconcerned with these earthly events, gazed at the distant sky.

A trumpet sounded. Suddenly even Skhâ could see, for thousands of Kushites around the square were throwing themselves prone. The king had come out of his palace. "You had better get down, too, if you are fain to keep your heads," said the low but penetrating voice of Kothar. Myron folded up on the ground, but not before he had obtained a good look at the king, who stood less than fifty paces away.

Saas-herqa, King of the Two Lands, was a slight, ineffectual-looking man. Myron would have guessed that he was in his thirties. His skin was lighter than that of most Kushites. On each of the king's brown cheeks was cut a pair of zigzag tribal scars, like twin serpents.

The king's personal presence, however, was dwarfed by the magnificence of his attire. For his regalia was copied after that of the Egyptian kings of the great days of the Egyptian Empire. From his head rose a great golden tiara, fronted with the head of the lion god Apizemek, of whom the king was the incarnation. Golden horns rose

236

from the sides, and golden wings covered the monarch's ears. Round his neck spread a golden gorget agleam with jewels. A jeweled baldric supported a sword with a jeweled hilt. The king's kilt and the high-crossed lacings of his tasseled sandals glistened with golden thread. He made a gesture with a small golden battle-ax, and the prostrate thousands rose.

Behind King Saas-herqa stood his fat queen, wearing an ornate crown of golden horns, wings, and a rearing cobra. Like the king, she was nude above the waist save for ornaments. Instead of a kilt she wore about her massive hips an ankle-length skirt, embroidered with golden wings and flowers.

Beside the queen stood an elderly man in plain white linen and a tall hat like the Persian cidaris. Though as dark as most Kushites, he was taller, with strongly aquiline features. These, together with his bald head and wattles, gave him a vulturine appearance. In response to Myron's whispered question, Kothar replied:

"That is Osorkon, high priest of Amon of Meroê. He and Puerma are the mightiest men in the kingdom."

Other Kushites crowded the doorway behind the king. All were clad like Egyptian nobles of three hundred years before.

Having dismounted, General Puerma strode up the steps to the portico of the palace and prostrated himself before the king. Rising, he turned so that he faced partly towards the king and partly towards the throng and began a speech.

Puerma spoke in Egyptian, as it was the affectation of the Kushite Court always to use that language in public. Puerma, however, paused between sentences for little Barga, the usher, to translate his words into Kushite for the benefit of the crowd. As Barga did this, Kothar likewise translated into Aramaic for his companions:

". . . he has collected tribute from the Sembritae . . . crushed the Critensi . . . raided the Dochi for slaves. . . ."

237

At a signal from Puerma, the loot and captives were paraded past the king. As a crowning touch, the man with the basket of brown objects poured his load in a heap before the king. The multitude screamed its cheers. Myron asked:

"O Kothar, what are those things that look like large brown slugs?"

"Phalli," said the Syrian. "The Kushites cut them off slain foes to keep count of the number of dead." Seeing Myron wince, he shrugged. "It is more practical than collecting heads, which are much heavier. Anyway, what do you expect of such crass barbarians, lacking spiritual enlightenment?"

Bessas and his companions had barely returned to their tents when a messenger from the palace announced that General Puerma commanded their presence forthwith.

When they had made what feeble toilet they could, the messenger guided Bessas, Myron, and Kothar back to the palace. On the way, Bessas growled:

"Enough of this crawling on our bellies! I care not what the local custom may be; I will give the general but one good bow."

General Puerma sat on a leopard skin spread on a low throne, while a page boy fanned him with a long-handled ostrich-plume fan. He beamed at Bessas' bow, his black eyes dancing in his round brown face. The Bactrian, with Kothar translating into Egyptian, began the polite formulas:

"May the gods give Your Highness long life and wealth! Your slave brings a letter of greeting from the Great King to the King of the Two Lands. . . ."

The general waited until Bessas ran out of breath or compliments, then said in passable Aramaic:

"Thank you for the good words; the gods prosper you also." At Bessas' startled expression, a broad smile creased the general's full-jowled face. "You surprise I speak the

238

Syrian tongue? Many years ago I serve in the Persian army. I march all through Egypt, Syria, Cappadocia, and Thrace to Greece. I march with King Xerxes. Of course, my speech is out of practice now. What is this about you going up the River of Darkness?"

Bessas told of his mission. Puerma drummed on the arm of his chair, then said:

"I do not know about this dragon. Is said that in the mountains east of the River of Darkness, in country of the Asachae, race of serpent kings rules the people. But your animal is something else, eh? Let me think." After a long silence, the general said: "You plan do anything else? Like catch slaves or hunt treasure?"

"Nay, my lord." Bessas grinned. "Though of course if I stumbled across a treasure I would not turn my back upon it."

The general smiled back. Myron felt that Puerma was an intelligent and forceful man who could be helpful if he chose. But it still behooved them to tread warily. Puerma said:

"You ever hear of the treasure of Takarta?"

"Aye." Bessas repeated what he had heard from Yehosha in Yeb. "But, as you see, sir, your servant cannot take time to search Africa for this box of baubles—even supposing that it exists—with my mother's life in the balance."

Puerma, his fat face suddenly grim, leaned forward. "You know, without permission from me, you not get up the river. Even if you get up, you never get through Kush on way back. You understand?"

"I understand. But what are you coming to?"

"This. If you want go up the river, you make pledge with me to bring back treasure of Takarta——"

"But General! We cannot spend years hunting the length and breadth of Africa——"

"You not hunt far. I make it easy for you to find this hoard."

239

"Know you where it is?"

"More or less. I tell you some things that make it easy to find. Otherwise, go back to Persia!"

"Why ask you me to fetch your treasure? Why not one of your own folk?"

Puerma twiddled his fingers. "I think you have better chance of getting to source of the river. We Kushites have raid the savage tribes of the south for slaves until now these dirty dogs attack us on sight. With your pale skins, they maybe take you for gods and let you pass. Besides, you find it harder to run away with treasure than one of my own people. Everybody notice foreigners and talk about them."

"If you have known where the stuff is, why have you waited until now to seek it?"

"Have been busy fighting Persians and wild tribes. Also, you are the first foreigner I see in Meroê who I think is strong enough to get treasure and honest enough not to try to cheat me afterwards."

"I thank Your Excellency." Bessas stroked his beard. "Of course, my lord, you mean for us to share the treasure equally, do you not?"

Puerma raised his eyebrows. "I not mean that at all. But I suppose you deserve some pay for work. You take one quarter, me three quarter."

"Nay, sir; half or nought. . . ."

After a haggle, Puerma said: "Tell you what. Is one valuable gem in the treasure: big red stone, call—how you say——"

"The True Anthrax?" asked Kothar.

"That is it. You give me the True Anthrax; then we divide rest of the treasure half and half."

"Agreed," said Bessas. Puerma clapped his hands and said: "Fetch Akinazaz the rain maker."

Akinazaz was a skinny old Kushite, naked but for a loin-cloth and a leopard skin hung around his neck. His body was covered with powdered ash, giving him a ghostly look.

240

"Now," said Puerma, "we swear great oaths, by my gods and your gods. . . ."

As there was no written contract, Myron suspected that Puerma could not read. When the oaths had been sworn and the rain maker had uttered hideous curses on him who should break them, Puerma said:

"Now I tell you how to find this treasure. Listen well. The kings of Kush rule from Napata from time of the great Kashta down to the reign of King Karkamon, in days of your King Darius.

"The royal line of King Kashta had two branches. The old branch rule in Napata, and the young branch rule the southern provinces as viceroys from Meroê. King Karkamon had son, Takarta. At that time, the senior member of the younger family, in Meroê, was Astabarqamon. When King Karkamon die, his son, Takarta, become king. But then he get message from King Darius, saying bow down to the king of the world and send him earth and water, for the god Auramazda choose him king over you and all other men. King Takarta say, ha-ha! And he cut off the messengers' hands and send these men back to say to King Darius: that is what happen to you if you come to my country. We beat King Cambyses, so we can beat you, too.

"So the Persians come and defeat King Takarta in one great battle. They seize Napata. King Takarta escape with treasure. But then he hear that his cousin Astabarqamon, in Meroê, has declare himself king, because now he has army and Takarta does not. Takarta know that if he go to Meroê as he is, his cousin kill him. So he and few faithful friends dress like poor peasants, all cover with lice and dirt. They walk right through Meroê, with treasure on back of ass, and nobody stop them.

"Then Takarta and his men go up the River of Darkness—far, far—three months' journey——"

"Mithra!" burst out Bessas. "Do you mean that after all our striving, we are only halfway to our goal?"

Puerma laughed and spread his hands. "I not know

241

the exact distance. Maybe is only half as far as to Persia; but is much harder going, with no roads and many wild men. Besides, your animals die of *nagana,* and then you have to walk."

Bessas growled: "I know not if my agreement with you was well-advised."

"Ah, but your Aryan sense of honor make you carry it out anyway!" Puerma chuckled. "Anyway, Takarta and friends go on up this river. Some die, but some live. After three months they find one lake, which the River of Darkness flow out of. There they build castle and take wives from the local tribes."

Myron asked: "If Takarta went to this unknown country to live, how did news of his fate get back to Kush?"

"Some of the followers quarrel with Takarta, who say he is still king and make everyone prostrate himself before speaking to him. When one friend forget, Takarta kill him. Or maybe some of them are just homesick. Anyway, four of the followers run away and come back down the River of Darkness. One by one they die of hardship and sickness, but one of them get to Meroê and tell his story, and that story come down to me."

Bessas: "Will this exiled king and his followers still be in their castle when we arrive?"

"I think not. All these things happen maybe forty year ago, and Takarta was not young man then. The man who came back to Meroê say there were only a few followers left in castle, and what of sickness and lions and wild hunters and quarrels he not think those live long. If these old men still live and try to stop you from taking the treasure, kill them."

Myron said: "But Napata is in Kushite hands now, is it not?"

"Aye; King Astabarqamon drive out the Persians. Napata is holy place. All our kings are bury there. There you can see pyramids, like those in Egypt, that kings are bury under. But Persians still rule the Nile as far south as Third Cataract, so Astabarqamon keep his capital at Meroê. Napata is too near the enemy.

"Well, that is the story. Follow the river for three months to one big lake and look for castle on small hill near this lake.

"Now we go to the victory banquet. You are my guests. Will be in pavilion outside. Some people"—he spat—"not like jolly parties, Kushite style."

Puerma clapped his hands and rose. An escort of soldiers in horned helmets, armed with broad-bladed spears and long-hafted axes like those of Pharaonic Egypt, came running. Surrounded by these warriors and followed by his guests, he swaggered out of the palace and through the streets of Meroê towards his pavilion outside the city walls.

"O Zayd!" said Bessas. "It seems a shame that your lovely daughter should miss this feast. Shall I run over to the camp and fetch the lass? Methinks Puerma would not mind——"

"Nay, nay, my son," said Zayd with a chuckle. "From all I hear, a Kushite party is no place for a virtuous Arab maiden. Besides, you seek to spoil the baggage. She is too haughty now, with every man in the clan dangling after her and beseeching me to give her to him to wife."

On the grass mats that floored the general's pavilion, Myron and his companions sat cross-legged in a semicircle, with Puerma and a score of Kushite officers. A woman sat between each man and the next.

Not knowing Kushite, Myron could not converse with either of his dinner companions. This fact did not stop them from talking to him and to each other about him. Seemingly they were cracking broad jokes, for they laughed uproariously and rubbed their bare breasts against him. Myron tried to learn a few words of their speech but found it hard going.

He downed a mug of beer, belched, and said: "Be-

243

shrew me if I am not coming to like the stuff, O Bessas!"

" 'Tis weaker than Egyptian beer," said Bessas. "By the wheels of the sun chariot, they're bringing in a live ox! Are we supposed to rend it asunder with nails and teeth?" He turned to General Puerma and changed from Greek to Aramaic. "My lord, is this beast our dinner?"

Puerma, who had discarded most of his regalia, grinned and scratched his paunch. "You see soon."

"Poor Kothar looks sick," said Myron.

Bessas: "What said you? I cannot hear over this din."

"I said, poor Kothar looks sick!"

"He probably fears that those wenches on his flanks will rape him."

"By Herakles, that were an interesting problem——" began Myron, but a bellow from the ox and an outburst of shouts from the Kushites cut him off.

The beast had been tripped and thrown at the entrance of the pavilion. Despite its thrashing, servitors swarmed around it and held it down with ropes. A pair with knives began to cut into the haunch of the living animal. The ox bellowed frantically; the Kushites shouted encouragement.

"*Papai!*" said Myron. "This is new to me, and I do not know that I like it."

Bessas grunted. "I have eaten raw meat ere this, when I was caught without food or fire on the Sakan steppes."

"Well, let's hold back and watch the others when we are served, so as to comply with their code of table manners."

"If you can call it that," said Bessas.

A swarm of slaves now crowded round the ox, which continued to moan and bawl as it was flayed and cut up. Blood spread around the entrance of the pavilion in a widening puddle; flies gathered in humming swarms. Nevertheless, the carvers skillfully avoided cutting any major blood vessel, so that the animal's agony went on without cease. The Kushites whooped and cheered at each bellow.

244

The slaves began to stream into the pavilion with heaped platters. Each platter bore a stack of thin flat disks of leathery bread, half a foot in diameter, and chunks of raw meat, still bleeding and warm. Each slave put his platter down in front of a woman.

As she received her platter, each woman attacked the meat with a small knife. When she had cut the meat into cubes the size of dice, she piled a number of these on a disk of bread, rolled the bread into a cylinder, and thrust the end of the cylinder into the mouth of the man on her left. It was, it seemed, a point of Kushite honor for a man to be fed with his arms hanging limply at his sides, not using his own hands at all. It was also good manners to chew with one's mouth open, making loud smacking and slobbering sounds. Myron murmured:

"Somehow my appetite is not what it was——"

A cylinder of bread and meat, jammed into Myron's open mouth, ended his speech. He almost gagged, but Bessas said:

"If you throw up, I'll break your neck. The stuff is not bad."

The slaves kept coming, refilling the platters as fast as they were emptied. The women fed the men until the latter signified that they had had enough. When the men were finished, each of them fed his woman partner in the same manner. Myron clumsily dropped his meat the first time he tried to roll a cartridge of bread, but the woman took it as a joke. With a final groan, the ox expired.

The noise subsided as the platters were cleared away. Now the slaves came round with huge pitchers of beer. The sun set; rushlights glimmered. The drinking went on and on. The noise of speech and laughter rose until Myron gave up trying to talk.

The Kushites drank incredible quantities. As the sky darkened, pairs of dining partners became more and more familiar. They shouted, screamed, slapped backs, and burst into hysterical howls. The men nuzzled and fondled the women. Myron's woman seemed to expect

245

the same; but Myron, fearing to pick up another load of vermin and disliking the whole procedure, held aloof.

A little muzzy with beer, he blinked and shook his ringing head. All over the floor of the pavilion, men and women were throwing off their few garments. The scene became one of unbridled satyrism. The chorus of grunts, snorts, belches, gasps, and giggles gave the impression of a vast and agitated farmyard. The mixture of smells was indescribable.

Although Myron sometimes scorned Kothar for the latter's prudishness, he now found that his own most compelling desire was to escape. Looking about for his comrades, he was taken aback to see that Bessas, Kothar, and General Puerma had all disappeared. The thought of being alone in the midst of a barbarous orgy, unable even to speak to those about him, terrified Myron. To the woman, who now lay expectantly beside him, he shouted:

"General Puerma? Where Puerma?"

At first she shouted back uncomprehendingly, making coitary gestures. At last she rose with a muttered execration and pointed to the rear of the room.

Myron got unsteadily to his feet. He picked his way carefully among the pairs of horizontal bodies to the curtains at the rear of the room. A last glance back showed him that many Kushites had fallen into sottish slumber, though here and there a pair of shiny black buttocks still rhythmically rose and fell in the wan, flickering rushlight. He stumbled through the curtains.

A dimly lit corridor ran back into the private parts of the pavilion. Myron followed this until familiar voices and the rattle of a dice box brought his attention to one of the compartments opening on the corridor.

Myron peeked through the crack in the door curtain. Seeing Puerma, Bessas, and Kothar within, he entered with a greeting. Bessas and the general were throwing dice.

246

There was another person in the room, a serving maid. She was a rather tall, large girl with a white skin, blue eyes, and light-brown hair. Like an Egyptian maid-servant, she wore nothing but a string of beads about her hips. She bore a tray on which sat mugs of beer.

Myron stared. He had not seen a person of such coloring since leaving Palestine. He knew that such hair and eyes sometimes occurred, albeit not very often, among Greeks and Syrians. He wondered if the young woman were of more northerly origin—a Thracian, say, or a Getes. In any case, while he realized that her features were not extraordinary, it was so long since he had seen a woman of more or less his own racial type that she looked as radiant as Aphrodite. At hazard he spoke:

"Ei Hellênis?"

"Malista," she replied. *"Eimai Makedonikê. Onomazomai Phyllis."*

"Ah, ah, no fair!" said General Puerma, wagging a fat forefinger. "If you must flirt with my slaves, do it in language I understand. You enjoy the party?"

Myron repressed a grimace of disgust. "It is different from anything I have ever seen, my lord. I shall always remember it. How is it that you people left early?"

Puerma said: "Your gallant captain"—he nodded at Bessas—"explain that he is in love and does not lust after any other woman. As for me, I can futter any time, but I do not have many chances to massacre one foreigner at gaming."

As Myron looked more closely at the low table on which the game was in progress, his eyes widened with horror. On each end of the table was piled the wealth of the player. On Puerma's side lay a heap of golden rings, chains, brooches, and other gauds. In the middle of the table stood a delicate balance for weighing out this gold. Two darics and a bracelet, the current stake, reposed beside the balance.

On Bessas' side lay the darics of King Xerxes—or rather

they had lain there. Most of them had now moved over to Puerma's side. As Myron watched, Puerma rattled the three dice in the box and threw.

"Isis!" cried the general, for three sixes showed. He swept up the stake.

"Bessas!" cried Myron. "Your mother——"

"Let me alone," grumbled Bessas. "I am so far down now that I must needs go on."

"But we shall be destitute!"

"That matters not; Takarta's treasure will make it up to us."

"If we obtain it! You must be mad, to——"

"Fear not, Master Myron," said Puerma soothingly. "His luck surely turn. Not fair, not to give him chance to win back his wealth."

After several more throws, during which the stake grew again, Puerma threw a six. He picked up the other two dice and threw again, getting another six; a throw with the remaining die brought forth a third six, making another Isis. Bessas glared as his money departed.

"The Corpse Fiend take these dice!" he growled. "All I can throw tonight are dogs!"

"In the name of Zeus the king!" cried Myron. "Use some sense, man. Another of those and we shall be beggars!"

Bessas' bloodshot eyes flamed dangerously. "I told you to leave me alone!"

"Well, I won't! If you're a fool, I am not! Drop that nonsense, come back to camp, and sober up!"

"Curse you, I suffer no man to speak to me thus!" shouted Bessas, beginning to lurch drunkenly to his feet.

"Gentlemen! Gentlemen!" cried Puerma.

"Excuse your slave," said Kothar.

As if by magic, the sound of the growing quarrel died away. All three men turned to stare at the Syrian, who had been sitting cross-legged, silent, and immobile throughout the altercation. But his voice possessed its strange authority.

"I made a small study of the stars and other omens this evening after I left the rout," he said. "Know that the mystical cosmic forces have combined against Master Bessas. He had no chance of winning this night."

"Why didn't you say so sooner?" groaned Bessas.

"You would not have believed me without a demonstration, and such a claim would only have caused discord. However, if you like, I will take your place; for I believe that my chances are fair."

"Very well. But your winnings shall belong to the expedition, not to you."

"I understand, sir. Let us play, General."

For a few throws the relative positions of the two players did not change. Each made small winnings and sustained small losses.

Then Kothar began to win consistently. Piece by piece, the archers flowed back across the table. The general's pile of winnings melted like the snows of Mount Libanos in spring.

Phyllis brought more beer. Puerma drank in great gulps. But Kothar, Myron suspected, only pretended to sip.

Kothar's winnings continued. Although he sustained an occasional setback, these losses were small and were followed by heavy winnings. Soon Puerma had, besides his golden ornaments, only a few darics left. He yawned and said:

"I wax too sleepy to continue. Besides, you will soon have wrested the treasury of Kush from me."

Kothar looked up with raised eyebrows. "Indeed, sir? Then I believe I am entitled to claim a forfeit from you, as I am ready and willing to continue the game until sunrise."

"Oh? That is right." Puerma gazed at the Syrian with a bleary and wavering stare. Then he shouted: "Phyllis!"

"Yes, master?" said the girl, appearing through the curtain.

"I give you to this man, whatever his cursed foreign

name be, as forfeit for breaking off the game. You are his. Obey him in all things. And now good night, my friends. Let us go out the back, so as not to stumble over those who sleep on floor of the dining room."

In parting, Puerma spoke to Myron in a conspiratorial whisper. "Truth to tell, I give away Phyllis because I cannot abide her pale skin. It seem unhealthy; remind me of corpses and leprosy. But you northrons are used to such. Fare you well!"

Outside, Myron said: "The gods keep us from another such coil! Verily, fortune rules men, not men fortune. Tell me, Kothar, did you not substitute, at suitable times, a set of your trained dice?"

Kothar smiled faintly in the moonlight. "I owe you thanks for the suggestion you made in Tahapanes, to bore holes in the sides of dice and install therein small leaden weights. I had a set made up for me in Opet. In sooth, the material betimes must serve the spiritual. My only regret is that I did not recover all our leader's losings."

"You really owe thanks to a suggestion of my friend Uni, an Egyptian priest, which started me to thinking."

Bessas mumbled something about a stain on his Aryan honor, to win by such trickery. Then he burst into sobs. Tears gleamed like pearls in the moonlight on his rugged, scarred face.

"I—I am nought but a stupid, drunken boor! I thought I could drink Puerma down, but he must be the champion toper of Kush; or else the demon Aeshma possessed me. I should never have gone so far from my mother!" He bent over. "O Myron, give me, I pray, a good hard kick in the arse!"

Myron, knowing his friend's strange moods, complied. His boot thudded home. Bessas straightened up, saying: "Now I feel better. But to whom belongs the lass?" He indicated Phyllis who, now decently clad, followed them.

"To me," said Kothar.

"Nay! We agreed that your winnings should belong to the expedition, and she is part of your winnings."

"Your slave begs to differ. The maiden was given to me as a forfeit, that is to say as a gift to compensate me for the breaking off of the game. She is not exactly what I should have chosen—I am not a lustful man—but the general gave me no choice. In any case, she is a gift, not a winning."

They argued some more, until Bessas appealed to Myron. "Why should the beauty of this woman be wasted on Kothar, who cares for nought but his spirits and spells, when others in the group would enjoy her far more?"

Myron thought. "I can see arguments either way. Why not ask the young lady what she prefers?"

"Ask a slave?" snorted Bessas. "Well, go ahead. I care not what become of her, for my heart is elsewhere."

Myron explained the situation to Phyllis, who said: "It is bad enough to be a slave to one man, Master Myron, but to be the common property of several were little better than being sent to the mines."

When Myron had translated Phyllis' Greek, Kothar said: "Very well, as I have no use for such property, I give her to you, Myron. To possess her would distract me from my quest for cosmic wisdom."

Bessas burst into a guffaw. Phyllis looked bewildered.

"Thank you," said Myron, "but now that I own her, what shall I do with her?"

"You ask?" said Bessas.

"No, seriously! If the journey southward prove as difficult as Puerma warned us, she is likely to perish. On the other hand, it goes against my grain to sell her to another Kushite, because these folk are not what one would call tenderhearted."

"By Ghu's bronzen bottom!" said Bessas, "you might as well pile a Pelion of folly on an Ossa of impulse and free her."

"Would you care to be free, my dear?" said Myron.

Phyllis burst into tears. "You m-mock me! After the pirates plucked me from the beach at Aineia, I would have given aught in my power to be freed whilst I still had some chance of regaining my home. But how could I ever return to Macedonia from here, hundreds of leagues from the Inner Sea? As I have no family or protector here, the first slaver who saw me could seize me. Or else I should starve. My only hope would be to become a public woman, or give myself as a concubine to some rich Kushite in hope that he would not use me too cruelly. Abandon me not in this savage country!"

"There, there, my dear girl," said Myron. "You shall remain with me as long as you like, though I warn you that the way ahead is hard and perilous." He put his arm around her, finding her as tall as he was.

As they walked towards their camp, Kothar said: "Whilst Captain Bessas was seeking to gamble away our substance and Master Myron was watching the mating time of the menagerie, I learnt some facts of interest."

"Speak!" said Bessas.

"I found an old Kushite officer who spoke Egyptian and was too rich in years to enjoy that mass rut. From him I learnt the state of affairs in Meroê.

"Two groups contest fiercely for power: one headed by General Puerma, the other by High Priest Osorkon. Now, Puerma is a man who loves the old. He worships the old Kushite gods: Apizemek, Anuqet, Tua, and the rest. To Amon-Ra he pays no heed. Also, he maintains the ancient custom of banquets of raw meat.

"Osorkon hates the old Kushite ways, deeming them unclean and barbarous. Fain would he make cultured Egyptians of the folk of Kush. He would subordinate all other gods to Amon-Ra, and he holds the eating of raw meat in particular horror. That is why tonight's feast was held outside the city instead of in Puerma's quarters in the palace."

"We Bactrians have had the same trouble with Persian rulers who follow the cult of Zoroaster," said Bessas. "Go on."

"You know the custom whereby the priests of Amon of Meroe, when a king ages or does badly, send him an embroidered napkin, called the Cloth of Death. When the king receives this grim gift, he calls in his guards and commands them to strangle him, and they do."

Bessas burst out: "By Anahita's womb, if any priest told me to slay myself, I'd hew his head from his shoulders ere his tongue had completed its clack!"

"No doubt you, not being a slave of custom as are most men, would do just that. But in all the centuries since Kashta founded the Kushite kingdom, no king has ever defied the priests' command. To be sure, only a few kings have ended their days thus, because most of them died in battle, or were murdered, or fell sick, or otherwise perished before the priests got around to them.

"Howsomever, here we have King Saas-herqa, a well-meaning wight of no great force or wisdom. He dotes on General Puerma, because Puerma is brave, loyal, and a splendid general. On the other hand, he fears to offend Osorkon, lest he receive the Cloth of Death. And Osorkon had been urging the king, more and more openly, to rid himself of Puerma, quickly and for good, so that the true religion shall prevail and the vile customs of raw-meat eating and promiscuous fornication shall be extirpated.

"Now Puerma, through his spies, knows about this. Being no more eager than the next man to be stabbed, poisoned, or otherwise disposed of, he casts about for the best course to follow. One possibility is to bribe the lesser priests, not all of whom are so fanatically pious as the holy Osorkon, to throw their weight against the high priest or even to slay him. Another is to raise the banner of revolt.

"Both of these courses, however, require wealth. As you have seen, Puerma is a gambling man, who has always let gold slip out the bottom of his scrip as fast as he puts it in the top. That is why he has lately acquired a burning interest in the treasure of Takarta."

Bessas said: "Suppose we did fetch this treasure back. Would Puerma keep his bargain, or would he slay us to possess himself of the whole?"

"Who knows what secrets the heart of a man can hold? Men make promises according to their hopes and keep them according to their fears. But from all I can learn, the Kushites are an honest folk, and Puerma is deemed a man of integrity even amongst the Kushites."

Bessas pondered. "That may be, but I still would not trust him to the point of playing odds-and-evens with him in the dark. However, tomorrow we'll try again for information and guides to the River of Darkness. Methinks the word will have gone out that we be hindered no more."

When they got back to the camp, Myron said: "O Bessas,—ah—I wonder——"

"Say no more, teacher. I shall move in with the boys."

In the tent that Bessas had vacated, Phyllis submitted, without resistance but without enthusiasm, to Myron's caresses.

"I know my duties, master," she said. "But, slave though I be, I am no wanton who pants with lust at the sight of every man. So take your pleasure and do not wait upon me."

Afterwards she told him her story. "I am the daughter of Philippos, a small landowner of Aineia. Being of pure Corinthian descent, my family deems itself a cut above the folk of those parts."

"I wondered why you spoke pure Doric without the Macedonian accent," said Myron. "Go on."

"Three years ago, celebrating our local Mysteries, I went with other maidens of Aineia to the seashore near the town. Whilst we bathed, a crew of pirates rushed upon us from behind the rocks of a headland.

254

Some of us escaped, but one other girl and I were caught. They dragged us to where a forty-oared craft was beached. There a host of hairy pirates set upon us and raped us, one after the other, until we could scarcely move. Then they put to sea with us.

"The pirates, who were Karians, had been raiding the coast and had sacked the town of Skapsa. So they had many other captives. As there is little room aboard such a craft, we were dreadfully crowded, huddled between the rowers' benches in the after part of the ship. Then the pirates decided to sail for home across the Aegean.

"We had been sailing but a short while when an outcry arose, for a ship was coming up astern. From other captives I learnt that this was a Macedonian trireme. No doubt someone had ridden to Therma to give the alarm.

"So the crew put out the oars and bent their backs. We flew over the waves, but ever that black-hulled trireme came closer. Men took the places of rowers whose strength failed, while others readied the pirates' weapons.

"Whilst this was happening, the captain pushed into the crowd of captives and spoke to me in broken Greek. 'Girl,' he said, 'I have been watching you, and I think I could like you. How say you?'

"I was tempted to spit in his face, but fear won the day. My tears had ceased and I managed a smile and a murmured assent.

"'It is well for you,' he said, 'because we are about to lighten the ship. I shall have to hide you because, if they knew, the crew would throw you overboard with the rest.'

"Then the captain rushed about, moving the captives hither and yon on the pretext of getting them out of the way of the rowers. In the confusion thus created he pushed me into his cabin. This was a mere kennel at the after end of the ship, but it was the only place for sleeping.

"Then I heard a frightful cry amongst the captives. Shrieks and splashes told of their fate. Between one splash and the next, I heard my poor friend Klea scream: 'I lay the evil eye upon you, Captain! I come from a line of Thessalian witches! I curse you in the name of the triple Hekate! Never shall you see your home again——' and then another splash cut short her voice.

"After a while the outcries ceased, though the splashes continued as the pirates threw over their bulkier loot. Huddled in the cabin, I expected to see the beak of the pursuing warship come tearing through the walls. But hours later, the captain came in again.

" 'We have shaken them off,' said he. 'Now hold your tongue and make yourself invisible until we reach our home port.'

"Throughout the rest of the day and the following night, the captain, whose name was Mavaen, spent much time with me. I found him not unkindly; for, though he had a strong lust for me, he reined himself back when I told him how sore I was from my treatment by his crew.

" 'A day or two to recover, lass,' said he, 'and then you shall learn what real loving is.'

"During the following day the ship gave a lurch and came to rest at a slant. I guessed that we had run ashore. Then sounds of altercation came through the cabin door. The door flew open and two pirates pounced upon me and dragged me forth.

"We were beached on a rocky island to rest the crew and pick up water. Captain Mavaen was quarreling with the boatswain. Although I could not understand their speech, I gathered that this officer had seen Mavaen thrust me into his cabin and now taxed the captain with perfidy towards his crew. To a sea thief it is a dreadful offense to secrete a part of the loot for one's own benefit, instead of throwing it into the common store to be divided at the share-out. Captain Mavaen had not only done this; he had also risked the freebooters' lives by

keeping a bulky, heavy piece of loot—meaning me—
aboard when the rest was abandoned.

"The boatswain, therefore, challenged Mavaen to fight
him to the death. So the pirates climbed down over the
bow, hustling me with them. They marked out a place
for the fight, and Mavaen and the boatswain went at it
with swords and bucklers.

"For a time they circled, leaping, slashing, thrusting,
and parrying, without either's gaining the advantage.
Then Mavaen lightly wounded the boatswain on the leg.
The boatswain could no longer leap so swiftly, and
soon Mavaen wounded him again, on the left shoulder.

"Now the boatswain had much ado to defend himself,
as he could no longer move his buckler swiftly enough
to guard his vitals. But he fought on, limping and gasping. The crew began to cheer Captain Mavaen and urge
him to finish the fellow off, though methinks they would
have cheered as loudly for the boatswain if he had held
the vantage.

"Mavaen began a mighty attack, slashing and thrusting and striking at his antagonist with his shield. He
drove the boatswain around the circle like a dog driving
sheep. I hoped to see the boatswain soon fall; for,
while both were bloody ruffians, at least Mavaen had tried
to save my life.

"But then a gull, flying overhead, let fall a bit of offal,
which struck Mavaen in the face. As the disconcerted captain gave back, the other plunged his sword into Mavaen's breast. The captain fell to the sand and soon
gasped out his life.

"The pirates chose the boatswain to be their new captain. But then another dispute arose. For some who
knew Greek had understood the curse which Klea had
hurled at the captain; and it was plain to the veriest
dunce, from the act of the gull, that the gods had taken
a hand in the fight. Fearing lest the curse should damn
them all, they were troubled as to what to do with me.
One faction was for cutting my throat then and there;

another for returning me to my home, at whatever risk; and a third for speedily selling me.

"Whilst the argument raged, another ship drew up offshore and anchored. The pirates flew to arms, but the new vessel neither attacked nor showed fear. She was a Phoenician trader, of the kind sometimes called a mussel boat, with more oars than a regular merchantman but fewer than a war galley. We could see from the shore that her people were well-armed. After some shouting across the water, her captain came ashore in the ship's boat.

"This captain, a big ox of a man in a shirt of lizard mail, said he was Baalram of Arvad. Seeing the pirates beached, he had bethought him that they might have some lately acquired merchandise to sell. Lest they get any clever ideas, he was not in the least afraid of them, because his ship had a beak like that of a warship and could smash the stern of the beached pirate craft as easily as a man crumples a sheet of papyrus.

"Since their cruise had not proved very profitable, the pirates were glad to dispose of their remaining loot so quickly. They sold me to Baalram, who took me back to Phoenicia. I was sold again, and taken to Egypt, where I was bought by a Persian colonel on his way to command the frontier fortress of Buhen on the Upper Nile.

"I had been a few months in Buhen, working as lady's maid to the colonel's wife, when the Kushites captured the fortress by a sudden attack at dawn. The colonel died sword in hand before the spears of a hundred foes, and the women—those not butchered in the excitement —were dragged away across the desert. General Puerma, who commanded the raid, set his eye on me; and that is how I came to Meroê."

"How did you find Puerma?"

"Not bad; certainly preferable to the cruel Baalram or the peevish Persian colonel. He summoned me to his bed but once. I do not think he liked me much that way, preferring his dark beauties. When he dismissed me, he said: 'You are a good girl, Phyllis, though I do not think that armies will march and thrones will topple on your account. You are too sweet and placid. Some day I shall find you a husband, of a good steady type like yourself.'" She began to weep. "And now, I fear, such hope is forever beyond me. I was betrothed to a rich youth of Aineia, but even if with the help of the gods I regained my home, his family would no longer even look at me after my shameful fate. I shall never have a home of my own."

Myron, too, wiped away a tear. For a wild instant he thought of offering her marriage himself; but prudence prevailed. No sensible, rational, temperate Hellene, he told himself, ever married for love alone, and certainly not for pity. Marriage was a serious matter, involving property and family, not to be entered into on a mere gust of emotion.

"Don't give up hope, my dear girl," he said. "Some day I may be able to do for you what Puerma said he would."

XIII The River of Darkness

BESSAS, MYRON, KOTHAR, SKHÂ, AND SHIMRI sat on the edge of a steep brown bluff near Meroê. Below them the azure Nile flowed placidly northward, while above, thin white veils of cirrus wafted across the face of the high hot sun. Bessas spoke:

"Men, I have brought you out here so that we could talk freely without our Arabian friends' overhearing. I have asked in Meroê how travel hence to southward is managed, and this is what I have learnt.

"He who would journey up the River of Darkness meets a peculiar hindrance, to wit: ignorance of the value of silver and gold. To one of Myron's philosophers this might seem an ideal state of affairs, but it makes the way hard for the farer. The distances are too great and the country too difficult for the traveler to take all his food with him; but wherewith shall he buy more from the locals?

"The usual trade goods, I am told, are iron hoes and spearheads, beads, and salt, which comes in little brown cones. Howsomever, these trifles are exceedingly heavy and bulky for their worth.

"Moreover, not all kinds are acceptable everywhere. Thus one tribe may refuse iron spearheads for some superstitious reason; another will accept red beads but not those of any other hue. Therefore the traveler must needs carry a vast fardel of trade goods of all kinds, to ward against being stranded and perishing of starvation.

"So it seems we shall have to bear much more dead weight than before. The established method is to hire fifty or a hundred Kushites as bearers, and another score or more of soldiers to guard the bearers. And these must all be fed.

"Now, Zayd means to return to his oasis as soon as I pay him off on the morrow. But our reckonings show that one of his camels can easily bear seven, eight, or even ten times as much as a human porter. Therefore, these beasts can carry more than can a hundred Kushites, even counting the weight of their riders.

"Moreover, camels will not desert, or mutiny, or rob and rape the natives and thus embroil us in unwanted conflict. They live off the leaves of thorn trees, whereas the Kushites must be fed and led, bullied and cajoled. Dip me in dung, but it seems pure folly to hire scores of wayward, lustful, and foolish men when these docile beasts can do the work!

"Since our plans have perforce been changed by the matter of Takarta's treasure, I therefore purpose to make Zayd a sporting offer: to carry us to the sources of the Nile, in return for half of the part of the treasure remaining after Puerma has taken his moiety; that is to say, one quarter of the total."

260

The men looked at one another. Skhâ asked: "How much will the treasure come to?"

"By the thousand senses of Azi Dahaka, how should I know? The tale avers it was borne through Meroê on the back of an ass, so it could hardly come to more than three talents of gold."

All fell to discussing how much three talents of gold would be. The two younger men became wildly excited when calculations, made by drawing figures in the dirt, showed that this would be the equivalent of about a hundred and thirty thousand shekels of silver.

"A kingly fortune!" cried Skhâ. "By Ashtarth's pubic zone; do you mean you would give half of that to a lot of flea-bitten sand thieves? The whole crew and their beasts cost us less than five shekels a day!"

Bessas smiled grimly. "When you can fare over waterless wastes as ably as these men do, Skhâ, it will be time enough to scorn them. And you forget several things. One is that Puerma gets half of the total, leaving half for Zayd and me to divide betwixt us. The other is that the sum I gave was but the upper limit. We may find that this fabled treasure is nought but a handful of tarnished silver, or that it has been scattered or destroyed, or that it never existed save in some flap-tongued fellow's fancy."

Myron looked at his friend with new respect. Ever since his disastrous game with Puerma, Bessas had seemed more mature. The big fellow was now less the roistering, reckless ruffian and more the thoughtful and responsible leader.

Skhâ said: "Of course, we can promise them aught and give them the slip later——"

"Enough!" barked Bessas. "I keep my word, whatever others may do." He continued: "Now, I have formed an opinion of Zayd, having dealt with men of his ilk in the deserts of Aryana. I am sure that, if I try to haggle with him and compel him to go on with us at his present rate of pay, he'll refuse. He waxes impatient to see his clan and get his hands once more on the reins of his tribal affairs. But offer him a chance at a daring exploit, with a hope of vast wealth at the end, and methinks he'll come."

Shimri, chewing a stalk of grass, asked: "How—how about us? What share have we of this treasure?"

"I propose that we divide the quarter remaining to us into eight parts. Of these, I as captain shall receive three parts, Myron as my lieutenant shall have two, and the rest of you one each. At least, that's how the pirates of the Hyrkanian Sea divide their loot. Is any man so hardy as to gainsay me? Good; we have decided."

On the last day of Duuzu, the expedition assembled for the march to southward. Besides Bessas, his four men, and Phyllis, there were the shaykh and his daughter, each riding a camel, and five other Arabs of the Banu Khalaf, riding and leading nineteen more of the beasts. One Arab and a camel had been sent back to the Fifty-League Oasis, while one new man had been added to the party. This was Merqetek the guide. Merqetek was a Dankala from Karutjet, a slight man with a sly grin that bent the tribal scars on his raisin-colored cheeks.

"Well," said Bessas, walking up and down before the line of waiting men and laden beasts, "henceforth we shall have no letters from princes and politicians to smooth our way. I'll wager no man south of here can read. Tighten that girth, Shimri."

Myron mused: "I wonder if we did right to decline those soldiers Puerma offered us. At a ha'penny a day, we could surely have afforded them."

" 'Tis not the money but the time. They'd have wended afoot and halved our speed."

"Suppose ten thousand naked blacks assail us——"

"Then we should be no stronger with forty than with fourteen. As we stand, we have at least a chance to out-run them on our beasts." Bessas shook his massive head. "Nay, for speed give me a small party. Further, I have had somewhat to do with unlettered tribesmen on the other

262

frontiers. Unless you drag an army with you, your best protection is to move swiftly and mind your own business. If you linger, you give the barbarians time to think, and they may think either that you mean them ill, or that they can profit by robbing you."

"At least, I am not sorry to see the last of fabled Meroê. For a capital city, it's the dullest and dirtiest place of my experience."

Shaykh Zayd, astride his kneeling camel, caught the drift of Myron's words and said: "You Hellenes are spoilt with your city-dwelling! By Ilâh and Ilât, only we *badawîn* know how to live so that such things are not needed. Bide with us for a year and you will never wish to sleep within walls again!"

Bessas poetized:

> Some men prefer to sleep in tents, while some
> In palace walls alone to sleep succumb;
> But tent or palace, 'tis the same to me,
> For when I wish to slumber, sleep shall come!

The Bactrian was in high good humor. The ten-day of waiting in Meroê for Puerma to return had jut him into his foulest mood, but since that low point he had steadily waxed more cheerful.

It was well, thought Myron, that someone felt thus. He himself had swallowed a knot of apprehension, which stubbornly remained in his stomach. A dozen times a day he told himself that he had been a fool to come on this jaunt and should begin devising excuses for turning back. And a dozen times a day he berated himself for cowardice, inconstancy, and neglect of a matchless opportunity to advance the knowledge of man.

"Where in demon land is Skhâ?" demanded Bessas. "I'll wager the whoreson little knave is off having a final canter on a pallet."

"Here he comes," said Myron. "But—who's that with him?"

263

Skhâ, approaching from the gate, led by the hand a tall, slender young woman in a Kushite kilt. "Here we are!" he cried gaily. "This is Katimar, the wench of whom I told you. Some of the Arabs and I clubbed together to buy her."

"And what," rumbled Bessas, "do you purpose to do with her?"

"Bring her along, of course, to serve us."

"Who said you might add servants to our company? And afoot, too, so that they would slow us?"

"That is no matter. She can keep up with us."

Myron, looking the girl over, realized that she was six feet tall and well-built. She grinned amiably, showing a large mouthful of gleaming white teeth.

"Take her back," said Bessas.

"But captain! We have paid good silver——"

"Take her back, I said! If her former owner will not give you back the full price, that is your ill luck."

"I will not! We will not face the wilderness without a woman to comfort us! Myron has his Macedonian, and you have the Arab wench——"

"Why, you foul-minded little——", snarled Bessas, starting for Skhâ with hand on hilt and murder in his eyes.

"Gentlemen!" cried Myron, throwing himself between them. "Let's not quarrel just as we are setting forth. I think we can come to a reasonable agreement."

"Well?" said Bessas, holding himself in with effort.

"Permit the girl to accompany us as far as Soba, to see how things work out. If it transpire that she does in fact encumber us, we can dispose of her there."

Bessas glowered at Skhâ, who had dodged behind the donkey purchased for Phyllis. "Very well. But I shall make the final decision, and no one who knows what is good for him shall gainsay me."

The road south to Soba led through a broad flat plain of pink sandy soil, covered by a sparse fuzz of dry golden-yellow grass. This pastel plain was stippled with large grayish-green trees, armed with millions of long straight thorns, as white as serpents' fangs and fully as sharp.

Here and there rose isolated outcrops, towering up to a height of a hundred feet. They were weathered into strange forms, like the ruins of castles built by giants. Others resembled pieces of unfinished statuary, with separated blocks in the shapes of cubes, spheres, and cones.

On this leg of the journey, the three girls spent much time together, even though Salîmat and Katimar had no language in common. Phyllis and Salîmat could converse in bad Aramaic, while Phyllis and Katimar could talk in broken Kushite.

Despite the wide differences of race and background among the three, the fact of being the only women in a large and motley band of men drew them close together. All were kept busy, Salîmat with managing the camels and their riders, Katimar with cookery, and Phyllis with the mending of garments. The black girl had turned out to be a better cook than the Macedonian, whose only culinary method was to fry everything in oil.

Myron was greatly pleased with Phyllis, who made life much more comfortable for him. Once he even thought he was falling in love with her. The prospect alarmed him, as he deemed this state of mind unwholesome and dangerous, as well as unsuited to his age.

On the other hand, he was just as happy not to have too much of Phyllis' company at any one time. She was a tireless talker, filling his ears with pointless tales of her very ordinary life in Aineia and ever boasting of her Corinthian ancestry. The gentle flow of verbiage kept on even when Myron wanted silence in which to think deep thoughts.

For the first two days out of Meroê, Katimar kept up with the company. Her long stride matched the walk of the beasts of burden, and when they trotted she trotted with them. Finding her skirt a hindrance, she stowed it among the baggage and ran naked.

On the third day, however, she developed a sore foot. An hour was wasted in vociferous argument as to which animal she should ride and how the loads should be shifted to accommodate her. At last she was placed behind Salîmat on the latter's camel. She screeched with terror as the beast rose with its rocking-horse motion, and she clung fearfully to the shaykh's daughter as she stared down from her vertiginous height.

On the afternoon of the fourth day they came to the junction of the two great rivers that make up the Nile: the Astapous and the Astasobas. A large sandy island, ribbed with palms, lay in the midst of the confluence.

Birds swarmed by millions; their clamor made the ears ring. Thousands of ducks and geese flew over the river. Cranes, herons, egrets, ibis, storks, and spoonbills waded in the shallows. Pelicans plunged for fish. Darters perched on trees, drying their half-opened wings. Hawks, eagles, and eagle-hawks wheeled high overhead.

Enormous crocodiles lay on the beaches with their mouths open, while small birds cleaned their fangs. The shores were heavily thicketed with thorny acacias and mimosas. From an overcast sky a light rain—the first that Myron had seen since leaving Persepolis—pattered down upon the dusty plain.

Merqetek led the company up the Astapous for two leagues to Soba, a mud-walled village. Here, said Merqetek, a ferry crossed the Astapous. Thereby they could gain its south side and resume their march along the Astasobas.

Camped outside Soba, Bessas called his people together. " 'Tis as I warned you, lads. The black wench cannot keep up with us. So, since speed is of the essence, she cannot continue with us."

"What shall we do with her?" wailed Skhâ.

Bessas shrugged. "She is your property. Sell her, give

266

her away, or free her; it is all one to me. But tomorrow we wend without her."

"You could buy another beast, like the ass you purchased for Phyllis."

"Belike, but I will not. I'll not further clutter our company with unneeded people, and that is my final word." He stalked off, muttering to Myron, who walked beside him: "A pox on this business of bringing women on an expedition! If you let one in, somebody will surely find an excuse for fetching another, until we have a troop of them."

"What else could I have done with Phyllis?"

"I blame you not; but see how this thing grows! Were there no woman at all, the knaves might forego their horizontal sports, at least outside of cities; but let the leaders enjoy the company of women and the rest will think of nothing else—especially a billygoat of a man like Skhâ, who makes a career of what should be only a healthy hobby."

They walked on up the Astapous, talking of many things, until the setting of the sun and the emptiness of their stomachs reminded them to return to camp. They had almost reached it when they were brought up short by the sound of screams. Salîmat and Phyllis appeared, running towards them. As the girls came near, they panted:

"C-come quickly! They are slaying Katimar!"

Bessas and Myron ran and soon burst upon the scene. Three Arabs held the screaming and struggling Katimar, so that her neck lay across a log. Standing beside the group with his sword out, Skhâ prepared to cut off the young woman's head. At the sight of Bessas, however, he stepped back.

"What is this?" demanded the Bactrian.

"We are killing the wench, that is all," said Skhâ.

"Why?"

"Because no one in Soba will buy her. Rather than loose her for some other man to enjoy without paying,

267

we decided to kill her. She is after all our property."

"You mother-futtering sons of serpents!" roared Bessas, while the Karian gaped in astonishment. "Dung-eating defilers of holy places! Let her up forthwith!" Bessas kicked one of the Arabs in the ribs, so that all quickly scrambled up. Katimar threw herself at Bessas' feet, kissing the toes of his boots.

"You said we might do with her as we liked!" cried Skhâ hotly.

"Shut up, you bloody little swine! O Shaykh, why did you not put a stop to this?"

"But, my lord, she is only a woman, a slave, and a black! What is the fate of such a contemptible creature to me?"

"How about you, Kothar?"

"I did protest, sir, but they paid me no heed."

"A fine pack of murderers," snorted Bessas. "Kothar, ask her whether, if we free her now, she can find her way home."

Katimar dried her tears and burst into an eager smile. "She says she can easily do so, if given a little food to take with her."

Bessas gave Katimar not only some food, but also a good knife and a fistful of trade copper. The last Myron saw of her, she was limping up the Astapous towards the land of the Megabarri, scores of leagues to the east. And for many days Skhâ sulked, refusing to speak either to Bessas or to Myron save in line of duty.

The ferry at Soba was a rickety little boat of sycamore planks sewn together with cords of palm fiber, holding three including the boatman. Half a day was spent in taking travelers and baggage across and towing beasts of burden by their bridles.

South of Soba the vegetation thickened. A forest of towering gum trees lined the banks of the Astasobas. The sausage tree, the soap tree, and the tamarind appeared. In the shallows of the river grew clumps of papyrus, lifting its feathery fronds eight or ten cubits above the flood.

This gallery forest hid the river from the travelers, save when they stamped and hacked a way through the tangle to reach the water. Their coming disturbed the crocodiles and the herds of hippopotami, which floated with only their eyes, ears, and nostrils showing. Although the greenery was a relief after so many leagues of desert, the insects became annoying.

Outside the forested strips along the river, the land stretched away in a grassy steppe. This plain, rarely interrupted by low hills, was dotted with squat, flat-topped, thorny acacias and deep-red termite hills. Across the river, sand dunes formed the skyline. Antelopes, wild asses, and giraffes appeared in the distance. At night, lions roared, leopards snarled, bushbucks barked, reedbucks whistled, and hyenas uttered their mirthful yells.

Once a great slate-colored rhinoceros lumbered out from behind a thicket, blinking and twitching its ears. It uttered a volcanic snort, lowered its head, and took a few menacing steps towards the travelers. The horses began to neigh, the asses to bray, and the camels to roar, while all the animals danced with terror. Bessas unsheathed his bow, but Merqetek rode up, shouting in Kushite and Egyptian. Kotar translated:

"He says not to shoot; it will but enrage the brute! He says for all of us to shout and scream!"

The travelers howled and hallooed, while Merqetek, producing a pair of wooden billets, beat them together with a valiant clatter. The rhinoceros snorted, turned, and trotted off across the plain, with its little cloud of tick birds fluttering after it.

The days and the river crept past. The monotonous plain stretched weary leagues to the flat horizon. As they proceeded south, the grass of the prairie lengthened and the thorny trees of the scrub grew larger.

Myron found himself a little disillusioned with Phyllis. Tiring of her gentle but never-ending talk of life in

269

Aineia and her noble ancestry, he tried to educate her by lectures on the world and the theories of priests and philosophers about it. But he quit when he saw that such talk bored her as much as her chatter of home and pedigree bored him.

So Phyllis spent more time with Salîmat. Bessas often joined them when they were resting or eating, sending them into gales of giggles with his chaff and beguiling them with tales of his adventurous past.

"Sit down and join us, old man," said Bessas genially to Myron one day. "I was telling the lassies about the time my half brother Moccus and I journeyed across Hind. This country is so stocked with gods that it is easier to meet a god than a man, and Mithra knows the land has a plenty of men.

"After we left mighty Pataliputra, we beat our way to Supara, near the western coast. On the way we fell in with another wanderer, named Shunga, from the Persian provinces of Hind. Gods, but he was a rascal! He dyed his whiskers blue and put on an air of the gravest piety, but he'd steal a bowl of porridge from a puppy dog.

"If a man tell you that the streets of India are paved with pearls, cast the lie back in his teeth. Nor do pigs run about the streets ready roasted. To be sure, the kings and priests are rich, but that is the case in other lands, and the vulgus has as much ado to keep ahead of hunger as elsewhere.

"It is hard for the traveler in Hind to earn an honest living, because all occupations are regulated by ancestry. Every man must follow his father's trade, according to the class into which he is born, and there is nothing left for the stranger to do. Nor will they ever change their ways. When an Indian says, 'This is not according to custom,' that ends the matter.

"Hence we reached Supara nigh to starving, having run out of gold and silver and failing to find a way to get our hands on more. We were reduced to filching melons in the market place when Shunga told us of a great cave

270

temple near Supara. This temple was, he said, full of gold and jewels to be had for the taking.

"Now, I am not uncommonly pious, but I like not to meddle with gods, especially strange gods on whose mercy I have no claim. But Shunga talked us round. He was worse than you Greeks at finding fancy reasons for doing things one wants but ought not to do.

"This temple was quarried out of the side of a mountain. Behind an ornamental stone gateway lay a short corridor, which widened out into a series of chambers: first the hall of offerings, then the dancing hall, then the hall of assembly, and lastly the shrine, a small room wherein stood the statue of the god Vishnu.

"Shunga had a scheme for getting into the shrine, namely: to make friends with the guard on duty at the entrance, ply him with rice wine laced with a decoction of poppy seeds, and thus put him to sleep. Shunga assured us that on this particular night there would be no ceremony, so all we had to do was to wait until the priests were asleep, pry loose a few kings' ransoms' worth of jewels from the statue, and flit out again.

"Getting in proved easy. With my heart beating like a blacksmith's hammer, I followed Shunga through the halls and into the shrine, where rose the great four-armed statue of the god, with a shawl of cloth of gold draped over his shoulders. Shunga lit a tiny lamp, set it in a corner, and covered it with a cone of oiled sheepskin, so that enough light came through to keep us from stumbling over our own feet.

"We were prowling around the statue, trying to decide which of the glorious rubies and emeralds and sapphires and opals and sardonyxes and topazes and other baubles to pry out first, when Moccus gave a little yelp and whispered: 'Ye gods, what is that?'

" 'That is only the sacred python,' said Shunga. 'Pay it no heed; it is probably drugged. Boost me up so that I can get at the jewels on the statue's girdle.'

"We had begun to do this when light and sound from

the outer chambers warned us that something was toward. And there we were, trapped at the bottom of a bag, just as Myron and I were in that damned Egyptian tomb.

"Shunga put out his light, and we clustered behind the statue. Soon the audience hall was lit by torches, brightly enough to read by. Peering around the legs of the god, we saw a gallant procession coming towards us. Shunga whispered: 'The gods have mercy on us, but that fat fellow with the fancy feathers in his turban is the king of Supara! He has come to ask the god some question.'

The king's soldiers stood at attention in rows on the sides of the audience chamber, and the king and his ministers stood in a glittering knot in the center. The priests banged on gongs and blew on conchs and danced and chanted. It was a brave spectacle, albeit I should have enjoyed it more under other circumstances. I said:

" 'What will they do? Say a prayer and go away?'

" 'No such luck,' said Shunga. 'See, they are melting butter over that lamp to the right. The high priest will bring the bowl of melted butter in here and daub the statue with it. Then he will pray to the god for guidance and tell the king what he thinks the god has put into his mind to say.'

" 'We had better do something quickly, then,' quoth I.

" 'Aye, but what?' said Shunga. 'I have been praying, but in view of the sacrilege we were about to perpetrate, I do not think the gods will extend themselves to help us.' Then he glanced from me to the statue and back. 'Make me a spider in my next incarnation, but you are the spit and image of Vishnu! Look!'

"I durst not peer around the statue, lest I discover myself to the throng in the audience hall, but I saw what he meant. Aside from the fact that the god had twice as many arms as I, we looked not unlike. Shunga said: 'We will put this likeness to use. Have you heard the legend of the churning of the Sea of Milk?'

" 'Nay,' said I. So, whilst arraying me as much like the

272

god as he could, Shunga told us how, acting in concert, the gods and the demons once churned the Sea of Milk, using Mount Mandara as the churn and the cosmic serpent Vasuki as the churn rope. Thus they created the Nectar of Immortality and other delightsome things.

"Meanwhile Shunga stripped me to the waist, took from his wallet the blue dye that he used on his beard, and rubbed it on my face and arms until I was blue all over. For a crown he crushed in the point of that cone of sheepskin wherewith he had covered the lamp and set the thing on my head. He hung round my neck his own necklace of beads, which was all the jewelry we had left amongst us. And he draped the god's golden shawl about my waist and made me doff my boots. Then he altered his own costume and that of Moccus.

"Following his instructions, we lifted the sacred serpent out of its cage. Then, as the priest approached the shrine with his bowl of butter, we stepped forth into the torchlight and went into our dance, which depicted the myth of the churning of the Sea of Milk.

"Shunga and Moccus each held one end of the snake and sawed it back and forth as if working one of those Indian churns, which is twirled by means of a rope twisted about its shaft. Between the two I did an Indian dance, waving my sword in one hand and the lamp in the other. I was a lively dancer in those days and had watched many Indian dances, so my imitation was not too bad.

"When we appeared, everyone in the audience room went rigid. We had done a dozen steps when the high priest screamed: 'Great god Vishnu!' and cast himself down on his face. So did the king and the ministers and the soldiers and whoever else was there. I was too busy with the steps of my dance to count the audience.

"What convinced the Indians of my divinity, I think, was my size. The folk of Supara are rather small. But Shunga, being from the Land of Five Rivers, and my half brother were both over six feet, and I overtopped them both.

273

"We went on dancing, never hurrying a step, through the audience hall and the outer chambers and out into the night. Now and then we passed a priest or a layman lying on his face and praying with all his might.

"Outside the entrance lay the king's riding elephant, draped and painted like King Xerxes on New Year's Day. Around it the mahouts and the grooms who held the horses and the rest of the royal crowd lay also prone.

"Shunga looked from the elephant to me and jerked his head. I climbed into the hawdah, followed by Moccus, whilst Shunga bestrode the animal's neck. He kicked the elephant under the ear, so that it got to its feet and shambled off into the night. But we had gone but half a league when Shunga stopped the elephant.

" 'Here we take to our own feet again,' said he. 'The king and the priest may begin to have doubts about the divine visitation and start hunting for us, and we could hardly be more conspicuous.'

"So we left the beast pulling branches off trees and stuffing the foliage into its maw. We left the cloth-of-gold shawl and the sacred python in the hawdah and set out afoot for Supara. Shunga said: 'Try not to step on a serpent, for many perish thus.' This was comforting advice to a barefoot man trudging a dusty road on a pitch-black night.

"We stopped at a stream to wash the blue dye off me, then scaled the city wall and regained our quarters without detection. Though glad to have saved our hides, we were disgruntled at not having brought one single jewel out of the temple. Worse, Moccus and I had lost our jackets and boots.

"Next day the market place buzzed with the news of this wondrous theophany. Whilst we were looking for a melon to steal, the high priest himself came strolling through, acclaimed by all and beaming like a tiger that has just swallowed a tax gatherer.

"Shunga pushed through the crowd, placed his palms together and bowed over them, and spoke to the priest.

274

I could not understand him, for he spoke in an ancient dialect called Sanskrit. In any case, the twain stepped aside and conversed in low voices. I saw the priest look in my direction and pass something to Shunga.

"Back at our lodgings, Shunga brought out a bag of golden rings and slugs, and square silver coins enough to see us all to our homes and have something left over. When we asked him how he had done it, he said with a chuckle:

" 'I told the holy father that I had a heinous sin to confess. Having obtained his ear, I told him the tale of our raid. He was greatly shocked by the sacrilege and spoke of having us seized and trampled by elephants. Then I reminded him that the temple had done very nicely from the manifestation of the god and doubtless would do even better in the future. But, if our little fraud were exposed, all this would cease.

" 'He saw the point at once and assured me that, as nought had been stolen, the gods could take care of themselves. In my case, they would probably do no more than degrade me to the untouchable class for a thousand incarnations.

" 'No doubt, I said. But meanwhile it were well, so as not to shake the faith of the masses in the true religion, to get my companions and me away from Supara forthwith. Otherwise we might be recognized, or my harddrinking comrades might boast of their feat in their cups. And, although we were willing to go home quietly, we could not do so in our present penury. Well, this priest can tell a tiger from a toadstool, so here we are.' "

On the eleventh stop after leaving Soba, they found a backwater of the Astasobas with a sandy bottom. Careful inspection and poking with spears having shown that no crocodiles lurked therein, they bathed.

After the sun had set, Myron and Bessas patrolled the margins of the backwater while the two young women washed themselves. Glancing towards the pair of lithe female bodies splashing about at the far end of the pool, pale in the light of the rising moon, Bessas said:

"I wonder—Myron!"

"Eh? What's that? Your pardon, O Bessas. My mind was on these strange stars we see and their bearing upon the question of the shape of the earth."

"Have the gods vouchsafed you the answer to this problem yet?"

"No, curse it. Sometimes I feel I almost have the solution, but then it always eludes my grasp. How goes your suit?"

"What suit?"

"Any ninny can see that you're infatuated with Salî-mat bint-Zayd."

Bessas heaved a gusty sigh. "It is as plain as all that? I had thought it a secret betwixt my soul and me."

"Is the fullness of yonder moon patent to the casual eye?"

"Ah, me! For days I have striven to work up my courage to speak to the shaykh of a possible alliance. But at this prospect I, who have waded through rivers of gore, do quail like a slave girl under the lash. Will you do it for me, old friend? Will you serve as go-between?"

"Certainly," said Myron.

The girls completed their baths, and all returned to the camp. Myron ate, squatting with the rest. Shimri, across the fire from him, looked up with popping eyes. For an instant the Judaean, his mouth too full for speech, could only point and gurgle. Myron looked around and scrambled up.

A dark shape, rising to an incredible height, towered over Myron's head. The eyes alone, showing their whites in the firelight, seemed to be at twice the height of a man. Myron had to lean back a little to see to the top of the thing. From each side of the central mass spread a pair of objects that looked at first like bat's wings, save that they were a hundred times the size of those of a proper bat.

276

As Myron's eyes adapted themselves to looking away from the fire, he saw that from the central mass sprang another feature. This was like an enormous blind snake, which reared and weaved this way and that, as if questing for a victim. The mass seemed to be perched on the trunks of a pair of great gray trees, which had not been there when Myron sat down.

The women screamed; an Arab shouted: *"Fîl!"*—Somebody threw a stick of firewood, whirling so that its burning end etched a looping curve of ruddy light in the darkness.

Below the questing serpent, a great red mouth fell open. A high-pitched bellow, between a scream and a roar, like the blast of a bronzen trumpet befouled with spittle, came from the cavernous opening. As the monster turned, the moonlight flashed on a pair of long white tusks.

Then the elephant was gone with a crashing of vegetation, leaving a frantic jabber of voices behind it. Myron looked for his leader. Bessas had leaped for his Parthian bow and now stood with arrow nocked.

"Praise Mithra, at least we were not stamped flat!" said the Bactrian. " 'Twas bigger than any elephants they have in Hind."

"D-did you see the horns on it?" cried Shimri.

Myron reproved the young man: "Those were not horns; they were tusks."

Bessas snorted. "Some day our beloved Myron will be trampled by one of these great African monsters. And when somebody runs for help, crying: 'A hippopotamus is killing Myron!' he will look up, and his dying words will be: 'You err, my dear fellow. This is not a hippopotamus; it is a rhinoceros!' " He glared around the camp. "Where in the seven Babylonian hells is Skhâ? He was supposed to patrol."

They found the Karian asleep against a tree trunk. Despite his howls that the crocodiles would devour him, they threw him into the Astasobas.

The next day, Myron took the shaykh aside and broached Bessas' proposal. Zayd thoughtfully pulled his beard.

"The Banu Khalaf is flattered that so great a lord and hero should ask for one of our daughters," said the shaykh. "Natheless, I must tell you that it may not be."

"She is surely old enough," said Myron.

"True, but that is not the issue. She should have been wed to some good clansman years ago, but she has overblown thoughts as to what sort of man she wishes. I fear that even becoming wife to Xerxes would scarcely satisfy her; and, being less strong in my dealings with her than a proper Arab father, I have not compelled her. Besides, she has threatened to stab in his sleep any man to whom I gave her against her will."

"She seems to like Bessas well enough."

"True, Master Myron, but that is not the point."

"What is the point, then?" said Myron with a touch of impatience, for the aged Arab showed a tendency to ramble.

"Craving your pardon, we are most particular about the purity of our blood. Lord Bessas is not an Arab, let alone a Khalafi. So pray tell him thanks, and thanks again, but let him seek a wife elsewhere than in the tents of the Banu Khalaf." The old man sighed. "Betimes I wish he were a Khalafi. I shall not live forever. I have no living sons; my brother Naamil, though well-loved in the clan, is too mild and indolent. Moreover he, too, has daughters only. No other man in the clan has the strength and wisdom required to ward us from disaster in this wicked world."

"Your daughter seems to be a better man than most men."

"Ah, true. But stones will sprout leaves or ever the *badawin* submit to being ruled by a woman. And that is why I should like some magician to turn Captain Bessas into an authentic Arab, complete with pedigree."

When Myron reported back to Bessas, his news cast the

other into the deepest gloom. "Of what avail my noble achievements, if there be no sweet woman to share them with?" said the Bactrian, wiping away a tear.

Myron suggested: "If you want a wife so badly, you could have Phyllis. She is desperately eager to find a husband, and she gazes upon you with that same gods-but-he's-wonderful look that you bend upon Salîmat."

"Phyllis is a good lass and I like her. For a second wife she would suit me well—that is, if you did not wish to keep her for yourself. But for the first, I will have Salîmat bint-Zayd and no other. I burn for her like an iron founder's furnace." He sighed. "It never occurred to me that the lesser races might hold the same interdicts regarding purity of blood as we Aryans do."

"Live and learn. I trust you'll keep your passions well reined in. For, if a man lay lustful hands on Salîmat, Zayd and his lads would think themselves in honor bound to have the fellow's heart. Not to mention that she's quick as a snake with a dagger herself."

"Fear not. In my younger days as a soldier on the frontier, I committed a few rapes with the rest, at the taking of towns. But when I saw the dole I thus made, I swore never again to take a woman against her will. This is between you and me, of course; for some might deem such self-denying resolutions unmanly." Bessas managed a wan smile. "So Zayd thinks I should make a good shaykh, eh, but for the detail that I'm no Arab? One could fare farther and do worse. Betimes I weary of forever flitting about the world like a bat in a banquet hall, without home or ties."

On the twenty-fifth of Abu, a weary column reached the point on the east bank of the river opposite Tenupsis, the capital of the southern Nubae. A large village with huts of wattle and thatch swam into view across the flume. A low stockade surrounded it, and a pair of skulls grinned from lofty poles at the sides of the gate.

Gazing at Bessas' party, Myron thought they looked

279

travel-worn and exhausted after nearly a month of marching. Their clothes were faded from the sun and stained from the rain, which became ever heavier and more frequent as they proceeded south. He himself felt that he would be in the Elysian fields, could he but lie down and do nothing for a fortnight. And if he could do his loafing in a good library, reading for hours every day, he would be on Olympos itself.

The march had borne heavily on men and beasts. One camel and one more horse had died. One Arab was sick with a persistent cough. Large biting flies buzzed menacingly about the caravan.

A grinning, naked Nuba scrambled up the river bank and spoke in broken Kushite to Merqetek, who translated to Kothar, who translated to Bessas. "He says he will ferry us across for one string of beads a passenger."

Bessas looked towards a distant cluster of conical huts, rising from the grassy plain on the eastern side of the river, where grazed a huge herd of cattle. "Myron, you and Merqetek go across to buy food ere we starve. I must needs think on how to set up a defensible camp. Or do you need Kothar as well to make yourself understood?"

"No," said Myron. "I now know enough Egyptian and Kushite to converse with Merqetek. Don't you find it curious that in Egypt the official language is Syrian, in Kush the official language is Egyptian, and here, where they speak the gods know what tongues, the language of trade is Kushite?"

"Get me a proper store of victuals, and one day I'll talk about the theory of languages all you like. But go."

Myron gathered a bag of trade goods and scrambled down the river bank. His heart sank when he saw the boat. It consisted of two large bundles of dried reeds lashed together. Each bundle was about the size and shape of the tusk of a big bull elephant.

The boatman launched the craft with the pointed ends of the bundles forward and settled himself astride the bow, with his legs hanging down into the water. He indicated that Myron and Merqetek should sit directly behind him, with their legs, also, in the water.

Myron pointed at the water, saying: "*Seka?* Do you not fear crocodiles?"

Merqetek listened to the boatman and laughed. "He says, when the crocodile will take us, it will take us, and there is nought we can do."

Myron climbed into his place. The boatman leaned forward and propelled the boat by paddling vigorously with his hands.

Around the landing on the far side a pack of young Nubae splashed and swam. Instead of swimming like all the other folk that Myron had seen, thrusting both arms forward and bringing them back to the sides at the same time, while kicking like a frog, these boys raised each arm in turn, stretched it forward out of water, and brought it down and back. Although the stroke looked fatiguing, it sent the youths shooting through the water at an amazing speed. Myron resolved to try this stroke, for in these crocodile-infested waters such a sprinter's pace might save one's life.

Two hours later, Myron returned with his purchases. It took two trips to ferry them across. His usually even temper was roiled by his getting caught in a sudden shower. He set down before Bessas a trussed young pig, squirming and grunting, and a round dark-brown object.

"This," he said, "is all I could find for sale in Tenupsis. I spoke to the Nubian king, and he said to return on market day, five days hence, to obtain a better choice."

"The pig I recognize, but what is this?" said Bessas, touching the brown thing with the toe of his boot.

"Cheese."

"I have never seen cheese of such a color."

"It's packed in cow dung to preserve it. It is also prepared with cow's urine."

281

"Ugh!" said Bessas. "By Mithra's mace, we had better not tell the others, lest their appetites be ruined. And what is in those bags which Merqetek is fetching?"

"One contains dried grasshoppers. The other is a kind of millet. You eat it as a porridge. I have tried it. It's repulsive, but it is the only corn grown hereabouts. One thing more: the king urged that you stockade your camp." He pointed towards the distant cluster of huts. "The Anderae, who occupy this bank of the river, will give you endless trouble otherwise. Oh, oh! Here they come."

Bessas blew a blast on his whistle. "Stand to arms!" he bellowed, unwrapping his bow case, which had been swaddled to protect it from the damp.

Twenty-odd Anderae advanced from the distant village, followed by a few of their women, Each bore a cowhide shield and either a club or a wooden spear with a head of antelope's horn. Like most of the folk along the Astasobas, all were completely naked, save that the older women wore about their hips a single ornamental string of beads. The tribal marking of the men consisted of several parallel horizontal scars across the forehead.

As the Anderae neared, Myron saw that they were tremendously tall, like some of the captives who had been paraded by General Puerma's army. Every person in the group towered over Myron, and most of the men were at least Bessas' height. Though well-muscled, they were rather slender for their height. Each had the two lower center front teeth missing, and the bodies of most were covered with the ash of burnt cow dung. Otherwise, Myron could not but admit that they were splendid-looking people.

These tall blacks marched straight up to the camp, ignoring the weapons raised against them. The tallest man stepped forward, casually trailing his shield and spear. He spoke in a harsh, staccato tongue, and Merqetek said:

"He says, give him a gift."

"Fiends! Who is he?" said Bessas.

"His name is Gwek."

"Is he the chief?"

The Andera laughed scornfully. "He says the Anderae have no chiefs. A real man, he says, takes care of himself and obeys no one. When will you give him his present?"

"By the warts on Ahriman's nose, why should I give him aught? What will he give me?"

"He says the Anderae do not barter. They take what they want."

"Well, if he thinks he can take anything of mine—ha, Shimri, *watch out!*"

The Judaean dove at a pile of luggage, in which another Andera had begun to rummage while the party's attention was elsewhere. The black leaped back, clutching a handful of strings of trade beads, and fled laughing.

"Come back, Shimri!" shouted Bessas. The Judaean, sword in hand, had started across the plain in pursuit of the thief. Bessas continued:

"Skhâ! Labîd! Amr! Drag all the baggage together in one pile, sit on it, and kill the next of these knaves who touches it!"

Gwek repeated his demand for gifts, more and more loudly. The other Anderae joined in, bellowing, holding out eager hands, and edging closer. The women added their screams to the tumult.

Bessas roared: "If they want to fight, we'll give them a bellyful! Tell them to stand back, or we shall begin!"

Instead of complying, the Anderae closed in around the travelers, covetously clutching at their possessions and shouting and laughing more uproariously than before. Bessas put his whistle to his lips and nocked an arrow.

Then Kothar, holding a lighted lamp, paraded forward and blew a blast of flame from his mouth. The Anderae scrambled back with wild yells. The noise died down. Bessas pushed his men into a fighting formation.

The Anderae trailed back towards their village, shouting back over their shoulders. Merqetek translated:

"They say you will be sorry that you were so stingy with them!"

Bessas said: "The Nubian chief is right. By nightfall I want our camp surrounded by seven-foot stakes. There are enough saplings along the river to furnish them. Jump to it!"

An hour later, weary from driving stakes into the rain-softened soil, Shimri said: "Wh-why do we not attack these savages tonight and teach them a lesson?"

Myron replied: "For the same reason that a wise mouse bites not a lion's nose. Thousands of these barbarians dwell within a few leagues of here, scattered about the plain. Do you see that village in the distance? And that one? Merqetek informs us that they have no government and live in universal discord, with each village raiding and fighting the next. But let an outsider attack one, and all assemble like a swarm of hornets to repel the invader."

That night, as Merqetek had taught them, they kindled several fires within the stockade and piled grass on them to make smoke. These smudge fires kept the swarming myriads of mosquitoes from driving men and beasts mad, although the dense blue smoke was scarcely less of a torment. All night the sound of the company's coughing mingled with the susurration of insects and the roars, howls, snarls, snorts, and trumpetings of the beasts that roamed the Astasobian plain.

Next morning the camp was surrounded by a five-foot fence, strengthened by withes interwoven among the palings. Then Bessas set his men to whittling sharp points on the tops of the stakes. The palisade was no defense against a serious assault, but it afforded cover for archers and enabled those within to control the flow of visitors.

And visitors soon arrived. Delegations came from many villages, until there were hundreds of ebon giants swarming around the stockade and shouting demands for gifts. Their clamor filled the air; their pungent odor

284

wafted through the encampment. Their threatening presence kept the expedition on edge, day and night.

When one was admitted, he would insult and berate the travelers as niggards, pounce upon some piece of portable property, and run for the gate. One of them escaped with an Arab's kaffiyya before those within learned to trip and pin their visitors at the first sign of larceny. After a few Anderae had been whipped out of the camp, attempts at theft fell off.

But the bloodless siege continued. Glowering over his stockade, Bessas said to Myron the next day:

"By the demons of Mazana, these churls give our folk no rest! I meant to stop here for them to gather strength for the next march, but they look wearier than ever. Look at that son of a toad! He has been at it for hours."

He pointed to a muscular Andera, who stood twenty paces away, shouting demands. Nearby, Salîmat said softly:

"Good Captain Bessas, if you let that mighty mendicant in, methinks I can use him."

The man was Nyakong, from one of the more distant villages. After Salîmat had spoken with him through Merqetek for an hour, he departed, scowling and muttering. Bessas asked:

"What said you to that lout, my lady?"

Salîmat smiled enigmatically. "We spoke of the leading men of the villages of the Anderae: which would do us good and which ill."

Late the same day, Gwek returned, shouting angrily. At Salîmat's request, he was admitted. Soon he, too, departed, frowning and growling.

The following day, small parties of the Anderae were seen from the camp, hurrying hither and thither across the savanna. Fighting broke out among them. Smoke rose from burning villages. Men, tiny in the distance, were seen pursuing and slaying other men. But the Anderae let the encampment alone. Bessas sought out Salîmat and said:

285

"By the flames of Atar, lass, you've worked a magic as strong as Kothar's! Tell me what you did."

"It was simple. First I told Nyakong that we could give him no gifts, because gifts were only for the brave, and Gwek had told us that Nyakong was the greatest coward of his village, whose men were the worst cravens among the Anderae.

"Then Gwek came, demanding to know what we had said to Nyakong to cause him to shout taunts at Gwek. And I told a similar tale, but with the rôles reversed. So now another feud has burst amongst the villages, half siding with Gwek and half with Nyakong. By the time they come to their senses, I trust that we shall be far away."

Bessas looked sharply at the shaykh's daughter. "My dear Salîmat," he said, "you belong, not in the clean, simple desert, but at the Achaemenid Court, where the threads of intrigue spread as thickly as cobwebs in a haunted house!"

XIV   The Pestilential Plain

KING AKOL, who ruled the southern Nubae from his thatched-hut palace in Tenupsis, proved friendly although possessed of a voracious appetite for gifts. He sold the travelers food, rented them women, and gave them advice.

They could not follow the river farther south, he said, because of the swamp that spread for many leagues in every direction. As the rains were now at their height, the river overflowed and flooded the plain, making it impassable. Nor was it practicable to go up the stream by boat, because the river lost itself in many channels, often blocked by floating masses of weed. Moreover, one would need the help of the fierce and hostile Syrbotae, who lived in the swamp.

Therefore one had to make a wide swing away from the Astasobas, around the swamp, returning to the river farther south. Somewhere in the misty distances of the unknown southland, Akol understood, lay the town of Boron, capital of the Alabi.

So Bessas' company darned their garments, sharpened their blades, tested their harness straps, laid in food, and prepared to march once more.

As the camels and mules were being loaded, Shaykh Zayd plucked at Bessas' sleeve. "The blacks come!"

"Plague!" Bessas ran to the edge of the stockade and peered over. Several furlongs off on the grassy plain, an irregular dark mass flickered and pulsated, flowing ever closer. Bessas blew his whistle. "Stand to arms!"

By the time the Anderae came within bowshot, the loaded camels had been unloaded. Every man, grasping a spear, was mounted on horse, mule, or camel. As the Anderae neared, looking ghostly with their hides smeared with cow-dung ash, they shouted and screamed in a frenzy of belligerence. Bessas asked:

"What say they?"

"They say we shall not go," replied Merqetek. "They will slay us and take all our nice things: our weapons, our ornaments, and our women. Their rain maker has given them a charm that protects them from our weapons."

"Follow me in column!" cried Bessas. He spurred at a canter out the gate. When the last camel cleared the gate, he commanded:

"By the left flank, turn!"

As a result of the differences in mounts and languages, and the lack of practice, the maneuver was raggedly carried out. Bessas pulled back to a walk while he bellowed curses and commands at his straggling troop. At last they were gotten into some sort of line.

"We are vastly outnumbered!" wailed an Arab. "What can twelve men do against hundreds?"

287

"By Mithra, you whoresons shall see!" said Bessas. "Many they may be, but they have never faced a mounted charge. Forward, walk! . . . Canter! . . . Charge! And Verethraghna aid us!"

His heart beating painfully, Myron charged with the rest, sighting on the foe over the point of his spear. The Anderae were scattered loosely about the plain. They ran towards the stockade, shaking their crude weapons and screaming war cries.

As the handful of mounted men bore down upon them, many of them threw spears. But these horn-tipped weapons had no great penetrating power. Most of them either missed or glanced harmlessly off leathern corselets.

When the mounts of their foes loomed over them, most of the Anderae broke and scattered. Of the few who struck or thrust at the mounted men, most were speared or ridden down. Bessas' horse Vayu, eyes rolling and teeth bared, assailed any foe who strove to stand before him, snorting and trampling like a four-legged demon.

Myron's horse knocked over one Andera. Myron, with a small prayer to Ares, couched his spear towards the ash-smeared chest of another black giant, who threw himself forward with upraised club. The club struck the horse's off shoulder with a thump, causing the animal to shy and almost unseat his rider. But Myron's spearhead went home. As the Andera fell, he dragged down the spearhead; the weapon was twisted out of Myron's grasp. Myron tugged out his bronze-headed mace and looked for another foe.

The Anderae were running in all directions, colliding and falling over one another in their haste. A widening gap formed in the center of their array as the troop galloped through. Here and there a man shrieked as the point of a spear found his back. Before he could come within reach of another antagonist, Myron had ridden completely through the hostile host. He drew rein.

Between him and the stockade the mass of Negroes

still milled, split by the charge into two separate crowds. Some were running away, some were hopping and screaming defiance, some were shouting advice to the others, and some were stolidly standing about as if wondering what to do next. They seemed to have no organization whatever.

"Form your line!" roared Bessas.

He led them in another charge. The Anderae scattered even faster than before. From the outer parts of their host, men began to stream away across the plain.

"Another charge; form your line!"

Myron pulled up beside Bessas, whose spear ran blood a yard back from the tip. "They are breaking; why kill more of them?"

"We must harry them from the field, lest they rally. Forward, walk! . . ."

Myron rode with the rest. With his mace he smote a black woolly head that bobbed into sight near his right knee.

Then there were no more Anderae within reach. The tribesmen were streaming away in all directions, bounding through the grass on their long legs almost as fast as a horse's canter. A score lay about the field, half hidden by the grass.

"Line up!" said Bessas.

He inspected his men. There were a few minor wounds on man and beast from the horn-headed spears. The Bactrian gave gruff directions for binding each wound and handed out praise and blame for actions during the fight. He scrutinized Kothar's unstained spear and shouted:

"Damn you for a sniveling coward! I saw you hold back your beast, so that you never got within striking distance! I ought to flog you!"

"Whatever my lord wishes," said Kothar with a shrug. "I have never pretended to be a warrior."

"*Ê!*" shouted Myron, pointing.

A group of Anderae were coming out of the stockade. Four of them dragged the women by the arms, while the other three were laden with plunder.

Myron spurred towards the plunderers. The sound of hooves and the clank of equipment told him that others followed.

As Myron came closer, the blacks looked around. Some began to run with their loot. Then, seeing how fast their foes were nearing them, they dropped the things to run faster.

One of the two dragging Phyllis released her arm while the other seized her from behind and held her fast. The man who had released her swung his club up to dash out the girl's brains.

Myron could not possibly reach the struggling group in time. He had no missile weapon available. To throw the mace would be useless, as he might hit Phyllis. His bow case was strapped to his saddle behind him; but he had never learnt to shoot from horseback, and he had no time to dismount.

Just as the club began to fall, the club wielder staggered as a feathered shaft sprouted from his flank. While the man reeled, dropping his bludgeon, the other released Phyllis and ran.

In an instant it was over. Seven more long ash-gray naked corpses cumbered the savanna.

Bessas, who had loosed the shot that saved Phyllis, rode up and leaped to the ground. The girl rushed upon him and embraced him. He seemed embarrassed, saying:

"There, there; give credit to old Myron, who first saw your plight and led the charge. The rest of you, back to the stockade and take up your loading again. We must be out of here within the hour!"

Then he stood for a little while, looking down at the bodies. Myron said: "I should call it an execution rather than a battle."

"Aye; I would never ask promotion for slaughtering naked and almost unarmed men. It is a pity in a way.

With modern weapons and civilized discipline, methinks these Anderae would make magnificent mercenaries. Could I but. . . ." He broke off. "Myron, where's your spear? Well, go back and fetch it. By the bones of Rustam, must I remind you to bring your head with you? Let's be on our way, my bullies!"

The next month was the most terrible that Myron had ever experienced. Leaving the river a few leagues south of Tenupsis, they struck southeastward, trying to skirt the edges of the gigantic swamp of which Akol had warned them. This, however, was not easy, for the entire land was flooded, ankle to calf deep, and the swamp sent out tendrils and outliers for many leagues. League upon league they splashed through stagnant surface water. The watery plain, covered with long, brown, dead grass, stretched as far as eye could cast. Only rarely a low flat-topped ridge or hummock, crowned with trees and termite hills, raised itself above the morass. The elevations were not dry either, as the leaden skies poured rain incessantly upon the land.

From time to time they had to avoid a patch of swamp. Many leagues they wasted, blundering among the bogs and starting marsh buck with grotesquely long, pointed hooves. Although Merqetek claimed to have been through this land before, he had not learnt his way. He was therefore useless as a guide, though still valuable as an interpreter.

Bessas said: "By the claws of the Corpse Fiend, this damnable country reminds me of the swamps of the Upper Oxus, near Zariaspa. They are good for marsh demons and venomous serpents but for nought else."

On the elevations they often found a village, with a group of naked, club-hefting villagers glowering at them. Sometimes they had to retreat to avoid attack, as they were now in no condition for battle.

They never knew how they would be received. Sometimes the villagers were implacably hostile. Sometimes

291

they were suspicious but willing to live and let live. Sometimes they were friendly. One never could tell in advance.

Because the sun and the stars were hidden most of the time, the travelers often found themselves headed in the wrong direction. When the rain let up, biting flies appeared in swarms. One striped devil with an orange body and black and white wings bore a proboscis over half the length of its body, standing out before it like a lance. A man attacked by it leaped and yelled as though stuck with a hot needle.

Food and water were not yet problems, as Bessas sometimes shot a game animal: a bounding tiang, a droop-eared roan antelope, or a burly waterbuck. For these hunts he borrowed one of the others' bows, not wishing to expose his precious Parthian war bow to the wet and risk having its laminations come unglued.

But the dampness and the attacks of insects began to tell. A camel died, and then a horse, and then another camel. The Arab who had been ailing weakened until he could hardly sit a camel. Then one night he, too, died. They mourned him, for of all the Arabs in the company he had been the most likable.

Shkâ, his taste for travel sated, wept for his distant home. Shimri glared, grimaced, twitched, and often muttered to himself.

Instead of letting up as Akol had promised, the rain became heavier. It rusted their weapons despite all the oiling and polishing they did. It got into their food and spoilt it. It got into some of the salt they had brought to trade and melted it together into solid blocks. It got into Myron's precious notes and made most of them illegible. At this, the Milesian burst into tears.

Bessas put an arm around Myron's shoulders and said: "Cheer up, old man. When we reach a dry clime, you can rewrite them from memory."

Myron gulped. "Never can I remember all those native names for plants and beasts!"

The ordeal brought out the best in Bessas. He was gentle with the weak, stern with the slack, and hearty with the willing. He was the first to leap to any difficult task. He drove his men, but he drove himself twice as hard. When they were utterly downhearted, he cheered with boisterous songs and crude jokes. Myron remarked:

"You are a greater man than I suspected, my boy. You seem to have learnt that there is more to leadership than hitting people over the head. Now, could I but persuade you to give serious thought to the nature of man and the universe——"

Bessas wagged a finger: "Flattery will gain you nought, teacher! I know you would fain make me over into a philosopher like yourself, but that were like teaching a horse to play the harp. A man of action I have always been; a man of action I shall always be."

"Well, Cyrus and Darius didn't get the name of 'great' solely by bashing in the skulls of miscreants, so why should you expect to?"

"Who said I wanted to be Cyrus or Darius? I enjoy life too much as Bessas of Zariaspa to wish to change."

Myron said: "Let me see if I cannot express your meaning by one of your Persian quatrains." He struggled with his muse for a few ush, then recited:

> *Behold the gallant Aryan hero true,*
> *Of little wit and mighty, bulging thew:*
> *He slays a dragon or a thousand foes,*
> *Then trips and breaks his neck without ado!*

Bessas guffawed, slapping his thighs. "You're an able versifier, even in Persian. But I think I can top you."

> *Here comes the sage from Hellas, grave and wise,*
> *Whose eagle gaze doth scan the starry skies;*
> *With eyes aloft, on a cockadrill he treads,*
> *And so concludes his heavenly surmise!*

293

On and on they slopped, with the south wind blowing the rain in their faces. The beasts of burden sickened and died, one by one, until all the company were walking. Bessas wept bitterly when his charger, Vayu, perished like the others.

Their shoes rotted faster than Shimri could cobble them; their threadbare garments fell into holes faster than Phyllis and Salîmat could patch and darn them. Soon they were tramping through the long grass in rags and tatters. They tried to make garments of antelope skins but, lacking means for properly tanning the hides, they found them slimy when wet and stiff as armor when dry. And the hides stank as they rotted.

They came to a river. While they disputed as to whether it was the Upper Nile, a hunting party of Shaikaru came upon them. The naked black giants proved friendly. They explained that this was but an eastern branch of the Astasobas; Boron, which they sought, lay on the larger, western branch. To reach it they had to cross the stream before them and ascend a smaller tributary to its source. The hunters not only pointed the way but went with them for several days to set them on the proper path.

On the last day of Ululu they were ascending this tributary. Rain came less often; new green grass sprouted vigorously among the brown stems of yesteryear, which often rose as high as a man. The land was less depressingly flat and featureless. Here and there from the higher ground arose a huge baobab tree, with a thick squat tublike elephant-colored trunk and long slender sparsely-leaved antlerlike branches. Sometimes, in rain or bad light, they were thrown into panic by mistaking a hillock for one of the elephant-eating serpents of which Yehosha had warned them.

They saw clumps of giraffes and great heards of antelopes. They passed a herd of elephants, moving slowly on vast columnar legs like rheumatic old men and stuffing themselves with everything green in reach of their trunks.

294

In the bright steamy sunshine the animals were mouse-colored on their backs and black on their lower parts. The elephants, a bowshot away, paid the travelers no heed until a puff of breeze carried human scent to their trunks and sent them lumbering off with squeals of alarm.

In beasts of burden, the company was now down to one horse, two mules, and three camels. Everybody walked and some carried loads on their backs as well. Much gear that Bessas judged not essential had been abandoned. Myron said:

"Puerma said something in Meroê about domestic animals' dying of a sickness in this region. We should have paid him closer attention at the time."

Kothar, brooding on supernatural influences, explained: "My familiars tell me that the gods of our homeland do not reign here. The gods of this land are dark, cruel, and dangerous. They are angry with us because we, not knowing their language and rites, do not worship them."

Bessas snorted: "If the local gods are any bloodthirstier than those Phoenician Baals, I want nought to do with them."

During a noon halt, a scream from behind a thicket made Myron whirl. For an instant he wondered if this were the cry of an animal, or of one of the party attacked by an animal. He dashed around the thicket.

Skhâ and an Arab were holding Phyllis down on her back, while another Arab was preparing to ravish her.

Myron tore out his sword and plunged towards the group. Sensing his approach, the two who held the girl released her and sprang to their feet. Skhâ drew his sword —a short blade like Myron's—and the Arabs their daggers.

"Abuse my slave, will you!" panted Myron, rushing at Skhâ.

"If you want trouble, grandpa, you shall have it!" said Skhâ, his round face red. Sidestepping Myron's rush, he

295

spoke to the Arabs: "Slay him quickly, brothers, or he will have the big chief down upon us!"

Skhâ parried one slash from Myron while the Arabs closed in from side and rear. Myron realized that they could easily destroy him by attacking from different directions, unless he kept whirling and dancing to keep them off. He, who had attacked so boldly, was now on the defensive. Lacking his buckler, he drew his dagger with his left hand. Phyllis had disappeared.

"Old fool, making such a fuss over a mere slave!" panted Skhâ, lunging.

Myron, beginning to breathe hard, stumbled back against the thicket. Here, in the shelter of its thorny branches, they at least could not come at him from behind. None of the three was very aggressive in pushing home an attack, though they all kept urging one another on:

"Close in, Labîd!" "Cut off his sword hand, Skhâ!" "Stab him in the leg to bring him down, Amr!" "Go on, fight, you two! He is old and weak!"

Amr got close enough to prick Myron in the left forearm, though Myron lightly wounded the Arab's shoulder as the latter jerked back.

It occurred to Myron that he had not shouted for help. Perhaps he had been too busy to think of it, or perhaps self-esteem had stilled his tongue. Now he raised his voice:

"Help! I am beset!"

Bessas' heavy footsteps sounded as the giant Bactrian rounded the thicket, sword in hand. Phyllis followed in her scanty rags. Taking a long stride, Bessas hit Labîd on the side of the head with the flat of his sword. The Arab fell sprawling into the grass, then scrambled up and fled with Amr.

Skhâ, whirling to face Bessas, whipped up his sword for a backhanded slash. "You, too, eh?" he snarled, and swung, gripping the string of amulets round his neck with his left hand.

Bessas took a step back, out of the range of the short sword. As the force of Skhâ's swing spun him around, Bessas' long blade shot out like a striking serpent and slid between the Karian's ribs.

Skhâ fell to hands and knees, then flat, coughing bloody froth. He blinked, rolled his eyes, and tried to speak. But his last choked-out words were in his native Karian, which none understood.

Bessas stared briefly down at the body, wiped his blade, and turned to the panting Myron. "What in the name of Ahriman is all this?"

Myron explained; Bessas nodded, saying: "What shall we do with those rogues?" He pointed to the two fugitive Arabs, hovering on the horizon. "Shall we saddle up and ride them down? Had I a proper rope I could catch them for flogging, for I used to have some skill with the lariat."

Myron said: "Arabs are fierce feudists. If you flog one, the others will think it their tribal duty to stab you. Call upon Zayd to order them back and flog them instead."

"O subtle one! So shall it be."

When Amr and Labîd were persuaded to return and take their punishment, they volubly explained that the whole attempted rape had been Skhâ's idea. The Karian had complained that his lusts were driving him mad, and nothing serious would befall them if they indulged their cravings on a slave.

"This," said Kothar darkly, "is but the first part of the serpent goddess' revenge, for our participation in the raid on Siptah's tomb. You shall see."

After Skhâ had been buried, Bessas walked somberly over the plain with Myron, slashing at weeds with a stick.

"As if my lusts were not doing the same to me," said the Bactrian, casting a burning glance back to where Salîmat busied herself with camp chores. "But I have sense enough to know that my choice is either to seize her and break up the expedition in a brawl, or contain myself in

297

patience. You need not worry; you can always have your cow-eyed Macedonian wench."

Myron tossed his head in a negative. "Middle age has its compensations, my boy. I have been so exhausted during the last month that I couldn't raise a stand if Aphroditê herself appeared before me. Perhaps it is just as well; a pregnant woman were no asset to our expedition."

"You have a point. Some folk in such a case would simply cut the woman's throat, but I think it wrong to use the poor little creatures so." Bessas slashed at a flower. "I blame myself for Skhâ's death. Had I taken time to think, I should have disarmed him and had him flogged with the others. Then he would still have been useful to us; for he was not a bad lad, despite his everlasting clack. But my lifelong habit has been, when a man assails me with steel, to slay him as expeditiously as I can."

"You couldn't help it. If you had stopped to think, I should have been dead, and what would Xerxes have done for his report?"

XV   The Hills of Iron

ON THE NINTH of Tashritu, twelve human beings and four beasts of burden straggled across the green flatlands of Boron. The traveler's rags flapped loosely about their bodies, so that their wearers were not much better covered than the naked Alabi who, standing storklike on one leg and watching their cattle, stolidly looked around as they passed.

The wayfarers' skins were burnt to deep bronze, spotted by insects bites, and seamed by scratches from thorns. Their ribs showed, as Bessas had harried them on for several days without taking time to hunt fresh meat. All bore loads on their backs, and four led two mules and two camels. Of the thirty-five beasts of burden with which they had left Meroê, only these survived. In the last few days, one more camel had died, and a lion had taken the horse. The surviving animals moved slowly and feebly, with hanging heads, despite the plentiful grass of the country through which they had come.

Some of Bessas' party limped, and all reeled with fatigue as they pushed along with sticks cut from saplings. Bessas, who bore by far the heaviest load, ranged from one end of the column to the other like a sheepdog, barking:

"Close up there! Straighten up, Umayya! We near the city, and we must march as if we were strong and fearless. Hurry up, Merqetek, if you do not crave a cut of my stick! Shimri, what in Arallu are you doing?"

The Judaean had paused, where the path crossed a stony patch of ground, to stoop under his load and pick up some reddish-black pebbles.

"Iron ore, by the Lord of the Waters!" he said, grinning up.

"What of it? We are not going into the ironmongery business. Get along!"

They passed through groves of small trees with enormous pale-green leaves, each leaf comprising a whole branch. From these trees hung huge bunches of finger-shaped fruits.

More and more of the Alabi—men who had been loafing and women who had been working the vegetable gardens—left their tasks to gape at the strangers. Soon the travelers were surrounded by a crowd of Negroes, pointing, gesticulating, and shouting. Children shrieked and dogs barked. Myron said to Bessas:

"I do not suppose that Ethiopians are more prone to violence than men of other races. But they are so noisy that it is difficult to ascertain whether they intend violence or not."

The Alabi were, like the Anderae, very tall and rather slender. They were coated with cow-dung ash and colored clays, which pigmented their bodies in an endless variety

299

of hues—various shades of red, orange, yellow, gray, and white.

The Alabi, like the Anderae, removed the two lower center front teeth. Besides their ornaments of bone, wood, and ivory, their hair was dressed with the help of dried mud into bizarre horns, crests, and helmets. Ostrich plumes sprouted from many of these coiffures.

Ahead of the party, the stockade of Boron spread along the banks of the Astasobas. Skulls topped a dozen poles about the gate, from which a group of spearmen issued, marching towards the newcomers.

"Ground your loads in a circle," said Bessas. "Sit on them and keep these knaves from pilfering, but do not strike or wound one without my command."

The Alabi crowded round, poking at the loads, fingering the travelers' tattered garments, trying to thrust fingers into the visitors' ears and mouths, and laughing loudly. They showed neither hostility nor a desire to steal, but simple curiosity and vast amusement. Their heavy body odor offended Myron's nostrils.

Then the group from the town arrived. A man shouted and whacked a few shoulders with a stick, whereupon the crowd divided to let the dignitaries through. A tall, grave Alab with a necklace of cane-rat bones spoke in a sharp, authoritative tone. Merqetek said:

"I cannot understand him, for I have never been so far south."

"Try all the tongues you know," said Bessas.

At length someone fetched an Alab who had lived among the Nubae. Explanations began. He of the rat-bone necklace said:

"I am Dimo, general of King Gau of the Alabi."

Bessas told who he was, adding that he wished to stop at Boron to rest and then pass on through King Gau's dominions.

"In that case," said General Dimo, "you must give King Gau a hundred strings of beads, fifty iron spearheads, fifty iron hoes, and one man-load of salt."

300

Bessas said: "O Myron, you are a better haggler than I. Chaffer this knave down, for the tribute he demands would clean us out."

Myron addressed himself, through the interpreters, to the general: "Unfortunately we lost our salt in the Shaikaru country. We could give ten strings of beads. . . ."

The haggling went on for an hour. Dimo sometimes spoke threateningly, and the spearmen frowned and hefted their horn-tipped weapons. But the travelers, on Bessas' orders, remained calm. The Alabi surged about, laughing and gabbling. When one group drifted off, another took their place.

At length Dimo accepted a fraction of the tribute he had first demanded. He signaled a drummer, who struck up a rhythm to show that the travelers were now under the king's protection.

King Gau sat on an ivory-legged bench in the royal hut and looked at his visitors from under heavy lids. As nude as all the other Alabi, he wore a necklace of crocodile teeth and, on each wrist, a heavy bracelet of ebony set with ivory spikes. Spearmen stood about; messengers came and went. A page held a gourd and, at a signal from the king, presented the vessel so that the king might drink of the contents through a straw.

Gau fingered a short sword, one of several cheap blades that Bessas had bought in Meroê. In response to Bessas' question, he said:

"We have no such beast as this sirrush in our land, although I have heard of strange creatures in other countries, such as men without mouths, and men with serpents for legs. The only strange creatures in Alabia are witches, whereof we have a plenty; we have burnt thirty-seven in the last moon.

"For that matter, I was always told that the men who dwelt beyond Kush had noses like those of elephants. Yet now I see that this is not true, however strange you may appear."

"Are we then the first men of our race to reach your land, O King?"

"Aye. The Kushites come hither once or twice in a generation. Sometimes they come to trade, which we welcome; sometimes they come to steal our folk for slaves, in which case we fight them. Why do you men of the North need slaves, when you have beasts like those you brought with you to bear your burdens?"

"Because, I suppose, men like to compel others to do their will. And speaking of animals, we started out with many more, but sickness has struck them down."

"That is the nagana," said the king. "We never drive our cattle very far to the east or the south, because they then catch the nagana and die."

"Well, I see that we shall have to hire men to carry our baggage. Can your subjects be retained for this purpose, King?"

King Gau took a pull at his gourd. Other pages presented gourds to the visitors. Myron found the liquid to be a fermented fruit juice, sweet and bland.

"Have you never drunk banana wine before?" asked King Gau. "Now, about those porters——"

One of the ruler's women burst in and hurled a rattle of speech at him. With an angry roar, Gau leaped up, swung his arm, and smote the woman on the shoulder blade with one of his spiky bracelets. The woman screamed and ran out of the audience room with red blood starting from the wounds in her back. Myron glimpsed the scars of other such wounds.

"Women!" said the king. "As I was saying, I think not that you can hire my people for porterage. They are too proud, holding the raising of cattle to be the only manly occupation. However, five days' journey down the river live the Ptoemphani, who worship a dog. Being but dogs themselves, they care not what they do. I will send a messenger, asking for—how many will you need?"

"Fifty or sixty, King."

"I will ask for sixty bearers, then. Of course they must

302

needs consult their god ere they embark upon any such enterprise, and unless he wag his tail they will do nought."

Bessas said: "King Gau, know you aught of a party of Kushites who fled south through this land, upwards of forty years ago? The story runs that they went on until they came to a great lake, where they built a house of stone."

Gau smiled thinly. "Oh, aye. I was a child when they passed through Boron, and I remember when four of them returned, going north on their way to Kush. I have heard of these lakes, which lie south of the Mattitaean country, at the foot of the Mountains of the Moon."

"Said you Mountains of the Moon, O King?"

"Aye. It is said that the tops of these mountains are covered with salt, so that they shine like the moon at its fullness. But no man dares to climb to the region of salt, for fear of the giants of salt that dwell there."

"What of the Kushites, sire?"

"They say the chief of these Kushites told a local hunting tribe that he and his men were gods. As gods, they commanded these hunters to build their stone house, which was a great wonder. But then the chief turned himself into a great black demon and slew his fellows. The hunters fled, and the demon still haunts the house of stone. Now no one goes nigh to the place, for fear of the demon."

Bessas arranged to buy food. "And another thing, if you please, sire. Could I obtain some tanned hides for new tents and clothes?"

The king had some trouble, through his translators, in understanding the word "clothes." At last he said:

"I suppose I can arrange it; though I cannot understand why you foreigners cover your bodies with those dirty, ugly things. Are you maimed or deformed in some of your parts, that you seek to hide them?"

The following morning, the day after their arrival,

King Gau summoned his visitors again. He greeted them with grave courtesy, inquiring whether they were well-fed and womaned.

"I have sent a messenger to the Ptoemphani," he said. "The ancestral spirits willing, he will be back in ten days. When you set out, I will also send one of my people with you as a guide and interpreter. You must avoid the land of the Mattitae, up the river, because we are at war with them and they would slay you if you entered their land from ours."

"Which way shall we take to avoid them?" asked Bessas.

"To the west. The route to the east is not good, because great swamps cover the land." King Gau brought out the sword that Bessas had given him and fingered the blade. "Strangers, I have been thinking about this thing, and also about the iron hoes and spearheads that we sometimes get in trade from the northern peoples. Long have I wondered how this stuff is made. You, coming from lands where they make many strange things, must know. What great spell is needed to create iron?"

Shimri bounded to his feet, sputtering. "Your M-Majesty! I—I can tell you. Iron is mmm—it is made from a kind of heavy red stone, with fire and hammering." He wiped the drool from his chin.

Bessas muttered in Greek: "Ye gods, Myron, can't you shut the fool up? If the king believes he can use him, he'll mew him up here like a caged bird forever."

"Too late," said Myron. "The king has already grasped the idea."

Gau smiled. "You interest me, man with a small chin. Is this red stone to be found in our land?"

"Aye, sir, it is. Behold!" Shimri drew from his pouch a couple of ironstone pebbles. "I found these within a furlong of Boron. I could make iron for you."

Gau fingered the pebbles. "Meseems I have seen rock of this kind in the hills to the west of the river. If I send a man with you, will you cross over there now and tell

304

me if there be enough of this stone to enable us to make our own iron?"

"Why, Your Majesty, I—ah——"

"Good!" King Gau snapped his fingers. A stalwart spearman stepped up, to whom the king gave careful instructions. "If you go now, you will be back for dinner. May the ancestral spirits favor your search!"

As Shimri departed, Bessas muttered: "He cleverly gives us no chance to talk to Shimri in private and prompt him to report no ore. If King Xerxes asks me, I shall advise him to leave the Alabi alone, for while they are but savages their king is as shrewd as Oroxaeus."

The principal hardship of life in Boron, Myron found, was neither the creeping things nor the smells, but the insatiable curiosity of the inhabitants. A ring of them surrounded the travelers' encampment, watching every action day and night and commenting upon them with animated gestures and loud, rich laughs. Sometimes an Alab would stand on one leg, with the foot of his other leg resting against his knee, leaning on his spear, and watching the camp from sunrise to sunset.

The evening after the second audience, Shimri limped in late for his dinner, his eyes bulging. "Oh, what a fuffool I was!" he burst out. "Do you know what this pork-eating king says?"

"That you are commanded to tarry in Boron and teach his people smithery," said Bessas, chewing.

"How in Dagon's name knew you that?"

"We are not all quite so addlewitted as you, my lad. Tell us the bad news."

"Well, I—I went with the black man, as the king said, and I found a muchel of ore. It begins three or four leagues from the river. When I returned and told the king of this, he asked me about the making of iron. I answered, and he said: 'Friend Shimri, the gods have sent you to teach us this art. You shall remain here whilst your comrades go looking for their crocodile-pard. When they return downriver you may rejoin them—if you have

305

carried out your part of the bargain.' I did not recall ever having made any bargain, but I thought it well not to argue with the king."

"You showed one glimmering of sense, anyway," said Myron.

"But what shall I d-d-do? I cannot—I cannot remain here amongst these uncircumcised savages, whose language I do not even speak! You must smuggle me out somehow!"

"It was not our doing," said Bessas heavily, "that you sounded off so eloquently to the king this morning. Having cooked your stew you must eat it. As for smuggling you out, we cannot. King Gau holds us in the hollow of his hand; and, even if we escaped his wrath now, we should face it on our return."

"But I lack the proper tools! I have no picks and shovels for digging the ore, no flux or charcoal for smelting, and no hammers, anvils, pincers, and tongs for working."

"You should have thought of that ere you told the king you could make iron for him. A word is like a bird: once sent forth it is never recaptured. If you now go and protest that you did but utter empty boasts, he will surely visit his wrath upon you. You will have to make your own picks of horn and shovels of wood, burn your own charcoal, and construct your own hammers of stone and tongs of green branches."

Shimri burst into sobs.

Ten days later King Gau, with his bodyguards and pages, rode past the camp astride an ox. For a time he watched Bessas' party, all of whom, under their leader's frowning gaze, were busily making or mending. Some worked on garments, some on tents, and some on weapons. Through interpreters, the king spoke to Myron:

"Could I make my own folk as diligent as that, I could conquer all the tribes along my borders. I could in-

306

vade Kush and enslave its people! Come with me to where the man Shimri works and explain what he does."

Myron accompanied the king to the smelting pit, which Shimri, stripped to a loincloth, was lining with clay. A pair of Alabi helped him, though in a fumbling manner because they had hardly any words in common with him. Another pair appeared, bearing a pole whence a basket-load of iron ore from across the river was slung. They dumped the contents of the basket atop the growing pile of ore.

Shimri, his shoulders peeling from sunburn, wiped the sweat from his forehead and turned his red face up. "I have hunted all over this neighborhood without finding any good limestone for flux. Without flux, you lose half your iron in the slag." He gave his shrill, unbalanced laugh. "I know; I shall—ah—work a miracle! I am the great Dagon!" He resumed his work, singing a Dagonite hymn.

"Sometimes," said King Gau, "I think that some god or spirit has taken possession of Shimri." The king looked up, his eyes straining northward. "Your porters come."

Up the river, along the path that lined the eastern bank, came a procession of men with gaudy patterns of red and white painted on their sable skins. Led by Ajang, King Gau's tall, grave messenger, they appeared comparatively small and gaunt.

"Their crops have been bad," said King Gau.

The newcomers crowded together, giggling nervously as the Alabi pressed around them, uttering gibes and threats. Myron counted; there were forty-four instead of sixty.

"And withal," said Bessas' familiar growl, "many look not as if they could bear a full talent apiece. But we live as we can, not as we list, as the camel said who tried to fly. Who commands?"

Yilthak, leader of the Ptoemphani, was a mild, middle-aged Negro. When his crew began to scream demands

307

that they be made spearmen instead of simple carriers, Yilthak proved unable to control them. Bessas had to knock a few heads together to restore quiet.

"You think spearmen will have life easy!" he cried. "Well, you shall take turns at these different duties. Myron, make a list of these men, so that we shall know who deserts or misbehaves."

Then Kothar spoke to Merqetek, who spoke to Ajang the messenger, who spoke to Yilthak, who spoke to the porters, who looked serious.

"I merely told them," said Kothar, "that you had made a magic whereby any evildoer shall be eaten by large purple snakes that will grow in his intestines and devour him from the inside."

"King Gaul!" said Bessas. "How many of those riding oxen, pray, are there? As all of our animals have died, we could make good use of such steeds."

"I have many," said the king. "Take such as you wish; it is only a fair return for Shimri's services to us."

Myron spent an hour learning to ride an ox. The animals' gait was easy enough, but they could not be controlled by the rider. Another man had to lead them.

The company also took time to worship Kwoth, the god of the Alabi. "It may do no good," said Bessas, "but we do not want to miss any chances."

"By Zeus the king!" swore Myron the following morning, as the sun rose over the wide green Alabian plain. "Bessas, if I ever thought Zayd's boys a little unruly, I now retract that opinion. They are demigods of order and discipline compared to these whipworthy rascals."

The twain had been trying for a Babylonian double hour to get the expedition under way. But the Ptoemphani made endless difficulties. Every man argued at the top of his lungs that his load was too heavy, or that he had a sore foot, or that his pay should be greater. Men were forever wandering off. They demanded that departure be postponed for an hour—a day—a month.

They threatened to throw down their loads, to refuse to move, to return home.

The Alabi stood on one leg, leaning on their spears, with smug aristocratic smiles on their faces.

"Hereafter," said Bessas, "I swear by Mithra's ten thousand eyes to do my exploring in decent lands, where they have camels and other proper beasts of burden to bear the loads. Trying to use these witlings for the purpose is like trying to pick fleas off a dog with mittens. Come on, you swabs, on the road! Last man gets a cut of the stick!"

A few whacks got the column into motion. There were half a dozen riding oxen, led by armed Ptoemphani; Zayd's four surviving Arabs, also armed and afoot; and the remaining Ptoemphani carrying gear in bags and long reed baskets on their heads and shoulders. Shimri, red of face and eye, stood in the crowd forlornly waving.

A fortnight later they were still marching. They crossed the Nile and struck southwest, into a country of broad plains broken by groups of low hills, of tree-dotted savanna interrupted by patches of solid forest, in which long-tailed monkeys scampered and large black apes with bare behinds chattered and screamed and threw filth at the travelers.

On the higher ground, euphorbias lifted their many long green fingers heavenwards. Dragon trees bristled with sharp sword-shaped leaves. Enormous lobelias rose like the jade and emerald spires of ancient eastern temples, built back in the days when gods still walked the earth. The explorers plowed through stands of thick grass higher than their heads, where a man could see twenty feet along a trail and no more than five athwart it.

Ajang showed the travelers a small tree with glossy, dark-green leaves and clusters of red berries. When chewed, he explained, the berries of the kahawa tree had the property of banishing sleep.

The continuous rain at last let up, though they still encountered violent thunderstorms. Enormous storm clouds towered miles into the sky. Lightning flashed and thunder boomed as if quarrelsome gods were having it out.

Animals swarmed in the plains, and birds of strange forms and hues filled the air. Swarms of scarlet bee eaters incarnadined entire trees. Grotesque black hornbills flapped heavily past with raucous cries. Ring-necked crows cawed, slender little gray plovers daintily paced the grass for insects, and big brown eagle-hawks hung fearlessly about the company in hopes of offal. At night, cuckoos and barbets sounded the hours with bell-like notes.

The party shrank. Three Ptoemphani ran away, and Amr the Arab stepped on a thick-bodied venomous serpent and died of the bite.

Otherwise, compared with the haggard, exhausted state in which Bessas' people had come to Boron, they were in good health. Dinner seldom lacked a cut of antelope, brought down by Bessas' mighty bow. Besides too many kinds of antelope to remember, they saw herds of wild horses with gaudy black and white stripes.

"Is that the man-eating bull with the movable horns?" asked Myron, pointing.

Half a furlong away, scattered over a low hill, were a score of massive black wild cattle. Unlike the elephant, the rhinoceros, and the hippopotamus, which paid no heed to anything more than a plethron distant, the buffalo saw the travelers as soon as they came into sight. Up came all twenty heads to stare fixedly, so that both curling horns could be seen on the sides of each black muzzle. They stood like statues, except for the slow swing of their heads to keep the travelers in view.

"The horns do not look movable to me," said Bessas, reaching for his bow case. "But we might try cow steak for a change."

However, when the black interpreters saw what the Bactrian was up to, they loudly protested. This was no mere cow, they insisted. Although the buffalo usually let people alone, when wounded it was more to be feared

310

than any other beast. It would trail its foe for leagues for a chance to kill him. At last Bessas sighed and put away his bow.

"This damned responsibility is making an old woman of me," he grumbled. "A year ago, 'twould have taken more than the plaints of a few fearful savages to turn me from my purpose."

One clear night, Myron climbed a hill and stood looking at the strange stars that circled the sky to the south. Long he stood, thinking. He felt that the answer to the problem of the shape of the earth was inside him, trying to burst from his heart—or from his head, if the Egyptians were right in locating the mind in the brain. His mind was pregnant with this solution, but somehow he could not quite bring it to birth.

He paced back and forth, ignoring the roar of a lion. He bit his lips and beat his head with his knuckles. He threw himself down and beat the earth with his fists. Then he leaped up with a yelp, because he had thrown himself on top of a nest of stinging ants. While he was picking the angry insects out of his clothes and skin, a touch on his arm made him start.

It was Umayya. "They sent me to fetch you back," said the Arab. "Elephants are all around, and they feared for your safety."

"Elephants?" said Myron, bringing his mind with an effort back to present reality.

A tree as thick as a man's thigh went over with a crash a few reeds away, and a pair of tusks showed pale against the starlit darkness. Another great black form eclipsed the campfire. A shrill trumpet blast made Myron jump. From all around came other elephantine noises: Squeals, grunts, groans, grumbles, snorts, snores, and the rumble of elephantine stomachs. Mixed with these was the swish of grass and the crackle and crash of branches torn off and trees overthrown.

"Ye gods and spirits!" said Myron. "There do seem to be a few of them. Let us——"

311

"Yalla!" screamed Umayya, and ran.

Myron smelled elephant and glimpsed a flapping ear that blotted out the stars. The beast, looking as big as the Ishtar Gate, was almost on top of him.

Myron ran after Umayya, following the Arab by the pallor of his loincloth. Although he ran headlong into a baby elephant and mistook a grown one for a tree, he at last arrived back at the camp. Bessas said:

"How in the name of Mithra did you fail to hear them? They've been making a fiendish alarum around us for hours."

"I was thinking about the stars," panted Myron.

"Well, if that's what it is to be a philosopher, I will stick to my sword and bow. Of what avail great thoughts if they allow the thinker to be squashed like an insect?"

But Myron could not give up his private quest. The following day, they halted by the banks of a stream. Myron went off to find a place to wash a dirty shirt.

A clump of trees spread their branches over the stream; from these branches hung masses of globular nests. Hundreds of yellow weaver birds clambered and fluttered about these nests, casting the din of their chatter abroad. As Myron approached, they flew up in golden clouds. He passed the clump and found a half-submerged boulder that would serve for laundering. Little by little the birds returned to their city.

Myron's gaze rested upon the weaver-bird colony. Thinking of the odd ways of men and beasts, Myron watched as one of the golden birds scrambled upside down about the lower half of its bag-shaped nest.

Myron's mind wandered to similar scenes from the world of nature. He thought of a fly creeping about a fruit, running sure-footedly over the lower as well as the upper surface; or the lizards that swarmed in the Negroes' huts, scuttling upside down across the ceilings of thatch. Now, suppose the world were like such a fruit—spherical, as Bessas had once jestingly suggested—and men were like

312

the fly. Then they could walk on all sides, bottom as well as top, without falling off.

But how would this be possible? Well, how did a fly manage? No doubt a fly had sticky feet, and men did not. But the forces that bound men fast to the earth's surface might work down towards the center of such a ball-earth from all sides. In that case, the direction of "down" would be one of those relative things whereof Herakleitos hinted. Why should one believe that there is any universal direction of "down," the same for gods and men? Why indeed, save that it was one of those things one had always taken for granted?

My "down," he thought, need not be the same as your "down," nor is my "up" your "up." It all depends upon where we stand. If we stand on opposite sides of this fantastic ball-earth, your "down" is my "up" and vice versa.

Myron leaped up and began to pace, striking his palm with his fist. The theory seemed at first utterly insane. But, the longer one thought about it, the more sense it made. Why did one see different stars, the farther south one went? Because one was farther around the bulge of the sphere. Where did the sun go at night? Why, around to the other side of the sphere. Why could one not see clear to the edge of the earth from a high mountain? Because one could not see around the curvature of the sphere. Why did the sun pass directly overhead in this clime, but not farther north? Because this was the part of the earth directly beneath the path of the sun, whereas in Hellas one viewed the sun from outside this zone.

Myron started back for the camp, so filled with his marvelous idea that twice he tripped over buttress roots and fell. At the camp, men were napping or performing small chores. Bessas looked up casually; then his deep-set eyes hardened as he saw that something was up.

"*Heurêka auto!*" cried Myron.

"You have found what?"

"I know! I know it! At last! It's wonderful!"

313

"Have you gone mad?"

Myron caught his breath. "The shape of the earth! I have found it! I know it! My dear fellow, this is the greatest d-day of my life!" He seized Bessas' massive arm and squeezed, shaking the arm as a dog shakes its prey. "It is shaped like a ball, a sphere! It is round! This explains everything! I am a made man! At last!"

He poured out a stream of impassioned Greek, arguing and explaining, shaking his fists, slapping Kothar's back, kissing Phyllis, hugging a startled Zayd, then leaping and capering about the camp like one bereft of his senses. He threw himself on the ground and rolled, laughing and crying.

"It's wonderful, wonderful, wonderful, wonderful. . . ."

Zayd asked Bessas: "Have the gods taken away our poor friend's wits?"

Bessas shook his head. "Nay. This is a seizure of what the Hellenes call philosophy."

"Is it then a kind of religious frenzy?"

"You might say so, though this religion has no temples. If we pay him no heed, it will pass." Bessas blew his whistle. "Time to pick up our loads! Jump to it, whoresons!"

"I—I was just washing my shirt," said Myron, "and watching these little yellow birds, when—where in Tartaros is my shirt, anyway? I must have left it by the stream!"

He ran off to recover the garment.

That night Myron said to Phyllis: "Come here, my girl."

With a small sigh she came. Afterwards he asked: "Didn't you enjoy it at all?"

"It did not hurt, master. You are a kind man."

"But you are really assotted with that roaring young friend of mine, who makes the ground smoke under him, eh?"

"What if I am, sir? I can do nought. A woman torn

314

from her family is like an insect, floating on a chip which is tossed on a stormy sea, and a slave must obey her master." She wept.

"Well, some day we must do something for you; for you have made my life more pleasant. But for now, we have all we can do to stay alive."

XVI   The Land of the Eaters

SOUTH, SOUTH, south they wended. Three of the riding oxen died, but otherwise the company kept its health.

Myron found the Ptoemphani a trial. They were always shirking and quarreling, always finding a thousand excuses for putting off the start of the march in the morning and another thousand for ending it early in the afternoon. Then, having persuaded Bessas to let them stop before they dropped from exhaustion, as soon as the sun went down they began pounding a hollow log, clapping hands in rhythm, dancing, and singing at the tops of their lungs. This they would keep up for hours.

Myron, who liked a reasonable quiet in which to think and write, chafed with annoyance. But Bessas merely said:

"These oafs won't mind my whacking them now and then if I let them have their fun. You cannot run an expedition as if it were a lecture course." Then he went off to join the dance, whooping and capering with the best.

During this time, Myron moved like a man in a daze, for all he could think and talk about was his wonderful new theory of the shape of the earth. At last, during a noonday halt, Bessas said:

"O Myron, yours may indeed be the discovery of the age. But you are becoming as bad, in ever talking about your conceit, as you say I am about horses. Besides, it makes me dizzy to think of hanging head down from the bottom of the earth. So pray give that flapping tongue a rest. Set yourself, instead, to master the speech of the savages, in case some accident befall our sorcerous Syrian."

So Myron conversed with Merqetek, Ajang, and Yilthak, picking up smatterings of their languages and learning much about the men and beasts of this unknown land. For instance, he learnt to distinguish the two kinds of rhinoceros: the smaller and more dangerous kind, which browsed, and the larger, grazing kind, which merely blinked stupidly as the travelers passed.

"Have you ever heard of serpents big enough to swallow elephants, whereof they told us in Kush?" said Myron.

The interpreters laughed. "Nay," said Ajang. "In the Great Forest grow serpents big enough to engulf a man or a cow, but never big enough to swallow an elephant. You, master, have been swallowing lies."

"Then, save for venomous serpents, I do not see that the beasts of this land are greatly to be feared, for all their size and abundance, provided one exercises prudent caution and stays with one's comrades. I am more concerned with the men known as the Eaters, because I do not think I should enjoy being cut up and roasted by human beings any more than I should like being swallowed by a snake. It seems to me that we are headed towards the Eaters' country."

"Fear not," said Ajang. "We would not be eaten, either. Yonder"—he threw out an arm to westward—"lie the lands of the Eaters, many days' journey hence. Yonder"—he pointed southwest—"lies the Great Forest, where dwell little men no higher than your knee. Yonder"—he pointed south—"stand the Mountains of the Moon. Yonder"—he pointed southeast—"the River flows out of the lakes that lie at the foot of these mountains. And that way"—he jerked a thumb to the east—"dwell the Mattitae, with whom King Gau is at war. So, you see, you cannot really get lost. We can always find

316

the River by marching eastward. Now, however, we shall march to the southeast, so that. . . ."

The Alab's voice died. On both sides of the safari stood a long line of spearmen, who had silently sprung from the shrubbery.

The march came to a stumbling halt. Some of the Ptoemphani dropped their loads and made as if to run. However, they found that they were surrounded by the newcomers. Moreover, Bessas, an arrow nocked, threatened to shoot the first man who ran.

The new Africans were men of ordinary stature, about that of Myron himself. They were of stocky, muscular build, very black, very flat of nose and full of lip. Unlike the naked tribes of the Astasobas, they wore kilts of goatskin or tree-bark cloth. They had the tails of cows and other beasts fastened to the backs of their skirts, and antelopes' horns affixed to their heads, which gave them a wild and fiendish look. They also bore well-made weapons of polished stone.

The thing that most struck Myron about these men was their discipline. In this respect they differed from the turbulent Anderae, the impulsive Alabi, and the unmannerly Ptoemphani. They stood like so many ebony statues until their officers told them to move.

A man wearing a mantle of black and white monkey fur stepped forward and spoke. Ajang presented Bessas to Ongosi, general of the great king, Ravonga son of Mbomu.

"Bessas!" said Myron. "In the name of Zeus, tell him you're a son of Xerxes!"

Bessas scowled at the lie but let himself he presented as a son of the Great King, on his way to pay his respects to King Ravonga.

"That is good," said Ongosi. "You shall come with us to our city of Ravonga. Our king, the stamp of whose foot causes mountains to crumble, will be pleased to see such outlandish creatures as yourselves."

The general smiled, showing a set of teeth filed to

317

points. He barked an order, and the spearmen closed up around the travelers.

As he resumed his march, Myron cast a glance at Ajang. The Alabi interpreter's eyes bulged, his mouth hung slack, and he shambled along with drooping shoulders. The man looked terrified.

"What is the matter?" said Myron.

Ajang stuttered: "The-these are the Akulangba—the Eaters!"

"Oh!" Myron whistled. "I thought they dwelt several days' march to the west?"

"So did I!" wailed Ajang. "I do not understand how they come to dwell in this land. I know nothing!" The Alab began to blubber, as if he had lost whatever sense he possessed.

The country blazed with an intense, aggressive greenness. Huge trees were laden with flowers of flame red and flowers of gold. The sun beat down fiercely from high overhead, although the air was mild and springlike.

The city of Ravonga spread out over several low hills near a sluggish river. It was not a city in the sense in which Myron would have used the word. Rather, it was a royal stronghold surrounded by the scattered huts and garden patches of several thousand of King Ravonga's subjects. Myron was struck by the neatness and good order of these huts.

The king's compound stood on the largest of the hills, surrounded by a wooden stockade. Myron's eyes widened as they approached the stockade. Among the Astasobas, he had become used to seeing a few poles topped by skulls at the entrances to villages. King Ravonga, however, used these ominous objects as an artistic motif. Every alternate stake of the stockade bore a skull. There must have been over a thousand of them, all grinning outwards.

Ongosi pointed to a row of empty huts, explaining

318

that these were for the use of the party. Ajang interpreted:

"He says: Get ready to visit the king. A man will come for you when the king is ready."

A guard of spearmen were posted around the huts. Myron and Bessas took one of the huts and spent a lively time chasing out the resident snakes, lizards, scorpions, centipedes, spiders, and huge red crickets, while listening to the horrified laments of the rest of the company. Their comrades' courage had vanished utterly on learning that they had fallen into the hands of the dreaded Eaters.

"We are lost!" wailed Zayd. "My lads fear not to face death, so that they have a good chance of decent burial. But they cannot bear the hideous fate that now confronts us!"

Bessas grunted. "What recks it whether you are eaten by worms or by other men? You're dead either way. The Derbikkai of Hyrkania get rid of their old people thus, and it always seemed sound sense to me."

Kothar, equally agitated, protested: "My lords, to scoffing skeptics like you—if you will pardon the expression —the fate of your bodies may seem of small moment. But to pious persons like myself and the shaykh, such a fate were worse than death. We know that our souls would be condemned to wander, homeless and comfortless, for aye, perchance to be enslaved by some wicked witch and forced to commit nameless abominations at his behest."

"Rubbish! Anyway, nobody has eaten us yet. We have escaped from worse coils, and we shall get out of this one whole. You shall see."

When the others had gone, Bessas and Myron clad themselves in their only remaining presentable tunics and got out gifts for King Ravonga. Bessas muttered:

"Would that I truly felt as confident as I sounded just now!"

319

"They haven't asked for tribute yet," said Myron.

"True, but it may be that Ravonga plans to devour us and possess himself of all we have. So why should he ask, when he knows he can take?"

When a page boy in a bark-cloth garment arrived, Bessas, Myron, Kothar, and Zayd set forth with Merqetek and Ajang. With a sinking sensation, Myron ducked through the low portal in the skull-decked stockade. They proceeded along an avenue lined with the huts of officials and nobles, whose women sat in front of the huts, pounding meal in wooden mortars with wooden pestles.

Screams came from ahead, where a man was lashed to a post. A small crowd had gathered to watch two other men mutilate the bound man, cutting him to pieces a little at a time. But when the travelers appeared, the crowd left the execution to gape at the strangers instead.

"Why is this man being tortured?" asked Myron. The page replied:

"He was convicted of adultery."

"Sink me in the Vourukasha Sea!" said Bessas. "We seem to have fallen among strait-laced folk. Zayd, warn your lads not to try to borrow any more women."

"I don't like this place," said Myron as they marched on up the hill.

At last they came to the square in front of the palace. This structure was, like King Gau's palace, a glorified thatched hut. But it was larger and grander; its woodwork was painted blood red.

"You stand here," said the page.

Spearmen stood around the square in rigid rows. A stool in front of the principal entrance served as a throne. Around the throne, a score of Akulangba squatted in long tree-bark robes. Other members of the court huddled in front of the lines of spearmen. A swarm of pages stood around, and to one side squatted a group of drummers.

Myron stood for, he thought, at least half an hour, shifting from foot to foot and ignoring the stares of several hundred pairs of eyes. At last a page stepped out of the palace, crying:

"Bwana mkubwa anaja! Nyamazani! Chini!"

All the Akulangba in the square threw themselves prone. So did Ajang and Merqetek. Myron, Kothar, and Zayd might have done likewise, but Bessas held out a hand.

"I have my own thoughts on this," he said. "Do not prostrate yourselves unless I tell you to."

King Ravonga, followed by another horde of attendants, walked out of his palace. He walked with a peculiar strut, swinging each leg stiffly out sidewise in a semicircle before setting it down before him. He halted in front of his stool and stared across the open space at the four whites. Bessas and his companions bowed low.

Ravonga was taller than most of his people and powerful, with a long face and large luminous eyes. He looked not over thirty.

At last the long silence broke; one of the minor notables sneezed. Instantly the king turned his head and spoke:

"Kumwua!"

Several spearmen pounced upon the offender and dragged him off. The drums struck up a rhythmic roar, almost drowning the cries of the doomed man. A brawny man, with a large hardwood club over his shoulder, strolled after the struggling group as they disappeared around the end of a fence that extended out from one wing of the palace. The victim's cries were cut off sharply; the drumming ceased.

The king resumed staring at his visitors. He spoke again: *"Kwa nini hapana chini?"*

"He says," muttered Ajang, lifting his face from the dirt, "why have you not prostrated yourselves?"

"Tell him," said Bessas, "that it were unseemly for the son and ambassador of the Great King to grovel before any other mortal, even a ruler. Natheless, I present my earnest respects."

More translation; then: "Who is this Great King? Is he the king of Kush?"

"Nay." Bessas tried to tell about the Persian Empire, though Myron feared that much of the explanation was not getting through.

"The king says: Have you brought him gifts?"

"Aye." Bessas nudged Merqetek with his foot. The Dankala jumped up, picked up the assortment of gifts, and followed the Bactrian as he strode forward. Bessas handed Ravonga a fistful of beads, some copper ornaments, and another Kushite sword.

When he examined the last gift, Ravonga broke into a broad smile, which showed his pointed teeth. He swished the blade through the air and asked:

"Naweza kata shingo?"

"The king would know if he can cut off a head with it," said Ajang.

"Aye, he can," said Bessas.

"Mzuri," said the king, and pointed to one of the older pages. The youth was dragged forward, screeching. He was forced down so that his neck lay across the king's stool. A spearman squatted in front of the stool, gripped the wool of the lad's head, and held him securely in place.

The king took his stance, swung the blade with both hands, and brought it down. The guard holding the youth's hair sat down as the head came off. Blood sprayed over him. Myron shut his eyes in horror.

The king spoke rapidly. Ajang said: "He says these are good gifts. He says your king must be almost as powerful as he himself is. He will see you again tomorrow."

The king turned and strolled back into his palace with that strange waddling gait.

Back in the huts, Myron drew a long breath. "Ye gods, Bessas, it's merely our good fortune that he did not test that sword on our necks instead of on one of his own people, after you stood up to him!"

"On the contrary, if we had groveled before him, he

322

would have thought he might with impunity use us as he does his own folk. You have to take a firm stand with these barbarians." Bessas shrugged. "Of course, I might be wrong."

"You'd be wrong once only, old boy. In Hera's name, let's get away from this god-detested place! Xerxes may not be any god among men, but at least he does not kill people just for fun!"

"We must find out some things first. Ajang! Merqetek! Yilthak!" When the Africans came into the hut, he commanded them: "Make friends with these spearmen who guard us, and learn what you can of King Ravonga and his ways. Whence came he? How long has the city been here? . . ."

As the sun sank over the lush green landscape, a group of Akulangba came down the hill to the huts occupied by the travelers. They bore a trussed pig, a bunch of bananas, several gourds of banana wine, and a large wooden bowl full of millet porridge.

"Ajang! Merqetek!" shouted Bessas. When the interpreters came running, they translated:

"King Ravonga sends this food to his friend, King Bessas, in return for the gifts he has received."

"So now I'm a king?" murmured Bessas.

"King Ravonga will speak with King Bessas on the morrow. Tomorrow, also, there shall be a feast in honor of Mboli. The Great King has declared this feast in gratitude to the god for sending him such an interesting friend."

"Tell King Ravonga we thank him and look forward to another meeting with him. Now then, my lads, tell me what you have learnt."

Ajang spoke: "We found two spearmen who were glad to talk. Know that the city of Ravonga has been here but nine years. The story of its founding is this: The main body of the Akulangba live, as we told you, several days' march to the west. Ten years ago, King Mbomu, who ruled that nation, died, leaving seventy-five sons; for, of course, King Mbomu had many wives.

"Now the eldest of these sons, Ngura, at once caused all his seventy-four brothers to be seized. And he held a great celebration at which these brothers were all burnt alive; all but one: Ravonga, who escaped the night before the burning by slaying the men set to guard him.

"For several moons, Ravonga lived as an outlaw. He thought to gather enough followers to overthrow his brother; but Ngura proved too strong and crafty for that. However, as the Akulangba found Ngura a hard and cruel ruler, many stole away to join Ravonga."

Myron said: "If Ngura be any crueler than Ravonga, he must be a monster indeed."

Ajang continued: "At length Ravonga's band reached such size that it could no longer support itself by raiding and robbery. So, following the advice of a wizard, he marched his followers, together with the women they had stolen, three days' march to the east. Here they found a small settlement of the Mbaba-ntu, of whom they ate the men and children and took the women. Since then other fugitives from the tyranny of Ngura have come here, so that now Ravonga commands the strongest tribe for many days' march in any direction."

"What think these folk of Ravonga?"

"They worship him. They say he is the greatest king among the Akulangba for ten generations, since the divine Basenga, who was the son of the god Mboli."

"Why does he waddle?" Bessas imitated Ravonga's strut.

"He mimics the walk of the lion, to show his people that he has a lion's might and ferocity."

Myron turned to see another procession emerging from the royal stockade. Men walked in pairs, each pair carrying a corpse by wrists and ankles. They bore the man who had been haggled to death for adultery, and the youth whom the king had beheaded, and four others;

324

two men and two women. These last four had all had their skulls bashed in.

"What happens yonder?" said Myron.

"Those," said Ajang, "are the people who have today displeased King Ravonga. Their bodies are thrown into the river for the crocodiles to eat. When the great king has time, he causes felons to be bound and thrown into the river alive. Then he and his court walk downstream, following the victims, until they reach the place where the crocodiles seize them and twist off their limbs by rolling over and over in the water."

"You are right, O Myron," said Bessas. "I am hardly a simpering milksop, but this place is too violent for me. If the gods will, we shall march on the morrow."

Before dawn, Myron awoke from a dream of earthquakes to find Ajang shaking him.

"Great chiefs!" cried Merqetek, waking Bessas. "The Ptoemphani are gone!"

Bessas leaped up with a roar. "Gone? What mean you, man?"

"They stole away during the night. All, even Yilthak, have vanished."

Myron yawned and rubbed his eyes. "No doubt they heard about the forthcoming feast. Knowing their hosts, they foresaw that they might be served up as the main course, so they decamped. Perhaps they were wiser than we."

"Know you what they did?" said Ajang. "They saved up their pombé, drinking none themselves, and plied the sentries with it until these oafs all went to sleep."

"Well, that spills the perfume into the soup!" snarled Bessas. "That means that when we leave here——"

"If we do," murmured Myron.

"—we shall have to carry such gear as we can take on our own backs. That leaves—let me see—eleven of us, counting the women and these black lads. We can carry no gifts to barbarian princes and only enough food for

325

a few days. Nor do I think that old Zayd can endure this pace much longer."

A royal page put his head in at the door of the hut and spoke. Ajang said: "It is time to go to the king, my masters."

The sun was rising redly over the broken landscape of savanna patched with jungle, when King Ravonga issued from his palace. Again, Ravonga's subjects threw themselves flat in the dirt, while Bessas and his people bowed.

"The king asks if you have more presents for him."

Bessas produced more beads and bangles.

"The king knows that you have two women. The king wishes them as gifts, also."

Bessas and Myron exchanged glances. Bessas said: "Tell the king that these women are not in condition to give to such a great man as he. We must clean and deck them first." He added in an undertone to Myron: "This means we clear out as soon as we can."

"The king understands. He has also learnt that your porters all fled during the night."

"That is true."

"Then, says the king, since you will not be able to carry with you the other gifts you have brought, you might as well give them to him now."

"Tell His Majesty that we will do our best; but that some of these things we must keep to enable us to travel."

"Then, says the king, you must give him those oxen you brought with you, as otherwise there may not be enough meat to go round at the feast tonight."

"I gladly give the king these oxen. Now may I ask the king some questions?"

Bessas asked about the sirrush and was assured that no such creature dwelt near Ravogna. About the elephant-eating serpents he received the same reply. The king had heard of the demon-haunted stone castle on the edge of a lake at the foot of the Mountains of the Moon but could not add to what the explorers already knew.

326

"The king would like to show you his palace and grounds. Will you come with him?"

King Ravonga waddled back into the thatched palace. The explorers trailed after him, amid a buzz of translation: ". . . Here is the king's private retiring room. . . . Here is the shrine to Mboli, where he leads his wives and children in prayer. . . ."

They rambled into the women's section of the palace. A young woman, naked and apparently a little drunk, approached the king, giggling foolishly. The king barked for his executioner, who rushed up, threw a cord about the woman's neck, and dragged her off, wailing piteously.

Unmoved, King Ravonga continued his tour. He led his visitors out the rear entrance of the palace. Here a large area was devoted to many purposes connected with the palace. There were huts for the royal servants, the execution ground, the king's private vegetable garden, a playground for the royal children, and a huge pit with a low fence around it.

"What is this?" said Bessas. Myron, looking over the fence, felt another prickle of horror.

In the steaming sunlight lay seven human beings. All were alive, all were naked, and all had had one or both legs broken. Four were Negroes, three men and a woman, much like the Akulangba in physical type.

The remaining three were small men, about four feet in height and of a slightly lighter brown than the Akulangba. Myron thought that they were the ugliest little men he had seen, with their potbellies and scrawny limbs. Their wide mouths, receding chins, and button noses gave them a simian look. Seven pairs of eyelids rose and seven pairs of eyes looked dully up at the spectators.

"What are those people doing there?" inquired Bessas.

"The king says they are some foreigners whom his men have lately captured. They are being saved for tonight's feast."

Myron felt a surge of excitement. "Tell the king that I have heard of the Pygmies from afar, although I had expected them to be even smaller. The greatest poet of my people mentions them!"

"Oh?" said the king. "Does this poet mention me?"

"No."

The king frowned ominously. "Then he cannot be much of a poet."

Myron hastily said: "Tell His Majesty that this poet lived long ago, before our time."

"The king understands. He also says he fears the older two of the Tikki-Tikki are too scrawny and tough. The one with the gray hair is a chief, but that will make him no more toothsome." King Ravonga laughed heartily at his own humor.

Myron could not resist saying: "If the king executes so many of his subjects, why must he hunt abroad for human flesh?"

Bessas scowled a warning, but too late. When the question had been translated, King Ravonga's eyes widened with horror.

"The king says: Are you suggesting that we eat our fellow tribesmen? That were a bad thing to do! Do you eat your fellow tribesmen at home?"

"No. We do not eat men."

"The king says: King Bessas has told him what mighty warriors his Persians are, and what great wars they wage. If the dead are not eaten, then what is done with them?"

"Nought," said Bessas, "unless the victorious general can take the time to bury his fallen."

"The king says that you must indeed be a wicked folk, to wage war without a good reason!"

Bessas looked at Myron. "Do you know, old man, I never thought of it that way before? Tell the king he may well be right."

King Ravonga led them around to the front of the palace. "The king asks: Is the palace of your father, the Persian king, any larger or grander than mine?"

Bessas' face showed an inner struggle. Racial pride and

328

his Bactrian bias towards truthfulness struggled with prudence. At last Myron spoke:

"Tell the king that it is hard to judge the relative sizes of two such buildings unless one can place them side by side. We invite him to come to Persepolis and compare palaces with his own eyes."

"The king says he would like to do that, though many hostile nations imperil the way. After the feast, when the sun has set, he asks that King Bessas join him in the palace to drink pombé. He may bring one interpreter."

The king swaggered off.

The travelers dined well, though some had been fearful lest they eat human flesh unawares. Myron snorted.

"I'll wager this is nothing but good old beef—and from one of our own oxen, at that. Besides, what if you did swallow a mouthful of man? The man is dead, so it cannot matter to him."

"You are a desperate rogue, O Myron," said Zayd, pulling his long gray beard with his bony hand. "We cannot all face these horrors so cold-bloodedly as you do."

Myron hid a smile. "Bessas, why did you give up the oxen so easily? They'd have been useful——"

"Because they are all down with this sickness they call nagana and so will soon be dead anyway." Bessas rose, wiping his mouth. "Now I must go to drink pombé with our kindly king."

"Don't forget what happened with General Pu——"

"Yes, teacher. Belike Kothar knows a spell against drunkenness; eh, sir wizard? If so, start mumbling!"

Bessas departed. Within and without the royal stockade, the Akulangba capered in endless dances to the tune of drums and reed flutes. The flutes played the same simple phrase over and over, while the drums emitted complex and ever-shifting rhythms.

Myron paced nervously. He cursed King Ravonga, who had not invited him to this evening's drinking bout

329

so that he could keep an eye on Bessas. He cursed Bessas, who would probably try to drink down his host and end up in a snoring stupor. He cursed himself for getting into such a fix, and he cursed Phyllis for making him feel guilty about exposing her to such perils. Would it not be a fine irony, he thought, if the man who had made the greatest discovery of the age were chopped up and broiled to sate the hunger of savages?

Hours later, heavy breathing sounded outside. Bessas loomed in the doorway. The Bactrian stooped to enter, holding a large object cradled in his arm with his cloak wrapped around it. He spoke with quiet intensity:

"Merqetek, Ajang, stand in the doorway to block it! Look what I have!"

He unwrapped the object, which gave a groan. It was the oldest of the three Pygmies whom they had seen in the pit that morning.

"Divinity!" breathed Myron. "How did you ever get him?"

"I slipped out the back door of the palace whilst all the Akulangba were drunken, broke down the fence, and clambered down into the pit. They had taken all of those we saw but two Pygmies. I couldn't take both, so I chose the one most likely to be of use to us: the chief."

"What of the king?"

"Snoring soundly. He tried to drink me down. You need not look at me in that disapproving way. I chewed a fistful of kahawa berries, so it would take more than this wishy-washy banana juice to fuddle me. But I'm so full of pombé that I splash inside as I walk.

"Now, harken! We leave tonight. Most of the Akulangba have fallen asleep, and our guards will do the same. I have seen to it that they, too, got a ration of pombé. We shan't be able to carry much, as we may be pursued. Let each of you go over his gear and take what is most essential; all weapons, for instance, but no tents, beads, or extra garments. Do not try to carry more than half a talent.

330

"Meanwhile, I shall set this little fellow's leg; I know enough field surgery for that. Fetch me some walking sticks to make a splint and straps to tie it fast with."

Dawn saw twelve figures hurrying across the meadows and through the groves of the land to the south of Ravonga. Small antelope bounded out of their way; large ones raised their heads to gaze in wonder. Grotesque wart hogs trotted off, their tails held stiffly erect. A lion trailed the company for a while but slunk away when Bessas roared at it and waved a spear.

All the company bore packs on their backs. Besides his pack, Bessas carried the Pygmy chieftain on his shoulders. The little man's broken leg was swollen and discolored under the crude splint. Nevertheless, though the jarring must have greatly pained him, he gave no sign of his feelings save an occasional grunt.

When the Pygmy learnt that he was not to be eaten, he became talkative. Besides his tribal tongue, he also spoke Mbaba-ntu, the common speech of this region, so that Ajang and Merqetek could translate.

The Pygmy was Dzaka, chief of the eastern Tikki-Tikki. Ajang explained:

"He says: My band set up a hunting camp at a safe distance, they thought, from Ravonga. We went there because the Akulangba are unskillful hunters, and game is therefore plentiful in their land. But a war party of Akulangba found our camp and rushed us. I and two others tried to fight whilst the rest of the band fled into the bush, but the big men threw a net over us and caught us as if we had been so many bush pigs. They also caught one child, which they butchered and ate on the spot.

"Then they trussed us and carried us back to Ravonga, arriving two days ago. They broke one leg of each of us and threw us into that pit. Now, I am happy not to be eaten. But, if you do not mean to eat me, why then did you take me from the Akulangba?"

"Tell him a man cannot have too many friends in this wild country," said Bessas. "So we thought that if we rescued him, he might do us some good. We need guidance to the place we are going, and belike he can persuade his fellow tribesmen to help us."

"He says he will surely do that. But he knows not whither the rest of his band have gone, and you will need help ere he can find them. For the Akulangba will pursue you with dogs, and he cannot talk to his people because the Akulangba would hear the sound."

"What means he, talk to his people?"

"With a drum."

Bessas and Myron questioned Dzaka about his band and his way of life. They were purely hunters, although they sometimes traded meat to the Mbaba-ntu for vegetable foods and implements.

About the habits of animals, they discovered, Dzaka was a mine of sober, factual information. There were no sirrushes and no elephant-eating serpents, he assured them, at least within twenty or thirty leagues of where they were. He had roamed this entire country and knew it as well as he knew the palm of his hand.

And speaking of animals, said Dzaka, they had better make a detour to the left.

"Why?" said Bessas.

"*Mbogo.*"

Myron peered through the long grass but could not see any buffalo. Then, as the marchers wound their way in the direction that Dzaka showed them, there was a huge black bull, standing with its muzzle up and staring at them from a hundred paces off. As the party drew away, the bull resumed its grazing.

"You see," Dzaka explained, "a single buffalo is more dangerous than a herd and should therefore be given ample room."

"Why is that?" asked Bessas.

"Because," replied the Pygmy, "if you run at a herd, shouting and waving your arms, they will nearly always run away. In a herd there is sure to be at least one cow-

332

ardly animal, and when it runs the others run, too. But a single buffalo may not be a coward, and it can kill you if you annoy it."

Bessas asked: "What would you deem the most dangerous beast in this land?"

Dzaka thought awhile, then chuckled. "Guess," he said.

"The lion?"

"Nay."

"The elephant?"

"Nay. . . ."

When he had run through all the larger African animals that he knew of, Bessas gave up. "Well, what is it, then? Some monster that we have not yet met?"

"It is the *nyuki*."

"The what?"

Dzaka indicated a creature the length of a finger joint. "Bz-z-z-z! Bz-z-z-z!" he said, moving his index finger in circles. Then he touched himself and cried: "*Eh! Eh!*"

"I think he means a bee or wasp," said Myron.

"Bees?" said Bessas. "Aye, it might be. With all the other beasts, one can fight, bluff, run, hide, or climb, but none of these acts avails against a swarm of angry bees. Mithra grant that we stumble not upon such! Now tell me, Master Dzaka, where the Astasobas—the River as these folk call it—comes from."

When this had been translated, Dzaka said: Yes, the Astasobas did indeed flow out of a great lake, the Lutta Nzigé, or Shining Slayer of Locusts. Many other streams flowed into this lake and others in the region, so no man could say just where the Astasobas started, as the water from all these streams mingled into one.

"I see," said Myron. "We dispute over the question of where some river rises. But the question really means nothing, because a river rises in as many places as it has tributaries."

"Well, we can truthfully say we have been to the head-

333

waters of the Nile," said Bessas, "even if we do not trace every tributary back to its source. Master Dzaka, have you heard of the stone castle of King Takarta?"

Yes, said Dzaka; he knew of the castle and its guardian demon. But the Tikki-Tikki had not looked into the matter, because they had no reason to think they could slay the demon or, even if they could, that it would prove edible.

Bessas said: "A practical-minded race—Myron, my *fravashi* tells me we are followed. Now, I could run five leagues with this little fellow on my shoulders and not tire. But the shaykh and the girls are near exhaustion. So what in the seven Babylonian hells shall we do?"

"Keep on walking, I suppose," said Myron. "They haven't caught us yet. In fact, we don't even know that they are pursuing us."

"Let us hope——" began Bessas, but then Dzaka spoke: "I hear the barking of dogs behind us."

Nobody else could hear the sound. They straggled on for another hour. Then Bessas said:

"I hear it, too. You were too quick with your hopes, O Myron."

Myron asked: "Could it be a pack of these piebald wild dogs that we have seen pursuing antelope?"

"Nay," said Dzaka. "Wild dogs do not bark like that."

When they climbed a rise, Bessas sent Merqetek up a tree to spy. The Dankala stood in a crotch, shading his eyes against the sun. At last he called down: "I see them, far away. There are at least a hundred, with dogs. . . . Now they are out of sight again."

"Come down," said Bessas. The Bactrian stamped and swore in a fury of frustration. "May worms eat their guts! May the Corpse Fiend gnaw their bones! May they all be kinless! If there were a few more of us, or less of them, or if we had horses, I would chance a fight. Or, in a barren mountainous land, like Gandara, it were easy to find some rocky point that a handful could hold against a multitude struggling up from below. In thick jungle, such

334

as I have seen in Hind, one can ofttimes give the pursuer the slip, as by walking in a stream bed. But here. . . ." He helplessly waved towards the gently rolling, parklike landscape. "One can neither fight, nor hide, nor fly. By myself I could outrun them, but of this company only Ajang could keep up with me, and I cannot abandon my comrades."

"Would to Zeus that we had the Tower of the Snail here," said Myron. "That was an excellent fortress. How about Takarta's castle? How far is the Locust Killer?"

"Nine days' march," said Dzaka. Myron grunted.

"Could we climb trees?" asked Kothar.

"Certes," said Bessas, "until they shot us out of the branches or burnt the trees down. Keep marching!"

Another hour passed. Now all could hear the barking.

"Ere long," said Bessas grimly, "they will sight us. O Shaykh, shall we slay the women rather than let them fall into these devils' hands?"

"These women," said Salîmat, "will die fighting beside their men, if you will give us weapons to fight with."

"You shall have your chance," said Bessas.

"If we could find a dense thicket," panted Shaykh Zayd, "we could creep in, and then they could come at us only a few at a time."

"They'd set the thicket afire," said Myron.

"But the plants hereabouts are wet from last night's rain. Perchance the trees would not burn."

"Could we hold them off by archery?" said Myron. "We outrange them, because I doubt if these unfeathered African arrows are accurate."

"We haven't enough arrows left," growled Bessas. "Keep marching!"

The barking came louder.

Dzaka said: "There is a stream in these parts. I had thought to see it long since."

"Couldn't we walk along the stream bed to throw the dogs off the scent?" said Myron.

"If they were not so close upon us, belike," said Bessas. "As it is, they would espy us at our wading."

As they topped the next rise, a chorus of yells, tiny with distance, broke out behind them. Myron looked back. Atop the last rise, two or three furlongs back, swarmed a mass of human figures, looking like small black ants at the distance.

"Well," said Bessas, "that does it. They have seen us. Now we must run, casting about for some defensible place. A clump of large trees, if their trunks be close enough together, were better than this open greensward. *Yâ ahî!*"

Off went the Bactrian at a trot, with Dzaka bouncing on his shoulders.

XVII   *The Mountains of the Moon*

MYRON RAN, stumbled, and ran some more. His heart pounded and his knees shook. He gasped for breath. An iron band seemed to compress his lungs. He brushed a bee away from his face and ran on.

At that, he ran better than some. Bessas led the flight; next behind him loped the towering Ajang. Then Merqetek and the surviving Arabs—Labîd, Umayya, and Abras—ran in a knot. Myron panted after them. Behind him came Kothar, Phyllis, and Salîmat. Old Zayd tottered at the tail of the procession.

At the top of the next rise, Bessas halted. Myron thought it was simply to let the others catch up, but then he saw that Dzaka was excitedly pointing and jabbering. When Myron reached the crest, he perceived that the stream of which Dzaka had spoken lay just beyond, cutting through a narrow cleft. This was about one reed wide but shallow, gurgling around projecting rocks.

"There's hope," said Bessas gruffly. "See you yonder tree?"

"Yes," said Myron.

"Well, run your eye up to a height of ten cubits. See you those great holes in the trunk?"

"Yes."

"See you aught else?"

"I see what appears to be a cloud of insects buzzing around the holes."

"Well, those, says Master Dzaka, are bees. An arrow in one of those holes would rouse the horde. Now, peer over the bank of the stream. See you where that big tree has fallen half over, so that its roots are bared?"

Myron saw the corner of a natural cave created by the fall of the tree. The stream had eroded away the earth supporting the tree until a wind had toppled it. But it failed to fall completely, because its branches tangled in those of its neighbors. The huge half disk of roots, projecting up at an angle from the bank of the stream, formed the roof of the cave, and the undisturbed earth its floor.

Bessas tenderly handed Dzaka to Ajang. "Get down in that cave, all of you. Cover yourselves as best you can."

"If we had our tents——" grumbled Kothar.

"Hold your tongue and obey orders!" snapped Bessas. "Leave space for me, as I shall come in haste."

Ajang began to lay Dzaka in the cave, then backed out with a startled yell. *"Nyoka mkubwa!"* cried the Pygmy.

"What's the matter? Mice?" said Bessas.

"Big snake!" said Merqetek.

"Let's see. . . . By Ahriman's flaming eyeballs, it is! Is it venomous, Dzaka?"

Myron missed the reply, but Bessas bent over, crawled halfway into the cave, and backed out. Gripped by the neck, just behind the head, he dragged a seemingly endless python. The snake's jaws yawned widely, its forked tongue flickered, and it hissed like a boiling kettle. Its ten-foot body, as thick in the middle as Myron's forearm, writhed and thrashed, trying to throw a coil about its captor.

"Stand clear!" barked Bessas.

337

The women shrieked. Cries and gasps came from the men. Kothar screamed: "Mertseger!" and ran back a few steps.

With a tremendous heave, Bessas hurled the serpent across the stream. It struck the far bank in a mass of writhing coils, hissed again, slithered down the bank into the water, and whipped downstream and out of sight with the speed of an arrow.

"It may not be big enough to engulf an elephant," said Myron, "but by Herakles, it's big enough for me!"

"Now get in there!" said Bessas. "The Eaters will be upon us ere you can recite a quatrain."

Myron crept into the cave, disturbing a host of scorpions and centipedes. As the naked Ajang had no cloak, Myron shared his with the strong-smelling Alabian. Grunts and squeals told of the others' finding their places. Men cursed softly as they bumped against the roof and brought showers of dirt down upon their heads. Some muttered prayers to their various gods.

Silence fell. Myron could hear the drone of the bees and, faint but rising, the barking of the Akulangba dogs.

The barking grew louder and louder. Now Myron could hear the shouts of the cannibals, and an undertone of sounds of many men moving. He heard the swish of feet through the grass, the rattle of bows and spears against shields, and the clatter and jingle of ornaments, all blurred together like the sounds of nocturnal insects.

Another sound came to his ears: the twang of a Parthian bow. The sound came again and again. Then, with a thud of booted feet, Bessas was among them.

"They saw me, curse them," muttered the Bactrian. "But I made two good hits."

The cries of the Akulangba rose to triumphant whoops. Myron expected a torrent of shiny black bodies to pour at any moment over the edge of the stream bank.

Then the vigorous shouts of the pursuers changed to cries of pain and alarm. The buzz of the bees rose until

338

it sounded like the hum of a gigantic lute string, stroked with a bow in the Indian manner. The Akulangba shrieked and their dogs howled. The whole din receded, dwindled, and slowly died.

Somebody in the cave yelped: "I am stung!"

"Do not move," said Bessas.

"Ê!" cried Myron, as a sharp pain in his cheek told him that one of the small fiends had reached him, also.

"We must stay here until dark," said Bessas, "when the bees go to sleep."

Hours dragged by. Several more of the fugitives were stung. When the dimming of the outer light marked the end of the day. Bessas went out to scout. He returned to say:

"The bees are all tucked into bed. Three of the Akulangba failed to get away; their bodies lie on the next rise. There is no sign of the rest, so I think we may come out."

The explorers began to crawl out of the cave and stretch their cramped limbs. Salîmat shrieked:

"My father!"

Bessas gently lifted the old man out of the cave and set him on the bank of the stream. Although conscious, Zayd was breathing in gasps.

"My heart pains me," he croaked. "Let me rest for a while and I shall be well. I have had these before."

"Are the Akulangba likely to return?" Myron asked Bessas.

"I hope not, but one never knows."

After a while, the shaykh roused himself. "Good people," he said, "I must speak with my clansmen on gentile matters. So, if the rest of you love me, pray withdraw beyond hearing."

The non-Arabs withdrew and sat on the edge of the bank, munching their meager repast in the dusk, until Salîmat called Bessas, Myron, and Phyllis back to the council.

"Hear my father," she said.

"O Bessas of Zariaspa," said the old man, "is it still your wish to wed my daughter?"

"Aye, sir, if she be willing."

"She has made up her mind that she will gladly be your wife, on one condition. This is that at the same time you wed her friend Phyllis the Macedonian. For Salîmat wots that Phyllis is sore assotted with you. And Phyllis is her dearest friend, from whom she would not be parted."

Bessas swallowed like a man nonplused and glanced at Myron. "Ah—strictly speaking, Phyllis is Myron's slave."

Myron felt a slight pang—not exactly of unrequited love, though he was fond of Phyllis in a fatherly way. It was more a twinge of jealousy, that Bessas should garner both girls, by virtue of his youth, strength, and god-like vitality, while Myron's superior wisdom and learning should count for nothing.

But Myron stiffened his spirit. He could have done what he pleased with Phyllis, and he had chosen to let matters take care of themselves. Anyway, the girl was a bit of a bore.

"I shall be happy to manumit Phyllis and give her to you as your wife," said Myron. "That is, if she wishes it."

"May the gods rain blessings upon you, master," said Phyllis. "I am more than willing."

"I, too, have a condition to impose," said Zayd. He was now sitting up and his voice had become stronger. "Sickness and battle have slain my sons; Salîmat is my only remaining child. When I am gone, the Banu Khalaf will have no shaykh. In our clan, it is the custom for the shaykh, or his family if he die of a sudden, to present one of his sons or nephews or sons-in-law to the gentile assembly as a nominee for his successor. If the assembly reject this choice, the shaykh may make one more. If that, too, be rejected, then any man may propose himself for election.

340

"I have taken counsel with Salîmat and Labîd and Abras and Umayya. Because of our great love and esteem for you, we want you for shaykh of the Banu Khalaf after I am gone."

"But——" said Bessas.

"True, you are not a Khalafi; not even an Arab. But you speak our speech, albeit not well, and you understand our ways. I can adopt you, and you can perfect your Arabic. My men will witness this adoption and nomination. When you return to the Fifty-League Oasis, they will present your name to the clan. How say you?"

"You know that I must return to Persepolis," said Bessas.

"What of that? We are accustomed to thousand-league journeys. A Khalafi thinks nought of leaving the clan for a year's journey on some trading venture and then returning to take his place in the tents. So long as you regard the clan as your home, to which you will return, you will be one of us."

"Let me think," said Bessas. For several ush he paced the banks of the stream with measured tread. At last he turned to the Arabs. "I will do it!"

"*Tayyib!* Summon the others to witness these deeds. . . . Now, to make a marriage binding amongst us, you must pay me a bridal price. It should be in camels, but, as we have no camels here, anything will do."

Bessas brought out the waist cloth in which he carried his few remaining darics. He handed one to Zayd, who said:

"I, Zayd ibn-Harith, in return for this gold, do hereby give unto you, Bessas son of Phraates, my daughter Salîmat, to be your wife. Love and cherish her and, if you take other wives, treat her as well as you do any of the others, giving her a fair share of your company by day and by night. May al-Ilâh and al-Ilât send you many strong and fearless sons. Now repeat after me: 'Before these witnesses. . . .'"

Bessas said: "Before these witnesses, . . . I, Bessas son

341

of Phraates, . . . take Salîmat bint-Zayd to be my wife, . . . I will love and cherish her and treat her well, . . . not favoring any other wives before her."

"Now, then," said Zayd, "before these members of the Banu Khalaf, I do adopt you, Bessas, as my son, and nominate you to be the next shaykh of the Banu Khalaf in my place." He looked into the faces of his Arabs. "Is it well?"

"*Tayyib!*"

"Now you shall swear allegiance to Bessas for the rest of this journey, as if he were already your shaykh. Find me a sharp stone."

A flint-headed spear dropped by one of the Akulangba in flight served the purpose. Bessas sat close to Zayd, facing the three young Arabs, with seven stones between them. With the spear, Zayd made a slight cut in the palm of the hand of each, at the base of the middle finger. Zayd touched the corner of Bessas' shirt to Bessas' wound and touched the bloodstained cloth to the seven stones. Then he did the same for each of the Arabs, saying:

"If any of the parties to this pact shall forswear and violate it, may the curse of al-Ilâh and al-Ilât descend upon him; may his camels die of the murrain; may the demons of the waste play games with his bones. . . ."

When Zayd had finished, each of the Arabs in turn kissed the hem of Bessas' shirt, promising him loyalty and obedience. Bessas in turn promised them protection, justice, and a fair share of the loot of all raids and robberies. When that was over, Bessas kissed his bride tenderly and looked around, saying:

"What next, dear friends?"

Myron had been writing. Now he handed a scrap of parchment to Phyllis, saying:

"Before these witnesses I, Myron Perseôs of Miletos, do hereby completely and irrevocably free and manumit you, Phyllis daughter of Philippos of Aineia, without restriction or reservation of any kind. Here is a written statement to that effect." In a hurried undertone he

342

added: "Please guard it carefully, because it has part of my notes on the religions of Egypt on the other side, and I want to copy these notes when we get back to civilization. Now, let's see, will somebody lend me some money? This is to be a Greek ceremony, which means that Phyllis must have a dowry."

Zayd handed his daric to Myron, who handed it to Phyllis. He said:

"O Bessas son of Phraates, before these witnesses, I, Myron Perseôs, acting in lieu of the father of Phyllis daughter of Philippos, who is unable to perform this office, do hereby give this my freedwoman, the said Phyllis, to you as your wife. I also give into your care her dowry, being one daric stater of gold. This property, you shall have the management and the usufruct of. But it shall revert to her in the event of divorce or widowhood; or, if she predecease you, it shall descend to her children. Love, cherish, and respect her, and may Zeus and Hera and Hymen and Aphroditê and Artemis and the other gods and goddesses bless your union and grant you many happy years together. Now repeat after me: 'Before these witnesses, I, Bessas son of Phraates. . . .'"

Bessas cleared his throat. "Before these witnesses, I. . . ."

"Now," said Myron when Bessas had finished his oath, "we sing a hymn to Hymen. As Phyllis and I are the only ones who know it, and as I cannot carry a tune, I think one stanza will suffice us. Do you know *Tune the lyre and hang the garlands green,* Phyllis?"

"Yes."

"Then here we go":

Tune the lyre and hang the garlands green. . . .

In her nervousness Phyllis sang, "Hang the lyre and tune the garlands green," but nobody noticed save Myron. The company prayed to its various gods. The suggestion of a dance to celebrate the wedding was quickly

343

squelched for fear the noise should draw enemies, and they turned in early.

They made the shaykh, who seemed to have largely recovered, as comfortable as they could. Myron privately asked him: "What led you to change your mind about purity of blood, O Zayd?"

"My daughter made up her mind. Also, the gods whispered into my ear: 'O Zayd, you may not survive this journey, so it were well to put your house in order.' Such advice is not to be slighted, although I hope for many years yet."

But next morning the old man was dead. They buried him, wept for him briefly, and hurried on.

During the next day's march, Myron—one side of his face swollen like a melon from the bee sting—asked Bessas: "Did you enjoy your drinking bout with King Ravonga?"

"If you don't mind their constant manslaying and their curious taste in victuals, the Akulangba are gentlemen of a sort. They have a strict code of manners and morals; and Ravonga means to see that they keep to it, if he must have every man in his kingdom clubbed and thrown to the crocodiles.

"As he explained to me, after the banana wine had gone to his head: 'Most men are bad. They lie, cheat, steal, fornicate, and disobey the king whenever they think they can do so without punishment. Those whom men call good are mainly those too weak or too timid to be bad. Therefore the king must make himself feared if he is to exact any sort of moral conduct from his subjects. That is why I am strict with my people, and they respect me for it.'

"Belike there is something in what he says. At least, I shall bear his words in mind when I become shaykh. I have known worse drinking companions than Ravonga, but 'tis well that we did not prolong our stay. It would have taken but the slightest whim or flash of ire to have changed us from honored guests into the main course at dinner."

Having run out of writing materials, Myron lost track of the date. However, from the phase of the moon, he judged that they were in the second half of Kislimu when, toiling over an endless grassy plain, they came to the top of a long undulating incline. This slope led down for another league to a great inland sea, which sparkled like quicksilver. To the travelers' right rose a range of massive, jungle-covered mountains. To the left, the plain dipped slightly into a great papyrus marsh, through which the Astasobas, emerging from the lake, wound its way. Bessas asked:

"Dzaka, is this the Locust Killer?"

"Aye."

"Are those the Mountains of the Moon?" The Bactrian pointed to the range on the right.

"*Hapana.* The Mountains of the Moon lie beyond the Locust Killer, another moon's journey." The Pygmy pointed southwestward, towards the knife edge of the far horizon, where the steel-gray sea met the sky.

"Where is the castle of Takarta?"

Dzaka pointed south, towards the place where the shelving eastern shore of the lake vanished over the curve of the sea. "Five or six days' journey."

"Then must we cross the Astasobas again?"

"*Ndiyo sana.*"

"Well, it won't hurt us to get wet once more. Off we go!"

As they marched south along the eastern shore of the great lake, the water widened until they could no longer see the other shore line. Now and then they sighted, on the opposite side, a silvery thread of a waterfall descending the rugged slopes of the mountain range, or an equally slender thread of blue smoke rising from some human habitation.

Although men were few in this land, they passed,

about once a day, a squalid little fishing village, redolent of drying fish. These fishermen, whom Dzaka called Vakovi, also took water from the lake to make salt by filtering and evaporation. Bessas traded meat he had shot and some of their few remaining trinkets for fish and salt.

Dzaka continued a practice that he had begun soon after their escape from the Akulangba. Whenever they halted near a fallen tree that had lain long enough for its heartwood to have rotted out, he would squat by it, with his injured leg sticking awkwardly out, and pound elaborate rhythms on the hollow log with billets of wood.

"I talk to my people," he said.

The lake sparkled endlessly on their right, save when sudden, violent thunderstorms whipped its surface to froth and drenched the travelers. Floating islands of papyrus reed, torn loose from marshes by the storms, wafted about its surface. Hippopotami lay in great herds in the shallows. At night they came ashore to wander the land like ghostly black clouds, grunting and chomping the long grass.

On the fourth day after they reached the Locust Killer, two small brown naked figures rose out of the scrub, shouting, "Dzaka!"

They bore small bows, each with a featherless arrow nocked. The points of these arrows were smeared with a black tarry substance, and the arrows in their quivers were carefully covered lest their points touch the bearers. Bone daggers were thrust through their waist strings.

"Put me down," said Dzaka to Bessas. Hopping on one leg and holding the giant's hand, Dzaka called to the Pygmies. A swift rush of talk convinced the latter that they had nothing to fear.

"I told you I talked to my people," said Dzaka. "These men are not of my band, but they know of the Eaters' attack upon us. My people have fled in that direction." He pointed northwest. "They will follow on our trail when they learn whither I have gone."

The Pygmies examined the travelers, fingering the

remnants of their clothes and their shabby equipment. They reached up and patted Bessas' midriff.

"They say you are a good man," said Dzaka. "Now Jogo goes to find my band, and Adimoku stays with us. If you need meat, he will kill it for you."

Bessas started a rumbling laugh but checked it at once, so that it came out as a snort. "That will be good," he said. He spoke to Myron in Greek: "I almost laughed at the idea of this little whoreson's being a better hunter than I. But then it struck me that he makes his living thus, and those envenomed shafts are not to be despised. Besides, our own arrows are nearly exhausted."

They marched on to the south. As the lake widened, the nature of the eastern shore changed, rising from the water to bold cliffs and headlands. Adimoku proved as good as his word.

"I thought I knew stalking," said Bessas after he had gone out to hunt with the Pygmy, "but forsooth I know nought. This fellow wriggles through the grass like a serpent to within spitting distance of an antelope. Then—ping!—the little poisoned arrow pierces the animal's neck, and down it goes."

In addition, Adimoku proved a marvelous forager, producing strange tubers, fungi, lizards, and other unfamiliar foods by the basketful. Dzaka said:

"The stupid Mbaba-ntu put seeds in the ground, and plants grow up, and they eat the plants. Then one year all the plants die, and the Mbaba-ntu die, too, because they know not how to get food in other ways. We Tikki-Tikki never go hungry."

"Except," said Myron, "that a lion sometimes makes a repast off you, does he not?"

Dzaka thought. "That is true. But then, lions get hungry, too."

As they marched, Myron became aware of a new feature in the landscape. To the southwest, where the lake met the skyline, a pattern appeared in the sky, just above the horizon. At first it was no more than a tiny suggestion of distant clouds. But as they marched it grew and became more stable.

At last Myron realized that he was looking at a distant range of enormous snow-capped mountains. Most of the time they were so obscured by clouds that the snowy peaks could not be seen. But sometimes, especially early in the morning, they stood naked and clear, white above and deep blue beneath. To Myron they looked mysterious and menacing. Although he doubted the tale of the salt giants, he supposed that the mountains might be the abode of Zeus-only-knew what strange beings.

At the same time he found a certain stark beauty in the sight. He kept this feeling to himself, knowing that all sensible men would regard as mad a man who saw beauty in snow-covered mountains.

"Aye," said Dzaka, "those are the Kilima Mwezi—the Mountains of the Moon. See you the salt on top?"

Myron began to explain the nature of snow but thought better of it. Instead, he said:

"You see, Bessas, this proves my theory about the earth. Have you observed how these mountains seem to rise out of the lake as we near them? So the surface of the earth must indeed be curved like a sphere. I hope I survive the journey to report this discovery to Xerxes."

"Tell me more about this Great King," said Dzaka from his seat on Bessas' shoulders. The Pgymy seemed endlessly fascinated by stories of life in the Persian Empire, and it gave Myron a chance to improve his command of the elaborately inflected Mbaba-ntu tongue.

"You say this Great King stops the little kings from fighting one another," said Dzaka. "Could he stop the Akulangba and the Mbaba-ntu from killing the Tikki-Tikki?"

"I do not know," said Myron. "Hitherto, his rule has not extended to this country. He cannot command where his soldiers cannot go."

348

"But Bessas is one of his warriors," said Dzaka, pointing to his mount. "And he comes to this land."

"Well, I suppose we could ask the king about protecting the Tikki-Tikki."

Bessas grumbled: "Don't let us in for any more monstrous tasks! Capturing a dragon that seemingly is not and finding a demon-haunted royal treasure are quite enough, without trying to open diplomatic relations between Persepolis and the Mountains of the Moon!"

"Speaking of demon-haunted castles," said Myron, "what's that yonder, on that point?"

Under a gray overcast, a promontory jutted out into the waters of the Locust Killer, rising to a peak at its outer end. Steep cliffs fell away sheerly to the water on all sides of the peak, except for the narrow ridge that ran out from the land. On the tip of the peak, a small dark eminence, more regular than a natural formation of rock, indicated human construction.

"That's it," said Bessas grimly.

The Pygmies chattered in the Tikki-Tikki tongue. Dzaka said:

"Adimoku says, if you please, he will not enter the stone house. Although he has slain an elephant, demons are beyond his ken. I do not wish to enter this place, either."

"I think we can excuse you," said Bessas. "For that matter, 'tis too late in the day to assail that stronghold. It would be dark ere we reached it, and I am for fighting demons by daylight, if one must fight them at all."

They camped on the lip of a ravine, through which a stream trickled down from the plain to the Locust Killer. A furlong away, Takarta's castle frowned down upon them, a crude dark mass, sharp in outline but vague in detail. The overcast persisted. A moonless night came down upon them, blotting out everything beyond range of their campfire.

Myron could not remember a darker night. Standing

349

near the edge of the bluff, he could barely make out the ghostly pallor of the surface of the Locust Killer below. From afar came the snorting of hippopotami and the trumpeting of an elephant.

Beside him, Bessas stared into the unyielding darkness towards the unseen castle. "I feel," muttered the Bactrian, "that we are being watched from up yonder."

"If so," said Myron, "they are not human watchers. Men would show a light. Perhaps they have flaming eyeballs like your Ahriman to light the darkness. What's Kothar up to?"

"Exorcisms. I told him that, if he knew any really good spells against demons, now was the time to use them."

They stared towards the Syrian, who squatted in front of a small fire. He had set up a hideous little ivory image, which he had obtained in one of the African towns, and was muttering and making signs with his hands.

Bessas whirled to face the castle again, head lifted like that of a wild beast listening. "Hear you that?"

"No. What?"

"A drumming comes from the castle."

"Oh. Now I hear it," said Myron.

Out of the darkness, over the buzz and chirp of nocturnal insects, came a roll or tattoo of impact sounds, as if somebody or something were beating rapidly against a large resonant object with the palms of its hands.

"There is something——" said Bessas. He listened, then said: "Let's go closer!"

"My dear fellow!" said Myron. "Though I believe less in demons than you do, I'm sure I should blunder off the edge of a cliff in this murk."

"Belike you're right." The Bactrian sounded almost relieved; as if, having shown his courage, he welcomed an excuse not to exercise it to the full. "It is your turn to take first watch."

During his watch, Myron heard the drumming again. His viscera crawled at the sound, and he threw more wood on the fire. When his time to rest came, he tossed and turned. When he did get to sleep, it seemed to him that he stood at the entrance to the castle, and an African god, fanged and taloned, rushed out and chased him over the savanna. He awoke with a yell as the thing's claws sank into him.

Bessas, Myron, Kothar, Merqetek, Ajang, and the Arabs cautiously picked their way along the hog-backed ridge that led out to the point on which Takarta's castle stood. Bessas strode like a man without fear. Behind him, Kothar carried his African idol in one hand and a looped cross, made of twigs, in the other. He never ceased to mumble spells and prayers. The others all looked terrified. Myron, bringing up the rear, had to speak sharply to keep them moving.

Utter silence reigned over the stronghold of the fugitive Kushite king. As he neared, Myron saw that it was made of unmortared, unshaped fieldstone. The stones, ranging in size up to that of a man's head, were roughly fitted together. It was a redoubt of the sort that men, knowing stone construction but stranded in a wild country and forced to depend for labor on simple primitives, would build.

Nevertheless, it was an imposing structure. The walls were irregularly curved, following the contours of the peak. If the castle had been square, it would have measured about twenty-five or thirty paces on a side. The outer wall rose to a height of eight to ten cubits, varying because of the irregularities of the ground. Taller construction could be seen within its confines.

A gap in the wall before them showed where the main gate had stood. Bessas hesitated before this aperture, an arrow nocked on his bowstring. The others crowded up behind, curiosity vying with terror. All stood quietly, listening. Myron noticed crumbling fragments of wood, relics of the gate. Termites and mold had destroyed all the rest of the portal.

"I hear nought," muttered Bessas. "Kothar, perform your office."

Kothar raised his hands, chanting:

Whether thou be a spirit that hath come from the earth,
Or a spirit that hath come from the waters,
Or a spirit that hath come from fire,
Or a spirit that hath come from the air,
Or a god that hath come from the heavens,
Or a demon that hath come from the underworld,
Or the ghost of one that lieth unburied,
Or a ghost for whom none careth,
Or a ghost to whom none maketh offerings,
Or a ghost to whom none poureth libations,
Or the ghost of a wicked man,
Or the ghost of one that leaveth no progeny,
By the holy names, get thee hence!
In the name of El, get thee hence!
In the name of Ashtarth, get thee hence!
In the name of Hadad, get thee hence!
In the name of Anath, get thee hence!
In the name of Shamas, get thee hence!
In the name of Tammuz, get thee hence!
In the name of Sahar, get thee hence!
In the name of Reshap, get thee hence!
In the name of Dagon, get thee hence!
In the name of Atah, get thee hence!
In the name of all the baalîm and baalâth, get thee
hence!
An thou depart not, may El destroy thee utterly!
An thou depart not, may Ashtarth afflict thee with dis-
eases!
An thou depart not, may Hadad smite thee with thunder-
bolts!
An thou depart not, may Reshap burn thee with flame!
An thou depart not. . . .

Although his heart pounded with nervousness, Myron

could not help the wry thought that part of the art of exorcism was to bore the hostile spirit to death. Kothar droned on and on, describing all the things that would happen to the demon if it did not clear out:

> *Thou shalt have no food to eat;*
> *Thou shalt have no water to drink,*
> *Neither good water nor foul water,*
> *Neither fresh water nor sea water,*
> *Neither Serpentine water nor Euphrates water;*
> *Thou shalt have no place to rest,*
> *Neither by day nor by night. . . .*

Kothar ended with a tremendous curse:

> *Be thou accursed in the names of El and all the gods!*
> *Be thou accursed by the holy names, which may not be*
> * spoken!*
> *Be thou accursed henceforth, until the end of time!*
> *Be thou accursed. . . .*

"That," said Kothar at last, "ought to do it."

"Come on," said Bessas, and stepped through the entrance.

As he passed through the opening, Myron observed that the outer wall was tremendously thick, with a pronounced batter. From the inner side of this wall, several partitions of stone had been extended to form chambers. Gaps in the upper courses of these partitions showed where wooden beams had been set to hold up a roof.

In the center of the inclosure rose a two-story building, the upper story being a mere penthouse. All the rooms gaped roofless to the sky. In several places the partitions had slumped, piling up irregular heaps of stones on the ground. A curious musky odor, which Myron could not identify, hung over the stronghold.

A contrast of color caught Myron's eye. From the stone-paved flooring of the courtyard he picked up an ivory sword hilt, with a pommel carved in the form of a vulture's head. The blade had rusted away to a faint red-brown stain on the stones, and the ivory was discolored by weathering. But the weapon had once been a handsome one. Others picked up similar relics: a small golden earring, a copper amulet green with corrosion, a bronzen buckle. . . .

"Athtar love us, but what is this?" said one of the Arabs.

He pointed to a scattering of human bones, lying near the corner of the inner structure. Bessas bent over.

"They don't seem to have been broken or crushed, as by a wild beast," grunted the Bactrian. "But if the wight simply lay down and died, how did his bones get so scattered? Here are some of the ribs. There are more. There's the skull, as if somebody had kicked it in play——"

A high, horrible, ear-splitting yell smote their ears, making them leap convulsively. As Myron turned, he saw a sight that nearly stopped his heart. All cried out.

Around the end of one of the partition walls came a creature. Although this thing walked on all fours, it possessed an enormous manlike form. Long black hair, shot with gray, covered it save on the face. The skin of its face was black, below a skull that peaked to a high, hairy crest. Small, deep-set eyes glared out from beneath huge bony eyebrow ridges. Its nose was wide, flat, and flaring, with forward-opening nostrils.

The monster rose to its hindlegs. Although these legs were shorter than those of a man, its arms were far longer, and its stature was that of a tall man. It drummed on its chest with the flats of its hands, making the booming sound that Myron had heard during the night.

Somebody threw a spear, but awkwardly, so that the point gave the animal a slight wound on the shoulder. It opened its wide mouth, showing fangs like those of a lion, and screamed again.

The man nearest to the monster was Merqetek, armed only with a short sword. Amid general yells of terror, the Dankala stumbled back, fumbling for his weapon. The next closest was Myron.

"Get out of the way! Give me a shot!" roared Bessas. The demon dropped to all fours and loped forward with appalling speed, fangs bared. A swing of a long arm knocked Merqetek flying. Then it bore down upon Myron. At the last minute it reared up on its hindlegs again, spreading its arms.

Myron belatedly remembered what he had been taught in Miletos, many years ago, about the way for infantry to receive a charge of cavalry. Gripping his spear, he dropped to one knee and braced the butt of his weapon against an outcrop of rock. As the monster swooped upon him, the point entered its belly.

The demon screamed again but, instead of backing off, it hurled itself forward, still striving to reach its victim. The point of the spear came out the thing's back as it forced itself down the seven-foot shaft towards its foe. A long arm lashed out, and black nails gashed Myron's forearm. He had to slide his hands down almost to the butt to keep his wrist from being seized; still he held his spear firm.

The beast gave another heave and reached for Myron again. Now it was easily close enough to grasp him. But Bessas' bow twanged, and a feathered shaft sank into the monster's chest. An instant later, Bessas and Ajang drove spears into its trunk, pushing with all their might until the creature suddenly toppled backward, flopping, gasping, and snapping its great jaws. The other men gathered their courage to attack, and soon a spear thrust in the heart ended the monster's agony.

Merqetek picked himself up, bruised but not broken. Bessas said:

"So that is what King Takarta turned himself into! It may not be a true demon, since material weapons slay it. But then what in the Land of Silence is it?"

"Let's ask the Pygmies," said Myron, wiping the blood from his arm with his shirt tail. He stepped to the entrance and called.

The Pygmies came up timidly, Dzaka hopping on one leg and holding Adimoku about the neck. When they saw the monster, however, they burst into shrill laughter.

"That is no demon," said Dzaka. "That is but a *nyani mkubwa*—a great ape. Over yonder"—he pointed westward, towards the far forested shore of the great lake—"are many. We Tikki-Tikki leave them alone, and they likewise do not bother us. But now—*e!*—we shall feast!"

"Eat that?" said Bessas. "I should feel like a cannibal."

"And who," said Myron, "castigated us for being squeamish about eating man, when we were guests of the Akulangba?"

"True, little man. But now our next task faces us: to find the treasure of Takarta. Search, lads, and to him who finds it I will give a piece out of it. Well, what is it, girls?" he said with an air of mild annoyance as Salîmat and Phyllis rushed through the gateway.

"You live!" they screamed and seized him in a double strangle hold, covering his face with kisses. "We heard the shouting," they babbled, "and we feared to come look, lest the demon had slain you all. . . . And at last we could wait no longer. . . . So here we are. . . . And you are a wicked man not to let your poor wives know. . . ."

"Yes, yes," he said with affectionate gruffness, "but now lend a hand with our search."

With a dozen persons searching and burrowing, not over half an hour passed before Abras called: "Is this not it, father of arrows?"

The Arab had found the corner of a bronzen chest, green with age, sticking out of a pile of fallen stone, which many eager hands soon cleared away. The chest proved somewhat over a cubit long and closed by a sliding bolt. A stout bronze handle projected from each end. Abras grasped the handles and tugged, grunting, but the box did not move.

Bessas picked up the box, his muscles bulging. "It must weigh over a talent," said he, setting it down.

The bolt had corroded fast in place and had to be hammered open with the back of an ax head. The hinges were likewise stuck. A sword blade, inserted into the crack between lid and box, broke the seal of corrosion. With a groan and a creak the lid was raised at last.

"By the claws of Apizemek!" breathed Merqetek.

Before them lay a gleaming mass of gold and jewels, undimmed by time. Rings, necklaces, bracelets, coins, and small bricks of bullion were heaped indiscriminately.

Kothar pushed forward. "Let me see! Where is the True Anthrax?"

"Stand back," said Bessas. "You found it, Abras, so see if this armlet will fit one of your skinny arms." The Arab gave a yelp of delight.

Squatting before the chest, Bessas began picking among the pieces. Presently he held up a ruby the size of a duck's egg, to which a thin golden chain was attached.

"Is this your True Anthrax?"

Kothar cupped his hands to receive the jewel, in a gingerly manner, as if he feared it might shatter or vanish. Myron thought that a wierd light gleamed in the Syrian's eyes.

"The True Anthrax!" he murmured. "One of the world's most famous magical gems, lost to the sight of man for three hundred years, since the days of the Assyrian Empire, when the Kushites overran Khem and a feathered black barbarian sat on the throne of the Pharaohs. . . ."

Bessas held out a hand, but Kothar seemed entranced, gazing into the flaming depths of the gem. At last Bessas snapped his fingers sharply.

"Give!"

Kothar shook his head as if coming out of a dream and handed the gem back.

"This Anthrax belongs to General Puerma," said Bessas, piling the treasure back into the casket. "Ajang, you shall be warden of the chest. If you find anybody but me trying to open it, slay him." He glowered round the circle of faces. "I know you are all more or less good men, but the sight of great wealth saps the virtue of even the strongest nature."

Bessas closed the chest and slid back the bolt. He struck the bolt a sharp blow with the back of the ax.

"Now," he said, "The bolt is jammed, so that it will take doing to get it open again. Let us find a place where we can sit and take counsel. I do not enjoy the sight of that dead demon."

They found a place at the base of the point. Bessas, speaking slowly and pausing for translation, reviewed their adventures to date.

"We have now accomplished two thirds of our task. We have obtained the ear of a king." Bessas opened his wallet, glanced in, and resumed: "Still there, thank Mithra. We have also recovered the treasure of Takarta, as we promised Puerma.

"We have not, however, obtained our dragon. Does every one of you swear, by all his gods, that he knows nought of such a creature?"

All swore. Kothar said: "We cannot yet rule out the dragon's existence. You were told to seek at the headwaters of the Nile. But, if you take that command literally, you would have to explore the sources of all the many rivers that feed into the lakes of this region."

"That were a lifetime's work. O Myron, how much of the year and a quarter, which Xerxes granted unto us, has passed?"

Myron thought. "It is now about the end of Kislimu. That means that almost nine of our fifteen months have passed, or three fifths of the time."

"That's more than half, is it not?" said Bessas. "You see, my friends, we must scurry homeward forthwith, if I am to save my mother's life."

Umayya said: "Lord Bessas, you are our shaykh. Why do you not stop quietly at the Fifty-League Oasis and not return to Persepolis at all? The Great King were hard put to find you in a kaffiyya, speaking Arabic and bearing an Arab name."

"Because the Great King holds my mother hostage."

Dzaka spoke up: "Do I understand aright that, if you go back to your Great King without your beast, he will slay you?"

"Aye."

"And you, knowing this, would go natheless?"

"I have said so."

"By the sacred ipi, you must come of a fey race! But I have a thought to propose."

"Speak, small ruler."

"First tell me. In this Empire of yours, have you the same beasts that we have here: the elephant, the rhinoceros, and so on?"

"Some like the lion we have; but for the most part no. Howsomever, the folk of the Empire know of many of these beasts, because from time to time the Kushites capture them alive and send them to the Great King, who keeps them in cages in his park in Hagmatana."

"If your king want strange beasts, I can get you a beast whereof the Persians know not."

"What is this?"

"We call it the *okapi*. It dwells only in the Great Forest, where the men of the north never come." The Pygmy pointed across the Locust Killer to the jungle-clad mountains beyond.

"What sort of beast is this?"

"It is something like a giraffe and something like a zebra."

Bessas frowned. "I could wish for a flying crocodile or

359

a fire-breathing bull, but 'twill suffice. Tell him I accept with thanks."

"It is nothing," said Dzaka. "You saved me from death and restored my leg."

"By Mithra, these Pygmies are the only folk in Africa to know gratitude! The others think of nought but parting the traveler from his possessions as speedily as they can."

"That is not all," said Dzaka. "I pray that you will do something else for me."

"Speak."

"I would go with you to the hut of this great chief whom you call Xerxes, taking some of my people with me. I would declare myself a subject of this chief, asking in return his protection against the big men, the Akulangba and the Mbaba-ntu and the Vakovi and the rest, who ever bully and harass and slay us for no cause."

"I know not how good this protection would be. It is hard to come to your country from ours. Without free access, I do not see how, with the best intentions, King Xerxes could extend his protecting arm over you."

"That I will hazard. At least, it were some help to be able to declare ourselves friends and subjects of the Great King."

XVIII   The Dusty Road to Death

THE MOON of Tebetu was in its second quarter. Bessas and Myron stood at the edge of the camp at the northern end of the Locust Killer. Dzaka's band of Pygmies scuttled about the camp, while Dzaka sat on a log with his mending leg stretched out.

"Chief Bessas," said the Pygmy, "in these lands, one who waits upon a chief is expected to bring a gift. Is it the same with your Great King?"

"Aye."

"Well then, tell me if my gifts will be acceptable. As you know. I have chosen Tshabi and Begendwé to go with me. I intend that one of us shall lead the okapi, one shall bear an elephant's tusk, and one shall carry a pot of wild honey. The tusk is that of a cow elephant. That of a bull were of greater worth but too heavy for us to carry. Think you these gifts will suffice?"

"I am sure of it, O King. In fact—gods and devils, what's this? What ails you, Merqetek?"

The Dankala staggered towards the camp, holding his side. Blood ran down over and under his hand.

"Kothar!" he gasped.

"Kothar what? Has he knifed you?"

"Aye. He stabbed me when I would not flee with him."

Merqetek sank down. Bessas caught the guide in his arms, lowered him gently, and bellowed for his wives, who came running to wash and bind the wound. Merqetek said:

"It is no use. I am done for. Pray you, avenge me!"

"Nonsense, lad; you will get well. What happened?"

Merqetek spoke haltingly, pausing to spit blood. "He said he had that to say which I should wish to hear. He meant, he said, to flee to northward, to the land of the Alabi. If he could reach King Gau before you, he would earn a fortune. But he needed a companion, able at wilderness craft. If I would go with him, he would share this fortune with me.

"I refused, because I had promised to guide the Lord Bessas, and I should be no sort of guide if I deserted him. Besides, I thought that a man who so lightly betrays one comrade will betray another as readily, and that my share of Kothar's fortune were likely to be a dagger in my sleep.

"When he saw I would not come, he lunged to silence me. I pricked him back, and then he ran off and. . . ."

Merqetek's voice trailed off to a mumble. His eyelids

dropped. Although he still breathed, he seemed but half conscious.

"What chance has he?" asked Myron.

"Not much," said Bessas. "If we are to avenge him, we'd better be on our way."

"Is it not more important to care for him than to catch his slayer?"

Bessas shrugged. "What more can we do for him? And 'tis not solely a matter of vengeance. Methinks Master Kothar has some deep-laid plan to do us ill." He turned to his wives. "Take the best care you can of him, girls. Dzaka, your people boast that they can trail a man or a beast across bare rock, do they not?"

"Aye, we are skilled in that art."

"Well, I need a good tracker."

Dzaka whistled sharply. "Alianga!"

A Pygmy youth strutted up, a grin on his wide mouth. After a staccato conversation, Dzaka said:

"He will track for you. I have told him what to do."

Bessas told Myron and Ajang to arm themselves and come. At first Alianga led them back along the trail left by Merqetek on his way to the camp. Over the neighboring rise they came upon a trampled spot in the long grass, where the two men had fought. A gleam caught Myron's eye, and he picked up Merqetek's knife.

"Bring it," said Bessas.

The trail from there on was less clear, even though Myron could see an occasional drop of blood on the grass, or an occasional footprint in soft soil. Nevertheless, Alianga trotted ahead, rarely pausing to cast about.

For hours they toiled after the Pygmy. The sun rose to the zenith and began to decline. They took hasty swigs of water from a gourd and plunged on.

Late in the afternoon, Bessas warned his companions not to talk, as they might be nearing their quarry.

"How do you know?" said Myron.

"It is something we hunters learn by practice. Now

362

hold your tongue and keep watching ahead for a sign of our man."

Trying to watch ahead caused Myron to stumble twice, by stepping into holes. But he heaved himself up and struggled on, fighting off exhaustion.

At last the Pygmy muttered something, gesturing. "Down!" snapped Bessas.

"I see nobody," said Myron.

"You wouldn't. The rascal sits with his back to a tree, two furlongs ahead of us. If I can find a point of vantage, I'll watch to learn if he has seen us."

Bessas crawled about in the long grass. After an endless wait, during which Myron had to pluck a beetle the size of a mouse from inside his shirt, Bessas whispered:

"Methinks he sees us not. We'll ring him. You and Ajang creep around to the right and come at him from that side—not together, but converging upon him from widely separated points. Alianga and I will do the like from the left. Slay him not if you can possibly take him alive; for I would ask him some questions. Unless he starts to run, do not show yourselves until I cry the haro."

Myron and his tall black companion spent the next hour working around to the east of the fugitive, keeping enough dead ground between him and them so that they could not be seen. At last they stalked as close as they could without risking discovery. They crouched behind two thickets.

Kothar sat placidly eating. From time to time he sipped from his gourd, or grasped some object that hung around his neck, raising it before his eyes.

At last he brushed his hands together, rose, slung the gourd over his back with the rest of his gear, and started to turn.

The bowstring twanged. There was the sibilant whistle of an arrow and the sound of its impact. Kothar took one running stride and fell on his face, the arrow through his calf.

Bessas ran out from behind a thicket. When Myron

reached the scene, Bessas had come up to the fugitive, tossed his bow aside, and swept out his sword.

Kothar struggled erect, balancing unsteadily on his sound leg. He, too, drew his sword. But, even as he began to bring it up to the guard position, Bessas' blade flashed golden in the light of the low sun and clanged against Kothar's sword. The short blade flew out of the Syrian's hand, turning over and over before it fell into the long grass.

Kothar swallowed. "I said the goddess Mertseger would have her revenge. This is my turn, mortal; yours will come. If you mean to slay me, get it over with."

The Syrian managed a certain dignity despite his ragged appearance. The long blue robe in which he had left Syria still covered his lanky frame, though so many pieces had been cut off the lower edge for patches that the faded and threadbare garment now failed to reach his knees. The remnant was a mass of darns and un-mended holes. His tall spiral hat had long since been lost; a strip of dirty cloth confined his tangled hair. The neat little chin beard had given way to a straggly full beard and mustache of reddish hue. A rag was rudely knotted about his left arm where Merqetek had wounded him.

Bessas smiled unpleasantly. "Slay you? Nay! I have promised myself a long talk with you, and how should I talk with a corpse? True, a necromancer could raise your ghost, but you're the only necromancer here. So how could you raise yourself?" He laughed boisterously. "Turn around."

When Kothar obeyed, Bessas grabbed the collar of his robe and yanked downward, tearing the garment half off its wearer. As the robe was peeled off to the waist, there was a flash and a tinkle. Gold and glittering jewels cascaded out of the robe, in which they had been contained by Kothar's girdle.

"Well, well!" said Bessas. "Some of the treasure of Ta-karta seems to have escaped its coffer. You must have slept too soundly, Ajang. Pick that stuff up, Myron. And what's this? The True Anthrax around our unworldly mystic's neck?"

He removed the jewel on its chain and put it into his wallet. Kothar made a sudden limping lunge for freedom, but Ajang caught him with one long bound and held him fast.

Bessas stripped Kothar down to his loincloth, pulled the arrow out of his leg, and said: "Start a fire, boys."

"Nay!" cried Kothar. "Not that, you barbarian!"

"Who spoke of burning you? Your tender flesh shall not even be singed—provided you answer my questions."

Myron gathered up the treasure and kindled a fire with flint and steel. When it was crackling briskly, Ajang threw his man down flat and sat on him. Bessas brutally grabbed one of Kothar's feet and hauled it towards the flames.

"Now," he said, "what was this plan to which you tried to persuade Merqetek?"

"That is my affair."

Bessas pulled the foot closer and closer to the fire until Kothar began to scream. "I will tell!"

"What, then?"

"There is a meeting of mystics of my order in Memphis, which I wished to attend, and—*ai!*" He shrieked as his foot went into the fire. A smell of charred meat arose.

"That," said Bessas, "is what will happen every time you lie. I know more than you imagine. You wished to visit King Gau for a special purpose, did you not?"

Kothar sobbed rackingly. "I—I wished to get to Gau ahead of you. I know of his deathly fear of witches. If I could have wrought upon him for a few days, he would have seized the lot of you and burnt you as witches."

"Why did you wish us broiled?"

"You will not slay me if I tell you?"

"I will do what I deem just; one good turn deserves another. Go on."

"I had promised a colleague to compass your destruction in the lands south of Egypt."

"For what price?"

"Ten pounds of silver, wherewith to pursue my researches."

"A good, round sum, though probably no more than your share of Takarta's treasure would have been."

"I had given my word. Besides, I got more than a quarter of the treasure anyway."

"So you did. But you had also sworn an oath to me."

"What civilized man would keep his word to a brutal barbarian like you? I hate you for the times you shouted at me and shamed me before all, berating me because I am not a blood-bespattered butcher like yourself."

"Who is this colleague for whom you acted?"

"Belkishir, high priest of Marduk of Babylon."

"By the iron hooves of Apaosha! What has the holy Belkishir against us?"

Little by little, Bessas dragged out of Kothar the tale of the embarrassment of the temple of Marduk over the matter of the sirrush. Some of the story Kothar knew from the letter that Belkishir had sent him, and the rest his sharp mind inferred. The priests had passed off a large lizard on their gullible worshippers as a baby sirrush; they had told King Xerxes a thumping lie about having obtained this creature from the sources of the Nile; and then, to keep their deceit from coming to light, they had plotted to destroy Bessas' expedition.

"So," said Bessas, "you knew all the time we were on a quest for fish feathers! Why did you go so far and wait so long before you struck?"

"I wanted the treasure of Takarta, especially the Anthrax."

"Who sent the Arabs of the Banu Tarafa to slay us?"

"I know not—*ai!*—I truly know nothing of that! Believe me!"

The inquisition continued until the sun set and dusk

366

began to gather. Bessas was able only to fill out a few more details. At last he rose and said:

"That will suffice."

"What will you do to me?" whimpered Kothar, nursing his burnt foot.

"You shall see. Ajang, grab his arms. Hoist them up against this tree, so. Now hold him steady."

"Mercy! I will be your slave! I will do aught. . . ."

Bessas found a heavy stone. Taking Merqetek's dagger from Myron, he drove the point through both of Kothar's forearms, which Ajang held crossed above the Syrian's head and against the tree trunk. The knife pierced between ulna and radius and on into the wood. While Kothar struggled and screamed like a lost soul, Bessas hammered the hilt home with his stone.

Bessas stepped back. The Syrian stood with his back to the tree, pinned against the trunk by the dagger through his forearms. As his arms were nearly straight above his head, he had no slack for movement. Blood ran down his arms and tears ran down his sunburned face as he screamed:

"May Anath chew you to pulp, you son of a she-camel! May the eight wild boars of Aleyin gash you to death! May Terah drive you mad with his beams! May. . . ."

"Well," said Bessas, "if the snake can wriggle out of that and save himself in this wilderness, I'll admit he deserves to live."

"You are a hard, cruel man," said Myron. "Let me at least pull the dagger out of the tree."

"Nay, by the fiends of Varena! Would you that I kissed and forgave him, so that the villain could make others the victims of his perfidy? To be kind to the tiger is to be cruel to the lamb. Merqetek was a good lad; spend your sympathies on him." Bessas turned away, his face somber. " 'Blood-bespattered butcher,' eh? I suppose I am. But it is late to change that now."

"A man can only strive towards being the kind of man

367

he aspires to be, while he lives." Myron shrugged. "I don't ask for the scoundrel's life. But that"—he jerked his head—"is the sort of revenge that Queen Amestris would take. It is unworthy of you."

Bessas sighed. "You are right, as usual."

He drew his bow and an arrow from their case, turned and let fly at twenty paces. Kothar, struck cleanly in the heart, jerked and hung limply.

"Now," said Bessas with forced briskness, "let's be off and make some furlongs towards home ere we stop for the night."

Back at camp, Myron and Bessas hastened to examine the treasure chest. The bolt did not seem to have been tampered with, but at last Myron said:

"I see what he did. He drove the pins out of the hinges with the point of his dagger."

When they opened the chest, it seemed to be full. Kothar had taken out the treasure, put aside what he thought he could carry, placed stones deep in the box, and piled the remaining gold and jewels on top of the stones, so that no shrinkage should be noticed.

"A clever scoundrel," muttered Bessas. "There are, alas, men who would rather gain one shekel by trickery than earn two honestly."

The moon of Tebetu was full when a squad of the Tikki-Tikki marched into the camp. On a halter of grass rope they led the okapi, a half-grown young male.

The beast was somewhat like a mule in size and shape, but longer in the legs and shorter in the body, with cloven hooves. It wore a coat of glossy purplish black, with legs a creamy white below the knee and a pattern of narrow black and white stripes on the rump. It had large ears, always turning this way and that, a long slender muzzle, and a tongue of astonishing length, with which it grasped the leaves it ate.

"They had much trouble," said Dzaka. "For several days after they trapped him, he sought to butt and kick them. But now he has become tame. We must keep him well-fed and watered and not leave him in the hot sun."

"Good boys!" said Bessas. "Let us celebrate!" Soon the Bactrian was shuffling in the circles of the Pygmy dance with all the small brown folk.

Then the encampment broke up. All the Pygmies save Dzaka, Tshabi, and Begendwé vanished into the bush. Bessas' company started north along the Astasobas.

One night they stopped at a village of the Mbaba-ntu. These were simple black peasants who, once their original fright and suspicion had been overcome, proved genial hosts.

The three Pygmies, however, refused to enter the village, saying that they would be killed. Myron learnt why when he talked with the Mbaba-ntu headman. The man cried passionately:

"We hate them. I hate them. I would slay every one of those small devils!"

"Why?"

"Because they kill our goats and cattle with their poisoned arrows and eat them, as if they were wild game. Nothing we can say or do will stop them. The only good Pygmy is a dead Pygmy."

When he heard who was coming, King Gau of the Alabi went forth from his palace to meet the arrivals.

"I had to assure myself that you truly lived," he said. "The Ptoemphani told us that you had been slain and eaten by the Akulangba. I see no dragon, but you do appear to have found another strange beast. What gifts have you brought for me?"

"Give him that bronze-headed mace, Myron," said Bessas. "It is of little use to a man on foot."

The king asked: "And how did Ajang bear himself?"

"Like a true man," replied Bessas, clapping the towering Alabian guide on the back. "I count him among my trusty friends. And what of our man Shimri?"

"He lives, but you will find him much changed."

They came upon Shimri under the thatched roof of his

369

smithy, hammering a spearhead on a stone anvil. A pair of sweating young Alabi helped him. He paused to say:

"Hail, m-mortals. The great god Dagon accepts your worship."

"Shimri!" said Myron sharply. "Don't you know us?"

"Aye. I—I know you. I knew you in my former life. B-but that was before I, Dagon, took possession of the body of the mortal Shimri ben-Hanun."

"We are on our way home. You can return to Gaza with us."

"What is Gaza to me? To a god, all places are as home. My—ah—my task is here, in t-teaching these folk the arts of civilization. Now leave me, mortals, for I have work to do."

Later, Bessas asked King Gau: "Is he always like this?"

"Sometimes he sits staring and saying nought for a day at a time. Sometimes he walks about the town, talking and laughing to himself. Betimes he starts for the river, saying he means to swim down the stream to the great sea and sport with his friends the fishes. After we had fished him out twice, just before the crocodiles got him, I set men to watch him day and night. Does he always eat enough for two?"

"That he does."

"Do you think he really is a god?"

Myron shrugged. "Who knows? The question is, shall we try to take him home with us, willy-nilly?"

"Nay," said Gau. "He wishes to remain here, and he is useful. Leave him. I believe he is a god, or at least that a god dwells in his body. That explains his prodigious appetite, as he must eat enough for himself and the god as well. We shall tenderly care for him and devoutly worship him."

"Our duty——" began Myron, but Bessas cut him off.

"The king is right," he said. "We shall have enough trouble getting this rare beast home alive without also being burdened by a zany deity."

370

"I don't know——"

"Well, I do. After all, who is happier than one who thinks himself a god? So why should we interfere? Now, O King, how shall we get back to Kush? I care not to face those great swampy plains again."

"They are not so swampy now, in the dry season. But the easiest way to reach Kush is by floating down the River on a raft. I will send a message to the king of the Ptoemphani, asking him to arrange with the Syrbotae to have your raft guided through the Great Swamp. King Ochalo owes me something, after the way his men behaved towards my friends. Then, provided always that their divine dog wags his tail, we shall send you on your way."

Myron worried over leaving Shimri to live out his days in this wilderness. But, with Bessas, King Gau, and Shimri himself all determined that the Judaean should stay, Myron did not see what he could do about it.

"He's the last of the three who left Philistaea with us," he said to Bessas.

The Bactrian scowled with thought. "Think you we ought to devise their kin of their fate?"

Myron pondered. "It might be better to say nothing. None of the three left a wife at home, and it were more merciful to let their relatives think they still prosper in distant lands. Moreover, while I don't think Kothar's family will greatly lament him, I should not relish the task of telling old Malko bar-Daniel of his son's end."

In the middle of Nisanu, in the twenty-first year of Xerxes' reign, a raft grounded gently at the ferry landing, on the south side of the Nile near Meroê. The raft bore ten human beings: Myron, Bessas, the latter's two wives, three Pygmies, and three Arabs.

They were a wild and dangerous-looking lot. All were either naked or clad only in breechclouts of hide. Those not barefoot wore sandals of woven grass. Headbands of hide confined their long tangled hair. The whites were

371

bronzed by the sun until they were not much lighter of skin than the Pygmies. All were lean and hard-looking, and they appeared a good deal older than when they had set out. Myron's beard and brows had turned to silver.

The after part of the raft had been fitted out as a shelter for the okapi. Throughout the three months' river journey from Boron, the beast had lounged on a bed of papyrus reed, under a thatched canopy, and chewed its cud. The women had petted and fussed over it until it became as tame as a puppy.

When the raft was securely beached, Myron and Bessas donned cuirasses and helmets and strapped on swords and daggers. After months of arduous travel, their weapons were almost the only possessions they still retained besides the heavy bronzen box. Even Bessas' little silver whistle had gone, as a gift to the chief of the Syrbotae.

With a word of warning to those who stayed on guard, the two set their sandaled feet on the steep path up to the plain on which Meroê stood. They walked slowly towards the Soba Gate, wrinkling their leathery brows against the glare of the high bright sun.

As they neared the gate, Bessas put out a hand. Myron followed his companion's gaze towards a row of dark objects mounted on the wall beside the gate. Then the twain strode rapidly forward until they squinted up at a row of heads on spikes. A couple of big brown vultures flapped off, hissing.

Although the heads were somewhat the worse for wear, they were not yet unrecognizable. They included persons of both sexes and varying ages. One large jowly head seemed of more importance than the rest, for it stood on a taller spike.

"I think," said Bessas heavily, "that I know that one. Ask somebody."

Several Kushites approached the travelers to stare. Myron spoke to one and pointed.

"Is that General Puerma?"

"Aye, and his family. I know not why, but the king of a

sudden denounced him as a traitor and had the heads off them all before they could mumble a prayer."

Bessas muttered: "My *fravashi* tells me that we had better go quietly back to the raft and push off."

"Right." As they picked their way back down the path, Myron said: "So the high priest won out after all!"

"So he did. Well, at least we need not divide our treasure with Puerma."

"Poor Puerma! Perhaps he was wrong to oppose progress, but I'm sure he was a more congenial companion than that sour-faced Osorkon."

They cast off. For two days they drifted dreamily down the Nile, stopping at villages to buy food and clothing, because the nights were becoming cold. The new garments were of thin dyed leather and thick undyed sackcloth. The two girls at once began draping and altering and walking back and forth for each other's inspection, as if they were modeling the latest fashions from Babylon.

Towards evening on the second day, as they drifted along with Labîd at the steering oar, Bessas raised his head.

"Something?" said Myron, closely attuned to his friend's moods.

"I hear a sound—a kind of distant roar."

"Could we be nearing the highest of the cataracts?"

"Mithra, yes! I had forgotten them." Bessas raised his powerful voice. "Every man on the paddles, quickly! Head for the right bank!"

Sluggishly the raft responded to the frantic splashing of its crew. The roar grew louder and the river swifter. The raft plodded shoreward, but the river hurried it along at a rising pace.

Paddling for all he was worth, Myron wondered if, as a final irony, they were to be wrecked in sight of civilization: men, women, beast, and treasure poured over the falls in a tangle of destruction.

"Faster!" gasped Bessas.

"Too late!" wailed an Arab.

"Hold your tongue and work, curse you!"

The shore crept closer. Myron thought: *Rhyppapai! We shall make it!* Then a glance downstream showed him that the edge of the cataract, where the surface of the river dropped from sight, was nearing fast.

"One more effort, boys!" cried Bessas. "Swing the nose a little upstream, Labîd!"

The Pygmies jabbered with terror, while the okapi stood on trembling legs. The roar now drowned out speech. Downstream Myron saw the mist of falls and the fangs of rocks.

One more effort. . . . Myron reeled with fatigue and almost fell overboard. Evidently they were not going to make it, after all. The bank was still a good three reeds away, and the head of the cataract was hardly farther.

But one could only die trying. . . . He dug in his paddle again.

The raft started to tilt. The women screamed like hawks.

With an ominous grinding and crackling, the raft struck a rock at the top of the rapid. Men staggered; Phyllis fell down.

"Get everything ashore!" shouted Bessas.

The Bactrian had dropped his paddle and leaped overboard into thigh-deep water. Stooping and bracing his massive legs, Bessas seized the corner of the raft and held it. The raft was precariously balanced on the point of rock. The least swing to one side or the other, and the river would whirl it round and send it spinning down the cataract, and a hundred men could not then hold it. But, gripping the logs with panting lungs and straining muscles, the giant, with the help of the rock, was holding even the invincible river at bay.

"Didn't you hear me? Get everything off! I cannot hold much longer! The water is but knee deep to shore!"

Myron gathered Dzaka into his arms and stepped off the raft. Althought the water was, in truth, but knee deep, the swiftness of the current made the footing precarious.

A glance showed that Labîd and Umayya were wrestling with the treasure chest.

Myron dropped the Pygmy ashore and hurried back to untie the okapi. The beast balked at leaving the raft until Salîmat, ruthlessly practical as always, pricked it in the rump with her dagger. Then it bounded forward and dragged Myron off his feet. He struck the water on his back, went under, but kept a desperate grip on the halter until he could struggle up again.

By the time Myron got ashore with the beast, coughed water out of his lungs, and tethered the creature to a thorn bush, the raft had been cleared. Weapons, the Pygmies' gifts to the Great King, and all the other gear of any worth had been taken ashore.

"Get the poles!" shouted Bessas.

This seemed to Myron like carrying thrift to the point of lunacy, but he knew better than to argue. He and Abras waded out, pulled the poles that upheld the okapi's canopy out of their sockets, and carried them ashore.

Then, at last, Bessas straightened up. With a whoop of *"Yâ ahî!"* he pushed on his corner of the raft, so that the structure began to swing away from him, pivoting on its point of contact with the rock. It spun slowly around, tore loose from the rock, plunged down the fanged slope of water, and broke up with loud crashes. Some logs were thrown into the air; others piled up on rocks. Some shot down out of sight on the long journey to Memphis and the sea.

Bessas staggered to shore and sat down, breathing hard. "By Mithra's mittens!" he said at last. "That was a harder battle than when I was surrounded by the Sakai and cut my way out singlehanded." He threw a hairy arm around each wife. "Give me a kiss, you two, and we shall be on our way."

"What are the poles for?" asked Myron.

"To carry Dzaka and the treasure. Help me to rig a litter and a yoke."

A youth of the Banu Khalaf came bouncing into the Fifty-League Oasis on his camel, crying out: "Our people return from the South!"

The sleepy oasis awoke to life. Arabs rushed about, dove for their tents to don their finery, broke into wild gesticulatory arguments, and fell to their knees to thank their gods for the return of their folk.

Soon a procession of people on Kushite asses ambled into the oasis, with the okapi shambling at the tail. The Banu Khalaf looked and asked one another:

"Where, oh where is our shaykh?"

Salîmat swung off her mount, embraced her fat uncle Naamil, and climbed a log. With a cry of: *"Ya jama'aya!"* she launched into a heated oration. She told of the expedition's adventures. Myron, who could follow the language quite well, noted that she credited Bessas not only with the heroic deeds that he had done but with many that he had not, such as strangling a lion to death, felling an elephant with his fist, and putting to flight single-handed an army of cannibals.

When she came to Zayd's death, she had the entire clan in tears. When she told how Zayd had given her to Bessas, adopted Bessas, and nominated him for the next shaykh, the tribesmen looked wonderingly at one another. Then she called upon Bessas.

Bessas hooked his thumbs in his belt, mounted the log, and said in passable Arabic: "Shaykh Zayd—may he rest in peace—told me he wanted me for his successor. It was not my conceit, but peradventure not a bad one. If you want me, I will try to be a good and just chieftain. If not, there shall be no hard feelings. It is up to you. I will not tell you about myself, because Salîmat has already done so. Peace be with you!"

The tribe acclaimed Bessas, albeit hesitantly. They seemed not so much pleased or displeased as bewildered by the turn of events. But nobody objected. As they poured forward to kiss Bessas' hands, a figure in Persian dress strolled into view and said:

"Are you Myron son of Perseus?"

"Yes. And you, sir?"

"Gergis by name. Your slave brings a message from Embas."

"Embas? Oh, yes, that priest of Mithra in Babylon, who saved us from nocturnal attack."

"That is right. As soon as you can withdraw your comrade from his throng of worshipful subjects, I fain would speak with him."

That, however, was easier said than done. Half the Banu Khalaf, it seemed, had quarrels or claims which they had been saving up for months and which they wanted Bessas to judge. He put them off, saying:

"Dear friends, give me until the morrow! I shall have to think deeply ere I can judge such weighty matters, and I am weary."

He turned to Myron, who presented the Persian. Bessas and Gergis exchanged a quick, secret sign, and Bessas said:

"How knew you that we should return by this route?"

"Your slave knew not. Embas sent out three messengers. One awaits you at Buhen and another at Swenet. We thought that surely such a net would catch you in your flight; and behold it has done so!"

"And your message?"

"I bring you a warning of traps laid for you along the path of your return. But—was there not a man named Kothar bar-Malko, who attached himself to you?"

"Aye, there was. We learnt that he had been suborned by the priest Belkishir, in Babylon, to get us murdered. He has joined the majority."

"No loss. Since you know of that plot, I will go on to the other. Know you of the plans of the House of Daduchus for your future?"

"Was it not they who set Labashi's cutthroats upon us in Babylon and the Banu Tarafa upon us at Marath?"

"Aye."

"Are they still at this game?"

377

"They are. They have hired more gangs of desperate rogues, to lie in wait for you in the lands betwixt here and Persepolis."

"That is cheerful news, comrade. How shall we avoid these rascals?"

"We cannot tell you for certain where and who the assassins are, but we believe that they lurk in the smaller towns and cities along the way: places like Siout and Gaza and Tiphsah."

"Wherefore should they do that?"

"They reason that a traveler could too easily slip through their fingers in a great city like Opet or Babylon, whereas all travelers pass through small towns along the principal route and are easy to keep watch for."

Bessas stroked his beard, frowning. Then his weathered face broke into a broad grin. "They did not count upon my returning as an Arab shaykh. With our camels we can avoid the small towns, stopping only at cities when we must to buy supplies."

"You seem well-prepared to take care of yourself, and we have done what we can. Are your resources enough to take you to Persepolis?"

"Not only that, but I shall also call upon that banking fellow Murashu in Babylon and pay him back every daric. And how can I repay your kindness?"

"It is nothing; the treasury of the Mithraeum meets my expenses, and it is no more than the son of Phraates merits. But if you would care to make an offering on your way through Babylon, to carry on the holy work. . . ."

"It shall be done. Now let's wash the dust from our throats. Your slave can only offer the date wine of his new-found clan, but 'tis better than the slop I have been drinking for the past few months."

Bessas' wives served them in the shaykh's tent. Sitting cross-legged on the rugs and cushions that had belonged to Zayd, they drank and talked. Bessas and Myron told of their adventures, while Gergis recounted events at the Persian Court.

He told, for instance, about the great Athenian general Themistokles, architect of the defeat of the Persian fleet at Salamis. Themistokles, beset by political enemies out for his blood, had fled to the Persian Court and thrown himself on Xerxes' mercy. Some courtiers and royal relatives, whose kin had fallen in the ill-starred Greek campaign, wished the man slain. But Xerxes had deferred his decision until Themistokles should learn the Persian language and ways and thus make the best case for himself. So Themistokles now lived with the commander in chief Artabanus and studied Persian speech and manners with the same intensity that he had once applied to Athenian politics and military matters.

"Which," said Gergis, "one must admit is fair."

"Had Xerxes been as just in all matters, he had earned the title of 'great,' " growled Bessas.

"True. And now your slave must be on his way, to inform my comrades at Buhen and Swenet that I have conveyed our meessage. May the Sleepless One befriend you!"

"May the Lord of the Wide Pastures give you long life and wealth," said Bessas.

He and Myron helped the man to saddle up and mount, and Gergis cantered off across the desert to eastward.

"Well," said Bessas, "we must begin to prepare for departure. A dozen or so of my nomads would, methinks, make an adequate escort. Besides, it will give me a chance to know these knaves better. And speaking of money, step back with me into the shaykh's tent. Labîd! Abras! Umayya!"

When Bessas had gathered the three Arabs who had accompanied him to the Locust Killer, he opened the treasure chest. He dug in both hands, scooped up a glittering mass, and dumped it on the carpet.

"This," he said, "is your share of the loot. Divide it equally amongst yourselves."

"How shall we do that, lord?" said Umayya. "It is hard to value such things."

379

"Let one man divide the stuff into three portions, and the others get first choice of the piles. Flip a coin to determine which of the two shall be first and which second."

As the three pressed kisses on Bessas' hands and garments, he said: "Aye, I know you love me, and I love you also. Now take your stuff and go." When the Arabs had gone, he began taking out pieces of gold. "Confirm my judgment, old man; but meseems this pile ought to pay off Astes' Nubians; this should suffice Master Murashu; this should make the Mithraeum happy; this should replace the camels the clan lost on this venture. . . ."

Then he scooped out the rest of the treasure in handfuls and dumped it in piles, saying:

"Remember our covenant for division of the treasure? It still holds. Kothar and Skhâ are dead; Shimri, being a god, needs no such lucre. Salîmat, as Zayd's heir, gets five parts; I get three parts, and you two."

"What about the True Anthrax? It's the most valuable single piece, apart from any magical powers it may or may not possess."

"We'll count that as one of the ten parts, and I'll take it for myself." Bessas hung the great gem around his neck. "I am the one most likely to need its protection. Now, teacher, choose any two piles you like. I have not weighed the gold down to the last bean, nor yet taken the gems to a lapidary for evaluation. Life is too short for such finical arguments, now!"

"These will do nicely," said Myron, indicating the two piles nearest to him.

"You cheat yourself. Here, take some more!" Bessas dumped another jingling handful on Myron's piles. "No arguments, now!"

"What are you doing with the rest?"

"I shall leave it in charge of my wives. Salîmat knows the tribe and is a clever wench withal, so I trust her to choose trustworthy guards."

"Aren't you taking the girls?"

"Nay. I seem to have gotten both with child and, for

380

such, long camel rides were not good. Besides, methinks a sometime vacation from one's loved ones were not a bad thing." Bessas gave a low, rumbling laugh. "Know, O Myron, that my father—God welcome him—had three wives, of whom only my mother survives. These three quarreled all the time, so that my poor father was put to it to referee their strife. I swore that I would take but one wife, if any. Now I have these two. A fine span of fillies they are; they quarrel not but are dear friends and sisters in sentiment.

"Howsomever, that brings up another difficulty for the man of the house. When they wish to persuade me to some course of action, they can always wheedle it out of me by taking turns in working upon me, thus wearing me down as the drip of water wears away a stone. As I have told you, I can refuse nought to a woman I love, and when I love two I am as soft as millet mush. Belike when their babes are born, they'll have less time to plot such stratagems.

"So, old friend, unless you wish to throw in your lot with the Banu Khalaf—which would surprise me, as they are neither literate nor concerned with things of the mind —this will be our last long ride together. What was that doggerel I made up at the start of our journey?"

Though thieves and lions in my pathway lie,
And whores and merchants seek to wring me dry,
With iron-hearted friends to guard my back,
I'll stride the dusty road until I die!

"Know that this dusty road may be the road to death for me. Whatever else I may have done, I have not brought Xerxes his dragon, nor yet returned within the allotted time."

"My dear boy, do you really think he might have you killed for not catching a beast that does not exist?"

"Who says it exists not? I and my Pygmy friends, against the solemn averment of the holy priests of Marduk, who

381

certes will not avouch their fraud! And Xerxes, who loves me not, may seize upon such a pretext for seating me upon the stake."

"Must you make this journey to Persepolis, then? Why not stay here with your family, as one of the Arabs urged?"

Bessas quaffed deeply. "I must go. And even if all go well as regards old Popeyes, I dread what my mother will say when she learns of my marriages. For fifteen years she has striven to wed me to some girls of decent Aryan family. I'm as terrified when I think of her as I was that morning we invaded the lair of the devil ape."

"Were you really frightened? You concealed it most masterfully."

Bessas belched. "Ha! I all but had the piss scared out of me. But could I, as leader, show fear before that motley band of knaves? Ahriman, no! Their habit of obedience would have fallen from them like the shackles from a manumitted slave. So let's drown these fearsome fantasms of the future in the Banu Khalaf's lousy date wine."

> *When bogles grim before your footsteps rise,*
> *And lowering thunderclouds benight the skies,*
> *Drink, and the phantoms scatter into mist;*
> *Drink, and the juice your omen drear denies!*

The sound of a song and the rhythmic clapping of hands wafted into the tent. An Arab appeared in the opening, ducked his head in a little bow, and touched his finger tips to heart, lips, and forehead.

"*Ya Shaykh!* The dance begins!"

Bessas set down his cup with a sigh. "In truth, I had rather sit here and drink and talk with you, but I must needs forth to skip and stamp the long night through. Ah me, the pains of principate! Will you join the dance?"

Myron smiled. "No, thank you. One of the few compensations of age is that one need not engage in such antics if one doesn't wish to, and I mean to take advantage of it!"

382

XIX   The Palace of the King

ON THE afternoon of the sixteenth of Abu, in the twenty-first year of Xerxes' reign, a summer sun blazed in the clear blue Persian sky. The chief eunuch, Aspamitres, went in haste to the palace of Darius, where his master was closeted with the wizard Ostanas.

"Great King!" said Aspamitres. "A band of Arabs on camels has arrived, praying to see Your Majesty forthwith. They bring with them a curious beast, which they say is a gift."

Xerxes and Ostanas exchanged a stare of surmise. The king said: "By the God of the Aryans! Can this be that ruffian of Zariaspa? When the time limit passed without a word, I thought he had perished or fled. But better late than never. I will see these men."

"Will the King of All Kings receive the men inside the Apadana?" asked the eunuch.

"Nay; it is the beast that concerns me the most. Prepare a reception on the steps before the Apadana."

Half an hour later, trumpets cried out before the great audience hall. Lines of spearmen snapped to attention. Behind the Immortals churned a crowd as colorful as a Persian flower garden in bloom. Courtiers and officials and their wives had gathered to see the sight. The sun sparkled on jewels and gleamed on gilded armor.

On the pave below stood a score of men in Arabian garb, dusty from travel. Their sun-darkened faces were lean and weary. A pock-marked giant towered over the rest. In the rear stood three small brown men, in Arab children's garb, holding the bridle of an exotic beast.

Painted and scented, King Xerxes strode out upon the portico of the Apadana. Down went the courtiers, the officials, and the Arabs, to touch the ground with their foreheads.

"Rise," said the king.

An usher struck the stones with his staff and cried: "My lord King! Bessas of Zariaspa has returned from the mission on which you dispatched him!" He led the giant forward.

"Are you truly Bessas son of Phraates?" asked Xerxes, peering nearsightedly.

"Aye, sire." Bessas tucked his arms into his sleeves and bowed from the waist.

"As Auramazda lives, I had never known you! How fared your mission?"

"May it please the Great King, your slave has been to the headwaters of the Nile, even as you commanded, and I——"

"That is no sirrush," said Xerxes sharply, gesturing towards the okapi.

Ostanas whispered: "May your slave venture to suggest that the Great King let the young man finish?"

"Go on," said Xerxes.

"Your slave," Bessas resumed, "has attained the region of the great lakes, whence flows the Nile. There I diligently inquired amongst the peasants and hunters and fishermen, but all agreed that no such beast as the sirrush exists in those parts, or in any other region so far as I can tell. When Your Majesty commands, I can tell you somewhat of how the story of this beast began.

"Now, your slave begs leave to present those things that he did obtain. First, here is the ear of an authentic king. In Egypt I sliced it from King Siptah's mummy."

Bessas handed the ear to a eunuch, who passed it on to the king. Xerxes fingered it with an expression of distaste and handed it to Ostanas.

"Next, I present to the King of All Kings the chief of a hunting tribe of the region whence flows the Nile, who prays you to enroll him as one of your tributary rulers and extend to him your protection. This is Dzaka, chief of the eastern Tikki-Tikki. With Dzaka are two of his subjects, Tshabi and Begendwé, bearing gifts, which they hope Your Majesty will graciously condescend to accept. Stand forth, O Dzaka!"

With great dignity, Dzaka limped forward, holding up his pot of honey. Behind him came Tshabi with the tusk and Begendwé leading the okapi. An usher fell in before them and led them up the steps until Dzaka confronted the king. In broken Persian he said:

"This for you, King."

Xerxes smiled broadly, showing his bad teeth. "I am delighted, Master Dzaka! I welcome you to the noble company of tributary kings of the Empire. You shall have my protection henceforth, and here is my hand on it."

After the king had gravely clasped hands with the solemn Dzaka, Tshabi muttered in his native tongue and handed the tusk to Xerxes, who passed it to Aspamitres. Begendwé then pressed the okapi's halter into the king's hand.

"What call you this?" said Xerxes, looking uneasily into the animal's large liquid eyes.

"Okapi," said Dzaka. "Live in wood."

"My Majesty is grateful," said Xerxes; then to Bessas: "Well, young man, although you have overrun your limit of time and failed to capture a sirrush, I cannot deny that you have exerted yourself on my behalf more effectively than the late Sataspes. I am charmed by my new subjects and the curious beast they have brought me. In fact, I have a thought for rendering this moment immortal.

"As you see, on the walls of the northern and eastern stairways, my artists have carved the bearers of tribute from all the lands whereof I am king. Two spaces alone remain blank. I had intended these for the European Greeks, but—ah—there has been a slight delay in reducing these brigands to obedience. Therefore, these reliefs shall depict, instead, my new African subjects and their gifts. Aspamitres, see you to it. Fetch hither the artists and have the sketches executed forthwith.

385

"Now, O Bessas, what befell the other man who went with you—that Milesian tutor of my sons—ah"—Xerxes snapped his fingers—"Myron, was that not his name?"

"Here he is, sire. He has kept a record of our explorations."

"Good! I am glad, Master Myron, that you have survived this perilous journey. You shall be lodged at my expense whilst you prepare your report. And both of you shall dine with me this evening, together with the small chieftain."

Myron and Bessas bowed together, murmuring: "Your slaves are honored, sire."

At this there was a buzz among the crowding courtiers, for rarely indeed did the king dine with persons outside his own family, save on certain festivals. For the most part he lived in godlike seclusion that became the more remote as he grew older. The king turned to his commander in chief.

"Artabanus, find lodging for these men in the barracks: the Arabs among the enlisted men and Masters Myron and Bessas in the officers' quarters. Give an officer's room to the Africans and assign slaves to care for all these people. Guard them well.

"Find also a place for this whatever-you-call-it, this beast, and remove it thither when the artists have done their work. Find out what it eats and arrange for a supply until it can be taken to my menagerie at Hagmatana. Do not tether it where Rustam can come upon it. That is all."

The king turned to re-enter the Apadana, but Bessas called out tensely: "Great King! Before you withdraw, may I ask. . . ."

The king turned back, his bushy black brows drawn together in a frown. "Well? Speak."

"What of your slave's mother, sire?"

"Oh. I am sorry to inform you that the Lady Zarina died of natural causes, several months ago, despite the ministrations of my own physician. Her possessions are in

386

the custody of Chamberlain Aspamitres, who will turn them over to you. Until later, then!"

When Myron and Bessas reached the room to which General Artabanus conveyed them, Bessas burst into a torrrent of weeping. He sank down upon his knees, beating the floor with his fists while tears poured down into his beard. Norax, the slave he had left behind to care for his mother, câme in and threw himself down to kiss the hem of Bessas' robe and join in the lamentation.

"How did the mistress die?" sobbed Bessas. "If that long-nosed devil slew her, I'll—I'll——"

"Nay, master," said Norax. "She was kept in comfort. She had a sickness that pained her, inside. Little by little it grew worse, though your noble mother was never one to complain. The king sent his own physician, the learned Apollonides of Kôs, but even he knew no cure. And at last she died, on the second day of Shabatu."

"Are you sure she was not poisoned?"

"I have no reason to think she was, sir. Her last words were a prayer for your safety."

At last Bessas mastered himself and dried his tears. He muttered a prayer for his mother's soul and asked the slave:

"What befell my cousin Sataspes, who was sent to sail around Africa?"

"He returned three months ago, with some story that he had sailed a hundred leagues or so down the west coast, but there the winds and currents stopped him. The king thought it a case of simple cowardice, so Sataspes paid the original penalty imposed upon him."

"I mourn him not, considering all the trouble he caused me," said Bessas grimly. He turned to Myron. "This gracious reception would seem to bode well for us, but I know better than to trust any king too far. If some-one is fattening you, be sure he will soon slaughter you. How think you we fare? Is Xerxes likely to seat me, too, on the stake?"

387

"I think not. This inviting us to dine is an auspicious sign. After all, some men would cheerfully cut off their noses for the privilege."

Meanwhile, Xerxes had again retired to Ostanas' chamber, where he spoke: "My good Ostanas, is this then the end of our hopes of defeating the demon Death?"

Ostanas, who rested his elbows on the table and his mouth on his bony clasped fists, raised his head.

"Gracious lord, I have been thinking hard. Whether or no the sirrush exists, I doubt not that Master Bessas did indeed perform a deed of dought. Of this, the small black men and the beast that resembles an antelope crossed with an ass are living proof.

"It may be that the sirrush lives, but that the priests of the false god Marduk, because of their hatred of Your Majesty, lied to you as to its provenance. It might exist in some other quarter. But to track it down were a life's task in itself, and neither of us—be it as you wish—grows younger by the day."

"What then?"

"I fear we shall have to give up the blood of the sirrush as one of the ingredients of our elixir. Howsomever, as we possess the other two items, it were a shame not to use them. So let us see what we can substitute.

"Of the beasts whereof we know, the one whose blood most nearly approaches the dragon's in ardor is the gryphon, which dwells in the land of the one-eyed Arimaspians, beyond Suguda in the far Northeast."

"Ask me not to send another expedition forth and wait another year!"

"Nay, nay, sire. I did but mention it in passing. Now, the beast of rank that is nearest to that of the gryphon is the lion."

"Lion, eh? I can send to Hagmatana for a lion from my menagerie."

"May it please the Great King, but methinks even that

388

were too slow. The king's ear will keep, but what of the heart of the hero?"

"What mean you?"

"Your slave means that we now have Bessas within our grasp; but will he so remain whilst you send to Hagmatana?"

"Guards watch him now, and I can have him shackled so securely that not even the demon Azi Dahaka could escape."

"But consider, Great King! A true hero will fight like a demon ere letting himself be taken, and either escape or perish trying. And for our elixir we need the heart cut from a living hero."

"What, then, do you purpose?"

"That we take him forthwith, by a means that I shall discover to you. Then, for the blood of our lion, we must sacrifice your pet."

"Poor old Rustam? Never! I love the mangy monster."

"There is no help for it, sire. We must work with dispatch, whilst the Good God has provided us with the materials.

"Understand, my master, this elixir will be less effective than that made with dragon's blood. Instead of giving you eternal life, it can at best prolong your life—let us say—a thousand years. But if we can accomplish this much, further researches may solve our problem ere the effect of this draft subside."

"At the moment, a thousand years' respite seems like a plenty." The king sighed. "I sometimes wonder why I strive to prolong this life of dole and disappointment."

"Courage, sire! Think of all the great works you have set in motion, which need your guiding hand to complete!"

"You are right, of course, my friend. Forget my melancholy words. The world needs me, so I must be worthy of the world, whatever my private feelings. And—by the Holy Ox Soul, you are a clever rascal! It is plain that you,

389

too, must needs partake of this cordial if you are to conduct the researches whereof you speak, eh?" Xerxes smiled sardonically.

"Now that Your Highness mentions it, I do perceive that such is indeed the case. Well, sire, shall we to our task?"

The royal repast was served in one of the larger rooms of the palace of Darius. Flickering torches in wall brackets and wavering oil lamps suspended from the celing strove to take the place of departing day.

Myron, eating breast of pheasant from a plate of lapis lazuli, thought that a private dinner with the king would be classed as highly public elsewhere. Besides the king, the commander in chief Artabanus, the chamberlain Aspamitres, the wizard Ostanas, and the royal physician Apollonides, several other officials sat at the table. The lower end was occupied by Myron, Bessas, and Dzaka. A score of Immortals stood at attention around the walls. These were men from one of the Persian battalions, in long-sleeved, pleated, ankle-length robes, bearing spears and battle-axes, with bow cases slung over their shoulders.

Bessas, once more clad in Aryan coat and trousers, talked and ate and talked again. One of the officials took notes. Xerxes, picking his teeth with a golden toothpick, asked searching questions: What was the wealth of these newly discovered African lands? What the military strength of their peoples? Were they friendly or hostile? How practical was Dzaka's proposal to extend the Empire's protection to the Tikki-Tikki? How about the kingdom of Kush? What had been learnt of the strengths and weaknesses of its government?

The hours passed; torches sputtered. The calls of sentries, pacing the walls of the palatial platform with partisans on their shoulders, rang through the moonlit night. Strains of music wafted from the king's harem. But ever the king probed and pried, as if to wring every drop of information from Bessas while he was still to hand.

At last the king clapped his hands. "Enough of business; pour the wine and send in the musicians. . . . To your heroic journey, Captain Bessas!"

"I thank Your Majesty," said Bessas.

Slaves poured wine of Halpa from alabaster pitchers into crystal goblets. Conversation became general. Myron found himself in a warm discussion of the shape of the earth with his neighbor, an official named Pharnuchus.

Pharnuchus wagged a finger at Myron. "I am a plain, blunt Persian, Master Myron, with none of your Greek subtleties. And I am sure that your theory somehow contradicts the words of the inspired Zoroaster, although I cannot cite the precise gatha."

Myron recited some of his arguments for the earth's sphericity. Pharnuchus toyed with the curls of his beard and said:

"So, so, I can see some advantage, not to have to fear falling off the edge. Then the great Persian Empire, in extending its benevolent sway over the peoples of the earth, will some day meet itself on the farther side, will it not? By Auramazda, I should like to be there! The next expedition we send out should essay to circumnavigate, not Africa only, but the entire earth! What think you—why, what ails Captain Bessas?"

Myron whirled in his seat. Bessas was slumped against the back of his chair, breathing heavily. Sweat ran down his pockmarked face. Myron, his heart pounding with sudden terror, leaned over his friend, who looked at him with a curiously blank stare out of eyes whose pupils were contracted to pin points.

"Tell the king I'm sick," muttered Bessas. "Some damned villain has fed me poppy juice! Take Anthrax."

"Is our hero unwell?" asked Xerxes from the head of the table. "One goblet of wine should not afflict so famous a tosspot as Master Bessas!"

391

The music of lyre and flute fell silent.

"He is ill, Your Majesty," said Myron, slipping the chain that held the great red jewel over Bessas' head and hoping that Xerxes' nearsightedness would conceal this move from the king. "For over a year he has carried the burden of three men, and now his resources have failed him."

"This is indeed unfortunate." The king snapped his fingers. "Guards! Carry Captain Bessas away."

Four guards stepped forward, as if they had been awaiting a signal, and bore off the now unconscious Bessas.

"Gentlemen," said Xerxes smoothly, "alas that our pleasant party should be thus interrupted! Let us hope that Master Bessas will soon recover. I, too, shall now retire, for the cares of state bear heavily upon me. The rest of you remain where you are and drink your fill."

The king stood up; all rose and bowed. As he swept out, surrounded by Immortals, all the others sat down except Ostanas, who followed Xerxes.

A flash of understanding struck Myron. Without a word to his companions, he leaped up and hurried after the king.

"Great King! Your Majesty! Your slave begs a word!"

Xerxes, striding down the corridor with Ostanas, turned. The bodyguards whirled and barred the way with their weapons, but the king waved them aside.

Myron fumbled for the Anthrax. "Sire, I have here a gift, which I have not had a chance to present." He held out the great red gem. "It is a magical ruby called the True Anthrax. Besides its intrinsic value, I am told that it is unique among jewels, in that it protects its owner."

"How?" said the king.

"It darkens when its wearer is in danger."

"Know you aught of this, Ostanas?"

The wizard squinted in the unsteady light. "I have heard of such a thing, and this may forsooth be the jewel in question. If so, then Master Myron has made Your

Majesty a handsome present indeed. Where did you get it, sir?"

"At the sources of the Nile, where an exiled king of Kush had hidden it."

"Your king is truly grateful, Master Myron," said Xerxes. "Now what would you of me?"

"Sire, may your slave speak to you, not as a humble subject to the king of the world, but as man to man?"

"Speak. I have never yet punished the bearer of ill tidings or the purveyor of unwelcome advice, as lesser kings have been known to do."

"Sire, Bessas has accomplished more for your realm than ten other men could have done. He has carried the name and fame of the great Xerxes into the demon-haunted jungles of Farther Africa, where no civilized man had gone before him. He has gained you new subjects, not by violence but by moral authority.

"Now, I know that Bessas did not lose consciousness just now from some ordinary ague or phthisic, but as a result of the action of Your Majesty's servants." Myron realized that he had, by these words, taken his life in his hands, but he plunged on: "I think you mean to kill him. Great King, he deserves better. Spare him."

Myron held his breath, awaiting his doom. But the king only smiled sadly, saying:

"I could put you off with a quibble. But, as you have been frank with me, I will do the like. What you ask is impossible. Know, however, that your friend is condemned by no petty spite of mine, and not even for his part in the death of my servant Datas. He is doomed by weighty reasons of state, to which all private claims must yield.

"Still, I am grateful for this gem. Come to me tomorrow and ask a boon. I say not that I will give you whatever you ask—I have had unhappy results from such impulsive offers—but I will grant any reasonable request. God befriend you!"

King and wizard, followed by the guardsmen, vanished down the hall.

With a splitting headache and an evil taste in his mouth, Bessas awoke. Stripped to his loincloth, he lay spread-eagled and supine on a large wooden table. He flexed his muscles and found that his wrists and ankles were firmly strapped to the corners of the table.

Craning his neck, Bessas saw that he was in a long chamber of considerable size, littered with manuscripts and with apparatus of whose meaning he was ignorant. In one corner stood a cage in which there paced a striped hyena. A small fire burnt upon a hearth; an open door led into a smaller chamber. Another door—heavy, wooden, and copper-studded—presumably led outside.

Bessas tested his bonds. He strained his bulging muscles until they cracked, without making the least impression on the straps. He tried to reach strap or buckle with fingers, toes, and teeth, to no avail. He threw his body from side to side in hope of oversetting the table, but it stood firm.

At last he gave a hoarse yell: "Help! Help!"

Nobody came. With a snarl of frustration, Bessas resigned himself to a study of Ostanas' apartment. Most of the objects therein meant little to him, but he at least entertained himself with imagining to what lethal uses he could put them. That suffed crocodile, for instance, could be rammed up Xerxes'——

The copper-studded door swung silently open. Two men crowded in, carrying a kind of stretcher. Two other men followed, holding the other end of the structure. Bessas could not at first see clearly what was on the stretcher; but, as the men neared to the table on which he lay, he caught a glimpse of black mane and tawny hide. This must be Rustam, the king's pet lion!

Following the second pair of men, Xerxes and Ostanas entered the room. The men with the stretcher put down their burden and went away. Ostanas came close to Bessas.

"He is awake."

Prudence struggled with red rage in Bessas' soul, and prudence did not have the better of it. "What is this? What are you doing? What have I done to you?" he shouted at Xerxes.

The king merely glanced at him and said to Ostanas: "Is all prepared?"

"Aye, my master. The lion, as you see, still lives, though I drugged him heavily enough so that I need not fear his sudden awakening whilst I drain his blood. With the man, it matters not whether he sleeps or wakes."

"Do you not need a younger man to help you?" said Xerxes anxiously.

"Not yet, sire. The supernatural influences invoked in this art are so fell that an unskilled apprentice were worse than none."

The king bent over the unconscious lion. "Farewell, old Rustam! I shall miss you." He stroked the animal's mane.

Ostanas pottered with vessels and instruments. He fed the small fire and hung a pot of water over it to boil. He sharpened a knife and tested it with his thumb.

"Your slave is now ready to begin the great work," he said.

"Then I shall depart," said Xerxes.

"What in demon land are you up to?" yelled Bessas. "What kind of king are you, who gives his faithful servants to witches to carve up for potions?"

"Would Your Majesty not prefer to remain?" said Ostanas. "This work will make history in the occult sciences."

Xerxes smiled. "Dear old Ostanas, how little you understand me, after all these years! I hate bloodshed and death. I know that my commands have sent many thousands to their doom—not all, belike, so justly as I might

395

have wished. But in my heart"—he slapped his bosom—"I love life and peace for all, even for the humblest. I have fostered your researches in hopes of winning a final victory over the demon Death, not only for me, Xerxes, but perchance for all mankind. So I will not stay to watch you take the heart of this young man—who dies, if it be any comfort to him, in a worthy cause. Oh, remind me later to deal with those lying priests of Marduk. By the Good God, they shall rue their mendacity! I will make them long for death!"

The king went out. Bessas spat at him, although he was out of range.

Whistling through his remaining teeth, Ostanas resumed his work. Although Bessas could not see what he did with the lion, a trickling sound came to Bessas' ears.

Time passed. The trickling dwindled away to individual drops. Ostanas prayed, then took King Siptah's ear off a shelf, dropped it into a mortar, and brayed it vigorously with the pestle.

When the ear had been reduced to powder, the wizard knelt and uttered more prayers. Although Bessas could plainly hear the words, the gods or other spirits appealed to were none that he knew.

Ostanas drew a diagram on the floor with a piece of charcoal, stood in it, and went through a long rigmarole with a wand, facing this way and that and mumbling a rhythmic chant.

Then he stepped out of the diagram and sharpened his knife some more with a wheet-wheet sound.

"You lousy old catamite!" snarled Bessas. "You are no magician. You are nought but a dirty old mountebank, who had cozened the silly king into thinking a potion can prolong his life. Well, it will not work. I know magicians in Egypt and Kush who would make six of you, you lying snake! You will die, and the king will die, and nobody will even remember you! You shall be a kinless, wandering ghost! In Mithra's name, may you be dipped in dung! May dogs eat your privates! May you be flayed alive with a dull knife! May you fall from the Bridge of the Separator and dwell in eternal torment in the House of the Lie!"

Wheet-wheet went the knife.

Bessas cursed Ostanas unto the tenth generation of his ancestry, but the wizard answered never a word. Ostanas set down his whetstone and came forward, his eyes gleaming under his bushy white brows. The knife blade flashed yellow in the light of the golden lamps.

Ostanas suddenly halted, frozen to immobility with his mouth half open and his eyeballs rolled sidewise. He turned towards the door, through which wafted a rising murmur of sound. There came a noise of shouting and running and the metallic clash of arms.

With a curse, Ostanas laid down the knife and hastened to the door. Grasping the bronzen knob, he opened the door a crack, then wider. He slipped out while, in its cage, the hyena laughed.

In his bedchamber, King Xerxes suffered his eunuchs to disrobe him and help him into his dressing gown. He said to Aspamitres:

"Did not Master Myron say something this evening about a custom of the Africans, to chew a twig every night until it is frayed and then brush their teeth with it? Get me some twigs and we will try it. Nay, not now! In the next few days, I meant. Nay, I want no women tonight. Now out, all of you. Leave one light on. Good night!"

The eunuchs filed out, bearing the royal ewer, wash basin, towel, drinking cup, and chamber pot. Xerxes raised his hands and prayed:

"As Auramazda is the best lord, so is Zoroaster the judge according to holy righteousness, he who brings life's deed of good thought to Mazdah and the Kingdom to Ahura, he whom they have established as herder to the poor.

397

"Righteousness is the best good. According to our desire may it be, as we wish it shall be to us, righteousness for salvation.

"Let the beloved brotherhood come to the support of Zoroaster's men and women, to the support of good thought. Whatever self deserves the precious reward, for him I beg the coveted prize of righteousness, which Auramazda will bestow."

The king tossed off his dressing gown. For half an ush he stood, naked but for the scented purple bags that covered his hair and beard, looking down with displeasure at his potbelly. He sighed, kicked off his slippers, and sat down on the bed.

Xerxes took a long look at the True Anthrax, which hung around his neck, and slipped under the covers.

Scarcely had the king settled himself to sleep when his private knock sounded. "Enter!" he called.

Artabanus' darkly darting eyes appeared in the crack of the door.

"O King!" said the commander in chief in a low, tense tone. "Something of the utmost moment has occurred!"

"What in the name of Auramazda is it? Do not stand in the doorway, mumbling like a crone, but come hither and speak up!"

"You are in danger, sire!" said the Hyrkanian, coming forward. "So great is this peril that I have brought my sons to help me guard you. Come on in, boys. Hurry!"

Seven young Aryans filed into the room.

"Well, now," said Xerxes, peering at his ruby. "You must be mistaken. See the bright red of this magical gem —uk!"

The tallest of Artabanus' sons had shot out two long arms and gripped Xerxes by the throat, digging his powerful thumbs beneath the purple bag that held Xerxes' beard and choking off the royal windpipe. At the same instant four of the other sons threw themselves on Xerxes' limbs, each seizing one.

398

Xerxes' eyes bulged. His mouth opened, but only a wheezy rasp came forth. He thrashed and struggled, his face turning blue.

Artabanus drew a short court sword from under his garments and leaned over the king's writhing form. He drove the blade again and again into Xerxes' hairy chest, saying in a low tone:

"This is for your brother Masistes. . . . And this is for all the daily slights and insults I have taken from you. . . . And this is for the pigheaded stupidity that lost us Salamis. . . . And this——"

"He is dead," said one of the sons.

"Why, so he is!" said Artabanus, wiping his blade on the king's scented beard bag. "To our business, lads."

Thus died Xerxes son of Darius—a great reformer, a great administrator, and a great builder; but, because of basic flaws of character, not quite a great king.

Myron dashed into Ostanas' chamber. "Bessas! I have hunted through this whole polluted palace. Are you still alive?"

"I suspect so. What in the seven Babylonian hells goes on?"

"Xerxes has been murdered!"

"Good! Who did it?"

Myron sawed with his knife at the straps that held Bessas' wrists. "I know not. Some say Aspamitres, some— ea! What's that lion doing here?"

Bessas' low laugh rumbled. "Fear not. 'Tis old Rustam, dead. Here, give me the knife."

His wrists free, Bessas sat up and with two slashes severed the straps that bound his ankles. He rubbed his swollen hands and feet. "My members are full of ants, from the tightness of the straps. Let's get out, ere the Immortals run wild and start shooting and spearing everyone in sight."

Outside in the halls, utter confusion reigned. People

ran shrieking. Some tried to stop others, clutching at their garments and shouting questions. Those clutched at only ran the harder and shrieked the louder.

A fat old eunuch went puffing past, helping himself along with an ebony, gold-tipped staff of office. Bessas snatched away the staff, saying:

"I need it more sorely than you, grandfather. To the barracks!"

The Bactrian set off with great strides through the halls, familiar to him from his service in the Immortals. Myron trotted after.

"Oh, there you are!" cried a powerful voice.

Myron and Bessas whirled. Coming towards them, sword out, was Zopyrus son of Bagabyxas.

"You escaped my men, but you shall not escape me!" snarled the nobleman. "Suborn the rape of my little daughter, will you?"

"Well, drown me in the Bitter River!" cried Bessas. "Are you still seeking my head, Zopyrus? Here it is!"

Zopyrus came on with a whirl of steel. Myron, unarmed except for his little table knife, gave back helplessly. As he looked around for something to throw or use as a club, Zopyrus was upon Bessas.

The Bactrian, nearly naked and unarmed but for the eunuch's staff, gripped the staff as he had seen the Egyptians of Siout do: one hand at the center of the staff, the other a foot behind it. Thus Bessas had two ends, a longer and a shorter, to strike with.

He parried Zopyrus' first slash, and his second. Zopyrus lunged; Bessas knocked the point aside.

Bessas feinted and struck the Persian a sharp rap over the head. Zopyrus shook his head and blinked. Bessas feinted again. As Zopyrus parried Bessas drove the end of the staff into the pit of Zopyrus' stomach.

The Persian doubled over, coughing. Bessas swung mightily. The staff swished through the air and broke with a crash against Zopyrus' head. The Daduchid tum-

400

bled to the floor. His sword fell with a clang and slithered across the mtrble.

"I'll just take this knave's head——" began Bessas, picking up the sword.

"In the name of Zeus, no!" cried Myron. "You cannot kill all the Daduchids, and to kill one were to worsen our plight! Come on!"

"Oh, very well. But I warn you, old man, this soft-heartedness of yours will be the death of you yet!"

A fortnight later, Myron and Bessas sat at the board of Myron's friend Uni, the Egyptian priest, in Shushan. Winecups stood on the table before them. Bessas was speaking:

"So, you see, my dream was fulfilled after all. 'O man, who seeketh what is sought in vain,' and 'that which dwelleth far above the flood,' refer to the sirrush, which exists not. 'Red shall engender red, blood call to blood,' no doubt means the True Anthrax and Xerxes' blood. 'That to trust which were to grasp a wraith' means the magical powers falsely ascribed to the gem, which may have played a part in saving my gore. Methinks it gave Xerxes—a superstitious wight, though in many ways intelligent—a false sense of security, so that he gazed upon the gem to see if it had darkened when he should have been looking to make sure that his guards were at their posts."

Myron interjected: "I knew the thing didn't work, when I saw Kothar looking at it unperturbed at the moment when Bessas was stealing up to shoot him."

Bessas concluded: "And 'a dreadful deed within a narrow room' is of course Xerxcs' murder."

"I wouldn't call Xerxes' bedchamber exactly narrow," said Myron.

"Belike not. But it may be that the spirit of Artagnes had to use that word to make the rhyme come out right. That's a difficulty which we poets know all too well."

401

"Pray do not digress, my sons," said Uni. "I am all a-twitter to know what happened next."

Bessas took up the tale again. "Well, when Xerxes was dead, Artabanus and his sons ran to the quarters of Prince Artaxerxes. Him they awoke, and Artabanus told the lad that his brother Darius had just murdered the king, and he must needs avenge his sire.

"So Artaxerxes, being young and confused with sleep, armed himself and gathered his bodyguards. He did not doubt Artabanus' words, for it was notorious that young Darius hated his father, the king, for seducing his wife. So Artaxerxes went to his brother's apartment, dragged him out of bed, and butchered him."

"What a night of knives!" said Uni. "I am glad I was not there when such dreadful deeds were done. Then what happened?"

"Seeing that things were going so well, Artabanus, thinking to seize the throne for himself, called upon his sons: 'Strike for empire, boys!' They all attacked Artaxerxes and dealt him a wound, so that for half an ush the fate of the dynasty hung in the balance."

While Bessas drank a swallow of wine, Myron took up the tale: "Both Aspamitres the chamberlain and Lord Bagabyxas, I hear, were involved in the plot, though just how I am not informed. No doubt the chamberlain shuffled the palace guards so that none was within call of the king when Artabanus struck.

"Bagabyxas, too, had a grudge against Xerxes. You recall that he had wed Xerxes' daughter Amytis. Later, when he accused her to the king of adultery, Xerxes let her off with a scolding.

"Yet Bagabyxas, they say, had no desire to see the whole dynasty supplanted and the realm rent by civil war. So he came to the aid of young Artaxerxes. The two fought off the attackers for the instant needed until the guards came running and cut down Artabanus and his sons. Bagabyxas sustained a grave wound in the struggle but may recover. The new king sentenced the chamberlain Aspamitres to the boats. The wizard Ostanas, they say, has fled to Egypt."

"Ambition must have addled Artabanus' wits," said Uni. "Even had he slain Artaxerxes, Xerxes had another legitimate son, Hystaspes, in Bactria. To him the great nobles would have rallied."

Myron: "And even if he had disposed of Hystaspes, the pretender Orontes would have popped up to claim the throne."

"Not that," said Uni. "Orontes is dead."

"Indeed?"

"Whilst you were struggling through the African jungles, Orontes raised the standard of revolt in Syria. The sub-governor of Phoenicia gathered the local levies and marched up the valley of the River of Freedom to oppose him. To get his army—mostly Arab mercenaries—across the Serpentine, Orontes built a floating bridge. But at the first shock of battle his Arabs broke and fled. In his retreat, finding his bridge obstructed by fugitives, Orontes tried to swim his horse across the Serpentine and drowned."

"Strange that we heard no gossip of this revolt," said Bessas.

"Not so strange," said Myron. "You jounced us across endless deserts, avoiding towns and seldom stopping long enough to exchange six words with the local people."

Uni: "But what befell you two on this night of noble carnage?"

Bessas resumed: "We won back to the barracks, where we gathered our Arabs and Pygmies and barricaded a section of the building. We were prepared to fight if need be, for we could not get our camels out of the stables to flee. Luckily I had friends amongst the Immortals, who kept their excited troopers in order. Artaxerxes had nought against us; and the Daduchids, what of Bagabyxas' wound and the lump on Zopyrus' pate, had other

403

things to think of than making more mischief for us. So here we are."

Uni asked the Bactrian: "What are your plans, my son?"

"I shall wend my way to Thadamora, to buy camels from Shaykh Alman. Thence I go to my Fifty-League Oasis to take up the headship of my clan—if the Banu Khalaf have not risen in my absence and chosen another shaykh. I must also return Dzaka and his comrades—who are, I fear, somewhat disillusioned with civilization—to their ancestral jungle.

"Thereafter I shall carry on Zayd's work of building up the desert trade routes south of Eygpt. As we have the camel and no other traders in those parts do, we should make a good thing of it."

"Provided," said Uni, "that these competitors whom you will ruin do not combine to make trouble for you."

"True; and also provided that I can restrain my Arabs' love of pillage and murder. It shows how one learns. A few years past I should have happily joined my sand thieves in their forays. But now I have come to see that true wealth is not the loot of a raid, nor even the trove of a treasure like that of Takarta—from which the king's tax gatherers will speedily separate you if they catch you. It is, rather, a network of established trade routes and connections and satisfied customers, which if carefully fostered will yield a profit for aye."

He uttered a deep, rumbling laugh. "Two years ago I had contemned such thoughts as base commercialism, and averred that the only gentlemanly trades were fighting, piracy, and horse breeding. Now, by Mithra, I am as crassly mercenary as any Tyrian!"

Myron asked: "How about your estate in Bactria?"

"To the afterworld with that! I have an estate—my clan of Arabian cutthroats—and why should I give that up to grasp at a shadow? Didn't some Greek storyteller compose a fable about a dog with a bone, who saw his image in the water?" Bessas shook his head. "It is sinful to say

404

so, but ever since I learnt of my mother's death I see things more clearly."

"What of your future, Myron?" asked Uni.

"My plans are as follows: *Alpha,* I shall deposit my share of the treasure of Takarta in your temple for safe-keeping. *Beta,* I shall buy a couple of horses or mules to take me to the city of my birth."

"Will you not need a slave to fetch and carry?" asked Uni.

"Bessas has already given me Norax."

"Who," said Bessas, "will no doubt soon cajole our tenderhearted Myron into freeing him."

"*Gamma,* I shall betake me to Miletos, purchase a house, settle down, and try to locate some of the friends of my youth, if any now reside in those parts. *Delta,* I shall write two books, for which I have already selected the titles. One shall be called *Aithiopika,* telling of my observations in Africa. The other shall be *Peri tês morphês tês oikoumenês* or 'About the Shape of the Earth.' You shall yet hear of my fame as a discoverer. As for *epsilon*—we shall see. Perhaps I shall try my luck in the West, where I hear that Pythagoras of Samos established a whole brotherhood of philosophers."

Uni said: "Why not stay in Shushan to write your books?"

"Remain in this brick kiln of a town throughout the summer's heat? My dear Uni, the only comfortable place in the city is the deepest dungeon beneath the citadel, and its appointments leave much to be desired in other respects. But I shall be back here from time to time to draw upon my deposit."

Bessas said: "Why not come back to Egypt with me? I could use you in my new business, for you are shrewder at bargaining and quicker at reckoning than I shall ever be."

"Thank you, old boy, but my writings are the more compelling task. Besides, I have had my fill of travel, and I'm getting a trifle old for such exertions. I have had my

405

adventure. I have seen the Mountains of the Moon and fought the great black man-ape, and I have returned hale and whole. But let us not carry this antique pitcher to the well too often."

"Well, any time you are in Upper Egypt, there'll be a place for you in the tents of the Banu Khalaf. By Ishtar's navel, dawn brightens the sky! We have talked the whole night through. Now I must go."

Uni yawned. "Had you not better snatch some sleep?"

"Not I! I can doze on a camel's back."

"Take care that you fall not off in your sleep, for it is a long way down."

"Fear not——"

A knock on Uni's door resounded, followed by shouts of *"Ya Shaykh! Yalla!"*

"There are my sand thieves now," said Bessas. "Excuse me; I must awaken my brown imps." Bessas left the room.

Uni looked at Myron. "I still think you need a wife."

"The same old Uni, ever trying to marry me off! When I am doing so well without one, why change?"

"I wonder that you did not wed the Macedonian girl."

"I thought of it; in fact I believed at one time that I was in love with her. But she had little to say of interest. Nor would she have brought me either property or standing, which to a Greek are the principal reasons for marrying.

"Moreover, she was less than half my age; so it would have been the mournful tale of old Bagabyxas and his young princess Amytis over again. If I could find some good-natured widow, now—but for the present, my **true** love is Gaia, goddess of the earth, whose lovely shape I must make known to all mankind."

They went to the door to bid farewell to the Bactrian and his Arabs. Bessas adjusted his kaffiyya, touched noses with Uni, seized Myron in a hug that almost cracked the Hellene's ribs, and kissed his friend soundly. Then he threw a leg over the back of his kneeling camel.

"The gods befriend you!" he cried.

Belike the friend whom for an hour we leave,
Is gone forever, sadly though we grieve;
Whilst him to whom we bid farewell for aye,
We may yet meet again, by Fate's reprieve!

After a last look at his old tutor, he bellowed, *"Yâ ahî!"* His camel rose by jerks, stern first; so did those bearing the Pygmies. With a rattle of gear and a flutter of head shawls, the company jounced away at a trot towards the bridge across the Khavaspa. The rising sun, striking slant-wise down the narrow street, splashed the robes of the men and the rumps of the camels with crimson.

XX   Author's Note

FOR THE NAME of this novel, I am indebted to Willy Ley, who let me use the title of Chapter 9 of his book *The Lungfish, the Dodo, and the Unicorn.* Here you can read about the *sirrush* and the speculations that its discovery stirred up after Koldewey excavated the Ishtar Gate around 1900. My story is based partly upon Koldewey's surmise that the priests of Marduk used to pass off some reptile (probably a monitor lizard) on their credulous worshipers as a young sirrush.

The novel is also based upon the story of Sataspes, as told by Herodotus (IV, 43), and upon the fact that, of the twenty-three groups of tribute bearers sculptured on each of the two retaining walls of the Apadana at Persepolis, the last group of each set shows three unmistakable African Pygmies. One carries a pot, one an elephant's tusk, while the third leads an okapi. Although this relief has been known for decades, not until recently was its true nature realized. Even Olmstead's monumental *History of the Persian Empire* (1948) describes the animal depicted as "a curiously foreshortened giraffe."

This sculpture proves that in the reign of Xerxes (486-465 B.C.) somebody traveled from the Achaemenid Empire to a country where Pygmies and okapis dwelt and returned to tell the tale. Today this would mean that the traveler reached the Ituri Forest of the northeastern Congo. In Xerxes' time, Pygmies were widely spread about Africa and the okapi probably had a wider range than it does now. But, as the okapi is adapted to life in a dense tropical rain forest, it cannot have ranged very far outside the present Congo, because east of the Congo-Uganda line the country becomes open parkland except for gallery forests along the streams. (In ancient times, however, the forest may have been somewhat more extensive because the Africans had not deforested large areas by annual grass burnings.)

Nothing is known about the contact opened up at this time between the Mediterranean world and the Lake Region of Central Africa save the bare fact that it happened. Whoever fetched the three Pygmies and their beast to Xerxes' court must have adventures quite as hair-raising as those attributed to my fictional characters.

The unknown explorer's feat of bringing a living okapi to Persepolis is matched by a similar exploit from later times. D. N. Wilber informs me that, about 1402, the Sultan of Egypt gave a giraffe to Timur, the Tatar king. And that poor giraffe walked all the way, presumably from its home in the Sudan, to Samarqand—well over 3,000 miles.

Afterwards the episode of the okapi was forgotten, except for the knowledge, alluded to by classical authors (Aeschylus, Anaxagoras, Euripides, Aristotle, Poseidonius, Diodorus, Claudius Ptolemaeus, etc.), that the Nile originated in rain or melting snow on tall equatorial mountains. This range was sometimes called the "Silver Mountain" and sometimes the "Mountains of the Moon," probably because of the snows of Mount Ruwenzori. Until the invasion of the country by European explorers in the nineteenth century, it was not generally believed that mountains in so tropical a region could have snow on them. But the discovery of Mounts Kenya, Kilimanjaro, and Ruwenzori proved otherwise.

It seems as if the travel route between the Mediterranean world and Central Africa did not remain open long. I suspect that it closed when the Nilotic Negroes of the southern Sudan learned to smelt iron and put iron heads on their spears. They thus became more formidable than when their spears were tipped only with horn. Having been raided by slavers, they probably attacked any outsiders on sight.

For many centuries the Nilotics kept all foreigners at bay, until the gun gave the outlanders another great advantage. Then slave raiding on the Upper Nile was resumed by the Arabs, Turks, and Egyptians, and by adventurers and riffraff from many nations.

The definitely historical characters in this novel are King Xerxes and his officials and relatives: Achaemenes, Apollonides, Artabanus, Aspamitres, Bagabyxas, Tithraustes, and Zopyrus; Murashu the banker and his son Belhatin; King Saas-herqa (whose cartouche can be read in several ways, such as Sa'as-heriqa, Si'aspiqa, Asâs-heraq, etc.); and various offstage and deceased characters alluded to, such as Amestris, Artaxerxes, Darius, Iranu, Masistes, Nabu-rimanni, Sataspes, Themistokles, and Vaus.

King Takarta is imaginary, though his predecessor Karkamon and his successor Astabarqamon are real. The exact date and cause of the removal of Kushite capital from Napata to Meroê are not known, but the change may have taken place somewhat as set forth in the story.

Three characters are on the border line between history and legend. Salîmat is a legendary Arab warrior princess for whom the Selîma Oasis (called the Fifty-League Oasis in the story) is named. Ostanas (or Osthanes) is a half-legendary magician alluded to by Pliny and Diogenes Laërtius, whose story was further embroidered by later writers on alchemy.

Orontes is based upon two sentences, of no great historical weight, by ancient writers. Strabo the geographer says of the Orontes River (XVI, ii, 7) that: "Though formerly called Typhon, its name was changed to that of Orontes, the man who built a bridge across it." John Zonaras, the Byzantine historian, says of the Orontes (XIII, 8) that it was ". . . according to some formerly called the Ophites, later named after the son of Cambyses, king of the Persians, who was drowned therein."

Now, Typhon was a dragon of Greek mythology, and *ophites* is Greek for "serpentine." Other sources call the river the Draco, or dragon. So we can infer that the original Semitic name for the river probably meant something like "serpentine" or "reptilian"; wherefore I have called the river the "Serpentine" in the story. The legend of the channel's having been dug by a flying dragon is based upon that given by Strabo, *loc. cit.*

However, the river cannot have been really renamed for the supposititious Orontes, because the original name was already very much like Orontes. It appears in Egyptian inscriptions of the fifteenth century B.C. as the Yernet or Yerset (the latter probably a misspelling) and Assyrian inscriptions of the ninth call it the Arantu. If the man Orontes lived, the resemblance between his name (probably something like Auravanda in Old Persian) and that of the river could have given rise to the story of the river's being named for the man, although the name of the river is at least a thousand years older.

The main characters in the story—Myron, Bessas, and their comrades—are all imaginary. It is not known who first suggested that the earth is round, but the idea appeared some time in the century in which the story is laid. Some ancient writers, such as Aristotle, attribute it to one of the followers of the philosopher Pythagoras—possibly Philolaos of Crotona, who was probably born within a few years of the time of my story, but of whom very little is definitely known. It may well have been suggested by the changing aspect of the heavens during a journey of exploration that covered many degrees of latitude.

Although the names of Greek, Babylonian, and other non-Persian characters are given in the most convenient approximation of their original forms, those of the Persians are given in their Latinized Greek guise. The reason is that Old Persian names are difficult. In some cases the Old Persian forms are not known while in others they are inordinately long or hard to pronounce.

For those who are curious about the original forms of these names, I add a list of OP names appearing in the story, whose OP forms are known, both in classical and in OP forms. By the use of diacritical marks, the OP names can be spelled in various ways. As you can see, the Greeks and Romans did not use any consistent system of transliterating Persian names. Starred names I made up by analogy with known forms:

CLASSICAL	OLD PERSIAN
Achaemenes	Hakhamanish
Arsaces, -kes	Arshaka
Arsames	Arshama
Artabanus, -os, Arta-panus	Artabanush
Artaxerxes	Artakhshathra
Aryandes	Haruvanta
Aspamitres	Aspamithra
Astes	Ashta
Bagabyxas*, Bacabasus, Bagazos, Megabyzes, -myxos	Bagabukhsha
Bardias*, Mardos, Mer-dias, Smerdis	Bardiya
Bessas*, -us, -os, Besas	Besha
Cambyses, Kam-	Kambujiya
Cyaxares, Ky-	Uvakhshatra, Hua-
Cyrus, Kyros	Kurush
Daduchus, -ouchos, Daü-chas, Daou-	Datavahya, Daduhya

411

CLASSICAL	OLD PERSIAN
Darius, Dareios, -eiaios	Darayavahush, Dareyav-osh
Datas, -is	Data
Daurises	Davirisha
Embas	Emba
Gomates	Gaumata
Haraspes	Haraspa
Hydarnes	Vidarna
Hystaspes	Vishtaspa
Izates	Yazata
Masdaeus, Mazae-, -aios	Mazdai
Masistes	Mathishta
Ochus, -os	Vahauka
Pharnuchus, -nouchos	Farnukha
Phraates	Frahata
Sataspes	Sataspa
Teaspes	Chaispish
Tithraustes	Chithravahishta
Vaus*	Vahush
Xerxes	Khshayarsha
Zamaspes	Jamaspa
Zarina, -naia	Zarinari
Zoroaster, -astres, Zara-throustes, Zaravastes, Zathraustes, Zaratas	Zarathushtra

Readers who find the name "Skhâ" bothersome may pronounce it simply like "scar" without the *r*.

As for place names, in most of the area covered by the story there are three strata of names: pre-classical names (Babylonian, Aramaic, Egyptian, etc.); classical names (Greek or Latin); and post-classical—medieval or modern—names (mostly Arabic). I have usually given places in the story their oldest known names, except in cases where a more recent form is much better known. Hence Marath (not Marathus or Amrît) but Damascus (not Dar Mesheq or Damaskos or Dimishq or esh-Shams). For ancient and modern forms of these various places see Baedeker's *Egypt and the Sûdân* (1929) and *Palestine and Syria* (1912). The map at the end of the first volume of Baikie's *History of Egypt* (1929) and Map No. 20 in Shepherd's *Historical Atlas* also have many such variant forms of place names. The pre-classical forms of the names of Meroê and Napata were Barua and Nepita or (or Nept) respectively.

All the places named in the novel are real except Ravonga and the castle of Takarta, which are imaginary. However, it is pure surmise to have located Pliny's Tenupsis near modern Kaka, and to have identified his Boron with modern Bor, and ancient Karutjet with modern Korti, because the true locations of these places are not certainly known. The Tower of the Snail (Burj el-Bazzâq, more accurately "of snails") at Marath = Amrît exists, although I may have taken liberties with its date. While this date is not certainly known, some archaeologists believe it to be later than the time of my story. The tomb of King Siptah is as I described it.

Ancient geographers distinguished between the White Nile and the Blue Nile, calling them the Astapous and the Astasobas, but they differed as to which affluent bore which name. Since the Blue Nile once had a town named Soba on it, and the White Nile has a tributary called the Sobat, one can argue either way.

Most of the African tribes mentioned are from Pliny. As no more "authentic" forms of their names are known, I have left these names in their Latin form. I have assumed that the Alabi, Bugaitae or Bougaeitai, Dankala, Mattitae, Nubae or Nubians, Ophirites, and Shaikaru of ancient writings are identical with the modern Aliab Dinka, Bega or Bisharîn, Dongolavi, Madi, Nuba and Nubians, Afar or Danakil, and Shankalla. This may or may not be true in all cases.

The customs attributed to the Kushites and other peoples of the Upper Nile are based upon those reported by the first European explorers to penetrate those regions in the eighteenth and nineteenth centuries. Remarks of ancient writers about the customs of the Negroes of the White Nile of going naked, smearing themselves with ash or clay, extracting some of their teeth, and raising cattle indicate that the Nilotics have changed their ways but little in 2,000 years.

In the Central African episodes, the native words used by African characters are (with a few minor exceptions) in Swahili. Of course Swahili (properly Kiswahili) was not spoken in the fifth century B.C. It is a trade language, which grew up in recent centuries on the East African coast. Its basis is a simplified Bantu, but it also has a large minority of words of Arabic and other non-African origin.

On the other hand, nobody knows what sort of languages were spoken in the Lake Region of Africa 2,400 years ago. One can only guess that they were related to those used there today. So the Swahili phrases are meant to give the right fictional flavor but not to mislead the reader. *Kahawa* is Swahili for "coffee," from the Arabic *qahwa*. *Nagana* is a corruption of the modern Zulu name for the livestock disease caused by the flagellate *Trypanosoma brucei*, spread by the bite of the tsetse fly *Glossina rhodesiensis*.

The day on which the story starts, 3 Nisanu, 20 Xerxes in the Babylonian calendar, would be April 8, 466 B.C. in ours. Xerxes was murdered in 465 B.C., not sooner than August 4 and not later than August 8; I have assumed August 6 as the date. Diodorus, Ctesias (*apud* Photius), and Justin give somewhat divergent accounts of the murder; I have followed the first of these because it best suited my story. Dates are given throughout in the Babylonian calender, although the calendric situation in the Achaemenid Empire had been complicated by the attempt of Darius, some decades before, to make the Egyptian solar year standard for the whole Empire. A lunar calendar like the Babylonian has a great advantage for the historical novelist, namely: it is always easy to tell what the moon looked like on any date, without calling up the planetarium.

A "penny" in the story means "one twelfth of a shekel." The people of those days actually used such awkward expressions, or some even clumsier, such as "three twenty-fourths of a shekel." Distinctive names for small coins had not yet been invented, and the coins themselves had not yet come into wide use. As a weight, a shekel was one sixtieth of a pound (the Babylonian pound being 1.1 times ours). A silver coin of that weight was about the size of a U.S. quarter or a British shilling, but its purchasing power was something like that of ten or twenty dollars. The daric stater, the standard Achaemenid golden coin, was worth twenty silver shekels.

"The boats" and "the ashes" were two methods of capital punishment employed by the Achaemenids. In the former, the culprit was placed in a coffinlike structure with his extremities sticking out and then left in the sun to die. In "the ashes" he was placed on a beam above a deep bed of ashes and left until he fell off to smother.

The rules of Egyptian checkers, or tjau (later known to the Romans as *ludus latrunculorum,* "the game of robbers") were reconstructed by Edward Falkener in his book *Games Ancient and Oriental and How to Play Them* (1892, 1961). If Falkener is right, the game is played on a board twelve cells on a side. Each of the two players has thirty pieces ("dogs") arranged at the start in five rows on alternate squares as in modern checkers. Each piece may move one square in any direction, orthogonally or diagonally, and may jump a hostile piece if the cell beyond it is vacant. But the only way that a player can take a hostile piece is by placing two of his pieces on opposite sides of that piece, orthogonally or diagonally. (One may move a piece between two of one's opponent's without losing it.) It is not a bad game as board games go, though each game takes much longer than a game of modern checkers.

415

The research trip for this novel proved exceptionally lively. In Uganda I was chased by a camera-shy hippopotamus. In the Congo I unwisely tried to swing, like Tarzan, on one of those dangling jungle vines, and shook down on myself a swarm of venomous ants.

The thing I remember with the most amusement happened when I was driving from Khartoum to the ruins of Meroê (a fifteen-hour round trip, and you need a four-wheel drive because of the sand). Seeing dead camels by the roadside with vultures picturesquely perched upon them, I thought that what I needed to add to the junk in my study was a well-bleached Sudanese camel's skull.

Then I tried to explain to my driver what I wanted. Not knowing the Arabic for "skull," I said I wanted the head of a camel, *râs al-jamal*. Oh, said Tejani, that would be easy. We'd stop at Shendi, where I could buy a camel, cut off its head, and take it with me! My wife is heartily thankful that I did not follow up this suggestion.

L. Sprague de Camp